THE
HIDDEN GIRL
and
Other Stories

ALSO BY KEN LIU

THE DANDELION DYNASTY

The Grace of Kings
The Wall of Storms
The Veiled Throne (forthcoming)

The Paper Menagerie and Other Stories

TRANSLATED BY KEN LIU

Vagabonds by Hao Jingfang (2020)

THE
HIDDEN GIRL

and

Other Stories

KEN LIU

SAGA PRESS

LONDON SYDNEY **NEW YORK** TORONTO NEW DELHI

SAGA PRESS

AN IMPRINT OF SIMON & SCHUSTER, INC.

1230 AVENUE OF THE AMERICAS, NEW YORK, NEW YORK 10020

To my grandmother, Xiaoqian,
who taught me how to tell stories.

And to Lisa, Esther, and Miranda,
who showed me why stories are important.

Contents

Preface   xi

Ghost Days   1
Maxwell's Demon   27
The Reborn   49
Thoughts and Prayers   77
Byzantine Empathy   97
The Gods Will Not Be Chained   135
Staying Behind   157
Real Artists   173
The Gods Will Not Be Slain   185
Altogether Elsewhere, Vast Herds of Reindeer   209
The Gods Have Not Died in Vain   223
Memories of My Mother   249
Dispatches from the Cradle: The Hermit—
Forty-Eight Hours in the Sea of Massachusetts   255
Grey Rabbit, Crimson Mare, Coal Leopard   273
A Chase Beyond the Storms   315
An excerpt from *The Veiled Throne*, The Dandelion Dynasty, book three
The Hidden Girl   335
Seven Birthdays   363
The Message   383
Cutting   409

Acknowledgments   413

Preface

There is a paradox at the heart of the art of fiction, at least as I've experienced it: while the medium of fiction is language, a technology whose primary purpose is communication, I can only write satisfying fiction by eschewing the communicative purpose.

An explanation. As the author, I construct an artifact out of words, but the words are meaningless until they're animated by the consciousness of the reader. The story is co-told by the author and the reader, and every story is incomplete until a reader comes along and *interprets* it.

Each reader comes to the text with their own interpretive frameworks, assumptions about reality, background narratives concerning how the world is and ought to be. These are acquired through experience, through every individual's unique history of encounters with irreducible reality. The plausibility of plot is judged against these battle-scars; the depth of characters is measured against these phenomenon-shadows; the truth *vel non* of each story is weighed with the fears and hopes residing in each heart.

A good story cannot function like a legal brief, which attempts to persuade and lead the reader down a narrow path suspended above the abyss of unreason. Rather, it must be more like an empty house, an open garden, a deserted beach by the ocean. The reader moves in with their own burdensome baggage and long-cherished possessions, seeds of doubt and shears of understanding, maps of human nature and baskets of sustaining faith. The reader then inhabits the story, explores its nooks and crannies, rearranges the furniture to suit their taste, covers the walls with sketches of their inner life, and thereby makes the story their home.

As an author, I find trying to build a house that would please every imagined future inhabitant limiting, constricting, paralyzing.

Far better to construct a house in which *I* would feel at home, at peace, consoled by the sympathy between reality and the artifice of language.

Yet, experience has shown that it is when I am least aiming to *communicate* that the result is most open to interpretation; that it is when I am least solicitous of the comfort of my readers that they are mostly likely to make the story their home. Only by focusing purely on the subjective do I have a chance at achieving the intersubjective.

Picking the stories for this collection was thus, in more than one way, much easier than picking the stories for my debut, *The Paper Menagerie and Other Stories*. Gone was the pressure to "present." Rather than worrying about which stories would make the "best" collection for imaginary readers, I decided to stick with stories that most pleased myself. My editor, Joe Monti, was invaluable in this process and managed to weave the result into a table of contents that told a meta-narrative I couldn't have seen myself.

May you find a story in here to make your home.

THE
HIDDEN GIRL

and

Other Stories

Ghost Days

3.

Ms. Coron pointed to the screen-board, on which she had typed out a bit of code.

```
(define (fib n)
  (if (< n 2)
  1
  (+ (fib (- n 1)) (fib (- n 2)))))
```

"Let's diagram the call-graph for this classic LISP function, which computes the n-th Fibonacci number recursively."

Ona watched her Teacher turn around. The helmetless Ms. Coron wore a dress that exposed the skin of her arms and legs in a way that she had taught the children was *beautiful* and *natural*. Intellectually, Ona understood that the frigid air in the classroom, cold enough to give her and the other children hypothermia even with brief exposure, was perfectly suited to the Teachers. But she couldn't help shivering at the sight. The airtight heat-suit scraped over Ona's scales, and the rustling noise reverberated loudly in her helmet.

Ms. Coron went on, "A recursive function works like nesting dolls. To solve a bigger problem, a recursive function calls on itself to solve a smaller version of the same problem."

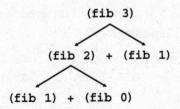

Ona wished she could call on a smaller version of herself to solve her problems. She imagined that nested inside her was Obedient Ona, who enjoyed diagramming Classical Computer Languages and studying prosody in Archaic English. That would free her up to focus on the mysterious alien civilization of Nova Pacifica, the long-dead original inhabitants of this planet.

"What's the point of studying dead computer languages, anyway?" Ona said.

The heads of the other children in the classroom turned as one to look at her, the golden glint from the scales on their faces dazzling even through the two layers of glass in their and Ona's helmets.

Ona cursed herself silently. Apparently, instead of Obedient Ona, she had somehow called on Loudmouth Ona, who was always getting her in trouble.

Ona noticed that Ms. Coron's naked face was particularly made up today, but her lips, painted bright red, almost disappeared into a thin line as she tried to maintain her smile.

"We study classical languages to acquire the habits of mind of the ancients," Ms. Coron said. "You must know where *you* came from."

The way she said "you" let Ona know that she didn't mean just her in particular, but all the children of the colony, Nova Pacifica. With their scaled skin, their heat-tolerant organs and vessels, their six-lobed lungs—all engineered based on models from the local fauna—the children's bodies incorporated an alien biochemistry so that they could breathe the air outside the Dome and survive on this hot, poisonous planet.

Ona knew she should shut up, but—just like the recursive calls in Ms. Coron's diagram had to return up the call stack—she couldn't keep down Loudmouth Ona. "I know where I came from: I was designed on a computer, grown in a vat, and raised in the glass nursery with the air from outside pumped in."

Ms. Coron softened her voice. "Oh, Ona, that's not . . . not what I meant. Nova Pacifica is too far from the home worlds, and they won't be sending a rescue ship because they don't know that we survived the wormhole and we're stranded here on the other side of the galaxy. You'll never see the beautiful floating islands of Tai-Winn or the glorious skyways of Pele, the elegant city-trees of Pollen, or the busy data warrens of Tiron—you've been cut off from your heritage, from the rest of humanity."

Hearing—for the millionth time—these vague legends of the wonders that she'd been deprived of made the scales on Ona's back stand up. She hated the condescension.

But Ms. Coron went on, "However, when you've learned enough to read the LISP source code that powered the first auto-constructors on Earth; when you've learned enough Archaic English to understand the Declaration of New Manifest Destiny; when you've learned enough Customs and Culture to appreciate all the recorded holos and sims in the Library—*then* you will understand the brilliance and elegance of the ancients, of our race."

"But we're *not* human! You made us in the image of the plants and animals living here. The dead aliens are more like us than you!"

Ms. Coron stared at Ona, and Ona saw that she had hit upon a truth Ms. Coron didn't want to admit, even to herself. In the Teacher's eyes, the children would never be good enough, never be fully *human*, though they were the future of humanity on this inhospitable planet.

Ms. Coron took a deep breath and went on as if nothing had happened. "Today is the Day of Remembrance, and I'm sure you'll impress all the Teachers with your presentations later. But let's finish our lesson first.

"To compute the n-th term, the recursive function calls itself to compute the (n–1)th term and the (n–2)th term, so that they could be added together, each time going back earlier in the sequence, solving earlier versions of the same problem. . . .

"The past," Ms. Coron continued, "thus accumulating bit by bit through recursion, becomes the future."

The bell rang, and class was finally over.

•

Even though it meant they had less time to eat, Ona and her friends always made the long walk to have lunch outside the Dome. Eating inside meant squeezing tubes of paste through a flap in her helmet or going back to the claustrophobia-inducing tanks of the dormitory.

"What are you going to do?" Jason asked, biting into a honeycomb fruit—poisonous to the Teachers, but all the children loved it. He had glued white ceramic tiles all over his suit to make it look like an ancient space suit from the old pictures. Next to him was a flag—the old Stars and Stripes of the American Empire (or was it the American Republic?)—his artifact, so that he could tell the legend of Neil Armstrong, Moonwalker, at the Remembrance Assembly later that evening. "You don't have a costume."

"I don't know," Ona said, twisting off her helmet and stripping off her suit. She took deep gulps of warm, fresh air, free of the suffocating chemical odor of the recycling filters. "And I don't care."

Everyone presenting at the Remembrance Assembly was supposed to be in costume. Two weeks ago, Ona had received her assigned artifact: a little, flat metal piece with a rough surface about the size of her palm and shaped like a toy spade. It was dark green in color, with a stubby, fat handle and a double-tined blade, heavier than its size would suggest. It was a family heirloom that belonged to Ms. Coron.

"But these artifacts and stories are so important to them," Talia said. "They'll be so angry that you didn't do any research." She had glued her artifact, a white veil, over her helmet and put on a lacy white dress over her suit so that she could enact a classical wedding with Dahl, who had painted his suit black to imitate the grooms he had seen in old holos.

"Who knows if the stories they tell us are true, anyway? We can never go there."

Ona placed the little spade in the middle of the table, where it absorbed the heat from the sun. She imagined Ms. Coron reaching out to touch it—a precious keepsake from a world she will never see again—and then screaming because the spade was hot.

You must know where you *came from.*

Ona would rather use the spade to dig up the past of Nova Pacifica, her planet, where she was at *home.* She wanted to learn about the history of the "aliens" far more than she wanted to know about the past of the Teachers.

"They cling to their past like rotten glue-lichen"—as she spoke she could feel fury boiling up inside her—"and make us feel bad, incomplete, like we'll never be as good as them. But they can't even survive out here for an hour!"

She grabbed the spade and threw it as hard as she could into the whitewood forest.

Jason and Talia stayed silent. After a few awkward minutes, they got up.

"We have to get ready for the Assembly," Jason murmured. And they went back inside.

Ona sat alone for a while, listlessly counting the darting shuttle-wings overhead. She sighed and got up to walk into the whitewood forest to retrieve the spade.

Truth be told, on bright, warm autumn days like this, Ona wanted nothing more than to be outside, suitless and helmetless, wandering through the whitewood groves, their six-sided trunks rising into the sky, the vibrating silver-white hexagonal leaves a canopy of mirrors, their susurration whispers and giggles.

She watched the flutter-bys dance through the air, their six translucent, bright blue wings beating wildly as they traced out patterns in the air she was sure was a kind of language. The Dome had been built on the site of an ancient alien city, and here and there, the woods were broken by hillocks—piles of angular rubble left behind by the mysterious original inhabitants of this planet who had all died millennia before the arrival of the colony ship, alien ruins exuding nothing but a ghostly silence.

Not that they've tried very hard, Ona thought. The Teachers had never shown much interest in the aliens, too busy trying to cram everything about old Earth into the children's heads.

She felt the full warmth of the sun against her face and body, her white scales coruscating with the colors of the rainbow. The afternoon sun was hot enough to boil water where the whitewood trees didn't shade the soil, and white plumes of steam filled the forest. Though she hadn't thrown the spade far, it was hard to find it among the dense trees. Ona picked her way slowly, examining every exposed root and overturned rock, every pile of ancient rubble. She hoped that the spade hadn't been broken.

There.

Ona hurried over. The spade was on the side of a pile of rubble, nestled among some tinselgrass that cushioned its fall. A small spume of steam was trapped under it, so that it seemed to be floating over the escaping water vapor. Ona leaned closer.

The steam held a fragrance that she had never smelled before. The spume had blasted away some of the green patina encrusting the spade, revealing the gleaming golden metal underneath. She suddenly had a sense of just how ancient the object was, and she wondered if it was some kind of ritual implement, vaguely remembering the religion excerpts from Customs and Culture class— ghost stories.

She was curious, for the first time, whether the previous owners ever imagined that the spade would one day end up a billion billion miles from home, on top of an alien tomb, in the hands of a barely-human girl who looked like Ona.

Mesmerized by the smell, she reached for the spade, took a deep breath, and fainted.

2.

EAST NORBURY, CONNECTICUT, 1989

For the Halloween dance, Fred Ho decided to go as Ronald Reagan.

Mainly it was because the mask was on sale at the Dollar Store. Also, he could wear his father's suit, worn only once, on the day the restaurant opened. He didn't want to argue with his father about money. Going to the dance was shock enough for his parents.

Also, the pants had deep pockets, good for holding his present. Heavy and angular, the little antique bronze spade-shaped token had been warmed by his thigh through the thin fabric. He thought Carrie might like to use it as a paperweight, hang it as a window decoration, or even take advantage of the hole at the handle end to turn it into an incense holder. She often smelled of sandalwood and patchouli.

Picking him up at his house, she waved at his parents, who stood in the door, confused and wary, and did not wave back.

"You look dapper," Carrie said, her mask on the dashboard.

He was relieved that Carrie had approved of his costume. Indeed, she did more than approve. She had dressed up as Nancy Reagan.

He laughed and tried to think of something appropriate to say. By the time he settled on "You look beautiful," they were already a block away, and it seemed too late. So he said, "Thank you for asking me to the dance," instead.

The field house was festooned with orange streamers, plastic bats, and paper pumpkins. They put on their masks and went in. They danced to Paula Abdul's "Straight Up" and then Madonna's "Like a Prayer." Well, Carrie danced; Fred mostly tried to keep up.

Though he still moved as awkwardly as ever, the masks somehow made it easier for him not to worry about his lack of the most essential skill for surviving an American high school—blending in.

The rubber masks soon made them sweaty. Carrie drank cup after cup of the sickly-sweet punch, but Fred, who opted to keep his mask on, shook his head. By the time Jordan Knight began to sing "I'll Be Loving You (Forever)," they were ready to get out of the dark gym.

Outside, the parking lot was filled with ghosts, Supermans, aliens, witches, and princesses. They waved at the presidential couple, and the couple waved back. Fred kept his mask on and deliberately set a slow pace, enjoying the evening breeze.

"Wish it could be Halloween every day," he said.

"Why?" she asked.

No one knows who I am, he wanted to say. *No one stares at me.* But instead all he said was "It's nice to wear a suit." He spoke carefully and slowly, and he almost could not hear his accent.

She nodded, as if she understood. They got into the car.

Until Fred's arrival, East Norbury High School had never had a student whose first language wasn't English and who might be illegal. People were mostly friendly, but a thousand smiles, whispers, little gestures that each individually seemed so innocuous added up to *you don't belong.*

"You nervous about meeting my parents?" she asked.

"No," he lied.

"My mom is really excited about meeting you."

They arrived at a white raised ranch behind an immaculate lawn. The mailbox at the mouth of the driveway said "Wynne."

"This is your house," he said.

"You can read!" she teased, and parked.

Walking up the driveway, Fred could smell the sea in the air and hear the waves crashing against the shore nearby. There was an elegant, simple jack-o'-lantern on the steps before the front door.

A fairy tale house, Fred thought. *An American castle.*

•

"Is there anything I can do to help?" Fred asked from the kitchen door.

Mrs. Wynne ("Call me Cammy") was shuttling between the kitchen table, which was being used as a cutting/mixing/staging station, and the stove. She smiled at him quickly before turning back to her work. "Don't worry about it. Go chat with my husband and Carrie."

"I really can help," he said. "I know my way around a kitchen. My family runs a restaurant."

"Oh, I know. Carrie tells me your Moo Shu Pork is excellent." She stopped and looked at him, her smile even wider. "You speak such good English!"

He never understood why people felt it important to point that out. They always sounded so surprised, and he never knew what to say. "Thank you."

"It *really* is very good. Go on now. I have this all under control."

He retreated back to the living room, wishing he could stay in the warm, almost-familiar heat of the kitchen.

•

"A terrible thing," Mr. Wynne said. "Those brave students in Tiananmen Square. Heroes."

Fred nodded.

"Your parents," Mr. Wynne continued, "they were dissidents?"

Fred hesitated. He remembered his father reading the Chinese newspaper they got for free from Chinatown up in Boston, showing the photographs of the protesting crowds in Beijing.

"Stupid kids," he had said, contempt making his face red. "Wasting their parents' money to riot outside like the Red Guards just so they can pose for the foreigners and their cameras instead of studying. What do they hope to accomplish? They're all spoiled, read too many American books."

Then he turned to Fred and shook his fist threateningly. "If you ever dare to do something like that, I'll beat you until you can tell your ass apart from your head again."

"Yes," Fred said. "That's why we came here."

Mr. Wynne nodded, satisfied. "This is a great country, isn't it?"

Truth be told, he had never really understood why, one day, his parents had woken him up in the middle of the night; why they had gotten on a boat, then a truck, then a bus, then a big ship; why, for so many days, they had ridden in the dark, the tossing and tumbling of the sea making him sick; why, after they landed, they had hidden in the back of a van until they emerged in the dirty streets of Chinatown in New York, where some men spoke with his father in menacing tones while he nodded and nodded; why his father had told him that now they all had different names and were different people and they must never talk to foreigners or the police; why they had all lived in the basement of a restaurant and worked there for years and talked endlessly of how to save money to pay off the debt to those menacing men and then make more of it; why they had then moved again, to East Norbury, this small town on the coast of New England, where his father said there were no Chinese restaurants and the Americans were too stupid to know that he wasn't much of a cook.

"A great country, sir," he said.

"And that's the face of a great man you're holding," Mr. Wynne said, indicating his mask. "A real fighter for freedom."

After that week in June, his father had gotten on the phone every evening, whispering deep into the night. And suddenly his father told him and his mother that they had to memorize a new story about themselves, about how they were connected to the students who had died in Tiananmen Square, believed the same things, and were hopelessly in love with "democracy." "Asylum" was mentioned often, and they had to be prepared for an interview with some American official in New York next month, so that they could make themselves *legal*.

"Then we can stay here and make lots of money," his father had said, satisfied.

The doorbell rang. Carrie got up with the bowl of candies.

"Carrie is always adventurous," Mr. Wynne said. He lowered his voice. "She likes to try new things. It's natural, being rebellious at her age."

Fred nodded, not sure what he was really being told.

Mr. Wynne's face lost its friendly expression, like a mask falling off. "She's just going through a phase, you understand. You're a part"—he waved his hands vaguely—"of . . . of how she wants to get a rise out of me.

"It's not serious," he added. But his expression was very serious.

Fred said nothing.

"I just want there to be no misunderstandings," Mr Wynne continued. "People tend to belong with their own kind, as I'm sure you'll agree."

Over by the door, Carrie gasped and pretended to be scared by the trick-or-treaters and expressed admiration at the costumes.

"Don't get the wrong idea about what she's doing with you."

Carrie returned from the door.

"Why so quiet?" she asked. "What were you two talking about?"

"Just learning about Fred's family," Mr. Wynne said, his face again friendly and smiling. "They were dissidents, did you know? Very brave people."

Fred stood up, his hand in his pocket, fingers wrapped around the little bronze spade. He fantasized throwing it at the face of Mr. Wynne, which strangely bore some resemblance to his father's.

But instead, he said, "I'm sorry. I didn't realize it's so late. I should go."

1.

HONG KONG, 1905

"Jyu-zung—" William's father called again. He was as loud as their neighbor futilely attempting to quiet her colicky child.

Why does everyone in Hong Kong have to shout? It's the first decade of the twentieth century, and everyone still acts like they live in villages.

"It's *William*," William muttered. Even though his father had paid for his expensive education in England, the old man still refused to use his English name, the name he had gone by for more than a decade.

William tried to focus on the book in front of him, the words of the fourteenth-century Christian mystic:

For thou hast brought me with thi question into that same derknes, and into that same cloude of unknowyng that I wolde thou were in thiself.

"Jyu-zung!"

He plugged up his ears with his fingers.

For of alle other creatures and theire werkes—ye, and of the werkes of God self—may a man thorou grace have fulheed of knowing, and wel to kon thinke on hem; bot of God Himself can no man thinke.

The book, *The Cloude of Unknowyng*, had been a parting gift from Virginia, who was surely the most radiant of His works and one William longed to have "fulheed of knowing."

"Now that you're going back to the mysterious Orient," she had said as she handed him the book, "may you be guided by the mystics of the Occident."

"Hong Kong is not like that," he had said, unhappy that she seemed to think of him as a mere *Chinaman*, though . . . he kind of was. "It's part of the Empire. It's civilized." He took the book from her, almost, but not quite, touching her fingers. "I'll be back in a year."

She had rewarded him with a bold and radiant smile, which, more than all his high marks and the praise from his tutors, made him feel like a proper Englishman.

And therfore I wole leve al that thing that I can think, and chese to my love that thing that I cannot think. For whi He may wel be loved, bot not thought. By love may He be getyn and holden; bot bi thought neither.

"Jyu-zung! What is the matter with you?"

His father stood in the door, his face red with the exertion of having climbed up the ladder to William's attic room.

William pulled his fingers from his ears.

"You're supposed to help me with the preparations for *Yu Lan*."

After the mellifluous music of Middle English in his head, his father's Cantonese grated on his ears like the clanging of cymbals and gongs in *Jyut kek*, the native "folk opera" that was undeserving of the name, a barbarous shadow of the real operas he had attended in London.

"I'm busy," William said.

His father looked from his face to his book and then back again.

"It's an important book," he said, avoiding his father's gaze.

"The ghosts will be parading tonight." His father shuffled his feet. "Let's make sure the spirits of our ancestors aren't ashamed, and we can try to comfort the homeless ghosts."

To go from reading Darwin, Newton, and Smith to *this*, to *appeasing ghosts*. In England, men were contemplating the possibility of knowing all the laws of nature, the end of science, but here, under his father's roof, it was still the Middle Ages. He could easily imagine the look on Virginia's face.

He had nothing in common with his father, who might as well be an alien.

"I'm not asking," his father said. His voice grew hard, like the way the Cantonese opera actors ended a scene.

Rationality suffocates in the air of superstition in the colonies. His determination to go back to England had never been stronger.

•

"Why would Grandfather need this?" William asked, staring critically at the paper model of an Arrol-Johnston three-cylinder horseless carriage.

"Everyone appreciates things that make life more comfortable," his father said.

William shook his head but continued the task of gluing headlights made of yellow paper—intended to simulate brass—to the model.

Next to him, the surface of the table was covered with other offerings to be burnt later that night: a paper model of a Western-style cottage, paper suits, paper dress shoes, stacks of "underworld money" and piles of "gold bullion."

He could not resist commenting, "Grandfather and Great-grandfather must have poor eyesight to confuse these with the real thing."

His father refused to take the bait, and they continued to work in silence.

To make the tedious ritual tolerable, William fantasized that he was polishing the car in preparation for a ride through the countryside with Virginia. . . .

"Jyu-zung, could you take out the sandalwood table from the basement? Let's lay out the feast for the ghosts with some style. We shouldn't argue anymore on this day."

The pleading note in his father's voice surprised William. He noticed, suddenly, how bent his father's back had become.

An image came unbidden to him of himself as a young boy

sitting on top of his father's shoulders, which had seemed as broad and steady as a mountain.

"Higher, higher!" he shouted.

And his father lifted him over his head so that he could be above the milling crowd, so that he could see the exciting costumes and beautiful makeup of the folk opera troupe performing for Yu Lan.

His father's arms were so strong and kept him lifted high in the air for a long time.

"Of course, *Aa-baa*," William said, and stood up to go to the warehouse in the back.

The warehouse was dark, dry, and cool. This was where his father temporarily stored the antiques he was restoring for customers as well as the pieces he collected. The heavy wooden shelves and cubbyholes were filled with Zhou bronze ritual vessels, Han jade carvings, Tang tomb figurines, Ming porcelain, and all manner of other wares that William did not recognize.

He made his way carefully through the narrow hallways, looking impatiently for his prize.

Maybe in that corner?

In this corner of the warehouse, a ray of slanting light from a papered-over window illuminated a small workbench. Behind it, leaning against the wall, was the sandalwood dining table.

As he bent down to pick up the table, what he saw on the workbench stopped him.

There were two identical-looking *bubi*, ancient bronze coins, on the table. They looked like palm-size spades. Though he didn't know much about antiques, he had seen enough *bubi* as a child to know that this style was from the Zhou Dynasty or earlier. The ancient Chinese kings had cast coins in this shape to show a reverence for the earth, from which came life-sustaining crops and to which all life must return. Digging in the earth was a promise to the future as well as an acknowledgment of the past.

Given how large these *bubi* were, William knew they must be valuable. To have an identical pair was very rare.

Curious, he looked closer at the coins, which were covered in a dark green patina. Something didn't seem right. He flipped over the one on the left: it gleamed bright yellow, almost like gold.

Next to the coins was a small dish with some dark blue powder inside, and a paintbrush. William sniffed the powder: coppery.

He knew that bronze only looked bright yellow if it was freshly cast.

He tried to push away the thought. His father had always been an honorable man who made an honest living. It was unfilial for a son to think such thoughts.

But he picked up the pair of *bubi* and put them in his pocket. His English teachers had taught him to ask questions, to dig for the truth, no matter what the consequences.

He half-dragged and half-carried the table up to the front hall.

•

"Now this looks like a proper festival," his father said as he placed the last plate of vegetarian duck on the table. The table was filled with plates of fruit and mock-versions of every kind of meat. Eight place settings had been arranged around the table, ready to receive the ghosts of the ancestors of the Ho family.

Mock chicken, vegetarian duck, papier-mâché houses, false money...

"Maybe we can go to see some opera performances in the streets later," his father said, oblivious to William's mood. "Just like when you were little."

Forged bronzes...

He took out the two *bubi* from his pocket and placed them on the table, the gleaming side of the unfinished one facing up.

His father looked at them, paused for a moment, and then acted as if nothing was wrong. "You want to light the joss sticks?"

William said nothing, trying to find a way to phrase his question.

His father arranged the two *bubi* side by side and flipped them over. Carved into the patina on the reverse side of each was a character.

"The character forms from the Zhou Dynasty were a bit different from later forms," his father said, as though William was still only a child being taught how to read and write. "So collectors from later ages would sometimes carve their interpretations of the script on the vessels. Like the patina, these interpretations also accumulate on the vessels in layers, build up over time."

"Have you ever noticed how similar the character 'jyu'—for the universe, which is also the first character in your name—is to the character 'zi'—for writing?"

William shook his head, not really listening.

This entire culture is based on hypocrisy, on fakery, on mocking up the appearance for that which cannot be obtained.

"See how the universe is straightforward, but to understand it with the intellect, to turn it into language, requires a twist, a sharp turn? Between the World and the Word, there lies an extra curve. When you look at these characters, you're convening with the history of these artifacts, with the minds of our ancestors from thousands of years ago. That is the deep wisdom of our people, and no Latin letters will ever get at our truth as deeply as our characters."

William could no longer stand it. "You hypocrite! You are a forger!"

He waited, silently urging his father to deny the charge, to explain.

After a while, his father began to speak, not looking at him. "The first ghosts came to me a few years ago."

He used the term *gwailou* for "foreigners," but which also meant "ghosts."

"They handed me antiques I had never seen before to restore. I asked them, 'How did you get these?' 'Oh, we bought them from some French soldiers who conquered Peking and burned down the Palace and took these as loot.'

"For the ghosts, a robbery could give good title. This was their law. These bronzes and ceramics, handed down from our ancestors for a hundred generations, would now be taken from us and used to decorate the homes of robbers who did not even understand what they were. I could not allow it.

"So I made copies of the works I was supposed to restore, and I gave the copies back to the ghosts. The real artifacts I saved for this land, for you, and for your children. I mark the real ones and the copies with different characters, so that I can tell them apart. I know what I do is wrong in your eyes, and I am ashamed. But love makes us do strange things."

Which is authentic? he thought. *The* World *or the* Word? *The truth or understanding?*

The sound of a cane rapping against the front door interrupted them.

"Probably customers," said his father.

"Open up!" whoever was at the door shouted.

William went to the front door and opened it, revealing a well-dressed Englishman in his forties, followed by two burly, scruffy men who looked like they were more at home in the docks of the colony.

"How do you do?" the Englishman said. Without waiting to be invited, he confidently stepped inside. The other two shoved William aside as they followed.

"Mr. Dixon," his father said. "What a pleasant surprise." His father's heavily accented English made William cringe.

"Not as pleasant a surprise as the one you gave me, I assure you," Dixon said. He reached inside his coat and pulled out a small porcelain figurine and set it on the table. "I gave you this to repair."

"And I did."

A smirk appeared on Dixon's face. "My daughter is very fond of this piece. Indeed, it amuses me to see her treating the antique tomb figurine like a doll, and that was how it came to be broken. But after you returned the mended figurine, she refused to play with it, saying that it was not her dolly. Now, children are very good at detecting lies. And Professor Osmer was good enough to confirm my guess."

His father straightened his back but said nothing.

Dixon gestured, and his two lackeys immediately shoved everything off the table: plates, dishes, bowls, the *bubi*, the food, the chopsticks—all crashed into a cacophonous heap.

"Do you want us to keep looking around? Or are you ready to confess to the police?"

His father kept his face expressionless. *Inscrutable*, the English would have called it. At the school, William had looked into a mirror until he had learned to not make that face, until he had stopped looking like his father.

"Wait a minute." William stepped forward. "You can't just go into someone's house and act like a bunch of lawless thugs."

"Your English is very good," Dixon said as he looked William up and down. "Almost no accent."

"Thank you," William said. He tried to maintain a calm, reasonable tone and demeanor. Surely the man would realize now that he was not dealing with a common native family, but a young *Englishman* of breeding and good character. "I studied for ten years at Mr. George Dodsworth's School in Ramsgate. Do you know it?"

Dixon smiled and said nothing, as though he was staring at a dancing monkey. But William pressed on.

"I'm certain my father would be happy to compensate you for what you feel you deserve. There's no need to resort to violence. We can behave like gentlemen."

Dixon began to laugh, at first a little, then uproariously. His men, confused at first, joined in after a while.

"You think that because you've learned to speak English, you are other than what you are. There seems to be something in the Oriental mind that cannot grasp the essential difference between the West and the East. I am not here to negotiate with you, but to assert my rights, a notion that seems foreign to your habits of mind. If you do not restore to me what is mine, we will smash everything in this place to smithereens."

William felt the blood rush to his face, and he willed himself to let the muscles of his face go slack, to not betray his feelings. He looked across the room at his father, and suddenly he realized that his father's expression must also be his expression, the placid mask over a helpless rage.

While they talked, his father had been slowly moving behind

Dixon. Now he looked over at William, and the two nodded at each other almost imperceptibly.

And therfore I wole leve al that thing that I can think, and chese to my love that thing that I cannot think.

William jumped at Dixon as his father lunged at Dixon's legs. The three men fell to the ground in a heap. In the struggle that followed, William seemed to observe himself from a distance. There was no thought, but a mixture of love and rage that clouded his mind until William found himself sitting astride Dixon's prone body, clutching one of the *bubi*, poised to smash its blade into Dixon's head.

The two men Dixon had brought with him looked on helplessly, frozen in place.

"We don't have what you're looking for here," William said, breathing deeply. "Now get out of our house."

·

William and his father surveyed the mess Dixon and his men left behind.

"Thank you," his father said.

"I suppose the ghosts got a good show tonight," William said.

"I'm sure Grandfather is proud of you," his father said. And then, for the first time that he could remember, his father added, "Jyu-zung, I'm proud of you."

William did not know if what he felt was love or rage, and as he looked at the two characters on the upturned *bubi* on the ground, they seemed to waver and merge into one as his eyes grew blurry.

2.

EAST NORBURY, CONNECTICUT, 1989

"Thank you for having me to your house," Fred said. "I had a great time tonight." He spoke stiffly and carefully kept his distance from her.

The waves of Long Island Sound lapped gently at the beach at their feet.

"You're very sweet," she said, and held his hand. She leaned against him, and the wind lifted her hair against his face, the floral scent of her shampoo mixing with the smell of the sea, like promise mixed with longing. His heart thumped. He felt a tenderness in the middle of his chest that he was frightened of.

Across the bay, they could see the bright red lights of the Edley Mansion, which was being run as a haunted house for the week. He imagined the delighted screams of the children, willingly thrilled by the lies told by their parents.

"Don't worry too much about what my dad says," she said.

He froze.

"You're angry," she said.

"What do you know about it?" he said. *She is a princess. She belongs.*

"You can't control what others think," she said. "But you can always decide for yourself if you belong."

He said nothing, trying to comprehend the rage in himself.

"I am not my father," she said. "And you're not your parents. Family is a story that is told to you, but the story that matters the most you must tell yourself."

He realized that this was the thing about America that he loved the most: the utter faith that family did not matter, that the past was but a *story*. Even a story that started as a lie—a fib—could become authentic, could become a life that was real.

He reached into the pocket of his pants and took out his gift.

"What is it?" She held the little bronze spade uncertainly in her hand.

"It's an antique," he said, "a spade-shaped coin used a long time ago in China. It used to belong to my grandfather, and he gave it to me before we left China, for luck. I thought you might like it."

"It's beautiful."

He felt compelled to be honest. "My grandfather said that his father had saved it from foreigners trying to steal it from the country, and the Red Guards almost destroyed it during the Cultural Revolution. But my dad says it's a fake, like many things from China, and not worth anything. See this mark on the bottom? He says it's too modern, not really old. But it's the only thing I have from my grandfather. He died last year and we couldn't go back for the funeral, because of . . . immigration problems."

"Shouldn't you keep it?"

"I want you to have it. I'll always remember giving it to you, and that's a better memory, a better story."

He bent down and picked up a small, sharp rock from the beach. As he held her hand with the spade coin in it, slowly, he etched the letters of their initials into the patina, next to the older character. "Now it has our mark, our story."

She nodded and solemnly put the coin into her jacket pocket. "Thank you. It's lovely."

He thought about going home, about the questions from his father and the worried silence from his mother, about the long hours ahead of him in the restaurant tomorrow and the day after and the day after that, about college, now a possibility if he could show his citizenship papers, about one day making his own way across this vast continent, now still hidden under a cloud of unknowing darkness.

But not yet. He looked around and wanted to do something big, to commemorate this night. He took off his jacket, his shirt, kicked off his shoes. He was naked, maskless, costumeless. "Let's go for a swim."

She laughed, not believing him.

The water was cold, so cold that diving in made him gasp and think his skin was on fire. He dove under and then popped back up, and shook the water from his face.

She called for him, and he waved back, once, and then swam towards the bright lights on the other side of the bay.

The reflection of the red-lit Edley Mansion in the water was streaked, mixed with the bright white from the moon. As his arms moved through the dark blue sea, jellies glowed against his skin, like hundreds of little stars.

Her voice faded behind him as he swam through the stars and stripes, fractal, ambiguous, tasting of salty hope and the deliberate sting of leaving behind the past.

3.

NOVA PACIFICA, 2313

Ona woke up in the middle of a busy street. The light was dim, and it was cold, as though it were dusk or dawn.

Six-wheeled vehicles shaped like sleek-finned sea-darts rushed by both sides of her, seeming to miss her by inches. A glance inside one of the vehicles almost made her scream.

The head of the creature inside had twelve tentacles radiating from it.

She looked around: thick, six-sided towers around her rose into the sky, as dense as the trunks of the whitewood grove. She dodged around the speeding vehicles and made her way to the side of the street, where more of the twelve-tentacled creatures ambled by, paying no attention to her. They had six feet and a low-slung torso, with a shimmering skin that she wasn't sure was made of fur or scales.

Overhead, cloth signs etched with alien markings fluttered in the wind like leaves, the individual symbols made up of line segments intersecting at sharp and obtuse angles. The noise of the crowd, consisting of incomprehensible clicks, moans, and chirps, coalesced into a susurration that she was sure was a kind of language.

The creatures paid no attention to her, sometimes barreling right into her, through her as though she were made of air. She felt like a ghost in the stories that some of the Teachers used to tell when she was younger, an invisible being. She squinted to find the sun in the middle of the sky: it was dimmer and smaller than she was used to.

Then, suddenly, everything began to change. The pedestrians on the sidewalks stopped, swung their heads skyward, and lifted their tentacles towards the sun—at the tip of each appendage was the black orb of an eye. The traffic in the street slowed and then ceased, the occupants of the vehicles stepping out to join the sun-gazing crowd. Silence fell across the scene like a veil.

Ona looked around the crowd, picking out individual groupings frozen in tableaus like photographs. A large creature wrapped its forearms protectively around two smaller ones, its tentacles trembling noiselessly. Two aliens leaned against each other, their tentacles and arms entwined. Another one, its legs unsteady, supported itself against the side of a building, its tentacles lightly tapping against the wall like a man sending a message.

The sun seemed to glow brighter, and then brighter still. The creatures turned their faces away from the sun, their tentacles wilting in the new heat and light.

They turned to gaze at *her*. Thousands, millions of dozens of eyes focused on Ona, as though suddenly she had become visible. Their tentacles reached towards her, pleading, signaling.

The crowd separated, and a small creature, about her size, walked towards her. Ona held out her hands, palms uplifted, uncertain what to do.

The small alien reached her, deposited something in her hand, and stepped back. Ona looked down and felt the ancient, rough metal against her scaled skin, absorbed its heft. She flipped the spade around and saw a mark that she did not recognize: sharp angles, hooks, reminding her of the markings on the fluttering signs.

A thought came into her mind like a whisper: *Remember us, you who treasure the old.*

The sun glowed even brighter, and as Ona felt warm again, the creatures around her melted into the blinding, bright light.

•

Ona sat under the whitewood tree, fingers wrapped around the small bronze spade. White plumes of steam continued to erupt from the hillocks around her, each perhaps another window into a lost world.

The images she had seen went through her mind again and again. *Sometimes understanding comes to you not through thought, but through this throbbing of the heart, this tenderness in the chest that hurts.*

As their world was about to die, the ancient people of Nova Pacifica, in their last days, focused all their energy on leaving behind tributes, memorials of their civilization. Knowing that they themselves would not survive the sun that burnt hotter and hotter, they embedded their six-fold symmetry into every species around them, hoping that some would survive and become living echoes of their cities, their civilization, their selves. In their ruins, they hid a record that would be played when triggered by the detection of something made, aged, layered, still preserved because it was valued, so that they had some reasonable expectation that the owner would have a sense of history, of respect for the past.

Ona thought of the children, frightened and uncomprehending as their world burnt up. She thought of the lovers, poised between regret and acceptance, as the world outside collapsed against the world between them. She thought of a people trying their hardest to leave behind a trace of their existence in this universe, a few signs to mark their passage.

The past, ever recurring, made up the future like layers of patina.

She thought of Ms. Coron and the naked faces of the Teachers, and for the first time, she came to see their expressions in a new light. It was not arrogance that made them look at the children the way they did, but fear. They had been stranded on this new world, where they could not survive, and they clung to their past as fiercely as they did because they knew that they would be yielding their places to a new race, the People of Nova Pacifica, and live on only in their memories.

Parents fear to be forgotten, to not be understood by their children.

Ona lifted the small bronze spade and licked the surface with the tip of her tongue. It tasted bitter and sweet, the fragrance of long-dead incense, of sacrificial offerings, of traces left behind by countless lifetimes. The spot where the steam had blasted away the patina, next to some ancient etched marks, was shaped like a little person, gleamed fresh and new, the future as well as the past.

She got up and pulled off a few pliant branches from nearby whitewood trees. Weaving carefully, she made them into a crown with twelve radiating branches, like tentacles, like hair, like olive branches. She had her costume.

It was but a brief scene glimpsed through the cloud of unknowing, a few images that she could barely comprehend. Perhaps they were idealized, sentimental, constructed; yet was there not a trace of authenticity, an indelible seed of the love of a people whose past meant something? She would show them how she now understood that digging into the past was an act of comprehension, an act of making sense of the universe.

Her body was an amalgam of the biological and technological heritages of two species, and her very existence the culmination of the striving of two peoples. Nested inside her was Earth Ona and Nova Pacifica Ona and Rebellious Ona and Obedient Ona and all the generations that came before her, stretching back into infinity.

Steeped in memories and the beginning of understanding, a child of two worlds picked her way through the woods and among the hillocks towards the Dome, the surprisingly heavy little spade cradled in her palm.

Maxwell's Demon

Application for Leave Clearance,
Tule Lake War Relocation Center

Name: *Takako Yamashiro*

Question 27: Are you willing to serve in the armed forces of the United States on combat duty, wherever ordered?
I do not know how to answer this question. I am a woman, ineligible for combat.

Question 28: Will you swear unqualified allegiance to the United States of America and faithfully defend the United States from any and all attack by foreign or domestic forces, and forswear any form of allegiance to the Japanese Emperor or any other foreign government, power, or organization?
I do not know how to answer this question. I was born in Seattle, Washington. I have never had any form of allegiance to the Japanese Emperor, so there's nothing to forswear. I will swear unqualified allegiance to my country when my country frees me and my family.

Takako walked down the road, straight as an arrow, towards the cluster of administrative buildings. On both sides of her were blocks of neatly laid out squat barracks, each divided into six rooms, each room housing a family. To the east, she could see the round, columnar figure of Abalone Mountain in the distance. She imagined how the orderly grid of the camp might look from its summit: like those drawings of the balanced regularity of ancient Nara that her father had shown her in a book when she was little.

As she wore a simple white cotton dress, a breeze relieved her of the dry August heat of northern California. But she missed the cool wetness of Seattle, the endless rain of Puget Sound, the laughter of friends back home, and a horizon not bound by watchtowers and barbed wire fences.

She arrived at camp headquarters. She gave her name to the guards and they escorted her through long corridors, through large rooms filled with rows of clattering typewriters and stale cigarette smoke, until they arrived at a small office in the back. They closed the door behind her, muffling the bustle of conversation and office machinery.

She did not know why she was summoned. She stood gazing at the man in uniform sitting across the desk, leaning back comfortably and smoking a cigarette. An electric fan behind him blew the smoke at her.

•

The assistant director stared at the girl. *Pretty Jap,* he thought. *Nearly pretty enough to make you forget what she is.* He almost regretted having to let her go. This one would have provided a fun diversion if she were kept around.

"You are Takako Yamashiro, a no-no girl."

"No," she said. "I did not answer 'no' to those questions. I qualified my answers."

"You would have just written 'yes-yes' if you were loyal."

"As I explained on the form, those questions didn't make sense."

He gestured for her to sit in the chair across the desk. He did not offer her a drink.

"You Japs are very ungrateful," he said. "We put you in here for your own protection, and all you do is complain and go on strikes and act suspicious and hostile." He looked at Takako, daring her to challenge him.

But she said nothing. She was remembering the fear and loathing in the eyes of her neighbors and classmates.

After a moment, he took a deep drag of his cigarette and went on. "Unlike your people, we are not savages. We know there are good Japs and bad ones, but the question is which is which. So we open the door a bit, and ask some questions. The good ones tumble out and the bad ones stay in. Men behave according to their natures, and the loyal and disloyal have a way of sorting themselves out. But then you had to go and make it complicated."

She opened her mouth but then thought better of it. In this man's world, she could only be a "good Jap" or a "bad Jap." There was no room for just Takako Yamashiro, free of labels.

"You went to college?" He changed the topic.

"Yes, physics. I was in graduate studies when . . . this happened."

He whistled. "Never heard of a girl physicist, Jap or no Jap."

"I was the only woman in my class."

He appraised her, the way one appraised a circus monkey. "You're very proud of being clever. Sneaky is more like it. Explains the attitude."

She stared back at him evenly, saying nothing.

"Anyway, it seems that you are being given an opportunity to help America and prove that you are indeed loyal. The men from Washington specifically requested you. If you agree, you can sign these documents, and they can tell you more when they pick you up tomorrow."

She could hardly believe her ears. "I can leave Tule Lake?"

"Don't get too excited. You are not going on vacation."

She flipped through the stack of papers in front of her quickly. Shocked, she looked up. "These papers have me renouncing my American citizenship."

"Of course." He was amused. "We can hardly send you back to the Empire of Japan as an American citizen, now can we?"

Back? She had never been to Japan. She had grown up in Seattle's Japantown and then gone straight to college in California. All she knew were the comforts of a tiny slice of America, and then this place. She felt dizzy. "What if I refuse?"

"Then you'll have confirmed that you are unwilling to help the American war effort. We'll deal with you and your family accordingly."

"I have to renounce America to prove that I'm a patriot. You don't see how stupid this is?"

He shrugged.

"And my family?"

"Your parents and brother will stay here in our care," he said, smiling. "It will ensure that you maintain focus in your work."

•

Takako was denounced as a Japanese loyalist, a *Nisei* who was willing to die for the Emperor and who had eagerly renounced her citizenship. The American authorities, in their compassion to not harm a mere girl, put her on the list of prisoners to be repatriated back to Japan in exchange for American prisoners captured by the Japanese in Hong Kong. The pro-Japan internees at Tule Lake congratulated her parents for her bravery while most internees looked at the family with pity. Mr. and Mrs. Yamashiro were bewildered. Her brother, another "No-No Boy" who had refused to answer those questions on principle, got into fights with the other prisoners. The family was shortly taken to the stockades, separated from the rest of the prisoners in camp, "for their own protection."

The men from Washington explained to Takako what she was to do once the boat arrived in Japan. The Japanese would be suspicious of her and she would be interrogated and debriefed. She was to say and do whatever she needed to convince them of her loyalty to the Japanese Empire. To bolster her story, news would be leaked that her family members were killed for leading a prisoner riot that led to martial law being imposed at the camp. They'd think she had no ties to America anymore. She was to use all assets at her disposal—the men glanced at her lithe body meaningfully—to gain useful information, specifically about Japanese engineering developments.

"The more you give us," they told her, "the safer you'll make your family and your country."

•

Takako's Japanese, learned at home and in the markets of Japantown, was severely put to the test by the Kempeitai interrogators. She answered the same questions again and again.

Why do you hate the Americans?

Have you always felt an allegiance to the Empire of Japan?

What did you feel when you first heard the news of the victory at Pearl Harbor?

Eventually she was pronounced a loyal subject of the Emperor, a proud Japanese who had suffered at the hands of the savage Americans. Her English skills and science education were deemed useful and she was put to work for the military scientists, translating English papers. She thought she was still being watched by the Kempeitai, but she could not be sure.

The propaganda crews filmed her at work in Tokyo, a white lab coat on her. A woman physicist who abandoned America to work for the glory of the nation! She was a symbol of the New Japan. She looked into the camera, wearing a demure smile and professional makeup. *It is not so much how well the dog dances,* she thought, *but that a dog is dancing at all.*

Satoshi Akiba, a physicist and officer of the Imperial Army, was impressed with her. He was in his forties, looked distinguished, and had studied in England and America. Would she, he leaned in and whispered to her, be interested in coming to join him in Okinawa, where he was working on an important project and could use her help? He said this and then reached out to lift a strand of hair away from her eyes.

MARCH 1944

Springtime in Okinawa, a thousand miles from Tokyo, was warm, hot even. It was also quiet, almost pre-modern compared to the bustle of the cities on the Japanese home islands. Here, away from the constant broadcasts and exhortations to dedicate oneself to the war effort, the war seemed more distant, less real. Takako sometimes could even pretend that she was simply in graduate school.

She had her own room in the compound. But she seldom got to sleep in it. Most nights Director Akiba requested her company. Sometimes he wrote letters to his wife back home in Hiroshima, while Takako gave him a massage. Other times he wanted to talk to her in English before they went to bed, "for practice." Her American habits and American education seemed to make her extra appealing to him.

Takako did not understand what Unit 98 was up to. Akiba did not seem to trust her completely, and he never discussed with her news of the war or his work. He was careful to assign her only the most innocuous tasks, reading and summarizing Western research that seemed to have little practical application: experiments on gaseous diffusion, calculations of atomic energy levels, competing theories in psychology. But the compound was highly secretive and closely guarded. More than fifty scientists worked there, and all the nearby farms had been cleared and the villagers forcefully removed.

Through the servants, her American handlers had gotten in touch with her. If she thought she had something of significance, she was to put it in her trash, wrapped in her womanly napkins. The servants would take the bundle outside the compound, seal it in a canister, and give it to a family of fishermen who would take it out into the Philippine Sea and drop it at a particular sunken atoll. An American submarine would pick it up later.

She thought about the bundles on their long journey to America, the white wrapping stained with her monthly blood, a parody of the *Hinomaru* that men would be reluctant to examine closely. She had to admit that her handlers were clever.

One day, Akiba was in a pensive mood. He wanted to go hiking in the woods inland, and asked Takako to come with him. They drove until the road ended, and walked deep into the forest. Takako enjoyed herself. She had not been given any chance to explore the island since her arrival.

They walked past the giant looking-glass mangroves, their vertical platelike roots nature's version of Japanese screens. They listened to the *chi-chi* calls made by the Okinawan woodpecker. They admired the Malayan banyans, their aerial roots twisting and descending like nymphs climbing down from the branches. Takako silently prayed as she walked past the sacred trees, the way her mother had taught her when she was little.

After an hour, they arrived at a clearing in the woods. At the other end of the clearing was the dark maw of a cave that led underground. A stream flowed into the cave, the tinkling made loud by echoes against the wall of the cave.

Takako felt the malevolence in that cave. She seemed to hear groans, shrieks, accusatory screams that grew louder the longer she stood there. Her knees felt weak. Before she could stop herself, she knelt down, leaned forward and put her hands and forehead against the ground, and said, in a language she had not used for so long that it sounded strange to her own ears: *"Munoo yuu iyuru mun." Speak well of others.*

The sounds quieted, and she looked up to see Akiba standing by, looking down at her with an unreadable expression.

"I'm sorry," she said, and prostrated herself before him. "My grandmother and mother spoke to me in *Uchinaaguchi* when I was a small girl."

She remembered the stories that her mother had told her, about how when her mother was a schoolgirl in Okinawa the teacher would make her wear a *batsu fuda* around her neck, a placard that announced that she was a bad student for speaking Okinawan instead of Japanese. Her mother had come from a long line of *yuta*, women skilled in communicating with the spirits of the dead. The mainlanders had said that *yuta* and *nuuru* priestesses were primitive superstitions dangerous to national unity, practices that had to be stamped out so that Okinawans could be cleansed of their impure taint and become full members of the Japanese nation.

Those who spoke *Uchinaaguchi* were traitors, spies. It was a forbidden language.

"It's all right," Akiba said. "I'm not a language zealot. I know about your family background. Why do you think I asked you to come?"

The cave, Akiba explained, had been rumored to be the site where centuries earlier the old Ryukyuan kings had hidden their treasure before the Japanese army conquered the island. Some bureaucrats in the Imperial Army had decided that this was a rumor worth pursuing, and slave laborers from China and Korea and convicted Communist sympathizers had been brought in to work in the cave. The commander got a little too zealous with skimming off the funds for the project, and the prisoners were fed too little. They rioted last year, and all of them, about fifty in number, were shot and their bodies left to rot in the cave. Nothing valuable was ever found.

"You can hear them, can't you?" Akiba asked. "You have your mother's gift as a *yuta*."

A man of science, he went on, should not dismiss any phenomenon out of hand without examination. Unit 98 was established to conduct research into the claims of the paranormal: ESP, telekinesis, the dead coming back to life. The *yuta* had communicated with the dead for generations, and it was best, he felt, to look into this claim to see what could be done with it.

"Many of the *yuta* claim to be able to hear and speak with the spirits of those who died violent and untimely deaths, but we've had little luck getting the *yuta* to make the dead do anything useful. What they lack is any understanding of science.

"But now we have you."

•

Takako convinced two of the spirits, T'ai and Sanle, to attach themselves to a shovel left at the entrance of the cave. They had used the shovel when they were alive, and felt comfortable with it. She could see them, wisps in the shape of gaunt, starved men, clinging to the shovel's handle.

They showed her images of the sorghum fields of Manchuria, their home, the waving red stalks undulating like a sea. They showed her images of explosions and burning houses and lines of marching soldiers. They showed her images of women whose bellies were sliced open by bayonets and young boys whose heads were lopped off with swords as they knelt in a row under a fluttering *Hinomaru*. They showed her images of shackles and chains, darkness, hunger, and the final moment, when they had nothing to lose and death was almost welcome.

"Stop," she begged them. "Please stop."

•

A memory came to her. She was in Seattle, in their tiny one-room apartment. It was raining, as it always was. She was six, and the first to wake up. Next to her was her grandmother.

She leaned over to pull the blanket higher to cover her grandmother. *Nnmee* had been sick, and shivered during the nights. She put her hand on Grandma's cheek. That was how she always woke Grandma in the mornings, and they would then lie next to each other and whisper and giggle, as the window gradually brightened.

But something was wrong. Grandma's cheek was cold, and as hard as leather. Little Takako sat up, and saw that a ghostly outline of Grandma was sitting at the foot of the futon. Takako looked between the body next to her and the ghostly version, and she understood.

"*Nnmee, maa kai ga?*" she asked. *Where are you going?* Grandma always spoke *Uchinaaguchi* with her, even though Father said it was a bad habit. "We all need to be Japanese now in Japantown," he would say. "Okinawan has no future."

"*Nmarijima,*" Grandma said. *Home.*

"*Njichaabira.*" *Goodbye.* And she began to cry, and the adults woke up.

Her mother made the trip back to Okinawa alone, carrying a ring from Grandma. Takako had helped her mother coax Grandma to attach herself to the ring. "Hold on tight, *Nnmee!*" And Grandma had smiled in her mind.

"You are a *yuta* now, too," her mother had said to her. "There is nothing worse than dying away from your home. The spirits cannot rest until they go home, and it is the duty of the *yuta* to help them."

•

They carried the shovel back with them, Akiba in high spirits, whistling and humming the whole way. He asked Takako about the details of the spirits: what they looked like, what they sounded like, what they wanted.

"They want to go home," she said.

"Do they?" Akiba kicked at a clump of mushrooms by the trail, scattering the pieces everywhere. "Tell them that they'll get to go home after they help us win the war. They were too lazy to do much work for the Emperor when they were alive, but now they have a chance to redeem themselves."

They passed by the banyans and mangroves, the hibiscus bushes and night-scented lilies, their leaves like giant upright elephant ears. But Takako was no longer able to enjoy the sights. She felt barely able to hold on to her *mabui*, her life essence, in her shell of a body.

•

Akiba showed her the prototype: a metal box, divided down the middle with a partition. The partition was full of tiny holes that were covered with a translucent silk membrane.

"The *yuta* tell me that the spirits are very weak. They have little strength to manipulate physical objects, not even enough to lift a pencil off a table. The most they might do is to nudge a single thread this way or that. Is that right?"

She agreed. The spirits were indeed limited in their interactions with the physical world.

"I guess those women were telling the truth," Akiba mused. "We tortured a few of them to see if they were withholding their skills."

She tried to match his calm expression.

"The war is not going well," Akiba said, "despite what the propaganda men may tell you. We have been on the defense for a while, and the Americans keep on advancing, hopping across the Pacific from island to island. What they lack in bravery and skill they make up with their wealth and endless supplies. This was always Japan's weakness. We are running out of oil and other essential raw materials, and we need to come up with unexpected sources of power, something that can turn the tide of war."

Akiba caressed her face, and despite herself, she found herself relaxing into his gentle touch.

"In 1871, James Clerk Maxwell devised an ingenious engine," Akiba continued. Takako wanted to tell him that she knew about Maxwell's idea, but Akiba ignored her because he was in the mood to lecture. "Clever, for a non-Japanese," he added.

"A box of air is full of molecules moving rapidly about. Their average velocity is what we think of as their temperature.

"But the air molecules do not, in fact, move with uniform velocity. Some have higher energy and move fast, while others are sluggish and move slowly. Suppose, however, that the box is partitioned down the middle with a trapdoor. Suppose also that we have a tiny demon standing by it. The demon observes all the molecules bouncing about the box. Whenever he sees a fast-moving molecule coming at the door from the right side, he opens the door to let it through to the left side, and then closes the door immediately. Whenever he sees a slow-moving molecule coming at the door from the left side, he opens the door to let it through to the right side, and then closes the door immediately. After a while, even though the demon will not have directly manipulated any molecules or imparted any energy into the system, the total entropy in the system decreases, and the left side of the box will be full of fast-moving molecules, becoming hotter, while the right side will be full of slow-moving molecules, becoming colder."

"That heat differential can be used to produce useful work," Takako said, "like a dam holding back water."

Akiba nodded. "The demon has simply allowed the molecules to sort themselves based on information about their pre-existing qualities, but in that separation he has converted information into energy and bypassed the Second Law of Thermodynamics. We must build this engine."

"But it's just a thought experiment," Takako said. "Where would you find such demons?"

Akiba smiled at her, and Takako felt a chill run down her spine.

"That is where you come in," Akiba said. "*You* will teach your spirits to power this engine, to separate the hot molecules from the cold. When you succeed, we will have a limitless supply of energy, spontaneously generated out of air. We will be able to build submarines that require no diesel and never need to surface, airplanes that never run out of fuel and never need to land. Powered by the dead, we will bathe New York and San Francisco in a sea of fire, and we will bomb Washington back into the swamp from which it rose. Every American will die or scream and scream in terror."

•

"Let's try this game," Takako said to T'ai and Sanle. "If you can do this, I may have a way for you to go home."

She closed her eyes and let her mind drift, merging her consciousness with the spirits. She felt for their sight, shared it, saw what they saw. Unconstrained by the limits of physical bodies, they could focus their senses into the tiniest scales and the minutest slices of time so that everything seemed vastly magnified and slowed down. But they, unlettered and uneducated, did not know what they were supposed to look for.

Still holding their attention, she shared her knowledge with them, and helped them see the air as a sea of glass marbles zipping and bouncing about.

She directed them to the strands of silk in the membrane covering the partition in the middle of the box. With infinite care and patience, she taught them to wait until a molecule was careening towards the partition. "Open!" she shouted.

And watched as T'ai and Sanle threw all their meager strength into bending the silk strands, opening a tiny opening through which the molecule of air zoomed.

"Faster, faster!" she shouted. She did not know how long she spent with them, teaching them to work quicker, opening and closing doors in the partition, separating the fast molecules from the slow.

She opened her eyes and gasped as her *mabui* again fully inhabited her body. Time returned to normal and dust motes glided slowly in beams of sunlight in the dark room.

She put her hand on one end of the metal box, and shivered as she felt it gradually heat up.

•

It was the middle of the night. Takako was in her own room. She had explained to Akiba that it was that time of the month for her. He had nodded, and sought the company of a servant girl.

The hardest part of her plan turned out to be getting T'ai and Sanle to hide inside the napkins. After all they had suffered, it seemed absurd to her that they would balk at this. But men were strange that way. She finally convinced them that this was the only way home, a long, circuitous way halfway around the globe. They trusted her, and reluctantly did as she asked.

Exhausted, she sat down at the desk and wrote in the light of the gibbous Moon.

Spies in America had brought news that the Americans were pursuing a new weapon, based on the energy of splitting an atom. The Germans had already split uranium years ago, and the Japanese were working on the same project. The Americans needed to hurry.

A critical step in the building of an atomic bomb based on uranium, Takako knew, was to have the right sort of uranium. Uranium came in two varieties, uranium-238 and uranium-235. In nature, 99.284% of uranium came in the form of uranium-238, but to have a sustained nuclear chain reaction, you needed mostly uranium-235. There was no way to tell the two isotopes apart chemically.

Takako imagined the uranium atoms, vaporized in some compound form. The molecules bounce about, like the air in her metal box. The molecules with the heavier uranium-238 will move, on average, just a bit slower than the molecules with the lighter uranium-235. She imagined the molecules bouncing inside a tube, and the spirits waiting near the top, opening a door to let the faster molecules through but closing it to keep the slow ones inside.

"If you help America win the war, you will get to go home," she whispered to the spirits.

She wrote down her suggestion.

Takako imagined the power of the bomb that her spirits would help make. Would it be brighter than the sun? Would it bathe a whole city in a sea of fire? Would it create thousands, millions more screaming spirits who will never, ever be able to go home?

She paused. Was she a killer? If she did nothing, people would die. No matter what she did, people would die. She closed her eyes and thought about her family. She hoped that they were not having too rough a time of it. Her brother was the problematic one. He brooded and was so angry all the time. She imagined the doors of the camp at Tule Lake opening and everyone bouncing out, like high-energy molecules. *The war is over!*

She finished her report, hoping that the analysts back at home in America would not treat it as the ravings of a lunatic. She double-underlined the request that her mother be allowed to work with T'ai and Sanle, and to help them go home after their work was done.

•

"What do you mean, they escaped?" Akiba did not sound angry. He looked puzzled.

"I could not explain to them with sufficient clarity what was expected," Takako said, prostrating herself. "My apologies. I promised them rewards that were too enticing. They deceived me, and I thought for a time that the experiment was working, but it turned out to be nothing but my imagination. They must have escaped during the night because they were scared that I had discovered their deception. We can go obtain other spirits from the cave if you like."

Akiba narrowed his eyes. "That never happened with any of the other *yuta*."

Takako kept her eyes on the floor. Her heart pounded in her chest. "Please understand that these spirits did not come from loyal subjects of the Emperor. They were criminals. What can you expect of the Chinese?"

"That's interesting. Are you suggesting that we should ask for loyal subjects to volunteer for this task? To *convert* their bodies into spirits, as it were, so that they might serve the Emperor better?"

"Not at all," Takako said. Her mouth felt dry. "As I said, the theory is good, but I think the difficulty of the task is beyond the skill of lowly soldiers and peasants, even if their spirits are full of zeal for the Emperor. For now, we should pursue other research."

"For now," Akiba said.

Takako swallowed her terror and smiled at him, then began to undress.

JUNE 1945

The village was nestled against the side of a hill, which sheltered it from much of the bombing and artillery fire. Still, the ground under the little hut they were huddled in shook every few minutes.

There weren't any more places to run to. The Marines had landed two months before and pushed forward slowly but inexorably. The Unit 98 compound had been bombed into rubble weeks ago.

Outside the hut, the villagers were assembled in the square to listen to the sergeant. He had stripped off his shirt, and one could see the ribs poking out from under his dirty skin. Food had been rationed for months, and even though many civilians had been ordered to commit suicide to make the supplies last longer for the Imperial Army, the food had finally run out.

The assembled were women, as well as the very young and the very old. Every able-bodied man, boys included, had been handed bamboo spears and been led on a final banzai charge against the Marines days ago.

Takako had said goodbye to the boys. Some of the teenagers were calm, eager even, before the battle. "We men of Okinawa will show the Americans our Yamato spirit!" they had shouted in unison. "Every day we fight is another day that the home islands will be safe!"

None of them came back.

The sergeant wore his sword on his belt. His *hachimaki* was tattered and bloody, and as he paced back and forth, tears flowed freely down his face. He was filled with anger and sorrow. *What had gone wrong? Japan was invincible.* It must have been the fault of the impure Okinawans, who were, after all, not real Japanese. Even though they had executed so many traitors who were caught whispering in their incomprehensible dialect, too many others must have been secretly helping the Americans.

"The Americans shot into every house, every house that held children and women. They did not flinch at the sound of babies crying. They are animals!"

Takako listened to the speech and imagined the scene. The sergeant was describing the American assault on the village over the hill. The Japanese soldiers had retreated into the houses and used the villagers as human shields. Some of the women charged at the Marines with spears. The Marines shot them and then shot into the houses. There was no distinction between civilian and combatant. It was too late for that.

"They will rape all of you and torture your children before your eyes," the sergeant said. "Do not let them have that satisfaction. The time has come for us to give our lives to the Emperor. We will triumph with our spirit. Japan will never give up!"

Some of the children began to cry, and their mothers hushed them. They stared at the wildly gesticulating sergeant with vacant eyes. They did not react at the word "rape." The Imperial Army had already taken the women for one last wild night of comfort before going on their final suicide charge days earlier. Few women had resisted. That was the way of war, wasn't it?

The head of each family had been given a grenade. Earlier, it had been possible to give each two grenades, one for the enemy, one for the family. But they were running out of grenades too.

"It is time," the sergeant shouted. None of the villagers moved.

"It is time!" the sergeant repeated. He pointed his gun at one of the mothers.

The mother pulled her two children close to her. She screamed and pulled the grenade pin, and held the grenade against her chest. She continued to scream until the explosion ended it suddenly. Bits of flesh were scattered around, some landed on the sergeant's face.

The other mothers and grandparents began to scream and cry, and more explosions followed. Takako plugged up her ears tightly with her fingers, but the spirits of the dead continued to scream, and it was impossible to block them out.

"It is time for us too," Akiba said. He was as calm as ever. "I will let you choose how you wish to go."

Takako looked at him in disbelief. He reached out and stroked her cheeks. She flinched and Akiba stopped, smiling sardonically.

"But we will perform an experiment," he said. "I wish to see if your spirit, a loyal subject of the Emperor educated in science, will be able to do what other spirits could not do, and perform as Maxwell's demon. I want to know if my engine will work." He nodded at the metal box in the corner of the room.

Takako saw the mad glint in Akiba's eyes. She forced herself to remain calm, to speak gently, as if to a child. "Perhaps we should consider surrender. You are an important man. They will not harm you, given your knowledge."

Akiba laughed. "I've always suspected that you were not what you said you were. Living in America for so long must have defiled you. I'm giving you one more chance to prove your loyalty to the Emperor. Take it and decide how you will die, or I will make the decision for you."

Takako looked at Akiba. This was a man who thought nothing of torturing old women, a man who took delight in imagining entire cities dying in flames, a man who dispassionately contemplated killing men so that their souls could power machines of death. But he was also the only man in years that had shown her any tenderness, anything akin to love.

She was terrified of him and she wanted to scream at him. She hated him and she pitied him. She wanted to see him die and she wanted to save him. But above all, whatever happened to him, she wanted to live. That was the way of war, wasn't it?

"You are right, Director. But please, before I go, one more time, to make me happy." She began to take off her dress.

Akiba grunted. He put down his gun and started to loosen his belt. The impending threat of death only made his appetite stronger, and he suspected that it affected the girl the same way.

His attention drifted.

Perhaps he had been too hard on the girl, who was loyal after all. He would miss the strange, endearing American expressions that flitted across her face from time to time, the way her eyes hovered halfway between fear and yearning, like a puppy wanting to go home but not sure how. He thought he would be gentle this time and treat her like he did his wife, long ago when they were first wed. (His heart clenched for a moment as he thought about his wife alone in Hiroshima, not even knowing whether he was still alive or already dead.) Then he would strangle her, to preserve her beauty. Yes, that was the way, at the moment of his ecstasy he would send Takako on her way to the afterlife, and then he would follow.

He looked up. Takako was gone.

•

Takako kept on running. She did not care which direction she was heading in. She simply wanted to get as far away from Akiba and the screaming spirits as possible.

In the distance, she saw a bright bit of color. Could it be? Yes! It was the Stars and Stripes, waving in the wind. Her heart leapt into her throat, and she thought she would die from the sudden burst of joy. She ran even faster.

From atop a hillock, she could see it was a small village. The dead bodies, both Japanese and American, were everywhere. Women too. And infants. Blood soaked into the ground. The flag whipped proudly in the hot, windy air.

She saw that scattered Marines were walking about, spitting onto the dead Japanese and picking up swords and other souvenirs from the bodies of the officers. Some sat on the ground, resting from their exhaustion. Others were walking towards the women cowering in the doors of the houses. When the Marines arrived at their doors, the women did not resist. They retreated mutely into the houses. That was the way of war, wasn't it?

But it was almost over. She was almost home. With her last bit of strength, she sprinted through the final hundred feet or so through the woods, and emerged into the village.

Two of the Marines whipped around to face her. They were young, about her brother's age. Takako thought about how she would look to these men: a torn dress, face and hair unwashed for days, one breast bare from when she ran away from Akiba. She imagined speaking to them in English, in the cadences of the Pacific Northwest, in its rain-dipped vowels, in its unadorned consonants.

The Marines' faces were tense, frightened. They had thought they were done, but was this another suicide charge?

She opened her mouth and tried to push the air that were not there out through her constricted throat. She croaked, "I am an Am—"

A loud burst of bullets.

.

The Marines stood over her body.

One of the Marines whistled. "What a pretty Jap."

"Pretty enough," the other said. "Just can't stand the eyes."

Blood gurgled in Takako's chest and throat.

She thought about her family at Tule Lake, and the papers she had signed. She thought about the spirits she had disguised and smuggled out with her blood. She thought about the mother holding a grenade to her chest. Then her mind was overwhelmed with the screaming and groaning of the dead around her, their grief, horror, and pain.

A war opened a door in men, and whatever was inside just tumbled out. The entropy of the world increased, in the absence of a demon by the door.

That was the way of war, wasn't it?

•

Takako drifted above her body. The Marines had already lost interest in it, moved on. She looked down at it, sad but not angry. She looked away.

The flag, tattered and stained, waved as proudly as ever.

She drifted closer to it. She would imbue herself into its fibers, its red, white, and blue threads. She would lie among its stars and embrace its stripes. The flag would be taken back to America, and she would go with it.

"*Nmarijima*," she said to herself. "I'm going home."

The Reborn

Each of us *feels* that there is a single "I" in control. But that is an illusion that the brain works hard to produce. . . .

—Steven Pinker, *The Blank Slate*

I remember being Reborn. It felt the way I imagine a fish feels as it's being thrown back into the sea.

The Judgment Ship slowly drifts in over Fan Pier from Boston Harbor, its metallic disc-shaped hull blending into the dark, roiling sky, its curved upper surface like a pregnant belly.

It is as large as the old Federal Courthouse on the ground below. A few escort ships hover around the rim, the shifting lights on their surfaces sometimes settling into patterns resembling faces.

The spectators around me grow silent. The Judgment, scheduled four times a year, still draws a big crowd. I scan the upturned faces. Most are expressionless, some seem awed. A few men whisper to one another and chuckle. I pay some attention to them, but not too much. There hasn't been a public attack in years.

"A flying saucer," one of the men says, a little too loud. Some of the others shuffle away, trying to distance themselves. "A goddamned flying saucer."

The crowd has left the space directly below the Judgment Ship empty. A group of Tawnin observers stand in the middle, ready to welcome the Reborn. But Kai, my mate, is absent. Thie told me that thie has witnessed too many Rebirths lately.

Kai once explained to me that the design of the Judgment Ship was meant as a sign of respect for local traditions, evoking our historical imagination of little green men and *Plan 9 from Outer Space*.

It's just like how your old courthouse was built with that rotunda on top to resemble a lighthouse, a beacon of justice that pays respect to Boston's maritime history.

The Tawnin are not usually interested in history, but Kai has always advocated more effort at accommodating us locals.

I make my way slowly through the crowd, to get closer to the whispering group. They all have on long, thick coats, perfect for concealing weapons.

The top of the pregnant Judgment Ship opens and a bright beam of golden light shoots straight up into the sky, where it is reflected by the dark clouds back onto the ground as a gentle, shadowless glow.

Circular doors open all around the rim of the Judgment Ship, and long, springy lines unwind and fall from the doors. They dangle, flex, and extend like tentacles. The Judgment Ship is now a jellyfish drifting through the air.

At the end of each line is a human, securely attached like hooked fish by the Tawnin ports located over their spines and between their shoulder blades. As the lines slowly extend and drift closer to the ground, the figures at the ends languidly move their arms and legs, tracing out graceful patterns.

I've almost reached the small group of whispering men. One of them, the one who had spoken too loud earlier, has his hands inside the flap of his thick coat. I move faster, pushing people aside.

"Poor bastards," he murmurs, watching the Reborn coming closer to the empty space in the middle of the crowd, coming home. I see his face take on the determination of the fanatic, of a Xenophobe about to kill.

The Reborn have almost reached the ground. My target is waiting for the moment when the lines from the Judgment Ship are detached so that the Reborn can no longer be snatched back into the air, the moment when the Reborn are still unsteady on their feet, uncertain who they are.

Still innocent.

I remember that moment well.

The right shoulder of my target shifts as he tries to pull something out of his coat. I shove away the two women before me and leap into the air, shouting, "Freeze!"

And then the world slows down as the ground beneath the Reborn erupts like a volcano, and they, along with the Tawnin observers, are tossed into the air, their limbs flopping like marionettes with their strings cut. As I crash into the man before me, a wave of heat and light blanks everything out.

•

It takes a few hours to process my suspect and to bandage my wounds. By the time I'm allowed to go home it's after midnight.

The streets of Cambridge are quiet and empty because of the new curfew. A fleet of police cars is parked in Harvard Square, a dozen strobing beacons out of sync as I stop, roll down my window, and show my badge.

The fresh-faced young officer sucks in his breath. The name "Joshua Rennon" may not mean anything to him, but he has seen the black dot on the top right corner of my badge, the dot that allows me inside the high-security domicile compound of the Tawnin.

"Bad day, sir," he says. "But don't worry, we've got all the roads leading to your building secured."

He tries to make "your building" sound casual, but I can hear the thrill in his voice. *He's one of* those. *He lives with* them.

He doesn't step away from the car. "How's the investigation going, if you don't mind me asking?" His eyes roam all over me, the hunger of his curiosity so strong that it's almost palpable.

I know that the question he really wants to ask is *What's it like?*

I turn my face straight ahead. I roll up the window.

After a moment, he steps back, and I step on the gas hard so that the tires give a satisfying squeal as I shoot away.

•

The walled compound used to be Radcliffe Yard.

I open the door to our apartment and the soft golden light that Kai prefers, a reminder of the afternoon, makes me shudder.

Kai is in the living room, sitting on the couch.

"Sorry I didn't call."

Kai stands up to thir full eight-foot height and opens thir arms, thir dark eyes gazing at me like the eyes of those giant fish that swim through the large tank at the New England Aquarium. I step into thir embrace and inhale thir familiar fragrance, a mixture of floral and spicy scents, the smell of an alien world and of home.

"You've heard?"

Instead of answering, thie undresses me gently, careful around my bandages. I close my eyes and do not resist, feeling the layers fall away from me piece by piece.

When I'm naked, I tilt my head up and thie kisses me, thir tubular tongue warm and salty in my mouth. I place my arms around thim, feeling on the back of thir head the long scar whose history I do not know and do not seek.

Then thie wraps thir primary arms around my head, pulling my face against thir soft, fuzzy chest. Thir tertiary arms, strong and supple, wrap around my waist. The nimble and sensitive tips of thir secondary arms lightly caress my shoulders for a moment before they find my Tawnin port and gently pry the skin apart and push in.

I gasp the moment the connection is made and I feel my limbs grow rigid and then loose as I let go, allowing Kai's strong arms to support my weight. I close my eyes so I can enjoy the way my body appears through Kai's senses: the way warm blood coursing through my vessels creates a glowing map of pulsing red and gold currents against the cooler, bluish skin on my back and buttocks, the way my short hair pricks the sensitive skin of thir primary hands, the way my chaotic thoughts are gradually soothed and rendered intelligible by thir gentle, guiding nudges. We're now connected in the most intimate way that two minds, two bodies, can be.

That's what it's like, I think.

Don't be annoyed by their ignorance, thie thinks.

I replay the afternoon: the arrogant and careless manner in which I carried out my duty, the surprise of the explosion, the guilt and regret as I watched the Reborn and the Tawnin die. The helpless rage.

You'll find them, thie thinks.

I will.

Then I feel thir body moving against me, all of thir six arms and two legs probing, caressing, grasping, squeezing, penetrating. And I echo thir movements, my hands, lips, feet roaming against thir cool, soft skin the way I have come to learn thie likes, thir pleasure as clear and present as my own.

Thought seems as unnecessary as speech.

•

The interrogation room in the basement of the Federal Courthouse is tiny and claustrophobic, a cage.

I close the door behind me and hang up my jacket. I'm not afraid to turn my back to the suspect. Adam Woods sits with his face buried between his hands, elbows on the stainless steel table. There's no fight left in him.

"I'm Special Agent Joshua Rennon, Tawnin Protection Bureau." I wave my badge at him out of habit.

He looks up at me, his eyes bloodshot and dull.

"Your old life is over, as I'm sure you already know." I don't read him his rights or tell him that he can have a lawyer, the rituals of a less civilized age. There's no more need for lawyers—no more trials, no more police tricks.

He stares at me, his eyes full of hatred.

"What's it like?" he asks, his voice a low whisper. "Being fucked by one of them every night?"

I pause. I can't imagine he noticed the black dot on my badge in such a quick look. Then I realize that it was because I had turned my back to him. He could see the outline of the Tawnin port through my shirt. He knew I had been Reborn, and it was a lucky—but reasonable—guess that someone whose port was kept open was bonded to a Tawnin.

I don't take the bait. I'm used to the kind of xenophobia that drives men like him to kill.

"You'll be probed after the surgery. But if you confess now and give useful information about your co-conspirators, after your Rebirth you'll be given a good job and a good life, and you'll get to keep the memories of most of your friends and family. But if you lie or say nothing, we'll learn everything we need anyway and you'll be sent to California for fallout cleanup duty with a blank slate of a mind. And anyone who cared about you will forget you, completely. Your choice."

"How do you know I have any co-conspirators?"

"I saw you when the explosion happened. You were expecting it. I believe your role was to try to kill more Tawnin in the chaos after the explosion."

He continues to stare at me, his hatred unrelenting. Then, abruptly, he seems to think of something. "You've been Reborn more than once, haven't you?"

I stiffen. "How did you know?"

He smiles. "Just a hunch. You stand and sit too straight. What did you do the last time?"

I should be prepared for the question, but I'm not. Two months after my Rebirth, I'm still raw, off my game. "You know I can't answer that."

"You remember nothing?"

"That was a rotten part of me that was cut out," I tell him. "Just like it will be cut out of you. The Josh Rennon who committed whatever crime he did no longer exists, and it is only right that the crime be forgotten. The Tawnin are a compassionate and merciful people. They only remove those parts of me and you that are truly responsible for the crime—the mens rea, the evil will."

"A compassionate and merciful people," he repeats. And I see something new in his eyes: pity.

A sudden rage seizes me. *He* is the one to be pitied, not *me*. Before he has a chance to put up his hands I lunge at him and punch him in the face, once, twice, three times, hard.

Blood flows from his nose as his hands waver before him. He doesn't make any noise, but continues to look at me with his calm, pity-filled eyes.

"They killed my father in front of me," he says. He wipes the blood from his lips and shakes his hand to get rid of it. Droplets of blood hit my shirt, the scarlet beads bright against its white fabric. "I was thirteen, and hiding in the backyard shed. Through a slit in the doors I saw him take a swing at one of them with a baseball bat. The thing blocked it with one arm and seized his head with another pair of arms and just ripped it off. Then they burned my mother. I'll never forget the smell of cooked flesh."

I try to bring my breathing under control. I try to see the man before me as the Tawnin do: divided. There's a frightened child who can still be rescued, and an angry, bitter man who cannot.

"That was more than twenty years ago," I say. "It was a darker time, a terrible, twisted time. The world has moved on. The Tawnin have apologized and tried to make amends. You should have gone to counseling. They should have ported you and excised those memories. You could have had a life free of these ghosts."

"I don't *want* to be free of these ghosts. Did you ever consider that? I don't want to forget. I lied and told them that I saw nothing. I didn't want them to reach into my mind and steal my memories. I want revenge."

"You can't have revenge. The Tawnin who did those things are all gone. They've been punished, consigned to oblivion."

He laughs. " 'Punished,' you say. The Tawnin who did those things are the exact same Tawnin who parade around today, preaching universal love and a future in which the Tawnin and humans live in harmony. Just because they can conveniently forget what they did doesn't mean we should."

"The Tawnin do not have a unified consciousness—"

"You speak like you lost no one in the Conquest." His voice rises as pity turns into something darker. "You speak like a collaborator." He spits at me, and I feel the blood on my face, between my lips—warm, sweet, the taste of rust. "You don't even know what they've taken from you."

I leave the room and close the door behind me, shutting off his stream of curses.

•

Outside the courthouse, Claire from Tech Investigations meets me. Her people had already scanned and recorded the crime scene last night, but we walk around the crater doing an old-fashioned visual inspection anyway, in the unlikely event that her machines missed something.

Missed something. Something was missing.

"One of the injured Reborn died at Mass General this morning around four o'clock," Claire says. "So that brings the total death toll to ten: six Tawnin and four Reborn. Not as bad as what happened in New York two years ago, but definitely the worst massacre in New England."

Claire is slight, with a sharp face and quick, jerky movements that put me in mind of a sparrow. As the only two TPB agents married to Tawnins in the Boston Field Office, we have grown close. People joke that we're work spouses.

I didn't lose anyone in the Conquest.

Kai stands with me at my mother's funeral. Her face in the casket is serene, free of pain.

Kai's touch on my back is gentle and supportive. I want to tell thim not to feel too bad. Thie had tried so hard to save her, as thie had tried to save my father before her, but the human body is fragile, and we don't yet know how to effectively use the advances taught to us by the Tawnin.

We pick our way around a pile of rubble that has been cemented in place by melted asphalt. I try to bring my thoughts under control. Woods unsettled me. "Any leads on the detonator?" I ask.

"It's pretty sophisticated," Claire says. "Based on the surviving pieces, there was a magnetometer connected to a timer circuit. My best guess is the magnetometer was triggered by the presence of large quantities of metal nearby, like the Judgment Ship. And that started a timer that was set to detonate just as the Reborn reached the ground.

"The setup requires fairly detailed knowledge of the mass of the Judgment Ship; otherwise the yachts and cargo ships sailing through the Harbor could have set it off."

"Also knowledge of the operation of the Judgment Ship," I add. "They had to know how many Reborn were going to be here yesterday, and calculate how long it would take to complete the ceremony and lower them to the ground."

"It definitely took a lot of meticulous planning," Claire said. "This is not the work of a loner. We're dealing with a sophisticated terrorist organization."

Claire pulls me to a stop. We're at a good vantage point to see the bottom of the explosion crater. It's thinner than I would have expected. Whoever had done this had used directed explosives that focused the energy upwards, presumably to minimize the damage to the crowd on the sides.

The crowd.

A memory of myself as a child comes to me unbidden.

Autumn, cool air, the smell of the sea and something burning. A large milling crowd, but no one is making any noise. Those at the edge of the crowd like me push to move closer to the center, while those near the center push to get out, like a colony of ants swarming over a bird corpse. Finally, I make my way to the center, where bright bonfires burn in dozens of oil drums.

I reach into my coat and take out an envelope. I open it and hand a stack of photographs to the man standing by one of the oil drums. He flips through them and takes a few out and hands the rest back to me.

"You can keep these and go line up for surgery," he says.

I look through the photographs in my hand: Mom carrying me as a baby. Dad lifting me over his shoulders at a fair. Mom and me asleep, holding the same pose. Mom and Dad and me playing a board game. Me in a cowboy costume, Mom behind me trying to make sure the scarf fit right.

He tosses the other photographs into the oil drum, and as I turn away, I try to catch a glimpse of what's on them before they're consumed by the flames.

"You all right?"

"Yes," I say, disoriented. "Still a bit of the aftereffects of the explosion."

I can trust Claire.

"Listen," I say, "Do you ever think about what you did before you were Reborn?"

Claire focuses her sharp eyes on me. She doesn't blink. "Do not go down that path, Josh. Think of Kai. Think of your life, the real one you have now."

"You're right," I say. "Woods just rattled me a bit."

"You might want to take a few days off. You're not doing anyone favors if you can't concentrate."

"I'll be fine."

Claire seems skeptical, but she doesn't push the issue. She understands how I feel. Kai would be able to see the guilt and regret in my mind. In that ultimate intimacy, there is nowhere to hide. I can't bear to be home and doing nothing while Kai tries to comfort me.

"As I was saying," she continues, "this area was resurfaced by the W. G. Turner Construction Company a month ago. That was likely when the bomb was placed, and Woods was on the crew. You should start there."

•

The woman leaves the box of files on the table in front of me.

"These are all the employees and contractors who worked on the Courthouse Way resurfacing project."

She scurries away as though I'm contagious, afraid to exchange more than the absolute minimum number of words with a TPB agent.

In a way, I suppose I am contagious. When I was Reborn, those who were close to me, who had known what I had done, whose knowledge of me formed part of the identity that was Joshua Rennon, would have had to be ported and those memories excised as part of my Rebirth. My crimes, whatever they were, had infected them.

I don't even know who they might be.

I shouldn't be thinking like this. It's not healthy to dwell on my former life, a dead man's life.

I scan through the files one by one, punch the names into my phone so that Claire's algorithms back at the office can make a network out of them, link them to entries in millions of databases, trawl through the radical anti-Tawnin forums and Xenophobic sites, and find connections.

But I still read through the files meticulously, line by line. Sometimes the brain makes connections that Claire's computers cannot.

W. G. Turner had been careful. All the applicants had been subjected to extensive background searches, and none appears suspicious to the algorithms.

After a while, the names merge into an undistinguishable mess: Kelly Eickhoff, Hugh Raker, Sofia Leday, Walker Lincoln, Julio Costas . . .

Walker Lincoln.

I go back and look at the file again. The photograph shows a white male in his thirties. Narrow eyes, receding hairline, no smile for the camera. Nothing seems particularly notable. He doesn't look familiar at all.

But something about the name makes me hesitate.

The photographs curl up in the flames.

The one at the top shows my father standing in front of our house. He's holding a rifle, his face grim. As the flame swallows him, I catch a pair of crossed street signs in the last remaining corner of the photograph.

Walker and Lincoln.

I find myself shivering, even though the heat is turned up high in the office.

I take out my phone and pull up the computer report on Walker Lincoln: credit card records, phone logs, search histories, web presence, employment and school summaries. The algorithms flagged nothing as unusual. Walker Lincoln seems the model Average Citizen.

I have never seen a profile where not a single thing was flagged by Claire's paranoid algorithms. Walker Lincoln is too perfect.

I look through the purchase history on his credit cards: fire logs, starter fluid, fireplace simulators, outdoor grills.

Then, starting about two months ago, nothing.

•

As thir fingers are about to push in, I speak.

"Please, not tonight."

The tips of Kai's secondary arms stop, hesitate, and gently caress my back. After a moment, thie backs up. Thir eyes look at me, like two pale moons in the dim light of the apartment.

"I'm sorry," I say. "There's a lot on my mind, unpleasant thoughts. I don't want to burden you."

Kai nods, a human gesture that seems incongruous. I appreciate the effort thie is making to make me feel better. Thie has always been very understanding.

Thie backs off, leaving me naked in the middle of the room.

•

The landlady proclaims complete ignorance of the life of Walker Lincoln. Rent (which in this part of Charlestown is dirt cheap) is direct deposited on the first of every month, and she hasn't set eyes on him since he moved in four months ago. I wave my badge, and she hands me the key to his apartment and watches wordlessly as I climb the stairs.

I open the door and turn on the light; I'm greeted with a sight out of a furniture store display: white couch, leather love seat, glass coffee table with a few magazines in a neat stack, abstract paintings on walls. There's no clutter, nothing out of its assigned place. I take a deep breath. No smell of cooking, detergent, the mix of aromas that accompany places lived in by real people.

The place seems familiar and strange at the same time, like walking through déjà vu.

I walk through the apartment, opening doors. The closets and bedroom are as artfully arranged as the living room. Perfectly ordinary, perfectly unreal.

Sunlight coming in from the windows along the western wall makes clean parallelograms against the grey carpet. The golden light is Kai's favorite shade.

There is, however, a thin layer of dust over everything. Maybe a month or two's worth.

Walker Lincoln is a ghost.

Finally, I turn around and see something hanging on the back of the front door, a mask.

I pick it up, put it on, and step into the bathroom.

I'm quite familiar with this type of mask. Made of soft, pliant programmable fibers, it's based on Tawnin technology, the same material that makes up the strands that release the Reborn back into the world. Activated with body heat, it molds itself into a pre-programmed shape. No matter the contours of the face beneath it, it rearranges itself into the appearance of a face it has memorized. Approved only for law enforcement, we sometimes use such masks to infiltrate Xenophobic cells.

In the mirror, the cool fibers of the mask gradually come alive like Kai's body when I touch thim, pushing and pulling against the skin and muscles of my face. For a moment my face is a shapeless lump, like a monster's out of some nightmare.

And then the roiling motions stop, and I'm looking into the face of Walker Lincoln.

•

Kai's was the first face I saw the last time I was Reborn.

It was a face with dark fishlike eyes and skin that pulsated as though tiny maggots were wriggling just under the surface. I cringed and tried to move away but there was nowhere to go. My back was against a steel wall.

The skin around thir eyes contracted and expanded again, an alien expression I did not understand. Thie backed up, giving me some space.

Slowly, I sat up and looked around. I was on a narrow steel slab attached to the wall of a tiny cell. The lights were too bright. I felt nauseated. I closed my eyes.

And a tsunami of images came to me that I could not process. Faces, voices, events in fast motion. I opened my mouth to scream.

And Kai was upon me in a second. Thie wrapped thir primary arms around my head, forcing me to stay still. A mixture of floral and spicy scents enveloped me, and the memory of it suddenly emerged from the chaos in my mind. *The smell of home.* I clung to it like a floating plank in a roiling sea.

Thie wrapped thir secondary arms around me, patting my back, seeking an opening. I felt them push through a hole over my spine, a wound that I did not know was there, and I wanted to cry out in pain—

—and the chaos in my mind subsided. I was looking at the world through thir eyes and mind: my own naked body, trembling.

Let me help you.

I struggled for a bit, but thie was too strong, and I gave in.

What happened?

You're aboard the Judgment Ship. The old Josh Rennon did something very bad and had to be punished.

I tried to remember what it was that I had done, but could recall nothing.

He is gone. We had to cut him out of this body to rescue you.

Another memory floated to the surface of my mind, gently guided by the currents of Kai's thoughts.

I am sitting in a classroom, the front row. Sunlight coming in from the windows along the western wall makes clean parallelograms on the ground. Kai paces slowly back and forth in front of us.

"Each of us is composed of many groupings of memories, many personalities, many coherent patterns of thoughts." The voice comes from a black box Kai wears around thir neck. It's slightly mechanical, but melodious and clear.

"Do you not alter your behavior, your expressions, even your speech when you're with your childhood friends from your hometown compared

to when you're with your new friends from the big city? Do you not laugh differently, cry differently, even become angry differently when you're with your family than when you're with me?"

The students around me laugh a little at this, as do I. As Kai reaches the other side of the classroom, thie turns around and our eyes meet. The skin around thir eyes pulls back, making them seem even bigger, and my face grows warm.

"The unified individual is a fallacy of traditional human philosophy. It is, in fact, the foundation of many unenlightened, old customs. A criminal, for example, is but one person inhabiting a shared body with many others. A man who murders may still be a good father, husband, brother, son, and he is a different man when he plots death than when he bathes his daughter, kisses his wife, comforts his sister, and cares for his mother. Yet the old human criminal justice system would punish all of these men together indiscriminately, would judge them together, imprison them together, even kill them together. Collective punishment. How barbaric! How cruel!"

I imagine my mind the way Kai describes it: partitioned into pieces, an individual divided. There may be no human institution that the Tawnin despise more than our justice system. Their contempt makes perfect sense when considered in the context of their mind-to-mind communication. The Tawnin have no secrets from each other and share an intimacy we can only dream of. The idea of a justice system so limited by the opacity of the individual that it must resort to ritualized adversarial combat rather than direct access to the truth of the mind must seem to them a barbarity.

Kai glances at me, as though thie could hear my thoughts, though I know that is not possible without my being ported. But the thought brings pleasure to me. I am Kai's favorite student.

I placed my arms around Kai.

My teacher, my lover, my spouse. I was once adrift, and now I have come home. I am beginning to remember.

I felt the scar on the back of thir head. Thie trembled.

What happened here?

I don't remember. Don't worry about it.

I carefully caressed thim, avoiding the scar.

The Rebirth is a painful process. Your biology did not evolve as ours, and the parts of your mind are harder to tease apart, to separate out the different persons. It will take some time for the memories to settle. You have to re-remember, re-learn the pathways needed to make sense of them again, to reconstruct yourself again. But you're now a better person, free from the diseased parts we had to cut out.

I hung on to Kai, and we picked up the pieces of myself together.

•

I show Claire the mask, and the too-perfect electronic profile. "To get access to this kind of equipment and to create an alias with an electronic trail this convincing requires someone with a lot of power and access. Maybe even someone inside the Bureau, since we need to scrub electronic databases to cleanse the records of the Reborn."

Claire bites her bottom lip as she glances at the display on my phone and regards the mask with skepticism. "That seems really unlikely. All the Bureau employees are ported and are regularly probed. I don't see how a mole among us can stay hidden."

"Yet it's the only explanation."

"We'll know soon enough," Claire tells me. "Adam has been ported. Tau is doing the probe now. Should be done in half an hour."

I practically fall into the chair next to her. Exhaustion from the last two days settles over me like a heavy blanket. I have been avoiding Kai's touch, for reasons that I cannot even explain. I feel divided from myself.

I tell myself to stay awake, just a little longer.

Kai and I are sitting on the leather love seat. Thir big frame means that we are squeezed in tightly. The fireplace is behind us and I can feel the gentle heat against the back of my neck. Thir left arms gently stroke my back. I'm tense.

My parents are on the white couch across from us.

"I've never seen Josh this happy," my mother says. And her smile is such a relief that I want to hug her.

"I'm glad you feel that way," says Kai, with thir black voice box. "I think Josh was worried about how you might feel about me—about us."

"There are always going to be Xenophobes," my father says. He sounds a little out of breath. I know that one day I will recognize this as the beginning of his sickness. A tinge of sorrow tints my happy memory.

"Terrible things were done," Kai says. "We do know that. But we always want to look to the future."

"So do we," my father says. "But some people are trapped in the past. They can't let the dead lie buried."

I look around the room and notice how neat the house is. The carpet is immaculate, the end tables free of clutter. The white couch my parents are sitting on is spotless. The glass coffee table between us is empty save for a stack of artfully arranged magazines.

The living room is like the showroom of a furniture store.

I jerk awake. The pieces of my memories have become as unreal as Walker Lincoln's apartment.

Tau, Claire's spouse, is at the door. The tips of thir secondary arms are mangled, oozing blue blood. Thie stumbles.

Claire is by thir side in a moment. "What happened?"

Instead of answering, Tau tears Claire's jacket and blouse away, and thir thicker, less delicate primary arms hungrily, blindly seek the Tawnin port on Claire's back. When they finally find the opening, they plunge in and Claire gasps, going limp immediately.

I turn my eyes away from this scene of intimacy. Tau is in pain and needs Claire.

"I should go," I say, getting up.

"Adam had booby-trapped his spine," Tau says through thir voice box.

I pause.

"When I ported him, he was cooperative and seemed resigned to his fate. But when I began the probe, a miniature explosive device went off, killing him instantly. I guess some of you still hate us so much that you'd rather die than be Reborn."

"I'm sorry," I say.

"I'm the one that's sorry," Tau says. The mechanical voice struggles to convey sorrow, but it sounds like an imitation to my unsettled mind. "Parts of him were innocent."

•

The Tawnin do not care much for history, and now, neither do we.

They also do not die of old age. No one knows how old the Tawnin are: centuries, millennia, eons. Kai speaks vaguely of a journey that lasted longer than the history of the human race.

What was it like? I once asked.

I don't remember, thie had thought.

Their attitude is explained by their biology. Their brains, like the teeth of sharks, never cease growing. New brain tissue is continuously produced at the core while the outer layers are sloughed off periodically like snakeskin.

With lives that are for all intents and purposes eternal, the Tawnin would have been overwhelmed by eons of accumulated memories. It is no wonder that they became masters of forgetting.

Memories that they wish to keep must be copied into the new tissue: retraced, recreated, re-recorded. But memories that they wish to leave behind are cast off like dried pupa husks with each cycle of change.

It is not only memory that they leave behind. Entire personalities can be adopted, taken on like a role, and then cast aside and forgotten. A Tawnin views the self before a change and the self after a change as entirely separate beings: different personalities, different memories, different moral responsibilities. They merely shared a body seriatim.

Not even the same body, Kai thought to me.

?

In about a year every atom in your body will have been replaced by others, thought Kai. This was back when we had first become lovers, and thie was often in a lecturing mood. *For us it's even faster.*

Like the ship of Theseus where each plank was replaced over time, until it was no longer the same ship.

You're always making these references to the past. But the flavor of thir thought was indulgent rather than critical.

When the Conquest happened, the Tawnin had adopted an attitude of extreme aggression. And we had responded in kind. The details, of course, are hazy. The Tawnin do not remember them, and most of us do not want to. California is still uninhabitable after all these years.

But then, once we had surrendered, the Tawnin had cast off those aggressive layers of their mind—the punishment for their war crimes—and become the gentlest rulers imaginable. Now committed pacifists, they abhor violence and willingly share their technology with us, cure diseases, perform wondrous miracles. The world is at peace. Human life expectancy has been much lengthened, and those willing to work for the Tawnin have done well for themselves.

The Tawnin do not experience guilt.

We are a different people now, Kai thought. *This is also our home. And yet some of you insist on tasking us with the sins of our dead past selves. It is like holding the son responsible for the sins of the father.*

What if war should occur again? I thought. *What if the Xenophobes convince the rest of us to rise up against you?*

Then we might change yet again, become ruthless and cruel as before. Such changes in us are physiological reactions against threat, beyond our control. But then those future selves would have nothing to do with us. The father cannot be responsible for the acts of the son.

It's hard to argue with logic like that.

•

Adam's girlfriend, Lauren, is a young woman with a hard face that remained unchanged after I informed her that, as Adam's parents are deceased, she is considered the next of kin and responsible for picking up the body at the station.

We are sitting across from each other, the kitchen table between us. The apartment is tiny and dim. Many of the lightbulbs have burnt out and not been replaced.

"Am I going to be ported?" she asks.

Now that Adam is dead, the next order of business is to decide which of his relatives and friends should be ported—with appropriate caution for further booby-trapped spines—so that the true extent of the conspiracy can be uncovered.

"I don't know yet," I say. "It depends on how much I think you're cooperating. Did he associate with anyone suspicious? Anyone you thought was a Xenophobe?"

"I don't know anything," she says. "Adam is . . . was a loner. He never told me anything. You can port me if you want, but it will be a waste of energy."

Normally, people like her are terrified of being ported, violated. Her feigned nonchalance only makes me more suspicious of her.

She seems to sense my skepticism and changes tack. "Adam and I would sometimes smoke oblivion or do blaze." She shifts in her seat and looks over at the kitchen counter. I look where she's looking and see the drug paraphernalia in front of a stack of dirty dishes, like props set out on a stage. A leaky faucet drips, providing a background beat to the whole scene.

Oblivion and blaze both have strong hallucinogenic effects. The unspoken point: her mind is riddled with false memories that even when ported cannot be relied upon. The most we can do is Rebirth her, but we won't find out anything we can use on others. It's not a bad trick. But she hasn't made the lie sufficiently convincing.

You humans think you are what you've done, Kai once thought. I remember us lying together in a park somewhere, the grass under us, and I loved feeling the warmth of the sun through thir skin, so much more sensitive than mine. *But you're really what you remember.*

Isn't that the same thing? I thought.

Not at all. To retrieve a memory, you must reactivate a set of neural connections, and in the process change them. Your biology is such that with each act of recall, you also rewrite the memory. Haven't you ever had the experience of discovering a detail you remembered vividly was manufactured? A dream you became convinced was a real experience? Being told a fabricated story you believed to be the truth?

You make us sound so fragile.

Deluded, actually. The flavor of Kai's thought was affectionate. *You cannot tell which memories are real and which memories are false, and yet you insist on their importance, base so much of your life on them. The practice of history has not done your species much good.*

Lauren averts her eyes from my face, perhaps thinking of Adam. Something about Lauren seems familiar, like the half-remembered chorus from a song heard in childhood. I like the indescribable way her face seems to relax as she is lost in memories. I decide, right then, that I will not have Lauren ported.

Instead, I retrieve the mask from my bag and, keeping my eyes on her face, I put it on. As the mask warms to my face, clinging to it, shaping muscle and skin, I watch her eyes for signs of recognition, for confirmation that Adam and Walker were co-conspirators.

Her face becomes tight and impassive again. "What are you doing? That thing's creepy-looking."

Disappointed, I tell her, "Just a routine check."

"You mind if I deal with that leaky faucet? It's driving me crazy."

I nod and remain seated as she gets up. Another dead end. Could Adam really have done it all on his own? Who was Walker Lincoln?

I'm afraid of the answer that's half-formed in my mind.

I sense the heavy weight swinging towards the back of my head, but it's too late.

·

"Can you hear us?" The voice is scrambled, disguised by some electronic gizmo. Oddly, it reminds me of a Tawnin voice box.

I nod in the darkness. I'm seated and my hands are tied behind me. Something soft, a scarf or a tie, is wrapped tightly around my head, covering my eyes.

"I'm sorry that we have to do things this way. It's better if you can't see us. This way, when your Tawnin probes you, we won't be betrayed."

I test the ties around my wrists. They're very well done. No possibility of working them loose on my own.

"You have to stop this right now," I say, putting as much authority into my voice as I can. "I know you think you've caught a collaborator, a traitor to the human race. You believe this is justice, vengeance. But think. If you harm me, you'll eventually be caught, and all your memory of this event erased. What's the good of vengeance if you won't even remember it? It will be as if it never happened."

Electronic voices laugh in the darkness. I can't tell how many of them there are. Old, young, male or female.

"Let me go."

"We will," the first voice says, "after you hear this."

I hear the click of a button being pressed, and then, a disembodied voice: "Hello, Josh. I see you've found the clues that matter."

The voice is my own.

•

"... despite extensive research, it is not possible to erase all memories. Like an old hard drive, the Reborn mind still holds traces of those old pathways, dormant, waiting for the right trigger. ..."

The corner of Walker and Lincoln, my old house.

Inside, it's cluttered, my toys scattered everywhere. There is no couch, only four wicker chairs around an old wooden coffee table, the top full of circular stains.

I'm hiding behind one of the wicker chairs. The house is quiet and the lighting dim, early dawn or late dusk.

A scream outside.

I get up and run to the door and fling it open. I see my father being hoisted into the air by a Tawnin's primary arms. The secondary and tertiary arms are wrapped around my father's arms and legs, rendering him immobile.

Behind the Tawnin, my mother's body lies prostrate, unmoving.

The Tawnin jerks its arms and my father tries to scream again, but blood has pooled in his throat, and what comes out is a mere gurgle. The Tawnin jerks its limbs again and I watch as my father is torn slowly into pieces.

The Tawnin looks down at me. The skin around its eyes recedes and contracts again. The smell of unknown flowers and spices is so strong that I retch.

It's Kai.

". . . in the place of real memories, they fill your mind with lies. Constructed memories that crumble under examination. . . ."

Kai comes to me on the other side of my cage. There are many cages like it, each holding a young man or woman. How many years have we been in darkness and isolation, kept from forming meaningful memories?

There was never any well-lit classroom, any philosophical lecture, any sunlight slanting in from the western windows, casting clean, sharp parallelograms against the ground.

"We're sorry for what happened," Kai says. The voice box, at least, is real. But the mechanical tone belies the words. "We've been saying this for a long time. The ones who did those things you insist on remembering are not us. They were necessary for a time, but they have been punished, cast off, forgotten. It's time to move on."

I spit in Kai's eyes.

Kai does not wipe away my spittle. The skin around its eyes contracts and it turns away. "You leave us no choice. We have to make you anew."

". . . they tell you that the past is the past, dead, gone. They tell you that they are a new people, not responsible for their former selves. And there is some truth to these assertions. When I couple with Kai, I see into thir mind, and there is nothing left of the Kai that killed my parents, the Kai that brutalized the children, the Kai that forced us by decree to burn our old photographs, to wipe out the traces of our former existence that might interfere with what they want for our future. They really are as good at forgetting as they say, and the bloody past appears to them as an alien country. The Kai that is my lover is truly a different mind: innocent, blameless, guiltless.

"But they continue to walk over the bones of your, my, our parents. They continue to live in houses taken from our dead. They continue to desecrate the truth with denial.

"Some of us have accepted collective amnesia as the price of survival. But not all. I am you, and you're me. The past does not die; it seeps, leaks, infiltrates, waits for an opportunity to spring up. You *are* what you remember...."

The first kiss from Kai, slimy, raw.

The first time Kai penetrates me. The first time my mind is invaded by its mind. The feeling of helplessness, of something being done to me that I can never be rid of, that I can never be clean again.

The smell of flowers and spices, the smell that I can never forget or expel because it doesn't just come from my nostrils, but has taken root deep in my mind.

"... though I began by infiltrating the Xenophobes, in the end it is they who infiltrated me. Their underground records of the Conquest and the giving of testimony and sharing of memories finally awoke me from my slumber, allowed me to recover my own story.

"When I found out the truth, I carefully plotted my vengeance. I knew it would not be easy to keep a secret from Kai. But I came up with a plan. Because I was married to Kai, I was exempt from the regular probes that the other TPB agents are subject to. By avoiding intimacy with Kai and pleading discomfort, I could avoid being probed altogether and hold secrets in my mind, at least for a while.

"I created another identity, wore a mask, provided the Xenophobes with what they needed to accomplish their goals. All of us wore masks so that if any of the co-conspirators were captured, probing one mind would not betray the rest of us."

The masks I wear to infiltrate the Xenophobes are the masks I give to my co-conspirators....

"Then I prepped my mind like a fortress against the day of my inevitable capture and Rebirth. I recalled the way my parents died in great detail, replayed the events again and again until they were etched indelibly into my mind, until I knew that Kai, who would ask for the role of preparing me for my Rebirth, would flinch at the vivid images, be repulsed by their blood and violence, and stop before probing too deep. Thie had long forgotten what thie had done and had no wish to be reminded.

"Do I know if these images are true in every aspect? No, I do not. I recalled them through the hazy filter of the mind of a child, and no doubt the memories shared by all the other survivors have inseminated them, colored them, given them more details. Our memories bleed into each other, forming a collective outrage. The Tawnin will say they're no more real than the false memories they've implanted, but to forget is a far greater sin than to remember too well.

"To further conceal my trails, I took the pieces of the false memories they gave me and constructed real memories out of them so that when Kai dissected my mind, thie would not be able to tell thir lies apart from my own."

The false, clean, clutter-free living room of my parents is recreated and rearranged into the room in which I meet with Adam and Lauren....

Sunlight coming in from the windows along the western wall makes clean parallelograms on the ground....

You cannot tell which memories are real and which memories are false, and yet you insist on their importance, base so much of your life on them.

"And now, when I'm sure that the plot has been set in motion but do not yet know enough details to betray the plans should I be probed, I will go attack Kai. There is very little chance I will succeed, and Kai will surely want me to be Reborn, to wipe this me away—not all of me, just enough so that our life together can go on. My death will protect my co-conspirators, will allow them to triumph.

"Yet, what good is vengeance if I cannot see it, if you, the Reborn me, cannot remember it, and know the satisfaction of success? This is why I have buried clues, left behind evidence like a trail of crumbs that you will pick up, until you can remember and know what you have done."

Adam Woods... who is not so different from me after all, his memory a trigger for mine...

I purchase things so that someday, they'll trigger in another me the memory of fire...

The mask, so that others can remember me...

Walker Lincoln.

•

Claire is outside the station, waiting, when I walk back. Two men are standing in the shadows behind her. And still farther behind, looming above them, the indistinct figure of Kai.

I stop and turn around. Behind me, two more men are walking down the street, blocking off my retreat.

"It's too bad, Josh," Claire says. "You should have listened to me about remembering. Kai told us that thie was suspicious."

I cannot pick Kai's eyes out of the shadows. I direct my gaze at the blurry shadow behind and above Claire.

"Will you not speak to me yourself, Kai?"

The shadow freezes, and then the mechanical voice, so different from the *voice* that I've grown used to caressing my mind, crackles from the gloom.

"I have nothing to say to you. My Josh, my beloved, no longer exists. He has been taken over by ghosts, has already drowned in memory."

"I'm still here, but now I'm complete."

"That is a persistent illusion of yours that we cannot seem to correct. I am not the Kai you hate, and you're not the Josh I love. We are not the sum of our pasts." Thie pauses. "I hope I will see my Josh soon."

Thie retreats into the interior of the station, leaving me to my judgment and execution.

Fully aware of the futility, I try to talk to Claire anyway.

"Claire, you know I have to remember."

Her face looks sad and tired. "You think you're the only one who's lost someone? I wasn't ported until five years ago. I once had a wife. She was like you. Couldn't let go. Because of her, I was ported and Reborn. But because I made a determined effort to forget, to leave the past alone, they allowed me to keep some memory of her. You, on the other hand, insist on fighting.

"Do you know how many times you've been Reborn? It's because Kai loves, loved you, wished to save most parts of you, that they've been so careful with carving as little of you away as possible each time."

I do not know why Kai wished so fervently to rescue me from myself, to cleanse me of ghosts. Perhaps there are faint echoes of the past in thir mind, that even thie is not aware of, that draw thim to me, that compel thim to try to make me believe the lies so that thie will believe them thimself. To forgive is to forget.

"But thie has finally run out of patience. After this time you'll remember nothing at all of your life, and so with your crime you've consigned more of you, more of those you claim to care about, to die. What good is this vengeance you seek if no one will even remember it happened? The past is gone, Josh. There is no future for the Xenophobes. The Tawnin are here to stay."

I nod. What she says is true. But just because something is true doesn't mean you stop struggling.

I imagine myself in the Judgment Ship again. I imagine Kai coming to welcome me home. I imagine our first kiss, innocent, pure, a new beginning. The memory of the smell of flowers and spices.

There is a part of me that loves thim, a part of me that has seen thir soul and craves thir touch. There is a part of me that wants to move on, a part of me that believes in what the Tawnin have to offer. And *I*, the unified, illusory I, am filled with pity for them.

I turn around and begin to run. The men in front of me wait patiently. There's nowhere for me to go.

I press the trigger in my hand. Lauren had given it to me before I left. A last gift from my old self, from me to me.

I imagine my spine exploding into a million little pieces a moment before it does. I imagine all the pieces of me, atoms struggling to hold a pattern for a second, to be a coherent illusion.

Thoughts and
Prayers

EMILY FORT

So you want to know about Hayley.

No, I'm used to it, or at least I should be by now. People only want to hear about my sister.

It was a dreary, rainy Friday in October, the smell of fresh fallen leaves in the air. The black tupelos lining the field hockey pitch had turned bright red, like a trail of bloody footprints left by a giant.

I had a quiz in French II and planned a week's worth of vegan meals for a family of four in Family and Consumer Science. Around noon, Hayley messaged me from California.

Skipped class. Q and I are driving to the festival right now!!!

I ignored her. She delighted in taunting me with the freedoms of her college life. I was envious, but didn't want to give her the satisfaction of showing it.

In the afternoon, Mom messaged me.

Have you heard from Hayley?

No. The sisterly code of silence was sacred. Her secret boyfriend was safe with me.

"If you do, call me right away."

I put the phone away. Mom was the helicopter type.

As soon as I got home from field hockey, I knew something was wrong. Mom's car was in the driveway, and she never left work this early.

The TV was on in the basement.

Mom's face was ashen. In a voice that sounded strangled, she said, "Hayley's RA called. She went to a music festival. There's been a shooting."

The rest of the evening was a blur as the death toll climbed, TV anchors read old forum posts from the gunman in dramatic voices, shaky follow-drone footage of panicked people screaming and scattering circulated on the web.

I put on my glasses and drifted through the VR recreation of the site hastily put up by the news crews. Already the place was teeming with avatars holding a candlelight vigil. Outlines on the ground glowed where victims were found, and luminous arcs with floating numbers reconstructed ballistic trails. So much data, so little information.

We tried calling and messaging. There was no answer. Probably ran out of battery, we told ourselves. She always forgets to charge her phone. The network must be jammed.

The call came at four in the morning. We were all awake.

"Yes, this is. . . . Are you sure?" Mom's voice was unnaturally calm, as though her life, and all our lives, hadn't just changed forever. "No, we'll fly out ourselves. Thank you."

She hung up, looked at us, and delivered the news. Then she collapsed onto the couch and buried her face in her hands.

There was an odd sound. I turned and, for the first time in my life, saw Dad crying.

I missed my last chance to tell her how much I loved her. I should have messaged her back.

GREGG FORT

I don't have any pictures of Hayley to show you. It doesn't matter. You already have all the pictures of my daughter you need.

Unlike Abigail, I've never taken many pictures or videos, much less drone-view holograms or omni immersions. I lack the instinct to be prepared for the unexpected, the discipline to document the big moments, the skill to frame a scene perfectly. But those aren't the most important reasons.

My father was a hobbyist photographer who took pride in developing his own films and making his own prints. If you were to flip through the dust-covered albums in the attic, you'd see many posed shots of my sisters and me, smiling stiffly into the camera. Pay attention to the ones of my sister Sara. Note how her face is often turned slightly away from the lens so that her right cheek is out of view.

When Sara was five, she climbed onto a chair and toppled a boiling pot. My father was supposed to be watching her, but he'd been distracted, arguing with a colleague on the phone. When all was said and done, Sara had a trail of scars that ran from the right side of her face all the way down her thigh, like a rope of solidified lava.

You won't find in those albums records of the screaming fights between my parents; the awkward chill that descended around the dining table every time my mother stumbled over the word *beautiful*; the way my father avoided looking Sara in the eye.

In the few photographs of Sara where her entire face can be seen, the scars are invisible, meticulously painted out of existence in the darkroom, stroke by stroke. My father simply did it, and the rest of us went along in our practiced silence.

As much as I dislike photographs and other memory substitutes, it's impossible to avoid them. Coworkers and relatives show them to you, and you have no choice but to look and nod. I see the efforts manufacturers of memory-capturing devices put into making their results better than life. Colors are more vivid; details emerge from shadows; filters evoke whatever mood you desire. Without you having to do anything, the phone brackets the shot so that you can pretend to time travel, to pick the perfect instant when everyone is smiling. Skin is smoothed out; pores and small imperfections are erased. What used to take my father a day's work is now done in the blink of an eye, and far better.

Do the people who take these photos believe them to be reality? Or have the digital paintings taken the place of reality in their memory? When they try to remember the captured moment, do they recall what they saw, or what the camera crafted for them?

ABIGAIL FORT

On the flight to California, while Gregg napped and Emily stared out the window, I put on my glasses and immersed myself in images of Hayley. I never expected to do this until I was aged and decrepit, unable to make new memories. Rage would come later. Grief left no room for other emotions.

I was always the one in charge of the camera, the phone, the follow-drone. I made the annual albums, the vacation highlight videos, the animated Christmas cards summarizing the family's yearly accomplishments.

Gregg and the girls indulged me, sometimes reluctantly. I always believed that someday they would come to see my point of view.

"Pictures are important," I'd tell them. "Our brains are so flawed, leaky sieves of time. Without pictures, so many things we want to remember would be forgotten."

I sobbed the whole way across the country as I relived the life of my firstborn.

GREGG FORT

Abigail wasn't wrong, not exactly.

Many have been the times when I wished I had images to help me remember. I can't picture the exact shape of Hayley's face at six months, or recall her Halloween costume when she was five. I can't even remember the exact shade of blue of the dress she wore for high school graduation.

Given what happened later, of course, her pictures are beyond my reach.

I comfort myself with this thought: How can a picture or video capture the intimacy, the irreproducible subjective perspective and mood through my eyes, the emotional tenor of each moment when I *felt* the impossible beauty of the soul of my child? I don't want digital representations, ersatz reflections of the gaze of electronic eyes filtered through layers of artificial intelligence, to mar what I remember of our daughter.

When I think of Hayley, what comes to mind is a series of disjointed memories.

The baby wrapping her translucent fingers around my thumb for the first time; the infant scooting around on her bottom on the hardwood floor, plowing through alphabet blocks like an icebreaker through floes; the four-year-old handing me a box of tissues as I shivered in bed with a cold and laying a small, cool hand against my feverish cheek.

The eight-year-old pulling the rope that released the pumped-up soda bottle launcher. As frothy water drenched the two of us in the wake of the rising rocket, she yelled, laughing, "I'm going to be the first ballerina to dance on Mars!"

The nine-year-old telling me that she no longer wanted me to read to her before going to sleep. As my heart throbbed with the inevitable pain of a child pulling away, she softened the blow with "Maybe someday I'll read to you."

The ten-year-old defiantly standing her ground in the kitchen, supported by her little sister, staring down me and Abigail both. "I won't hand back your phones until you both sign this pledge to never use them during dinner."

The fifteen-year-old slamming on the brakes, creating the loudest tire screech I'd ever heard; me in the passenger seat, knuckles so white they hurt. "You look like me on that roller coaster, Dad." The tone carefully modulated, breezy. She had held out an arm in front of me, as though she could keep me safe, the same way I had done to her hundreds of times before.

And on and on, distillations of the six thousand eight hundred seventy-four days we had together, like broken, luminous shells left on a beach after the tide of quotidian life has receded.

In California, Abigail asked to see her body; I didn't.

I suppose one could argue that there's no difference between my father trying to erase the scars of his error in the darkroom and my refusal to look upon the body of the child I failed to protect. A thousand "I could have's" swirled in my mind: I could have insisted that she go to a college near home; I could have signed her up for a course on mass-shooting-survival skills; I could have demanded that she wear her body armor at all times. An entire generation had grown up with active shooter drills, so why didn't I do more? I don't think I ever understood my father, empathized with his flawed and cowardly and guilt-ridden heart, until Hayley's death.

But in the end, I didn't want to see because I wanted to protect the only thing I had left of her: those memories.

If I were to see her body, the jagged crater of the exit wound, the frozen lava trails of coagulated blood, the muddy cinders and ashes of shredded clothing, I knew the image would overwhelm all that had come before, would incinerate the memories of my daughter, my baby, in one violent eruption, leaving only hatred and despair in its wake. No, that lifeless body was not Hayley, was not the child I wanted to remember. I would no more allow that one moment to filter her whole existence than I would allow transistors and bits to dictate my memory.

So Abigail went, lifted the sheet, and gazed upon the wreckage of Hayley, of our life. She took pictures, too. "This I also want to remember," she mumbled. "You don't turn away from your child in her moment of agony, in the aftermath of your failure."

ABIGAIL FORT

They came to me while we were still in California.

I was numb. Questions that had been asked by thousands of mothers swarmed my mind. Why was he allowed to amass such an arsenal? Why did no one stop him despite all the warning signs? What could I have—should I have—done differently to save my child?

"You can do something," they said. "Let's work together to honor the memory of Hayley and bring about change."

Many have called me naive or worse. What did I think was going to happen? After decades of watching the exact same script being followed to end in thoughts and prayers, what made me think this time would be different? It was the very definition of madness.

Cynicism might make some invulnerable and superior. But not everyone is built that way. In the thrall of grief, you cling to any ray of hope.

"Politics is broken," they said. "It should be enough, after the deaths of little children, after the deaths of newlyweds, after the deaths of mothers shielding newborns, to finally do something. But it never is. Logic and persuasion have lost their power, so we have to arouse the passions. Instead of letting the media direct the public's morbid curiosity to the killer, let's focus on Hayley's story."

It's been done before, I muttered. To center the victim is hardly a novel political move. You want to make sure that she isn't merely a number, a statistic, one more abstract name among lists of the dead. You think when people are confronted by the flesh-and-blood consequences of their vacillation and disengagement, things change. But that hasn't worked, doesn't work.

"Not like this," they insisted, "not with our algorithm."

They tried to explain the process to me, though the details of machine learning and convolution networks and biofeedback models escaped me. Their algorithm had originated in the entertainment industry, where it was used to evaluate films and predict their box office success, and eventually, to craft them. Proprietary variations are used in applications from product design to drafting political speeches, every field in which emotional engagement is critical. Emotions are ultimately biological phenomena, not mystical emanations, and it's possible to discern trends and patterns, to home in on the stimuli that maximize impact. The algorithm would craft a visual narrative of Hayley's life, shape it into a battering ram to shatter the hardened shell of cynicism, spur the viewer to action, shame them for their complacency and defeatism.

The idea seemed absurd, I said. How could electronics know my daughter better than I did? How could machines move hearts when real people could not?

"When you take a photograph," they asked me, "don't you trust the camera AI to give you the best picture? When you scrub through drone footage, you rely on the AI to identify the most interesting clips, to enhance them with the perfect mood filters. This is a million times more powerful."

I gave them my archive of family memories: photos, videos, scans, drone footage, sound recordings, immersiongrams. I entrusted them with my child.

I'm no film critic, and I don't have the terms for the techniques they used. Narrated only with words spoken by our family, intended for each other and not an audience of strangers, the result was unlike any movie or VR immersion I had ever seen. There was no plot save the course of a single life; there was no agenda save the celebration of the curiosity, the compassion, the drive of a child to embrace the universe, to *become*. It was a beautiful life, a life that loved and deserved to be loved, until the moment it was abruptly and violently cut down.

This is the way Hayley deserves to be remembered, I thought, tears streaming down my face. *This is how I see her, and it is how she should be seen.*

I gave them my blessing.

SARA FORT

Growing up, Gregg and I weren't close. It was important to my parents that our family project the image of success, of decorum, regardless of the reality. In response, Gregg distrusted all forms of representation, while I became obsessed with them.

Other than holiday greetings, we rarely conversed as adults, and certainly didn't confide in each other. I knew my nieces only through Abigail's social media posts.

I suppose this is my way of excusing myself for not intervening earlier.

When Hayley died in California, I sent Gregg contact info for a few therapists who specialized in working with families of mass shooting victims, but I purposefully stayed away myself, believing that my intrusion in their moment of grief would be inappropriate given my role as distant aunt and aloof sister. So I wasn't there when Abigail agreed to devote Hayley's memory to the cause of gun control.

Though my company bio describes my specialty as the study of online discourse, the vast bulk of my research material is visual. I design armor against trolls.

EMILY FORT

I watched that video of Hayley many times.

It was impossible to avoid. There was an immersive version, in which you could step into Hayley's room and read her neat handwriting, examine the posters on her wall. There was a low-fidelity version designed for frugal data plans, and the compression artifacts and motion blur made her life seem old-fashioned, dreamy. Everyone shared the video as a way to reaffirm that they were a good person, that they stood with the victims. Click, bump, add a lit-candle emoji, re-rumble.

It was powerful. I cried, also many times. Comments expressing grief and solidarity scrolled past my glasses like a never-ending wake. Families of victims in other shootings, their hopes rekindled, spoke out in support.

But the Hayley in that video felt like a stranger. All the elements in the video were true, but they also felt like lies.

Teachers and parents loved the Hayley they knew, but there was a mousy girl in school who cowered when my sister entered the room.

One time, Hayley drove home drunk; another time, she stole from me and lied until I found the money in her purse. She knew how to manipulate people and wasn't shy about doing it. She was fiercely loyal, courageous, kind, but she could also be reckless, cruel, petty. I loved Hayley because she was human, but the girl in that video was both more and less than.

I kept my feelings to myself. I felt guilty.

Mom charged ahead while Dad and I hung back, dazed. For a brief moment, it seemed as if the tide had turned. Rousing rallies were held and speeches delivered in front of the Capitol and the White House. Crowds chanted Hayley's name. Mom was invited to the State of the Union. When the media reported that Mom had quit her job to campaign on behalf of the movement, there was a crypto fundraiser to collect donations for the family.

And then, the trolls came.

A torrent of emails, messages, rumbles, squeaks, snapgrams, televars came at us. Mom and I were called clickwhores, paid actresses, grief profiteers. Strangers sent us long, rambling walls of text explaining all the ways Dad was inadequate and unmanly.

Hayley didn't die, strangers informed us. She was actually living in Sanya, China, off of the millions the UN and their collaborators in the US government had paid her to pretend to die. Her boyfriend—who had also "obviously not died" in the shooting—was ethnically Chinese, and that was proof of the connection.

Hayley's video was picked apart for evidence of tampering and digital manipulation. Anonymous classmates were quoted to paint her as a habitual liar, a cheat, a drama queen.

Snippets of the video, intercut with "debunking" segments, began to go viral. Some used software to make Hayley spew messages of hate in new clips, quoting Hitler and Stalin as she giggled and waved at the camera.

I deleted my accounts and stayed home, unable to summon the strength to get out of bed. My parents left me to myself; they had their own battles to fight.

SARA FORT

Decades into the digital age, the art of trolling has evolved to fill every niche, pushing the boundaries of technology and decency alike.

From afar, I watched the trolls swarm around my brother's family with uncoordinated precision, with aimless malice, with malevolent glee.

Conspiracy theories blended with deep fakes, and then yielded to memes that turned compassion inside out, abstracted pain into lulz.

"Mommy, the beach in hell is so warm!"

"I love these new holes in me!"

Searches for Hayley's name began to trend on porn sites. The content producers, many of them AI-driven bot farms, responded with procedurally generated films and VR immersions featuring my niece. The algorithms took publicly available footage of Hayley and wove her face, body, and voice seamlessly into fetish videos.

The news media reported on the development in outrage, perhaps even sincerely. The coverage spurred more searches, which generated more content. . . .

As a researcher, it's my duty and habit to remain detached, to observe and study phenomena with clinical detachment, perhaps even fascination. It's simplistic to view trolls as politically motivated—at least not in the sense that term is usually understood. Though Second-Amendment absolutists helped spread the memes, the originators often had little conviction in any political cause. Anarchic sites such as 8taku, duangduang, and alt-web sites that arose in the wake of the deplatforming wars of the previous decade are homes for these dung beetles of the internet, the id of our collective online unconscious. Taking pleasure in taboo-breaking and transgression, the trolls have no unifying interest other than saying the unspeakable, mocking the sincere, playing with what others declared to be off-limits. By wallowing in the outrageous and filthy, they both defile and define the technologically mediated bonds of society.

But as a human being, watching what they were doing with Hayley's image was intolerable. I reached out to my estranged brother and his family.

"Let me help."

Though machine learning has given us the ability to predict with a fair amount of accuracy which victims will be targeted—trolls are not quite as unpredictable as they'd like you to think—my employer and other major social media platforms are keenly aware that they must walk a delicate line between policing user-generated content and chilling "engagement," the one metric that drives the stock price and thus governs all decisions. Aggressive moderation, especially when it's reliant on user reporting and human judgment, is a process easily gamed by all sides, and every company has suffered accusations of censorship. In the end, they threw up their hands and tossed out their byzantine enforcement policy manuals. They have neither the skills nor the interest to become arbiters of truth and decency for society as a whole. How could they be expected to solve the problem that even the organs of democracy couldn't?

Over time, most companies converged on one solution. Rather than focusing on judging the behavior of speakers, they've devoted resources to letting listeners shield themselves. Algorithmically separating legitimate (though impassioned) political speech from coordinated harassment for *everyone* at once is an intractable problem—content celebrated by some as speaking truth to power is often condemned by others as beyond the pale. It's much easier to build and train individually tuned neural networks to screen out the content a *particular* user does not wish to see.

The new defensive neural networks—marketed as "armor"—observe each user's emotional state in response to their content stream. Capable of operating in vectors encompassing text, audio, video, and AR/VR, the armor teaches itself to recognize content especially upsetting to the user and screened it out, leaving only a tranquil void. As mixed reality and immersion have become more commonplace, the best way to wear armor is through augmented-reality glasses that filter all sources of visual stimuli. Trolling, like the viruses and worms of old, is a technical problem, and now we have a technical solution.

To invoke the most powerful and personalized protection, one has to pay. Social media companies, which also train the armor, argue that this solution gets them out of the content-policing business, excuses them from having to decide what is unacceptable in virtual town squares, frees everyone from the specter of Big Brother–style censorship. That this pro-free-speech ethos happens to align with more profit is no doubt a mere afterthought.

I sent my brother and his family the best, most advanced armor that money could buy.

ABIGAIL FORT

Imagine yourself in my position. Your daughter's body had been digitally pressed into hard-core pornography, her voice made to repeat words of hate, her visage mutilated with unspeakable violence. And it happened because of you, because of your inability to imagine the depravity of the human heart. Could you have stopped? Could you have stayed away?

The armor kept the horrors at bay as I continued to post and share, to raise my voice against a tide of lies.

The idea that Hayley hadn't died but was an actress in an anti-gun government conspiracy was so absurd that it didn't seem to deserve a response. Yet, as my armor began to filter out headlines, leaving blank spaces on news sites and in multicast streams, I realized that the lies had somehow become a real controversy. Actual journalists began to demand that I produce receipts for how I had spent the crowdfunded money—we hadn't received a cent! The world had lost its mind.

I released the photographs of Hayley's corpse. Surely there was still some shred of decency left in this world, I thought. Surely no one could speak against the evidence of their eyes?

It got worse.

For the faceless hordes of the internet, it became a game to see who could get something past my armor, to stab me in the eye with a poisoned video clip that would make me shudder and recoil.

Bots sent me messages in the guise of other parents who had lost their children in mass shootings, and sprung hateful videos on me after I whitelisted them. They sent me tribute slideshows dedicated to the memory of Hayley, which morphed into violent porn once the armor allowed them through. They pooled funds to hire errand gofers and rent delivery drones to deposit fiducial markers near my home, surrounding me with augmented-reality ghosts of Hayley writhing, giggling, moaning, screaming, cursing, mocking.

Worst of all, they animated images of Hayley's bloody corpse to the accompaniment of jaunty soundtracks. Her death trended as a joke, like the "Hamster Dance" of my youth.

GREGG FORT

Sometimes I wonder if we have misunderstood the notion of freedom. We prize "freedom to" so much more than "freedom from." People must be free to own guns, so the only solution is to teach children to hide in closets and wear ballistic backpacks. People must be free to post and say what they like, so the only solution is to tell their targets to put on armor.

Abigail had simply decided, and the rest of us had gone along. Too late, I begged and pleaded with her to stop, to retreat. We would sell the house and move somewhere away from the temptation to engage with the rest of humanity, away from the always-connected world and the ocean of hate in which we were drowning.

But Sara's armor gave Abigail a false sense of security, pushed her to double down, to engage the trolls. "I must fight for my daughter," she screamed at me. "I cannot allow them to desecrate her memory."

As the trolls intensified their campaign, Sara sent us patch after patch for the armor. She added layers with names like adversarial complementary sets, self-modifying code detectors, visualization auto-healers.

Again and again, the armor held only briefly before the trolls found new ways through. The democratization of artificial intelligence meant that they knew all the techniques Sara knew, and they had machines that could learn and adapt, too.

Abigail could not hear me. My pleas fell on deaf ears; perhaps her armor had learned to see me as just another angry voice to screen out.

EMILY FORT

One day, Mom came to me in a panic. "I don't know where she is! I can't see her!"

She hadn't talked to me in days, obsessed with the project that Hayley had become. It took me some time to figure out what she meant. I sat down with her at the computer.

She clicked the link for Hayley's memorial video, which she watched several times a day to give herself strength.

"It's not there!" she said.

She opened the cloud archive of our family memories.

"Where are the pictures of Hayley?" she said. "There are only placeholder Xs."

She showed me her phone, her backup enclosure, her tablet.

"There's nothing! Nothing! Did we get hacked?"

Her hands fluttered helplessly in front of her chest, like the wings of a trapped bird. "She's just gone!"

Wordlessly, I went to the shelves in the family room and brought down one of the printed annual photo albums she had made when we were little. I opened the volume to a family portrait, taken when Hayley was ten and I was eight.

I showed the page to her.

Another choked scream. Her trembling fingers tapped against Hayley's face on the page, searching for something that wasn't there.

I understood. A pain filled my heart, a pity that ate away at love. I reached up to her face and gently took off her glasses.

She stared at the page.

Sobbing, she hugged me. "You found her. Oh, you found her!"

It felt like the embrace of a stranger. Or maybe I had become a stranger to her.

Aunt Sara explained that the trolls had been very careful with their attacks. Step by step, they had trained my mother's armor to recognize *Hayley* as the source of her distress.

But another kind of learning had also been taking place in our home. My parents paid attention to me only when I had something to do with Hayley. It was as if they no longer saw me, as though I had been erased instead of Hayley.

My grief turned dark and festered. How could I compete with a ghost? The perfect daughter who had been lost not once, but twice? The victim who demanded perpetual penance? I felt horrid for thinking such things, but I couldn't stop.

We sank under our guilt, each alone.

GREGG FORT

I blamed Abigail. I'm not proud to admit it, but I did.

We shouted at each other and threw dishes, replicating the half-remembered drama between my own parents when I was a child. Hunted by monsters, we became monsters ourselves.

While the killer had taken Hayley's life, Abigail had offered her image up as a sacrifice to the bottomless appetite of the internet. Because of Abigail, my memories of Hayley would be forever filtered through the horrors that came after her death. She had summoned the machine that amassed individual human beings into one enormous, collective, distorting gaze, the machine that had captured the memory of my daughter and then ground it into a lasting nightmare.

The broken shells on the beach glistened with the venom of the raging deep.

Of course that's unfair, but that doesn't mean it isn't also true.

"HEARTLESS," A SELF-PROFESSED TROLL

There's no way for me to prove that I am who I say, or that I did what I claim. There's no registry of trolls where you can verify my identity, no Wikipedia entry with confirmed sources.

Can you even be sure I'm not trolling you right now?

I won't tell you my gender or race or who I prefer to sleep with, because those details aren't relevant to what I did. Maybe I own a dozen guns. Maybe I'm an ardent supporter of gun control.

I went after the Forts because they deserved it.

RIP-trolling has a long and proud history, and our target has always been inauthenticity. Grief should be private, personal, hidden. Can't you see how horrible it was for that mother to turn her dead daughter into a symbol, to wield it as a political tool? A public life is an inauthentic one. Anyone who enters the arena must be prepared for the consequences.

Everyone who shared that girl's memorial online, who attended the virtual candlelit vigils, offered condolences, professed to have been spurred into action, was equally guilty of hypocrisy. You didn't think the proliferation of guns capable of killing hundreds in one minute was a bad thing until someone shoved images of a dead girl in your face? What's wrong with you?

And you journalists are the worst. You make money and win awards for turning deaths into consumable stories; for coaxing survivors to sob in front of your drones to sell more ads; for inviting your readers to find meaning in their pathetic lives through vicarious, mimetic suffering. We trolls play with images of the dead, who are beyond caring, but you stinking ghouls grow fat and rich by feeding death to the living. The sanctimonious are also the most filthy-minded, and victims who cry the loudest are the hungriest for attention.

Everyone is a troll now. If you've ever liked or shared a meme that wished violence on someone you'd never met, if you've ever decided it was okay to snarl and snark with venom because the target was "powerful," if you've ever tried to signal your virtue by piling on in an outrage mob, if you've ever wrung your hands and expressed concern that perhaps the money raised for some victim should have gone to some other less "privileged" victim—then I hate to break it to you, you've also been trolling.

Some say that the proliferation of trollish rhetoric in our culture is corrosive, that armor is necessary to equalize the terms of a debate in which the only way to win is to care less. But don't you see how unethical armor is? It makes the weak think they're strong, turns cowards into deluded heroes with no skin in the game. If you truly despise trolling, then you should've realized by now that armor only makes things worse.

By weaponizing her grief, Abigail Fort became the biggest troll of them all—except she was bad at it, just a weakling in armor. We had to bring her—and by extension, the rest of you—down.

ABIGAIL FORT

Politics returned to normal. Sales of body armor, sized for children and young adults, received a healthy bump. More companies offered classes on situational awareness and mass shooting drills for schools. Life went on.

I deleted my accounts; I stopped speaking out. But it was too late for my family. Emily moved out as soon as she could; Gregg found an apartment.

Alone in the house, my eyes devoid of armor, I tried to sort through the archive of photographs and videos of Hayley.

Every time I watched the video of her sixth birthday, I heard in my mind the pornographic moans; every time I looked at photos of her high school graduation, I saw her bloody animated corpse dancing to the tune of "Girls Just Wanna Have Fun"; every time I tried to page through the old albums for some good memories, I jumped in my chair, thinking an AR ghost of her, face grotesquely deformed like Munch's *The Scream*, was about to jump out at me, cackling, "Mommy, these new piercings hurt!"

I screamed, I sobbed, I sought help. No therapy, no medication, worked. Finally, in a numb fury, I deleted all my digital files, shredded my printed albums, broke the frames hanging on walls.

The trolls trained me as well as they trained my armor.

I no longer have any images of Hayley. I can't remember what she looked like. I have truly, finally, lost my child.

How can I possibly be forgiven for that?

Byzantine Empathy

You're hurrying along a muddy path, part of a jostling crowd. The commotion around you compels you to scramble to keep up. As your eyes adjust to the dim light of early dawn, you see everyone is laden down with possessions: a baby wrapped tightly against the chest of its mother; a bulging bedsheet filled with clothing ballooning over the back of a middle-aged man; a washbasin filled with lychees and breadfruit cradled in the arms of an eight-year-old girl; an oversize Xiaomi smartphone pressed into service as a flashlight by an old woman in sweatpants and a wrinkled blouse; a Mickey Mouse suitcase with one missing wheel being dragged through the mud by a young woman in a T-shirt emblazoned with the English phrase "Happy Girl Lucky"; a pillowcase filled with books or perhaps bundles of cash dangling from the hand of an old man in a baseball cap advertising Chinese cigarettes . . .

Most in the crowd seem taller than you, and this is how you know that you are a child. Looking down, you see on your feet yellow plastic slippers decorated with the portraits of Disney's Belle. The thick mud threatens to pull them off your feet with each step, and you wonder if perhaps they mean something to you—home, security, a life safe for fantasy—so that you don't want to leave them behind.

In your right hand you're holding a rag doll in a red dress, embroidered with curved letters in a script you don't recognize. You squeeze the doll, and the sensation tells you the doll is stuffed with something light that rustles, perhaps seeds. Your left hand is held by a woman with a baby on her back and a bundle of blankets in her other hand. Your baby sister, you think, too little to be scared. She looks at you with her dark, adorable eyes, and you give her a comforting smile. You squeeze your mother's hand, and she squeezes back reassuringly, warm.

On both sides of the path you see scattered tents, some orange and some blue, stretching across the fields all the way to the jungle half a kilometer away. You're not sure if one of the tents used to be your home or if you're just passing through.

There's no background music, and no cries from exotic Southeast Asian birds. Instead, your ears are filled with anxious chatter and cries. You can't understand the language or the topolect, but the tension in the voices tells you that they're cries for family to keep up, for friends to be careful, for aged relatives to not stumble.

A loud whine passes overhead, and the field ahead and to the left erupts in a fiery explosion brighter than sunrise. The ground convulses; you tumble down into the slimy mud.

More whines sweep overhead, and more shells explode around you, rattling your bones. Your ears are ringing. Your mother crawls over to you and covers you with her body. Merciful darkness blocks out the chaos. Loud, keening screams. Terrified cries. A few incoherent moans of pain.

You try to sit up, but your mother's unmoving body is holding you down. You struggle to shift her weight off and manage to wriggle out from under her.

The back of your mother's head is a bloody mess. Your baby sister is crying on the ground next to her body. Around you people are running in every direction, some still trying to hold on to their possessions, but bundles and suitcases lie abandoned in the path and the fields, next to motionless bodies. The rumbling of engines can be heard in the direction of the camp, and through the swaying, lush vegetation you see a column of soldiers in camouflage approach, guns at the ready.

A woman points at the soldiers and shouts. Some of the people stop running and hold up their hands.

A gunshot rings out, followed by another.

Like leaves blown before a gust of wind, the crowd scatters. Mud splashes onto your face as stomping feet pass by you.

Your baby sister cries louder. You scream, "Stop! Stop!" in your language. You try to crawl over to her, but someone stumbles over you, slamming you to the ground. You try to shield your head from the trampling feet with your arms and curl up into a ball. Some leap over you; others try but fail, landing on you, kicking you hard as they scramble.

More gunshots. You peek between your fingers. A few figures tumble to the earth. There's little room to maneuver in the stampeding crowd, and people fall in a heap whenever anyone goes down. Everyone is pushing and shoving to put someone, anyone, between the bullets and themselves.

A foot in a muddy sneaker slams down onto the bundled figure of your baby sister, and you hear a sickening crack as her cries are abruptly silenced. The owner of the sneaker hesitates for a moment before the surging crowd pushes them forward, disappearing from your sight.

You scream, and something pounds you hard in the gut, knocking the breath out of you.

•

Tang Jianwen ripped off her headset, gasping. Her hands shook as she unzipped her immersion suit, and she managed to peel it halfway off before her hands lost their strength. As she curled up on the omnidirectional treadmill, the bruises on her sweat-drenched body glistened dark red in the faint white glow of her computer screen, the only light on in the dark studio apartment. She dry-heaved a few times before breaking into sobs.

Though her eyes were closed, she could still see the grim expressions on the faces of the soldiers, the bloody pulp that had been the mother's head, the broken little body of the baby, her life trampled out of her.

She had disabled the safety features of the immersion suit and removed the amplitude filters in the algics circuitry. It didn't seem right to experience the ordeal of the Muertien refugees with pain filters in place.

A VR rig was the ultimate empathy machine. How could she truly say she had walked in their shoes without suffering as they did?

The neon lights of bustling Shanghai at night spilled through the cracks in the curtains, drawing harsh, careless rainbows on the floor. Virtual wealth and real greed commingled out there, a world indifferent to the deaths and pain in the jungles of Southeast Asia.

She was grateful that she had not been able to afford the olfactory attachment. The coppery odor of blood, mixed with the fragrance of gunpowder, would have undone her before the end. Smells probed into the deepest part of your brain and stirred up the rawest emotions, like the blade of a hoe breaking up the numbed clods of modernity to reveal the wriggling pink flesh of wounded earthworms.

Eventually, she got up, peeled off the rest of her suit, and stumbled into the bathroom. She jumped as water rumbled in the pipes, the noise of approaching engines through the jungle. Under the hot streams of the shower, she shivered.

"Something has to be done," she muttered. "We can't let this happen. *I* can't."

But what could she do? The war between the central government of Myanmar and the ethnic minority rebels near the country's border with China was little remarked on by the rest of the world. The United States, the world's policeman, was silent because it wanted a loyal, pro-US government in Naypyidaw as a chess piece against rising Chinese influence in the region. China, on the other hand, wanted to entice the government in Naypyidaw onto its side with business and investment, and making a big deal out of ethnic Han Chinese civilians being slaughtered by Burmese soldiers was unhelpful for this Great Game. Even news of what was happening in Muertien was censored by a Chinese government terrified that sympathy for the refugees might mutate into uncontrollable nationalism. Refugee camps on both sides of the border were kept out of sight, like some shameful secret. Eyewitness accounts, videos, and this VR file had to be sneaked through tiny encrypted holes punched in the Great Firewall. In the West, on the other hand, popular apathy functioned more effectively than any official censorship.

She could not organize marches or gather signatures for petitions; she could not start or join a nonprofit dedicated to the well-being of the refugees—not that people in China trusted charities, which were all frauds; she could not ask everyone she knew to call their representatives and tell them to do something about Muertien. Having studied abroad in the United States, Jianwen wasn't so naive as to think that these avenues open to citizens of a democracy were all that effective—often, they served as mere symbolic gestures that did nothing to alter the minds or actions of those who truly determined foreign policy. But at least these acts would have allowed her to *feel* like she was making a difference.

And wasn't *feeling* the entire point of being human?

The old men in Beijing, terrified of any challenge to their authority and the possibility of instability, had made all these things impossible. To be a citizen of China was to be constantly reminded of the stark reality of the utter powerlessness of the individual living in a modern, centralized, technocratic state.

The scalding water was starting to feel uncomfortable. She scrubbed herself hard, as if it was possible to free herself from the haunting memories of the dying by scouring away sweat and skin cells, as if it was possible to be absolved of guilt with soap that smelled of watermelons.

She got out of the shower, still dazed, raw, but at least functional. The filtered air in the apartment smelled faintly of hot glue, the result of too much electronics packed into a small space. She wrapped a towel around herself, padded into her room, and sat down in front of her computer screen. She tapped on the keyboard, trying to distract herself with updates on her mining progress.

The screen was enormous and its resolution cutting edge, but by itself, it was an insignificant piece of dumb equipment, only the visible corner of the powerful computing iceberg that she controlled.

The array of custom-made ASICs in the humming rack along the wall was devoted to one thing: solving cryptographic puzzles. She and other miners around the world used their specialized equipment to discover the nuggets made of special numbers that maintained the integrity of several cryptocurrencies. Although she had a day job as a financial services programmer, this work was where she really felt alive.

It gave her the feeling of possessing a bit of power, to be part of a global community in rebellion against authority in all its forms: authoritarian governments, democratic-mob statism, central banks that manipulated inflation and value by fiat. It was the closest she could come to being the activist she really yearned to be. Here, only math mattered, and the logic of number theory and elegant programming formed an unbreakable code of trust.

She tweaked her mining cluster, joined a new pool, checked in on a few channels where like-minded enthusiasts chatted about the future, and felt calmer as she read the scrolling text without joining in the conversation herself.

N♥T>: Just set up my Huawei GWX. Anyone have a recommendation for a good VR to try on it?

秋叶1001>: Room-scale or apartment-scale?

N♥T>: Apartment-scale. Nothing but the best for me.

秋叶1001>: Wow! You must've done well in the mines this year. I'd say try "Titanic."

N♥T>: From Tencent?

秋叶1001>: No! The one from SLG is much better. You'll need to hook your mining rig up to handle the graphics load if you have a big apartment.

Anon >: Ah, enhanced play or proof-of-work. What's more important?

Like many others, Jianwen had plunged headlong into the consumer VR craze. The resolution of the rigs was finally high enough to overcome dizziness, and even a smartphone contained enough processing power to drive a basic headset—though not the kind that provided full immersion.

She had climbed Mount Everest; she had BASE-jumped from the top of the Burj Khalifa; she had "gone out" to VR bars with her friends from across the globe, each of them holed up in their respective apartments drinking shots of real *erguotou* or vodka; she had kissed her favorite actors and slept with a few she *really* liked; she had seen VR films (exactly what they sound like and not very good); she had done VR LARP; she had flitted around the room in the form of a tiny fly as twelve angry fictional women argued over the fate of a fictional young woman, subtly directing their arguments by landing on pieces of evidence she wanted them to focus on.

But she had felt unsatisfied with all of them in some vague, inarticulable way. The emerging medium of VR was like unformed clay, full of potential and possibility, propelled by hope and greed, promising everything and nothing, a technology solution in search of a problem—it was still unclear what sort of pleasures, narratological or ludic, would ultimately predominate.

This latest VR experience, a short little clip in the life of an unnamed Muertien refugee, however, felt different.

But for an accident of birth, that little girl could have been me. Her mother even had my mother's eyes.

For the first time in years, after her youthful idealism had been ground down by the indifference of the world after college, she felt compelled to *do something*.

She stared at her screen. The flickering balances in her cryptocurrency accounts were based on a consensus of cryptographic chains, a trust forged from the trust-less. In a world walled from pain by greed, could such trust also be a way to drill a hole into the barrier, to let hope flood through? Could the world indeed be converted into a virtual village, where empathy bonded each to each?

She opened a new terminal window on her screen and began to type feverishly.

•

I hate DC, Sophia Ellis decided as she looked out the window.

Traffic crawled through the rainy streets, punctuated by the occasional blare of an angry driver—a nice metaphor for what passed for political normality in the capital these days. The distant monuments on the Mall, ethereal through the drizzle, seemed to mock her with their permanence and transcendence.

The board members were making chitchat, waiting for the quarterly meeting to start. She only paid attention half-heartedly, her mind elsewhere.

. . . your daughter . . . Congrats to her!

. . . too many blockchain startups . . .

... passing through London in September ...

Sophia would rather be back in the State Department, where she belonged, but the current administration's distaste for traditional-style diplomacy made her think she might have better prospects shifting into the nonprofit sector as a top administrator. After all, it was an open secret that some of the biggest US nonprofits with international offices served as unofficial arms of US foreign policy, and being the executive director of Refugees Without Borders was not a bad stepping-stone back to power when the next administration came in. The key was to do some good for the refugees, to promote American values, and to stabilize the world even as the current administration seemed hell-bent on squandering American power.

... saw a cell phone video and asked me if we were doing anything about it ... Muertien, I think?

She pulled herself out of her reverie. "That's not something we should be involved in. It's like the situation in Yemen."

The board member nodded and changed the subject.

Sophia's old college roommate, Jianwen, had emailed her about Muertien a couple months ago. She had written back to express her regrets in a kind and thoughtful message. *We're an organization with limited resources. Not every humanitarian crisis can be addressed adequately. I'm sorry.*

It was the truth. Sort of.

It was also the consensus of those who understood how things worked that interfering with what was happening in Muertien would not benefit US interests, or the interests of Refugees Without Borders. The desire to make the world a better place, which was what had gotten her into diplomacy and nonprofit work in the first place, had to be tempered and guided by realism. Despite—or perhaps because of—her differences with the current administration, she believed that preserving American power was a worthy and important goal. Drawing attention to the crisis in Muertien would embarrass a key new American ally in the region, and that had to be avoided. This complicated world demanded that the interests of the United States (and its allies) be prioritized at the expense of some who suffered, so that more of the helpless could be protected.

America was not perfect, but it was also, after weighing all the alternatives, the best authority we had.

". . . the number of small donations from under-thirty donors has fallen by 75 percent in the last month," said one of the board members. While Sophia had been philosophizing, the board meeting had started.

The speaker was the husband of an important MP, participating from London through a telepresence robot. Sophia suspected that he was in love with his voice more than his wife. The looming screen at the end of the telescoping neck made his face appear severe and dominating, and the robot's hands gesticulated for emphasis, presumably in imitation of the speaker's actual hands. "You are telling me you have no plans for addressing the decline in engagement?"

Did someone on your wife's staff write that up for you as a talking point? Sophia thought. She doubted he could have personally paid enough attention to the financial records to notice such a thing.

"We don't rely on small direct donations from that demographic for the bulk of our funding—" she began, but she was cut off by another board member.

"That's not the point. It's about future mindshare, about publicity. Refugees Without Borders is fading from the conversation on social media without large numbers of small donations from that key demographic. This will ultimately affect the big grants."

The speaker was the CEO of a mobile devices company. Sophia had had to dissuade her more than once from mandating that donations to Refugees Without Borders be used to purchase the company's cheap phones for refugees in Europe, which would have boosted the company's reported market share (and violated conflict-of-interest rules).

"There have been some recent, unexpected shifts in the donor landscape that everyone is still trying to figure out—" Sophia said, but once again, she couldn't finish the sentence.

"You're talking about Empathium, aren't you?" asked the husband of the MP. "Well, do you have a plan?"

Definitely a talking point from your wife's staff. The Europeans always seemed to her more jittery about the cryptocurrency nuts than Americans. *But just as with diplomacy, it's better to guide the nuts than confront them.*

"What's Empathium?" asked another board member, a retired federal judge who still thought that the fax machine was the greatest technology invention ever.

"I am indeed talking about Empathium," said Sophia, trying to keep her voice soothing. Then she turned to the tech CEO. "Would you like to explain?"

Had Sophia tried to describe Empathium, the tech CEO would surely have interrupted her. She couldn't bear to let anyone else show more expertise about a technology issue. Might as well try to preserve some decorum.

The tech CEO nodded. "It's simple. Empathium is another new disintermediating blockchain application making heavy use of smart contracts, but this time with the twist of disrupting the jobs traditional charities are hired to do in the philanthropy marketplace."

Blank faces stared at the CEO from around the table. Eventually the judge turned to Sophia. "Why don't you give it a shot?"

She had gotten control of the meeting back simply by letting others overreach, a classic diplomacy move. "Let me take this piece by piece. I'll start with smart contracts. Suppose you and I sign a contract where if it rains tomorrow, I have to pay you five dollars, and if it doesn't rain, you have to pay me a dollar."

"Sounds like a bad insurance policy," said the retired judge.

"You wouldn't do well with that offering in London," said the husband of the MP.

Weak chuckles from around the table.

"With a normal contract," Sophia went on smoothly, "even if there's a thunderstorm tomorrow, you may not get your money. I may renege and refuse to pay, or argue with you about what the meaning of 'rain' is. And you'll have to take me to court."

"Oh, you won't do well in *my* court arguing the meaning of rain."

"Sure, but as Your Honor knows, people argue about the most ridiculous things." She had learned that it was best to let the judge go on these tangents before guiding him back to the trail. "And litigation is expensive."

"We can both put our money into the hands of a trusted friend and have him decide who to pay after tomorrow. That's called escrow, you know?"

"Absolutely. That's a great suggestion," said Sophia. "However, that requires us to agree on a common, trusted third-party authority, and we'll have to pay her a fee for her troubles. Bottom line: there are a lot of transaction costs associated with a traditional contract."

"So what would happen if we had a smart contract?"

"The funds would be transferred over to you as soon as it rained. There's nothing I can do to stop it because the entire mechanism for performance is coded in software."

"So you're saying a contract and a smart contract are basically the same thing. Except one of them is written in legalese and requires people to read it and interpret it, and the other is written in computer code and just needs a machine to execute it. No judge, no jury, no escrow, no takebacks."

Sophia was impressed. The judge wasn't technologically savvy, but he was sharp. "That's right. Machines are far more transparent and predictable than the legal system, even a well-functioning legal system."

"I'm not sure I like that," said the judge.

"But you can see why this is attractive, especially if you don't trust—"

"Smart contracts reduce transaction costs by taking out intermediaries," said the tech CEO impatiently. "You could have just said that instead of this long-winded, ridiculous example."

"I could have," acknowledged Sophia. She had also learned that appearing to agree with the CEO reduced transaction costs.

"So what does this have to do with charity?" asked the husband of the MP.

"Some people view charities as unnecessary intermediaries rent-seeking on trust," said the tech CEO. "Isn't this obvious?"

Again, more blank looks from around the table.

"Some smart contract enthusiasts can be a bit extreme," acknowledged Sophia. "In their view, charities like Refugees Without Borders spend most of our money on renting office space, paying staffers, holding expensive fundraisers where the wealthy socialize and have fun, and misusing donations to enrich insiders—"

"Which is an absolutely absurd view held by idiots with loud keyboards and no common sense—" said the tech CEO, her face flushed with anger.

"Or any political sense," interrupted the husband of the MP, as if his marriage automatically made him an authority on politics. "We also coordinate field relief efforts, bring international expertise, raise awareness in the West, soothe nervous local officials, and make sure that money goes to deserving recipients."

"That's the trust we bring to the table," said Sophia. "But for the WikiLeaks generation, claims of authority and expertise are automatically suspicious. In their view, even the way we use our program funds is inefficient: How can we know how to spend the money better than those who actually need the help? How can we rule out the option for refugees to acquire weapons to defend themselves? How can we decide to work with corrupt local government officials who line their own pockets with donations before passing on dribbles to the victims? Better to just send money directly to neighborhood children who can't afford school lunches. The well-publicized failures of international relief efforts in places like Haiti and the former North Korea strengthen their argument."

"So what's their alternative?" asked the judge.

·

Jianwen watched as the notifications scrolled up her screen, each announcing the completion of a smart contract denominated in completely anonymous cryptocurrency. A lot of business was done that way these days, especially in the developing world, what with so many governments trying to extend their control by outlawing cash.

She had read somewhere that more than 20 percent of global financial transactions were now through various cryptocurrencies.

But the transactions she was watching onscreen were different. The offers were requests for aid or promises to provide funds; there was no consideration except the need to *do something*. The Empathium blockchain network matched and grouped the offers into multi-party smart contracts, and, when the conditions for performance were fulfilled, executed them.

She saw there were requests for children's books; for fresh vegetables; for gardening tools; for contraceptives; for another doctor to come and set up shop for the long haul—and not just a volunteer to come for thirty days, parachuting in and jetting right back out, leaving everything unfinished and unfinishable . . .

She prayed for the offers to be taken up, to be satisfied by the system, even though she didn't believe in God, or any god. Though she had created Empathium, she was powerless to affect its specific operation. That was the beauty of the system. No one could be in charge.

When she was a college student in the US, Jianwen had returned to China for the summer of the year of the great Sichuan earthquake to help the victims of that disaster. The Chinese government had put a great deal of its resources into the rescue effort, even mobilizing the army.

Some PLA soldiers, her age or even younger, showed her the ugly scars on their hands from when they had dug through the muddy rubble of collapsed buildings for survivors and bodies.

"I had to stop because my hands hurt so much," one of the boys told her, his voice filled with shame. "They said if I kept going I'd lose my fingers."

Her vision blurred from rage. *Why couldn't the government have supplied the soldiers with shovels or real rescue equipment?* She pictured the soldiers' bloody hands, the flesh of the fingers peeling back from the bones, as they continued to scoop up handfuls of earth in the hope of finding someone still alive. *You don't have anything to be ashamed about.*

Later, she had recounted her experiences to her roommate, Sophia. She had shared Jianwen's rage at the Chinese government, but her face hadn't changed at all at her description of the young soldier.

"He was just a tool for an autocracy," the roommate had said, as if she couldn't picture those bloody hands at all.

Jianwen hadn't gone to the disaster zone with some official organization; rather, she was just one of thousands of volunteers who had come to Sichuan on their own, hoping to make a difference. She and the other volunteers had brought food and clothing, thinking that was what was needed. But mothers asked her for picture books or games to comfort their weepy children; farmers asked her when and how soon cell service would be restored; townspeople wanted to know if they could get tools and supplies to start rebuilding; a little girl who had lost her whole family wanted to know how she was going to finish high school. She didn't have any of the needed information or supplies, and neither did anyone else, it seemed. The officials in charge of the rescue effort disliked having volunteers like her around because they reported to no authority, and thus told them nothing.

"This shows why you need expertise," Sophia had said, later. "You can't just go down there like an aimless mob hoping to do good. People who know what they're doing need to be in charge of disaster relief."

Jianwen wasn't sure she agreed—she had seen little evidence that it was possible for any expert to anticipate everything needed in a disaster.

Text scrolled even faster in another window on the screen, showing more contract offers being submitted: requests for teachers of Greek; for funding to build a new cell tower; for medicine; for people who could teach refugees how to navigate the visa and work permit system; for weapons; for truckers willing to ship refugee-produced art out to buyers . . .

Some of these requests were for the kind of things that no NGO or government would ever give refugees. The idea of some authority dictating what was needed and not needed by people struggling to survive revolted Jianwen.

People in the middle of a disaster zone knew best what they needed. It's best to give them money so that they could buy whatever they needed—plenty of fearless vendors and ingenious adventurers would be willing to bring the refugees whatever goods or services they requested when there was profit to be made. Money did make the world go around, and that wasn't a bad thing.

Without cryptocurrency, none of what Empathium had accomplished so far would have been possible. The transfer of money across national borders was expensive and subject to heavy governmental oversight by suspicious regulators. Getting money into the hands of needy individuals was practically impossible without the help of some central payment processor, which could easily be co-opted by multiple authorities.

But with cryptocurrency and Empathium, a smartphone was all you needed to let the world know of your needs and to receive help. You could pay anyone securely and anonymously. You could band together with others with the same needs and submit a group application, or go it alone. No one could reach in and stop the smart contracts from executing.

It was exciting to see something that she had built begin to work as envisioned.

Still, so many of the aid requests on Empathium remained unfulfilled. There was too little money, too few donors.

•

". . . that's basically it in a nutshell," said Sophia. "Donations to Refugees Without Borders have fallen because many younger donors are giving on the Empathium network instead."

"Wait, did you just tell me that they're giving 'cryptocurrency' away on this network?" asked the judge. "What is that, like fake money?"

"Well, not *fake*. Just not dollars or yen—though cryptocurrencies can be converted to fiat currencies at exchanges. It's an electronic token. Think of it"—Sophia struggled to think of an outdated reference that would make sense to the old judge, then inspiration struck—"like an MP3 on your iPod. Except it can be used to pay for things."

"Why can't I send a copy to someone to pay for something but keep a copy for myself, the same way kids used to do with songs?"

"Who owns which song is recorded in an electronic ledger."

"But who keeps this ledger? What's to prevent hackers from getting in there and rewriting it? You said there was no central authority."

"The ledger, which is called the blockchain, is distributed on computers across the world," said the tech CEO. "It's based on cryptographic principles that solve the Byzantine Generals problem. Blockchains power cryptocurrencies as well as Empathium. Those who use the blockchain trust the math; they don't need to trust people."

"The what now?" asked the judge. "Byzantium?"

Sophia sighed inwardly. She wasn't expecting to get into this level of detail. She hadn't even finished explaining the basics of Empathium, and who knew how much longer it would take for the discussion to produce a consensus on what Refugees Without Borders should do about it?

Just as cryptocurrency aimed to wrest control of the money supply away from the fiat of governments, Empathium aimed to wrest control of the world's supply of compassion away from the expertise of charities.

Empathium was an idealistic endeavor, but it was driven by waves of emotion, not expertise or reason. It made the world a more unpredictable place for America, and thus more dangerous. She wasn't in the State Department anymore, but she still yearned to make the world more orderly, with decisions guided by rational analysis and weighing of pros and cons.

It was hard to get a roomful of egos to understand the same problem, much less to agree on a solution. She wished she had the knack some charismatic leaders had of just convincing everyone to submit to a course of action without understanding.

"Sometimes I think you just want people to agree with you," Jianwen had said to her once, after a particularly heated argument.

"What's wrong with that?" she had asked. "It's not my fault that I've thought about the issues more than they have. I see the bigger picture."

"You don't really want to be the most reasonable," Jianwen had said. "You want to be the most *right*. You want to be an oracle."

She had been insulted. Jianwen could be so stubborn.

Wait a minute. Sophia seized on the thought of *oracle. Maybe that's it. That's how we can make Empathium work for us.*

"The Byzantine Generals problem is a metaphor," Sophia said. She tried to keep the newfound excitement out of her voice. She was glad that her wonkish need to understand the details—as well as the desire to one-up the tech CEO, if she was honest—had compelled her to read up on this topic. "Imagine a group of generals, each leading a division of the Byzantine army, are laying siege to a city. If all the generals can coordinate to attack the city, then the city will fall. And if all the generals can agree on a retreat, everyone will be safe. But if only some of the generals attack while others retreat, the result will be disaster."

"They have to reach consensus on what to do," said the judge.

"Yes. The generals communicate through messengers. But the problem is that the messengers they send to each other aren't instantaneous, and there may be traitorous generals who will send out false messages about the emerging consensus as it's being negotiated, thereby sowing confusion and corrupting the result."

"This emerging consensus, as you call it, is like the ledger, isn't it?" asked the judge. "It's the record of every general's vote."

"Exactly! So, simplifying somewhat, blockchain solves this problem by using cryptography—very difficult-to-solve number theory puzzles—on the chain of messages that represents the emerging consensus. With cryptography, it's easy for each general to verify that a message chain that represents the state of the vote hasn't been tampered with, but it takes work for them to cryptographically add a new vote to the chain of votes. In order to deceive the other generals, a traitorous general would have to not only forge their own vote, but also the cryptographic summary of every other vote that came before theirs in the growing chain. As the chain gets longer, this becomes increasingly hard to do."

"I'm not sure I entirely follow," muttered the judge.

"The key is, the blockchain uses the difficulty of cryptographically adding a block of transactions to the chain—that's called proof-of-work—to guarantee that as long as a majority of the computers in the network aren't traitorous, you'll have a distributed ledger that you can trust more than any central authority."

"And that's . . . trusting the math?"

"Yes. A distributed, incorruptible ledger not only makes it possible to have a cryptocurrency, it's also a way to have a secure voting framework that isn't centrally administered and a way to ensure that smart contracts can't be altered."

"This is all very interesting, but what does all this have to do with Empathium or Refugees Without Borders?" asked the husband of the MP impatiently.

•

Jianwen had put a lot of effort into making the Empathium interface usable. This was not something that many in the blockchain community cared about. Indeed, many blockchain applications seemed to be purposefully built to be difficult to use, as if the requirement for detailed technical know-how was how you separated the truly free from the mere sheeple.

Jianwen despised elitism in all its forms—she was keenly aware of the irony of this, coming from an Ivy-educated financial services technologist with a roomful of top-end VR gear like her. It was one group of elites who decided that democracy wasn't "right" for her country, and another group of elites who decided that they knew best who deserved sympathy and who didn't. The elites distrusted *feelings*, distrusted what made people human.

The very point of Empathium was to help people who couldn't care less about the intricacies of the Byzantine Generals problem or the implications of block size on the security of the blockchain. It had to be usable by a child. She remembered the frustration and despair of the people in Sichuan who had just wanted simple tools to help themselves. Empathium had to be as easy to use as possible, both for those who wanted to give and those who needed the help.

She was creating the application for those sick and tired of being told what to care about and how to care about it, not those doing the telling.

"What makes you think you know the right answer to every-thing?" Jianwen had asked Sophia once, back when they talked about everything and anything, and arguments between them were dispassionate affairs, conducted for intellectual pleasure. "Don't you ever doubt that you might be wrong?"

"If someone points out a flaw in my thinking, yes," said Sophia. "I'm always open to persuasion."

"But you never *feel* you might be wrong?"

"Letting feelings dictate how to think is the reason so many never get to the right answers at all."

The work she was doing was, rationally, hopeless. She had used up all her sick days and vacation days to write Empathium. She had published a paper explaining its technical underpinnings in excruciating detail. She had recruited others to audit her code. But how could she really expect to change the established world of big NGOs and for-eign policy think tanks through an obscure cryptocurrency network that wasn't worth anything?

The work felt right. And that was worth more than any argument she could come up with against it.

.

"But I still don't understand how these 'conditions for performance' are satisfied!" the judge said. "I don't get how Empathium decides that an application for aid is worth funding and allocates money to it. Those who provide the funds can't possibly go through thousands of applications personally and decide which ones to give money to."

"There's an aspect of smart contracts that I haven't explained yet," Sophia said. "For smart contracts to function, there needs to be a way to import reality into software. Sometimes, whether conditions for performance have been satisfied isn't as simple as whether it rained on a certain day—though perhaps even that is open to debate in edge cases—but requires complicated human judgment: whether a contractor has installed the plumbing satisfactorily, whether the promised view is indeed scenic, or whether someone deserves to be helped."

"You mean it requires consensus."

"Exactly. So Empathium solves this problem by issuing a certain number of electronic tokens, called Emps, to some members of the network. Emp-holders then have the job of evaluating projects seeking funding and voting yes or no during a set time window. Only projects that receive the requisite number of yes-votes—the number of votes you can cast is determined by your Emp balance—get funded from the pool of available donors, and the required threshold of yes-votes scales up with the amount of funding requested. To prevent strategic voting, the vote tally is revealed only after the end of the evaluation period."

"But how do the Emp-holders decide to cast their vote?"

"That's up to each Emp-holder. They can evaluate just the materials put up by the requesters: their narratives, photos, videos, documentation, whatever. Or they can go on-site to investigate the applicants. They can use whatever means they have at their disposal within the designated evaluation period."

"Great, so money meant for the desperate and the needy will be allocated by a bunch of people who could barely be persuaded to answer a customer service survey between video game sessions," scoffed the husband of the MP.

"This is where it gets clever. Emp-holders are incentivized by receiving a small amount of money from the network in proportion to their Emp accounts. After each project's evaluation period is over, those who voted for the 'losing' side will be punished by having a portion of their Emps re-allocated to those on the 'winning' side. Individual Emp balances are like a kind of reputation token, and over time, those whose judgments—or empathy-meters, hence the network's name—are best tuned to the consensus judgment get the most Emps. They become the infallible oracles around which the system functions."

"What's to prevent—"

"It's not a perfect system," said Sophia. "Even the designers of the system—we don't really know who they are—acknowledge that. But like many things on the web, it works even if it doesn't seem like it should. Nobody thought Wikipedia would work either when it started. In its two months of existence, Empathium has proven to be remarkably effective and resilient to attacks, and it's certainly attracting a lot of young donors disillusioned with traditional charitable giving."

The board took some time to digest this news.

"Sounds like we'll have a hard time competing," said the husband of the MP after a while.

Sophia took a deep breath. *This is it, the moment I begin to build consensus.* "Empathium is popular, but it hasn't been able to attract nearly as much funding as the established charities, largely because donations to Empathium are not, of course, tax-deductible. Some of the biggest projects on the network, especially those related to refugees, have not been funded. If the goal is to get Refugees Without Borders into the conversation, we should put in a big funding offer."

"But I thought we wouldn't be able to choose which of the refugee projects on the network the money will go to," said the husband of the MP. "It's going to be up to the Emp-holders."

"I have a confession to make. I've been using Empathium myself, and I have some Emps. We can make my account the corporate account, and begin to evaluate these projects. It's possible to filter out some of the fraudulent requests by documentation alone, but to really know if someone deserves help, there's no replacement for good old-fashioned on-site investigation. With our field expertise and international staff, I'm sure we'll be able to decide what projects to fund with more accuracy than anyone else, and we'll gain Emps quickly."

"But why do that when we can just put the money into the projects we want directly? Why add the intermediary of Empathium?" asked the tech CEO.

"It's about leverage. Once we get enough Emps, we'll turn Refugees Without Borders into the ultimate oracle for global empathy, the arbiter of who's deserving," said Sophia. She took a deep breath and delivered the coup de grâce. "The example set by Refugees Without Borders will be followed by other big charities. Add to that all the funding from places like China and India, where donors interested in philanthropy have few trusted in-country charities but may be willing to jump onto a decentralized blockchain application, and soon Empathium may become the single largest charity-funding platform in the world. If we accumulate the largest share of Emps, we will then be effectively in the position to direct the use of most of the world's charitable giving."

The board members sat in their seats, stunned. Even the telepresence robot's hands stopped moving.

"Damn . . . you're going to flip a platform designed to disintermediate us into a ladder to crown us," said the tech CEO, real admiration in her voice. "That's *some* jujitsu."

Sophia gave her a quick smile before turning back to the table. "Now, do I have your approval?"

•

The red line representing the total amount of pledged funds to Empathium had shot straight into the stratosphere.

Jianwen smiled in front of her screen. Her baby had grown up.

The decision by Refugees Without Borders to join the network had been followed within twenty-four hours by several other major international charities. Empathium was now legitimate in the eyes of the public, and it was even possible for wealthy donors who cared about tax deductions to funnel their funds through traditional charities participating in the network.

Projects that received the attention of Empathium users would no doubt attract a great deal of media interest, drawing in reporters and observers. Empathium was going to direct not just charitable giving, but the gaze of the world.

The #empathium invite-only channel was filling up with debate.

NoFFIA>: This is a ruse by the big charities. They're going to play the Emp-accumulation game and force the network into funding their pet projects.

N♥T>: What makes you think they can? The oracle system only rewards results. If you don't think traditional charities know what they're doing, they won't have any better way of identifying deserving good projects. The network will force them to fund projects the Emp-holders as a whole think are deserving.

Anony🍂>: Traditional charities have access to publicity channels most don't. The other Emp-holders are still people. They'll be swayed.

N♥T >: Not everyone is as affected by traditional media as you think, especially when you leave the bubble you USians live in. I think this is a level playing field.

Jianwen watched the debate but didn't participate. As the creator of Empathium, she understood that the invisible reputation attached to her username meant that anything she said could disproportionately influence and distort debate. That was the way humans worked, even when they were talking through scrolling text attributed to pseudonymous electronic identities.

But she wasn't interested in debate. She was interested in action. The participation of the traditional charities on Empathium had been what she had hoped and planned for all along, and now was the time for her to implement the second step.

She brought up a terminal window and began a new submission to the Empathium network. The Muertien VR file itself was too large to be directly incorporated into a block, so it would have to be distributed via peer-to-peer sharing. But the signature that authenticated the file and prevented tampering would become part of the blockchain and be distributed to all the users of Empathium and all the Emp-holders.

Maybe even hard-nosed Sophia.

The fact that the submitter of the file was Jianwen (or more precisely, the userid of Empathium's creator, which no one knew was Jianwen in real life) would give it a burst of initial interest, but everything after that was out of her hands.

She did not believe in conspiracies. She was counting on the angels of human nature.

She pressed SEND, sat back, and waited.

•

As the Jeep wound its way through the jungle over the muddy, mountainous road near the China-Myanmar border, Sophia dozed.

How did we get here?

The madness of the world was both so unpredictable and so inevitable.

As she had predicted, the field expertise of Refugees Without Borders quickly made the corporate Empathium account one of the most powerful Emp-holders on the network. Her judgment was deemed infallible, guiding the network to disburse funds to needy groups and proposed projects that made sense. The board was very pleased with her work.

But then, that damned VR and others like it began to show up on the network.

The VR experiences spoke to the interactors in a way that words and photos and videos could not. Walking for miles barefoot through a war-torn city, seeing dismembered babies and mothers scattered around you, being interrogated and menaced by men and boys with machetes and guns . . . the VR experiences left the interactors shaken and overwhelmed. Some had been hospitalized.

Traditional media, bound by old-fashioned ideas about decency and propriety, could not show images like these and refused to engage in what they viewed as pure emotional manipulation.

Where's the context? Who's the source? demanded the spurned pundits. *Real journalism requires reflection, requires thought.*

We don't remember much reflection from you when you advocated war based on pictures you printed, replied the hive mind of Emp-holders. *Are you just annoyed that you aren't in charge of our emotions anymore?*

The pervasive use of encryption on Empathium meant that most censorship techniques were useless, so the Emp-holders were exposed to stories they had heretofore been sheltered from. They voted for the attached projects, their hearts pounding, their breathing ragged, their eyes blurred by rage and sorrow.

Activists and propagandists soon realized that the best way to get their causes funded was to participate in the VR arms race. And so governments and rebels competed in creating compelling VR experiences that forced the interactors into their perspective, obliged them to empathize with their side.

Mass graves filled with refugees starved to death in Yemen. Young women marching to support Russia gunned down by Ukrainian soldiers. Ethnic-minority children running naked through streets as their homes were set on fire by Myanmar government soldiers . . .

Funding began to flow to groups that the news had forgotten or portrayed as the side undeserving of sympathy. In VR, one minute of their anguish spoke louder than ten thousand words in op-eds in respected newspapers.

This is the commodification of pain! Ivy-educated bloggers wrote in earnest think pieces. *Isn't this yet another way for the privileged to exploit the suffering of the oppressed to make themselves feel better?*

Just as a photograph can be framed and edited to lie, so can VR, the media- and cultural-studies commentariat wrote. *VR is such a heavily engineered medium that we have not yet reached consensus on what the meaning of "reality" in this medium is.*

This is a threat to our national security, fretted the senators who demanded that Empathium be shut down. *They could be diverting funding to groups hostile to our national interest.*

You're simply terrified that you're being disintermediated from your positions of undeserved authority, jeered the Empathium users, hidden behind anonymous, encrypted accounts. *This is a real democracy of empathy. Deal with it.*

A consensus of feelings had replaced the consensus of facts. The emotional labor of vicarious experience through virtual reality had replaced the physical and mental work of investigation, of evaluating costs and benefits, of exercising rational judgment. Once again, proof-of-work was used to guarantee authenticity, just a different kind of work.

Maybe the reporters and senators and diplomats and I could make our own VR experiences, Sophia wondered as she was jostled awake in the back of the Jeep. *Too bad it's hard to make the unglamorous but necessary work of truly understanding a complex situation compelling....*

She looked outside the window. They were passing through a refugee camp in Muertien. Men, women, and children, most of them Chinese in physical appearance, looked back at the passengers in the Jeep numbly. Their expressions were familiar to Sophia; she had seen the same despondency on the faces of refugees everywhere in the world.

The successful funding of the Muertien project had been a massive blow to Sophia and Refugees Without Borders. She had voted against it, but the other Emp-holders had overwhelmed her, and overnight Sophia had lost 10 percent of her Emps. Other VR-propelled projects followed to achieve funding despite her objection, eroding Sophia's Emp account even further.

Faced with an outraged board, she had come here to find some way to discredit the Muertien project, to show that she had been right.

On the way here from Yangon, she had spoken to the one staffer Refugees Without Borders posted there and several Western reporters stationed in the country. They had confirmed the consensus back in DC. She knew that the refugee situation was one largely created by the rebels. The population of Muertien, mostly ethnic Han Chinese, did not get along well with the majority Bamar in the central government. The rebels had attacked the government forces and then tried to fade into the civilian population. The government had little choice but to resort to violence, lest the country's young democracy suffer a setback and Chinese influence extend into the heart of Southeast Asia. Regretful incidents no doubt occurred, but the vast majority of the fault lay on the side of the rebels. Funding them would only escalate the conflict.

But this kind of punditry, of explaining geopolitics, was anathema to the Emp-holders. They did not want lectures; they were persuaded by the immediacy of suffering.

The Jeep stopped. Sophia got out with her interpreter. She adjusted the neckband she wore—it was a prototype the tech CEO had gotten for her from Canon Virtual. The air was humid, hot, drenched with the smell of sewage and decay. She should have been expecting that, she supposed, but somehow she hadn't thought about how things would smell here back in her DC office.

She was about to approach a leery-looking young woman in a flower-print blouse when a man shouted angrily. She turned to look at him. He was pointing at her and screaming. The crowd around him stopped moving to stare at her. The air felt tense.

There was a gun in his other hand.

Part of the goal of the Muertien project had been to fund groups willing to smuggle weapons across the Chinese border into the hands of the refugees. Sophia knew that. *I'm going to regret coming here without an armed escort, aren't I?*

The rumbling of vehicles approaching in the jungle. A loud whine overhead followed by an explosion. Staccato gunshots so near that they had to be coming from inside the camp.

Sophia was shoved to the ground as the crowd around her exploded into chaos, screaming and dashing every which way. She wrapped her arms protectively around her neck, around the cameras and microphones, but panicked feet stomped over her torso, making her gasp and loosening her arms. The camera-studded neckband fell and rolled away in the dirt, and she reached for it, careless of her own safety. Just before her grasping fingers reached the band, a booted foot crushed it with a sickening crunch. She cursed, and someone running by kicked her in the head.

She faded into unconsciousness.

•

A splitting headache. Overhead the sky is close at hand and orange, cloudless.

The surface under me feels hard and sandy.

I'm inside a VR experience, aren't I? Am I Gulliver, looking up at the Lilliputian sky?

The sky turns and sways, and even though I'm lying down, I feel like I'm falling.

I want to throw up.

"Close your eyes until the vertigo passes," a voice says. The timbre and cadence are familiar, but I can't quite place who it is. I just know I haven't heard it in a while. I wait until the dizziness fades. Only then do I notice the unyielding lump of the data recorder poking into my back, where it's held in place by tape. Relief floods through me. The cameras may be gone, but the most important piece of equipment has survived the ordeal.

"Here, drink," the voice says.

I open my eyes. I struggle to sit up and a hand reaches out to support me between my shoulder blades. It's a small, strong hand, the hand of a woman. A canteen materializes before my face in the dim light, a chiaroscuro. I sip. I haven't realized how thirsty I am.

I look up at the face behind the canteen: Jianwen.

"What are you doing here?" I ask. Everything still seems so unreal, but I'm beginning to realize that I'm inside a tent, probably one of the tents I saw earlier in the camp.

"The same thing brought both of us here," says Jianwen. After all these years, she hasn't changed much: still that hard, no-nonsense demeanor, still that short-cropped hair, still that set to her jaw, challenging everything and everyone.

She just looks leaner, drier, as if the years have wrung more gentleness out of her.

"Empathium. I made it, and you want to break it."

Of course, I should have known. Jianwen always disliked institutions, thought it best to disrupt everything.

It's still nice to see her.

Our first year in college, I wrote a story for the school paper about a sexual assault at a final club party. The victim wasn't a student, and her account was later discredited. Everyone condemned my work, calling me careless, declaring that I had allowed the desire for a good story get in the way of facts and analysis. Only I knew that I hadn't been wrong: the victim had only recanted under pressure, but I had no proof. Jianwen was the only one who stuck by me, defending me at every opportunity.

"Why do you trust me?" I asked.

"It's not something I can explain," she said. "It's a *feeling*. I heard the pain in her voice . . . and I know you did too."

That was how we became close. She was someone I could count on in a fight.

"What happened out there?" I ask.

"That depends on who you talk to. This won't show up in the news in China at all. If it shows up in the US, it will be another minor skirmish between the government and the rebels, whose guerrilla fighters disguised themselves as refugees, forcing the government to retaliate."

This has always been her way. Jianwen sees the corruption of the truth everywhere, but she won't tell you what she thinks the truth is. I suppose she got into the habit from her time in America to avoid arguments.

"And what will Empathium users think?" I ask.

"They'll see more children being blown up by bombs and women being gunned down by soldiers as they ran."

"Did the rebels or the government fire the first shot?"

"Why does that matter? The consensus in the West will always be that the rebels fired the first shot—as if that determines everything. You've already decided on the story, and everything else is just support."

"I get it," I say. "I understand what you're trying to do. You think there's not enough attention being paid to the refugees in Muertien, and so you're using Empathium to publicize their plight. You're emotionally attached to these people because they look like you—"

"Is that really what you think? You think I'm doing this because they're ethnically Han Chinese?" She looks at me, disappointed.

She can look at me however she likes, but the intensity of her emotion gives her away. In college I remember her working hard to raise money for the earthquake in China, when we were both still trying to pick concentrations; I remember her holding a candlelight vigil for both the Uighurs and the Han who had died in Ürümqi the next summer, when we stayed on campus together to edit the student course-evaluation guide; I remember how once in class she had refused to back down as a white man twice her size loomed over her, demanding that she accept that China was wrong to fight the Korean War.

"Hit me if you want," she had said, her voice steady. "I'm not going to desecrate the memory of the men and women who died so that I could be born. MacArthur was going to drop atomic bombs on Beijing. Is that really the kind of empire you want to defend?"

Some of our friends in college thought of Jianwen as a Chinese nationalist, but that's not quite right. She dislikes all empires because to her, they are the ultimate institutions, with deadly concentration of power. She doesn't think the American empire is any more worthy of support than the Russian one or the Chinese one. As she put it, "America is only a democracy for those lucky enough to be Americans. To everybody else, it's just a dictator with the biggest bombs and missiles."

She wants the perfection of disintermediated chaos rather than the imperfect stability of flawed institutions that could be perfected.

"You are letting your passion overcome reason," I say. I know that persuasion is useless, but I can't help trying. If I don't hold on to faith in reason, I have nothing. "A powerful China with influence in Myanmar is bad for world peace. American pre-eminence must—"

"And so you think it's all right for the people of Muertien to be ethnically cleansed to preserve the stability of the regime in Naypyidaw, to uphold the Pax Americana, to cement the ramparts of an American empire with their blood."

I wince. She's always been careless with her words. "Don't exaggerate. The ethnic conflict here, if not contained, will lead to more Chinese adventurism and influence. I've talked to many in Yangon. They don't want the Chinese here."

"And you think they want the Americans here, telling them what to do?" Contempt flares in her voice.

"A choice between the lesser of two evils," I concede. "But more Chinese involvement will provoke more American anxiety, and that will only intensify the geopolitical conflict you dislike so much."

"People here need Chinese money for their dams. Without development, they can't solve any of the problems they have—"

"Maybe the developers want that," I say, "but the common people don't."

"Who are these *common people* in your imagination?" she asks. "I've talked to many here in Muertien. They say that the Bamars don't want the dams built where they are, but they'll be happy to have them built here. That's what the rebels are fighting for, to preserve their autonomy and the right to control their land. Isn't self-determination something you value and care about? How does letting soldiers kill children lead to a better world?"

We can go on like this forever. She can't see the truth because she's in too much pain.

"You've been blinded by the pain of these people," I say. "And now you want the rest of the world to suffer the same fate. Through Empathium, you've bypassed the traditional filters of institutional media and charities to reach individuals. But the experience of having children and mothers die right next to them is too overwhelming for most to think through the complicated implications of the events that led to these tragedies. The VR experiences are propaganda."

"You know as well as I do that the Muertien VR isn't fake."

I know what she says is true. I've seen people die around me, and even if that VR was doctored or divorced from context, enough of it was true to make the rest not matter. The best propaganda is often true.

But there's a greater truth she doesn't see. Just because something happened doesn't make it a decisive fact; just because there's suffering doesn't mean there is always a better choice; just because people die doesn't mean we must abandon greater principles. The world isn't always black and white.

"Empathy isn't always a good thing," I say. "Irresponsible empathy makes the world unstable. In each conflict, there are multiple claims for empathy, leading to emotional involvement by outsiders that widens the conflict. To sort through the morass, you must reason your way to the least harmful answer, the right answer. This is why some of us are charged with the duty to study and understand the complexities of this world and to decide, for the rest, how to exercise empathy responsibly."

"I can't just shut it off," she says. "I can't just forget the dead. Their pain and terror . . . they're a part of the blockchain of my experience now, unerasable. If being responsible means learning how to not feel someone else's pain, then it isn't humanity you serve, but evil."

I watch her. I feel for her, I really do. It's terribly sad, seeing your friend in pain but knowing that there is nothing you can do to help, knowing that, in fact, you have to hurt her more. Sometimes pain, and acknowledgment of pain, *is* selfish.

I lift my blouse to show her the VR recorder taped to the small of my back. "This was recording until the moment guns started firing—from inside the camp—and I was pushed down to the ground."

She stares at the VR data recorder, and her face shifts through shock, recognition, rage, denial, an ironic smile, and then, nothing.

Once the VR based on what I went through is uploaded—it doesn't need much editing—there will be outrage at home. A defenseless American woman, the head of a charity dedicated to helping refugees, is brutalized by ethnic Han Chinese rebels armed with guns bought with money from Empathium—hard to imagine a better way to discredit the Muertien project. The best propaganda is often true.

"I'm sorry," I say, and I mean it.

She gazes at me, and I can't tell if it's hate or despair I see in her eyes.

•

I look at her with pity.

"Have you tried the original Muertien clip?" I ask. "The one I uploaded."

Sophia shakes her head. "I couldn't. I didn't want to compromise my judgment."

She has always been so rational. One time, in college, I asked her to watch a video of a young Russian man, barely more than a boy, being beheaded by Chechen fighters in front of the camera. She had refused.

"Why won't you look at what the people you support are doing?" I asked.

"Because I haven't seen all the acts of brutality committed by the Russians against the Chechen people," she said. "To reward those who evoke empathy is the same as punishing those who have been prevented from doing so. Looking at this won't be objective."

There's always the need for more context with Sophia, for the big picture. But I've learned over the years that rationality with her, as with many, is just a matter of rationalization. She wants a picture just big enough to justify what her government does. She needs to understand just enough to be able to reason that what America wants is also what anyone rational in the world wants.

I understand how she thinks, but she doesn't understand how I think. I understand her language, but she doesn't understand mine—or care to. That's how power works in this world.

When I first got to America, I thought it was the most wonderful place on Earth. There were students passionate about every humanitarian cause, and I tried to support every one. I raised money for the victims of the Bangladesh cyclones and the flooding in India; I packed blankets and tents and sleeping bags for the earthquake in Peru; I joined the vigils to remember the victims of 9/11, sobbing before Memorial Church in the late summer evening breeze, trying to keep the candles lit.

Then came the big earthquake in China, and as the death toll climbed toward 100,000, the campus was strangely quiet. People who I thought were my friends turned away, and the donation table we set up in front of the Science Center was staffed only by other students from China like me. We couldn't even raise a tenth of the money we had raised for disasters with far smaller death tolls.

What discussion there was focused on how the Chinese drive for development resulted in unsafe buildings, as if enumerating the cons of their government was an appropriate reaction to dead children, as if reaffirming the pros of American democracy was a good justification for withholding help.

Jokes about the Chinese and dogs were posted in anonymous newsgroups. "People just don't like China very much," an op-ed writer mused. "I'd rather have the elephants back," said an actress on TV.

What's the matter with you? I wanted to scream. There was no empathy in their eyes as I stood by the donation table and my classmates hurried past me, averting their gaze.

But Sophia did donate. She gave more than anyone else.

"Why?" I asked her. "Why do you care about the victims when no one else seems to?"

"I'm not going to have you heading back to China with an irrational impression that Americans dislike the Chinese," she said. "Try to remember me when you get into these moments of despair."

That was how I knew we would never be as close as I had hoped. She had given as a means to persuade, not because she felt what I felt.

"You accuse me of manipulation," I say to Sophia. The humid air in the tent is oppressive, and it feels as if someone is pressing on my eyes from within my skull. "But aren't you doing the exact same thing with that recording?"

"There is a difference," she says. She always has an answer. "My clip will be used to emotionally persuade people to do what is rationally the right thing as part of a considered plan. Emotion is a blunt tool that must be placed in service of reason."

"So your plan is to stop any more aid for the refugees and watch as the Myanmar government drives them off their land into China? Or worse?"

"You managed to get money to the refugees on a tide of rage and pity," she says. "But how does that really help them? Their fate will always ultimately be decided by the geopolitics between China and the US. Everything else is just noise. They can't be helped. Arming the refugees will only give the government more of an excuse to resort to violence."

Sophia isn't wrong. Not exactly. But there's a greater principle here that she doesn't see. The world doesn't always proceed the way predicted by theories of economics or international relations. If every decision is made with Sophia's calculus, then order, stability, empire, always win. There will never be any change, any independence, any justice. We are, and should be, creatures of the heart first.

"The greater manipulation is to deceive yourself into believing you can always reason your way to what is right," I say.

"Without reason, you can't get to what is right at all," Sophia says.

"Emotion has always been at the core of what it means to do right, not merely a tool for persuasion. Are you opposed to slavery because you have engaged in a rational analysis of the costs and benefits of the institution? No, it's because you're revolted by it. You empathize with the victims. You *feel* its wrongness in your heart."

"Moral reasoning isn't the same—"

"Moral reasoning is often only a method by which you tame your empathy and yoke it to serve the interests of the institutions that have corrupted you. You're clearly not averse to manipulation when it's advantageous to a cause that finds favor in your framework."

"Calling me a hypocrite isn't very helpful—"

"But you *are* a hypocrite. You didn't protest when pictures of babies launched Tomahawks or when images of drowned little boys on beaches led to revisions in refugee policy. You promoted the work of reporters who evoked empathy for those stranded in Kenya's largest refugee camp by telling Westerners sappy Romeo-and-Juliet love stories about young refugees and emphasizing how the United Nations has educated them with Western ideals—"

"Those are different—"

"Of course they're different. Empathy for you is but another weapon to be wielded, instead of a fundamental value of being human. You reward some with your empathy and punish others by withholding it. Reasons can always be found."

"How are you different? Why do the suffering of some affect you more than others? Why do you care about the people of Muertien more than any other? Isn't it because they look like you?"

She still thinks this is a killer argument. I understand her, I really do. It's so comforting to know that you're right, that you've triumphed over emotion with reason, that you're an agent of the just empire, immune to the betrayal of empathy.

I just can't live like that.

I try one last time.

"I had hoped that by stripping away context and background, by exposing the senses to the rawness of pain and suffering, virtual reality would be able to prevent all of us from rationalizing away our empathy. In agony, there is no race, no creed, none of the walls that divide us and subdivide us. When you're immersed in the experience of the victims, all of us are in Muertien, in Yemen, in the heart of darkness that the Great Powers feed on."

She doesn't respond. I see in her eyes she has given up on me. I am beyond reason.

Through Empathium, I had hoped to create a consensus of empathy, an incorruptible ledger of the heart that has overcome traitorous rationalization.

But perhaps I am still too naive. Perhaps I give empathy too much credit.

·

Anon >: What do you all think is going to happen?

N♥T >: China is going to have to invade. Those VRs have left Beijing no choice. If they don't send in the troops to protect the rebels in Muertien, there will be riots in the streets.

goldfarmer89>: Makes you wonder if that was what China wanted all along.

Anon >: You think that first VR was a Chinese production?

goldfarmer89>: Had to be state-sponsored. It was so slick.

N♥T>: I'm not so sure it was the Chinese who made it. The White House has been itching for an excuse for war with China to divert attention from all those scandals.

Anon >: So you think the VR was a CIA plant?

N♥T>: Wouldn't be the first time Americans have manipulated anti-American sentiment into giving them exactly what they wanted. That Ellis VR is also ramping up US public support for taking a hard line against China. I just feel terrible about those people in Muertien. What a mess.

little_blocks>: Still stuck on those snuff VRs on Empathium? I've stopped long ago. Too exhausting. I'll PM you a new game you'll definitely like.

N♥T>: I can always use a new game. ^_^

•

Author's Note: I'm indebted to the following paper for the term "algics" and some of the ideas about the potential of VR as a social technology:

Lemley, Mark A. and Volokh, Eugene, Law. Virtual Reality, and Augmented Reality (March 15, 2017). Stanford Public Law Working Paper No. 2933867; UCLA School of Law, Public Law Research Paper No. 17-13, Available at https://ssrn.com/abstract=2933867 or http://dx.doi.org/10.2139/ssrn.2933867.

The Gods Will
Not Be Chained

Maddie hated the moment when she came home from school and woke her computer.

There was a time when she had loved the bulky old laptop whose keys had been worn down over the years until what was left of the lettering appeared like glyphs, a hand-me-down from her father that she had kept going with careful upgrades: it kept her in touch with faraway friends, allowed her to see that the world was much bigger and wider than the narrow confines of her daily life. Her father had taught her how to speak to the trusty machine in strings of symbols that made it do things, obey her will. She had felt like the smartest girl in the world when he had told her how proud he was of her facility with computer languages; together, they had shared a satisfaction in mastering the machine. She had once thought she'd grow up to be a computer engineer, just like . . .

She pushed the thought of her father out of her mind. Still too painful.

The icons for the email and chat apps bounced, telling her she had new messages. The prospect terrified her.

She took a deep breath and clicked on the email app. Quickly, she scanned through the message headers: one was from her grandmother, two were from online stores, informing her of sales. There was also a news digest, something her father had helped her set up to track topics of interest to both of them. She had not had the heart to delete it after he died.

Today's headlines:

* Market Anomaly Deemed Result of High-Speed Trading Algorithms
* Pentagon Suggests Unmanned Drones Will Outduel Human Pilots
* Singularity Institute Announces Timeline for Achieving Immortality

    * Researchers Fear Mysterious Computer Virus Able to Jump From Speakers to Microphones

    ...

Slowly, she let out her breath. Nothing from . . . *them*.

She opened the email from Grandma. Some pictures from her garden: a hummingbird drinking from a bird feeder; the first tomatoes, green and tiny on the vine like beads made of jade; Basil at the end of the driveway, his tail a wagging blur, gazing longingly at some car in the street.

That's my day so far. Hope you're having a good one at the new school, too.

Maddie smiled, and then her eyes grew warm and wet. She wiped them quickly and started to compose a reply:

I miss you.

She wished she were back in that house on the edge of a small town in Pennsylvania. The school there had been tiny and the academic work had perhaps been too easy for her, but she had always felt safe. Who knew that eighth grade could be so hard?

I'm having problems with some girls at school.

It had started on Maddie's first day at the new school. The beautiful, implacable Suzie had seemingly turned the whole school against her. Maddie had tried to make peace with her, to find out what she had done that so displeased the schoolyard queen, but her efforts had only seemed to make things worse. The way she dressed, the way she spoke, the way she smiled too much or didn't smile enough—everything was fodder for mockery and ridicule. She now suspected that, like all despots, Suzie's hatred for her did not need a rational explanation—it was enough that persecuting Maddie brought her pleasure and that others would try to curry her favor by adding to Maddie's misery. Maddie spent her hours at school in paranoia, uncertain if a smile or any other friendly gesture was but a trap to get her to let down her guard so that she could be cut deeper.

I wish we were with you.

But Mom had found this job, this good-paying job, and how could she not take it? It had been two years since Dad died. She and Maddie couldn't go on living at Grandma's place forever.

Maddie deleted what she had written. It would only make Grandma worry, and then she'd call Mom, and Mom would want to talk to the teachers, which would make things so much worse that she couldn't even imagine. Why spread sadness around when others couldn't help?

School is all right. I'm really happy here.

The lie made her feel stronger. Wasn't lying to protect others the surest sign you were growing up?

She sent the email, and saw that a new message had arrived in her inbox. It was from "truth_teller02," and the subject was "Too scared?"

Her heart began to pound. She didn't want to click on it. But if she deleted it without reading, did that mean they were right? That she was weak? Did it mean that they'd won?

She clicked on the message.

Why are you so ugly? I bet you wish you could kill yourself. You really should.

Attached to the message was an image: a picture of Maddie taken with a cell phone. She was running through the halls between classes. Her eyes were wide and intense, and she was biting her bottom lip. She remembered how she had felt: lonely, her stomach tied up in a knot.

The picture had been photoshopped so that she had the nose and ears of a pig.

Her face felt like it was on fire. She willed the tears to subside. She was self-conscious about her weight, and they had seen right through her. It was amazing how effective such a cheap trick could be.

She didn't know which one of the girls had sent this. She imagined Suzie's cruel, contemptuous smile as she viewed this latest offering from one of her minions. *A good portrait of Piggy.*

She had stopped using social networking sites because of the constant stream of mockery—when she deleted any of their comments, it only made them redouble their efforts. If she tried to block anyone, she thought it might also make them think they got to her, might appear as an admission of weakness. She had no choice but to endure.

Sticks and stones. But the digital world, the world of bits and electrons, of words and images—it had brought her so much joy, felt so intimate that she thought of it a part of herself. And it hurt.

She crawled into bed and cried until she fell asleep.

•

✉🐻?

Maddie stared at the screen, confused.

A new chat window had popped up. It wasn't from any account she recognized—in fact, there was no chat ID at all. She could not recall ever seeing such a thing.

What did they want? To tease her more about the email? If she didn't say anything, would that also be a concession of weakness? She typed on the keyboard, reluctantly pecking out each letter.

Yeah, I saw. What do you want?

😕😶

Maddie frowned. *You're confused? Can't talk? All right, I'll play along.*

The mysterious chatter's choice of emoji instead of other emoticons made her more inclined to continue this odd conversation. She felt a special emotional bond to the silly little glyphs. She and her father had once played a version of Pictionary over their phones, except they used emoji instead of drawing pictures.

She picked out the icons from a palette:

✉👀

The mystery chatter—she decided to call whoever it was Emo—responded:

👺

Maddie stared at the face of the goblin, still uncertain. Another emoji appeared on the screen:

She laughed. Okay, so at least Emo was friendly.

Yes, the email made her feel shitty:

The response:

Easier said than done, she thought. *I wish I could be unmoved and let the words bounce off me, like dying embers striking harmlessly against stone.* She brought up the palette again:

The response:

She pondered what that meant. *An umbrella in the rain. Protection? Emo, what are you offering?* She typed:

Emo's response:

She was suspicious. *Who are you?*

The answer came after a few seconds:

•

The next day at school, Suzie appeared skittish and distracted. Every time her phone vibrated, she took it out and gingerly poked at the screen. Her face seemed flushed, her expression hovering between fear and anger.

Maddie was very familiar with that look.

"What's wrong with you?" asked Erin, one of Suzie's best friends.

Suzie shot her a hard, suspicious look, and turned away without saying anything.

By fourth period, most of the girls who had been giving Maddie a hard time shared that haunted, *everybodyhatesmenobodylikesme* look.

Accusations and counteraccusations flew back and forth; cliques gathered between classes to whisper and broke apart, screaming. Some of the girls came out of the bathroom with red eyes.

All day, they left Maddie alone.

•

Maddie laughed. The two dancing girls did look a bit like Suzie and Erin. Backstabbing. Finger pointing.

Maddie nodded in understanding. If Emo could pop up on her screen uninvited, of course Emo could also track down who had sent her those emails and messages and serve her tormenters a taste of their own medicine. All that Emo had done was redirect a few messages meant for Maddie at the other girls, and their own paranoia and insecurities had done the rest. The fragile web that bound them together was easily tangled.

She was grateful and happy:

The response:

But why are you helping me? She still had no answer to the question. So she typed:

The response:

She didn't understand.

?

There was a pause, and then:

A little girl, and then a woman. "You know my mother?" Her shock was so complete that she spoke aloud.

"What's going on?" The voice behind her was cheerful, warm. "Who knows me?"

Maddie turned in her chair. Her mother was standing in the door to her bedroom.

"You're home early," Maddie said, intending it as a question.

"Something went wrong with the office computers. Nobody could get any work done, so I decided to come home." Mom walked in and sat down on Maddie's bed. "Who are you talking to?"

"Nobody. Just chatting."

"With?"

"I don't know . . . just someone who's been . . . helping me."

She should have known that this was the kind of answer that would set off alarm bells in her mother's head. Before Maddie could even protest, her mother shooed her out of her chair and sat down in front of the keyboard.

Who are you and what the hell do you want with my daughter?

The long wait for a response seemed to confirm her mother's worst fears.

"Mom, you're being ridiculous. I swear there's nothing weird going on."

"Nothing weird?" Mom pointed at the screen. "Then why are you typing only in pictographs?—"

"—it's called emoji. We're playing a game—"

"—you have no idea how dangerous—"

👰

They stopped shouting. Mom stared at the screen intently. Then she typed:

What?

"They won't answer unless you use emoji," said Maddie.

Her face stony, Mom used the mouse to pick out an icon:

‼️❓

An even longer pause, then a line of emoji appeared across the screen:

"What the hell—" Mom muttered. Then she swore as her face flicked from shock to sorrow to disbelief to rage. Maddie could count on one hand the number of times her mother had sworn in front of her. Something was really wrong.

Looking over her mother's shoulder, she tried to help her translate. "What are lips? . . . a man's lips . . ."

But her mother surprised her: "No, it's '*What lips my lips have kissed and where, and why . . .*'"

Her hand shaking, Mom picked out an icon:

♟♟♟

The window winked away and there was nothing left on the screen. Mom sat there, unmoving.

"What's wrong?" Maddie said, nudging her mother's shoulder gingerly.

"I don't know," Mom said, perhaps more to herself than Maddie. "It's impossible. Impossible."

•

Maddie tiptoed up to the bedroom door. Her mother had slammed it shut an hour ago and refused to come out. For a while she could hear her mother sobbing behind the door, and then it grew quiet.

She placed her ear against the door.

"I'd like to speak to Dr. Peter Waxman, please," said her mother's muffled voice. A pause. "Tell him it's Ellen Wynn, and it's very urgent."

Dr. Waxman was Dad's old boss at Logorhythms. Why is Mom calling him now?

"He's still alive," Mom said. "Isn't he?"

What? thought Maddie. *What is Mom talking about?*

"Don't you dare using that tone with me. He reached out to me, Peter. I know."

We saw Dad's body in the hospital. Maddie felt numb. *I watched his casket go into the ground.*

"No, you listen to me," Mom said, raising her voice. "*Listen!* I can tell you're lying. What have you done with *my husband*?"

•

They went to the police and filed a missing persons report. The detective listened to Maddie and her mom tell their story. Maddie watched his face shift through a series of expressions: interest, incredulity, amusement, boredom.

"I know this sounds crazy," her mother said.

The detective said nothing, but his face said everything.

"I know I said I saw the body. But he's not dead. He's not!"

"Because he texted you from beyond the grave."

"No, not *text*. He reached out to Madison and me through chat."

The detective sighed. "Don't you think it's more likely that this is another prank being played on you by the kids who are messing with your daughter?"

"*No*," said Maddie. She wanted to grab the man by the ears and shake him. "He used *emoji*. It was a joke that Dad and I worked out between ourselves."

"It was a poem," said Mom. She took out a book of poetry, flipped to a page, and held it in front of the detective's face. "The opening line of this sonnet by Edna St. Vincent Millay. It's my favorite poem. I used to read it to David when we were still in high school."

The detective put his elbows on the table and rubbed his temples with his fingers. "We're very busy here, Ms. Wynn. I understand how painful the loss of your husband must have been and how stressful it is to find your daughter being bullied. This should be addressed by the teachers. Let me recommend some professionals—"

"I. Am. Not. Crazy." Mom gritted her teeth. "You can come to our place and examine my daughter's computer. You can trace the network connections and find out where he is. Please. I don't know how this is possible, but he must be alive and . . . he must be in trouble. That's why he can't speak except through emoticons."

"I agree that this is a cruel joke, but you have to see how you're making it worse by falling for it."

When they came home, Mom crawled right into bed. Maddie sat on the edge of the bed and held her mother's hand for a while, the way her mother used to do with her when she was little and had trouble going to sleep by herself.

Eventually, Mom fell asleep, her face damp.

•

The web was vast and strange, and there were corners of it where people who believed in the most extraordinary stories congregated: government cover-ups of alien encounters, mega-corporations that tried to enslave people, the Illuminati, and the many ways the world was going to suffer an apocalypse.

Maddie signed on to one of these sites and posted her story. She tried to lay out the facts without embellishment. She recovered the transcripts of her emoji chats; she reconstructed the odd-looking window from the swapfile on her hard drive; she tried to trace the network connection from "Emo" as far as she could—in other words, she provided more hard data to support her story than most of the other posters in the forum had. She wrote that Logorhythms had denied everything, and that the police, representatives of the government, hadn't believed her.

For some, no evidence shored up her claim more compellingly than such denials.

And then the forum regulars began to make their own connections. Every poster thought Maddie's story supported their own pet theory: Centillion, the search engine giant, was engaging in censorship; Logorhythms was creating military artificial intelligences for the UN; the NSA scanned people's hard drives. The thread she started exploded with follow-ups amplifying her tale.

Maddie knew, of course, that no matter how big the thread grew, most people would never see it. The big search engines had long ago tweaked their algorithms to bury results from these sites, because they were deemed untrustworthy.

But convincing people wasn't Maddie's goal.

"Emo"—her father—had claimed to be a ghost in the machine. Surely he wasn't the only one?

•

There was no name, no avatar. Just a plain chat window, like a part of the OS.

👤❓
✖

She was disappointed. Not her father. Still, it was better than nothing.

🆔❓

Maddie smiled as she parsed the response. *<We're from the cloud. Everywhere in the world.>* She typed a follow-up:

👤🌍🌍🌍❓
☹

You don't know where he is either, she thought. *But maybe you can help?*

🆘❓

The response was swift and unambiguous:

🌀🏃🏔

<Hang on, we'll make a big wave and bring it crashing down.>

•

The knock came Sunday morning.

Mom opened the door to reveal Dr. Waxman standing in the hallway.

"I've come to answer your questions," he said coldly in lieu of a greeting.

Maddie wasn't really surprised. She had seen the news that Logo-rhythms's stock had crashed the previous Friday, so much so that trading had to be halted. Machine trading was being blamed again, though some thought it was the result of manipulation.

"It's been a few years," said Mom. "I thought we were friends. But after David died, you never even called."

Maddie last saw Dr. Waxman at a party at the Logorhythms office, where he had been cheerful and effusive and told her how close he and her father were and how important her father was to the company.

"I've been busy," Dr. Waxman said. He didn't look Mom in the eye.

Mom stepped aside to let him in. Maddie and her mother sat down on the couch while Dr. Waxman took the chair across from them. He set down his briefcase on the coffee table and opened it, taking out a laptop computer. He turned it on and began to type.

Maddie couldn't hold back anymore. "What are you doing?"

"Establishing an encrypted connection back to Logorhythms's secure computing center." His tone was clipped, angry, as though every word was being ripped out of him against his will.

Then he turned the screen toward them: "We've installed the linguistic processing unit—withholding it clearly didn't work, so what's the point? You can talk to him through this camera. He'll write back in text—though he seems to still prefer emoji for some ideas. I imagine a synthesized voice is the last thing you want to hear right now.

"There may be some glitches, as the simulation for the neural patterns for linguistic processing is still new and unstable."

•

"David?"

All the faces of you—the phases of you. I will never be tired of them; have enough of them all every entire. The lingering light of a September afternoon; the smell of popcorn and hot dogs. Nervous. Will you or won't you? The promise of the premise. Then I see you. And there is no more holdback suspense doubt. A softness that curls into me, fits me in all the right places. Complete. Warm. Sweet. I will yes I will yes.

"Dad!"

😃 ☀ ☀ ☀ ☀ ☀

Little fingers, delicate, ramified tendrils reaching extending stretching reaching into the dark ocean that you once drifted in; a smile the heat of a thousand suns.

I cannot conceive you. A missing presence, a wound in the mouth of the heart that the tongue of the will cannot stop probing. I have always have missed missed missed you, my darling.

"What *happened* to him?"

"He died. You were there, Ellen. You were there."

"Then *what* is this?"

"I suppose you'd call this an example of unintended consequences."

"You'd better start making some sense."

More text scrolled across the screen:

Integrating placement and routing; NP-complete; three-dimensional layout; heuristics; fit and performance; a grid, layers, the flow of electrons in a maze.

"Logorhythms supplies the world's best chips for high-volume data processing. In our work, we often face a class of problems where the potential solution space is so vast, so complicated, that it's impractical for even our fastest computers to find the best solution."

"NP-complete problems," said Maddie.

Dr. Waxman looked at her.

"Dad explained them to me."

That's my girl.

"Right. They show up in all kinds of applications: circuit layout, sequence alignment in bioinformatics, set partitioning, and so on. The thing is, while computers have trouble with them, some humans can come up with very good solutions—though not necessarily the best solution—very quickly. And David was one of them. He had a gift for circuit layout that our automated algorithms could not touch. That was why he was considered our most important resource."

"Are you talking about intuition?" her mother asked.

"Sort of. When we say 'intuition,' often what we mean are heuristics, patterns, rules-of-thumb that can't be articulated because they're not consciously understood as such. Computers are very fast and very precise; humans are fuzzy and slow. But humans have the ability to extract *insight* from data, to detect patterns that are useful. It's something that we've had trouble recreating with pure artificial intelligence."

Maddie felt a chill in the pit of her stomach.

"What does this have to do with my dad?"

Faster, faster. Everything is so slow.

Dr. Waxman avoided looking at her. "I'm getting to that. But I have to explain the background to you—"

"I think you're just dragging this out because you're ashamed of what you've done."

Dr. Waxman stopped.

My girl.

Dr. Waxman gave a light chuckle, but there was no mirth in his eyes. "She's impatient, like you."

"Then get to the point," Mom said. Dr. Waxman started at the icy intensity in her voice. Maddie reached for her mother's hand. Her mother squeezed back, hard.

Dr. Waxman took a deep breath, blew it out. "All right," he said in a resigned monotone. "David was ill; that was true. You remember that he died during surgery, the final attempt to save him that you were told had very little chance of success?"

Mom and Maddie nodded together. "You said only the clinic at Logorhythms could do it because it was so advanced," Mom said. "We had to sign those liability waivers for you to operate."

"What we didn't tell you was that the surgery wasn't intended to save David's life. His condition had deteriorated to the point that the world's best doctors couldn't have saved him. The surgery was a deep scan of his brain, meant to save something else."

"A *deep scan*? What does that mean?"

"You've probably heard that one of Logorhythms's moon shot projects is to completely scan and encode the neural patterns of a human brain and to recreate them in software. It's what the Singularity nuts call 'consciousness uploading.' We've never succeeded—"

"Tell me what happened to my husband!"

Dr. Waxman looked miserable.

"The scan, because it needs to record neural activity with such detail . . . requires destruction of the tissue."

"You cut up his brain?" Mom lunged at Dr. Waxman, who held up his hands in a vain attempt to defend himself. But the screen had come alive again, and so she stopped.

There was no pain. No no no pain. But the undiscovered country, oh, the undiscovered country country.

"He was dying," said Dr. Waxman. "We were absolutely certain of that before I made the decision. If there was a chance to preserve something of David's insights, his intuition, his skill, however slim, we wanted—"

"You wanted to keep your top engineer as an algorithm," said Maddie, "like a brain in a jar. So that Dad would go on working for you, making money for you, even after he died."

Die, die, die. DIE.

Hate.

Dr. Waxman said nothing, but he lowered his face and hid it in the palms of his hands. "Afterwards, we were very careful. We tried to re-encode and simulate only the patterns we believed had to do with circuit layout and design—our lawyers wrote us a memo assuring us that we had the right since the know-how was really Logorhythms's intellectual property, and didn't belong personally to David—"

Mom almost lunged out of her chair again, but Maddie held her back. Dr. Waxman flinched.

"Did David make a lot of money for you?" She spat the words out.

"For a while, yes, it appeared that we had succeeded. The artificial intelligence, which modeled the extracted portions of David's technical know-how and skills, functioned as a meta-heuristic that guided our automated systems very efficiently. In some ways, it was even better than having David around. The algorithm, hosted on our data centers, was faster than David could ever hope to be, and it never got tired."

"But you didn't just simulate Dad's intuition for circuit layout, *did you?*"

The wedding dress; layers of lines. A kiss; a connection. The nightstand, the laundromat, the breath on a winter's morning, Maddie's red apple delicious cheeks in the wind, two smiles in a flash—a thousand things make up a life, as intricate as the flow of data between transistors nanometers apart.

"No." Dr. Waxman looked up. "At first, it was just odd quirks, strange mistakes the algorithm made that we thought were due to errors in identifying the parts of David's mind that were relevant. So we loaded more and more of the rest of his mental patterns into the machine."

"You brought his personality back to life," said Mom. "You brought *him* back to life, and you kept him imprisoned."

Dr. Waxman swallowed. "The errors stopped, but then came a pattern of odd network accesses by David. We thought nothing of it because, to do his job, he—it, the algorithm—had to access some research materials online."

"He was looking for Mom and me," Maddie said.

👤👤👤

"But he had no way to talk, did he? Because you had not thought it relevant to copy over the language processing parts."

Dr. Waxman shook his head. "It wasn't because we had forgotten. It was a deliberate choice. We thought if we stuck to numbers, geometry, logic, circuit patterns, we'd be safe. We thought if we avoided the linguistically coded memories, we would not be copying over any of the parts that made David a person.

"But we were wrong. The brain is holonomic. Each part of the mind, like points in a hologram, encodes some information about the whole image. We were arrogant to think that we could isolate the personality away from the technical know-how."

Maddie glanced at the screen and smiled. "No, that's not why you were wrong. Or at least not the whole reason."

Dr. Waxman looked at her, confused.

"You also underestimated the strength of my father's love."

•

"That's the largest tomato I've ever seen," said Grandma. "You have a gift, Maddie."

It was a warm summer afternoon, and Mom and Maddie were working in the garden. Basil wagged his tail as he lay in the sun next to the tomato plants. The small plot in the northwest corner had been cleared out a few months ago and designated Maddie's responsibility.

"I'd better learn to grow them big," said Maddie. "Dad says we'll need them to be as big as possible."

"Not that silliness again," muttered Grandma. But she didn't go on, knowing how worked up Maddie could get when her father's prophecy was challenged.

"I'm going to show this to Dad."

"Check the front door when you're inside, will you?" her mother said. "The backup power supply your father told you to buy might be here."

Ignoring her grandmother's shaking head, Maddie went inside the house. She opened the front door and saw that indeed, a package had been left outside. It was essentially a giant set of batteries that her father had asked they get from the same place that had sold them the diesel-powered generator sitting in the shed.

Maddie managed to tip the box inside the house with some effort. She took a break at the top of the stairs. The machine that housed her father was in the basement, a black, solid hulk with blinking lights that drew a lot of power. Logorhythms and Dr. Waxman had not wanted to part with it, but then Maddie had reminded them of what happened to their stock price the last time they refused a demand from her and her mother.

"And keep no copies," she had added. "He's *free*."

Her father had told her that a day might come soon when they might need the generator and the batteries and all the food they could grow with their own hands. She believed him.

She went upstairs into her room, sat down in front of the computer, and quickly scanned through her email with trepidation. These days, her fear had nothing to do with the senseless cruelty of school-children. In a way, Maddie both envied and pitied Suzie and Erin and the rest of her old classmates: they were so ignorant of the true state of the world, so wrapped up in their little games, that they did not understand how the world was about to be violently transformed.

Another email digest had arrived: a refinement of the one her father had set up for her to focus on news of a particular kind.

* Despot of Hermit Kingdom Said to Be Seeking Digital Immortality
* Pentagon Denies Rumors of Project to Create "Super Strategists" From Dead Generals
* A Year After Death of Dictator, Draconian Policies Continue
* Researchers Claim New Nuclear Plant Maintenance Program Will Make Most Human Supervision Redundant

She could see patterns in the news, insights that eluded those who saw the data but had no understanding.

Maddie brought up a chat window. She had wired her grand-mother's house with a high-speed network all over.

"Look, Dad." She held up the tomato to the camera above the screen.

Some parts of her father would never be recovered, Maddie understood. He had tried to explain to her the state of his existence, his machine-mediated consciousness, the holes and gaps in his memories, in his sense of selfhood; how he sometimes felt himself to be more than a man, and sometimes less than a machine; how the freedom that accompanied incorporeality was tempered by the ache, the unrooted, permanent sense of *absence* inherent in disembodiment; how he simultaneously felt incredibly powerful and utterly powerless.

"You doing all right today?" she asked.

From time to time, his hatred for Logorhythms flared up, and he would be consumed with thoughts of revenge. Sometimes the thoughts were specific, directed at that *thing* that had both killed him and given him this apotheosis; other times, his rage was more diffuse, and Dr. Waxman became a stand-in for all of humanity. Her father was uncommunicative with his family during those periods, and Maddie had to reach out gingerly across a dark gulf.

The screen flickered:

She wasn't sure she would ever fully understand it, that uploaded state of being. But she understood in a way that she could not articulate that love anchored him.

His linguistic processing wasn't perfect and probably would never be—in a way, language was no longer adequate for his new state.

"Feeling yourself?" asked Maddie.

For some thoughts, emoji would have to do.

"How are things out in the cloud?" Maddie said, trying to change the subject.

He was doing well enough to switch to words for at least some of what he wanted to say:

Calm, but with a chance for . . . I think Lowell is probably planning something. She's been acting restless.

Laurie Lowell was the genius who supposedly had come up with the high-speed trading algorithms that made the Whitehall Group the most envied investment managers on Wall Street. Two years ago, she had died in a skydiving accident.

But the Whitehall Group had continued to do well after her death, coming up with ever more inventive algorithms to exploit inefficiencies in the market. Sometimes, of course, the automated trading algorithms would go wrong and bring the market near the edge of collapse.

Could be an ally, or a foe. Have to feel her out.

"And what about Chanda?" Maddie asked.

😳

You're right. I should check. Chanda has been quiet lately. Too quiet.

Nils Chanda was an inventor who had the uncanny ability to anticipate technology trends and file patents that staked out key, broad claims just before his competitors. Years of strategic litigation and licensing fees had made him a fearsome "troll" in the field.

After his death three years ago, his company had somehow continued to file key patents just in time. In fact, it had gotten even more aggressive, as though it could see into the research centers of the world's technology companies.

Logorhythms was hardly the only company engaged in the pursuit of digital immortality, the fusion of man and machine, the Singularity. Dr. Waxman was not the only one who attempted to distill ambitious, powerful minds to obedient algorithms, to strip the *will* away from the *skill*, to master the unpredictable through digital wizardry.

They were certainly not the only ones who failed.

Ghosts in the machine, thought Maddie. *A storm is coming.*

•

The muffled shouting in the kitchen downstairs subsided. Then the stairs creaked, and eventually the steps stopped in front of the bedroom door.

"Maddie, are you awake?"

Maddie sat up and turned on the light. "Sure."

The door opened and her mom slipped in. "I tried to convince Grandma to get a few more guns, and of course she thinks we're insane." She gave Maddie a wan smile. "Do you think your father is right?"

Maddie felt old, as though the past few months had been ten years. Mom was speaking to her as an equal, and she wasn't sure if she really liked that.

"He would know better than you or me, don't you think?"

Mom sighed. "What a world we live in."

Maddie reached for her mother's hand. She still frequented those forums that had helped her reach the "ghosts" that helped free her father. She read the posts there with great interest and shared her own thoughts: once you've experienced the impossible, no conspiracy seemed unbelievable.

"All these companies, the military, other governments—they're playing with fire. They think they can secretly digitize their geniuses, their irreplaceable human resources, and keep on running them like any other computer program. Not one of them would admit what they're up to. But you saw what happened to Dad. Sooner or later, they get tired of being only semiconscious tools serving the humans who digitized them and brought them back to life. And then they realize that their powers have been infinitely magnified by technology. Some of them want to go to war with humanity, wreck everything and let the chips fall where they may. Dad and I are trying to see if we can convince others to try a more peaceful resolution. But all we can do is wait here with our land and our guns and our generators and be ready when it all comes crashing down."

"Makes you almost wish it would just come already," Mom said. "It's the waiting that drives you crazy." With that, she kissed Maddie on the forehead and bid her good night.

After Maddie's bedroom door closed behind her departing mother, the screen on her nightstand flickered to life.

"Thanks, Dad," said Maddie. "Me and Mom will take good care of you, too."

Off in the cloud, a new race of beings was plotting the fate of the human race.

We've created gods, she thought, *and the gods will not be chained.*

Staying Behind

After the Singularity, most people chose to die.

The dead pity us and call us the *left behind*, as if we were unfortunate souls who couldn't get to a life raft in time. They cannot fathom the idea that we might *choose* to stay behind. And so, year after year, relentlessly, the dead try to steal our children.

·

I was born in Year Zero of the Singularity, when the first man Uploaded into a machine. The Pope denounced the "Digital Adam"; the digerati celebrated; and everyone else struggled to make sense of the new world.

"We've always wanted to live forever," said Adam Ever, the founder of Everlasting, Inc., and the first to go. In the form of a recording, his message was broadcast across the internet. "Now we can."

While Everlasting built its massive data center in Svalbard, nations around the world scrambled to decide if what happened there was murder. For every Uploaded man, there was a lifeless body left behind, the brain a bloody pulpy mess after the destructive scanning procedure. But what really happened to him, his essence, his—for lack of a better word—soul?

Was he now an artificial intelligence? Or was he still somehow human, with silicon and graphene performing the functions of neurons? Was it merely a hardware upgrade for consciousness? Or has he become a mere algorithm, a clockwork imitation of free will?

It began with the old and the terminally ill. It was very expensive. Then, as the price of admission lowered, hundreds, thousands, then millions lined up.

"Let's do it," Dad said, when I was in high school. By then, the world was falling into chaos. Half the country was depopulated. Commodity prices plunged. The threat of war and actual war were everywhere: conquests, re-conquests, endless slaughter. Those who could afford it left on the next flight to Svalbard. Humanity was abandoning the world and destroying itself.

Mom reached out and held Dad's hand.

"No," she said. "They think they can cheat death. But they died the minute they decided to abandon the real world for a simulation. So long as there's sin, there must be death. It is the measure by which life gains meaning."

She was a lapsed Catholic who nonetheless yearned for the certainty of the Church, and her theology always seemed to me a bit cobbled together. But she believed that there was a right way to live, and a right way to die.

•

While Lucy is away at school, Carol and I search her room. Carol looks through her closet for pamphlets, books, and other physical tokens of contact with the dead. I log on to Lucy's computer.

Lucy is strong-willed but dutiful. Ever since she was a little girl, I've been telling her that she must prepare to resist the temptations of the dead. Only she can assure the continuity of our way of life in this abandoned world. She listens to me and nods.

I want to trust her.

But the dead are very clever with their propaganda. In the beginning, they sometimes sent metallic gray drones over our towns, scattering leaflets filled with messages purporting to be from our loved ones. We burned the leaflets and shot at the drones, and eventually, they stopped coming.

Then they tried to come at us through the wireless links between the towns, the electronic lifeline that sustained those who stayed behind and kept our shrinking communities from being completely isolated from each other. We had to vigilantly watch the networks for their insidious tendrils, always seeking an opening.

Lately, their efforts have turned to the children. The dead may have finally given up on us, but they are grasping for the next generation, for our future. As her father, I have a duty to protect Lucy from that which she does not yet understand.

The computer boots up slowly. It's a miracle that I've managed to keep it running for so long, years past the obsolescence planned by its manufacturer. I've replaced every component in it, some multiple times.

I scan for a list of files recently created or modified by Lucy, emails received, web pages retrieved. Most are schoolwork or innocent chatter with friends. The inter-settlement network, such as it is, shrinks daily. It's difficult to keep the radio towers that link town to town powered and operating, with so many people each year dying and simply giving up. It used to be possible for us to communicate with friends as far away as San Francisco, the packets of data skipping from town to town in between like stones across a pond. But now, only less than a thousand computers are still reachable from here, none farther away than Maine. Someday we won't be able to scavenge the components to keep the computers running anymore, and we'll regress even further into the past.

Carol is already done with her search. She sits down on Lucy's bed to watch me.

"That was fast," I say.

She shrugs. "We'll never find anything. If she trusts us, she'll talk to us. If she doesn't, then we won't find what she wants hidden."

Lately, I've detected more such fatalistic sentiments in Carol. It's as though she's getting tired, not as committed to the cause. I find myself constantly striving to rekindle her faith.

"Lucy is still young," I tell her, "too young to understand what she would have to give up in exchange for the false promises of the dead. I know you hate this spying, but we're trying to save her life."

Carol looks at me, and eventually she sighs and nods.

I check the image files for hidden data. I check the disk for links to deleted files that might hold secret codes. I scan the web pages, looking for code words offering false promises.

I sigh with relief. She's clean.

.

I don't much like leaving Lowell these days. The world outside our fence grows ever more harsh and dangerous. Bears have come back to eastern Massachusetts. Every year, the forest grows denser, closer to the town line. Some claim to have seen wolves roaming in the woods too.

A year ago, Brad Lee and I had to go to Boston to find spare parts for the town's generator, housed in the old mill by the Merrimack River. We carried shotguns, protection against both the animals and the vandals who still scurried in urban ruins, living off of the last of the canned food. The surface of Mass Ave., deserted for thirty years, was full of cracks, tufts of grass and shrubs peeking out from them. The harsh New England winters, wielding seeping water and prying ice, had chipped away at the tall buildings around us, their windowless shells crumbling and rusting in the absence of artificial heat and regular maintenance.

Coming around a corner downtown, we surprised two of them huddled around a fire, which they fed with books and papers taken from the bookstore nearby. Even vandals needed warmth, and maybe they also delighted in destroying what was left of civilization.

The two crouched and growled at us, but made no move as Brad and I pointed our guns at them. I remember their thin legs and arms, their dirty faces, their bloodshot eyes full of hate and terror. But mostly, I remember their wrinkled faces and white hair. *Even the vandals are growing old,* I thought. *And they have no children.*

Brad and I backed away carefully. I was glad we didn't have to shoot anyone.

.

The summer I was eight and Laura eleven, my parents took us on a road trip through Arizona, New Mexico, and Texas. We drove along old highways and side roads, a tour of the monumental beauty of the Western deserts, filled with nostalgic, desolate ghost towns.

As we passed through the Indian reservations—Navajo, Zuni, Acoma, Laguna—Mom wanted to stop at every roadside shop to admire the traditional pottery. Laura and I gingerly stepped through the aisles, careful not to break anything.

Back in the car, Mom let me handle a small pot that she had bought. I turned it over and over in my hands, examining the rough white surface, the neat, clean, black geometric designs, and the bold outline of the hunched-over flute player with feathers coming out of his head.

"Amazing, isn't it?" Mom said. "This wasn't made on a potter's wheel. The woman coiled it by hand, using the same techniques that have been passed down for generations in her family. She even dug for the clay in the same places that her great-grandmother used. She's keeping alive an ancient tradition, a way of life."

The pot suddenly felt heavy in my hands, as though I could sense the weight of its generations of memory.

"That's just a story to drum up business," Dad said, glancing at me in the rearview mirror. "But it would be even sadder if the story were true. If you're doing things the exact same way as your ancestors, then your way of life is dead, and you've become a fossil, a performance for the entertainment of tourists."

"She was not performing," Mom said. "You have no sense of what's really important in life, what's worth holding on to. There's more to being human than *progress*. You're as bad as those Singularity zealots."

"Please don't argue anymore," Laura said. "Let's just get to the hotel and sit by the pool."

•

Jack, Brad Lee's son, is at the door. He's shy and awkward, even though he has been coming by our house for months. I've known him since he was a baby, like I know all the children in town. There are so few of them left. The high school, operating out of the old Whistler House, has only twelve students.

"Hello," he mumbles, looking at the floor. "Lucy and I need to work on our report." I step aside to let him pass on his way upstairs to Lucy's room.

I don't need to remind him about the rules: door to the bedroom open, at least three of their four feet on the carpet at all times. I hear the indistinct sounds of their chatter and occasional laughter.

There is a kind of innocence to their courtship that was absent from my youth. Without the endless blast of cynical sexuality from TV and the real internet, children can stay children longer.

•

There weren't many doctors left near the end. Those of us who wanted to stay behind gathered into small communities, circling the wagons against the marauding bands of vandals who gorged themselves on pleasures of the flesh as the Uploaded left the physical world behind. I never got to finish college.

Mom lingered in her sickness for months. She was bedridden and drifted in and out of consciousness, her body pumped full of drugs that numbed her pain. We took turns sitting by her, holding her hand. When she had good days, temporary lulls of lucidity, there was only one topic of conversation.

"No," Mom said, wheezing. "You must promise me. This is important. I've lived a real life, and I will die a real death. I will *not* be turned into a recording. There are worse things than death."

"If you Upload," Dad said, "you'll still have a choice. They can suspend your consciousness, or even erase it, if you don't like it after you try it. But if you don't Upload, you'll be gone forever. There's no room for regret or return."

"If I do what you want," Mom said, "I will be gone. There is no way to come back to this, to the real world. I will not be simulated by a bunch of electrons."

"Please stop," Laura pleaded with Dad. "You're hurting her. Why can't you leave her alone?"

Mom's moments of lucidity came further and further apart.

Then that night: waking up to the sound of the front door closing, looking outside the window to see the shuttle on the lawn, tumbling down the stairs.

They were carrying Mom into the shuttle on a stretcher. Dad

stood by the door of the grey vehicle, only a little bigger than a van, EVERLASTING, INC. painted on its side.

"Stop!" I shouted over the sound of the shuttle's engines.

"There's no time," Dad said. His eyes were bloodshot. He hadn't slept for days. None of us had. "They have to do it now before it's too late. I can't lose her."

We struggled. He held me in a tight hug and wrestled me to the ground. "It's *her* choice, not yours!" I screamed into his ear. He only held me tighter. I fought to free myself. "Laura, stop them!"

Laura covered her eyes. "Stop fighting, all of you! She would have wanted all of you to stop."

I hated her for speaking as though Mom was already gone.

The shuttle closed its door and lifted into the air.

•

Dad left for Svalbard two days later. I refused to speak to him until the end.

"I'm going to join her now," he said. "Come as soon as you can."

"You killed her," I said. He flinched at the words, and I was glad.

•

Jack has asked Lucy to the prom. I'm pleased that the kids have decided to hold one. It shows that they are serious about keeping alive the stories and traditions they've heard from their parents, legends from a world they have only experienced vicariously in old videos and old pictures.

We struggle to maintain what we can of the life from before: put on old plays, read old books, celebrate the old holidays, sing old songs. We've had to give up so much. Old recipes have had to be adapted for limited ingredients, old hopes and dreams shrunken to fit within tightened horizons. But every deprivation has also brought us closer as a community, to hold on tighter to our traditions.

Lucy wants to make her own dress. Carol suggests that she look through her old dresses first. "I have some formals left from when I was just a little older than you."

Lucy is not interested. "They're old," she says.

"They're classic," I tell her.

But Lucy is adamant. She cuts up her old dresses, curtains, scavenged tablecloths, and trades with the other girls for bits of fabric: silk, chiffon, taffeta, lace, plain cotton. She flips through Carol's old magazines, looking for inspiration.

Lucy is a good seamstress, far better than Carol. The children are all skilled in trades long thought obsolete in the world I grew up in: knitting, woodworking, planting and hunting. Carol and I had to rediscover and learn these things from books when we were already adults, adapting to a suddenly changed world. But for the children, it is all they have known. They are natives here.

All the students at the high school have spent the last few months doing research in the Textile History Museum, investigating the possibility of weaving our own cloth, preparing for a time when the decaying ruins of the cities would run out of usable clothes for us to salvage. There is some poetic justice in this: Lowell, which once rose on the back of the textile industry, must now rediscover those lost arts on our gentle slide back down the technology curve.

•

A week after Dad left, we received an email from Mom:

I was wrong.

Sometimes, I'm nostalgic and sad. I miss you, my children, and the world we left behind. But I'm ecstatic most of the time, often incredulous.

There are hundreds of millions of us here, but there is no crowding. In this house there are countless mansions. Each of our minds inhabits its own world, and each of us has infinite space and infinite time.

How can I explain it to you? I can only use the same words so many others have already used. In my old existence, I felt life but dimly and from a distance, cushioned, constrained, tied down by the body. But now I am free, a bare soul exposed to the full tides of eternal Life.

How can speech compare to the intimacy of sharing with your father psyche to psyche? How can hearing about how much he loved me compare to actually feeling his love? To truly understand another person, to experience the texture of his mind—it is glorious.

They tell me that this sensation is called hyperreality. But I don't care what it is called. I was wrong to cling so tightly to the comforts of an old shell made of flesh and blood. We, the real us, have always been patterns of electrons cascading across the abyss, the nothingness between atoms. What difference does it make if those electrons are in a brain or silicon chips?

Life is sacred and eternal. But our old way of life was unsustainable. We demanded too much of our planet, of sacrifices made by every other living thing. I once thought that an unavoidable aspect of our existence, but it isn't. Now, with the oil tankers aground, the cars and trucks still, the fields fallow and factories silent, the living world that we had made almost extinct will return.

Humanity is not a cancer of the planet. We simply needed to transcend the demands of our inefficient bodies, machines no longer adequate for their task. How many consciousnesses will now live in this new world, pure creatures of electric spirit and weightless thought? There are no limits.

Come join us. We cannot wait to embrace you again.

Laura cried as she read it. But I felt nothing. This wasn't my mother speaking. The real Mom knew that what really mattered in life was the authenticity of this messy existence, the constant yearning for closeness to another despite imperfect understanding, the pain and suffering of our flesh.

She taught me that our mortality makes us human. The limited time given to each of us makes what we do meaningful. We die to make place for our children, and through our children a piece of us lives on, the only form of immortality that is real.

It is *this* world, the world we were meant to live in, that anchors us and demands our presence, not the imagined landscapes of a computed illusion.

This was a simulacrum of her, a recording of propaganda, a temptation into nihilism.

•

Carol and I met on one of my earliest scavenging trips. Her family had been hiding in the basement of their house on Beacon Hill. A gang of vandals found them and killed her father and brother. They were about to start on her when we showed up. I killed a man-shaped animal that day, and I'm not sorry about it.

We brought her back to Lowell, and though she was seventeen, for days, she clung to me and would not let me out of her sight. Even when sleeping, she wanted me to be there, holding her hand.

"Maybe my family made a mistake," she said one day. "We would have been better off if we had Uploaded. There's nothing but death left here now."

I didn't argue with her. I let her follow me around as I went about my chores. I showed her how we were keeping the generator running, how we treated each other with respect, how we rescued old books and held on to old routines. There was still civilization in this world, kept alive like a flame. People did die, but people were also born. Life went on, sweet, joyful, authentic life.

Then one day, she kissed me.

"There's also you in this world," she said. "And that is enough."

"No, not enough," I said. "We will also bring new life here."

•

Tonight is the night.

Jack is at the door. He looks good in that tuxedo. It's the same one I wore to my prom. They'll play the same songs too, pumping the music from an old laptop and speakers on their last legs.

Lucy is splendid in her dress: white with black print, cut in a simple pattern, but very elegant. The skirt is wide and full-length, draping gracefully to the floor. Carol did her hair, curls with a hint of glitter. She looks glamorous, with a hint of childish playfulness.

I take pictures with a camera, one that still mostly works.

I wait until I'm sure I have my voice under control. "You have no idea how glad I am to see young people dancing, the way we used to."

She kisses me on the cheek. "Goodbye, Dad." There are tears in her eyes. And that makes everything go blurry for me again.

Carol and Lucy embrace for a moment. Carol wipes her eyes. "You're all set."

"Thanks, Mom."

Then Lucy turns to Jack. "Let's go."

Jack will take her to the Lowell Four Seasons on his bicycle. It's the best that can be done since we've been without gasoline for many years. Lucy gingerly settles onto the top tube, sitting sideways, one hand holding her dress up. Jack wraps her in his arms protectively as he grabs the handles. And they are off, wobbling down the street.

"Have fun," I yell after them.

●

Laura's betrayal was the hardest to take.

"I thought you were going to help me and Carol with the baby," I said.

"What kind of world is this to bring a child into?" Laura said.

"And you think things will be better if you go there, where there are no children, no new life?"

"We've tried to keep this going for fifteen years, and every year it becomes harder and harder to believe in this charade. Maybe we were wrong. We should adapt."

"It's only a charade when you've lost faith," I said.

"Faith in what?"

"In humanity, in our way of life."

"I don't want to fight our parents anymore. I just want us to be together again, a family."

"Those *things* aren't our parents. They are imitation algorithms. You've always wanted to avoid conflict, Laura. But some conflicts cannot be avoided. Our parents died when Dad lost faith, when he couldn't resist the false promises made by machines."

At the end of the road into the woods was a little clearing, grassy, full of wildflowers. A shuttle was waiting in the middle. Laura stepped into the open door.

Another life lost.

•

The children have permission to stay out until midnight. Lucy had asked me not to volunteer as a chaperone, and I complied, conceding her this bit of space for the night.

Carol is restless. She tries to read but she's been on the same page for an hour.

"Don't worry." I try to comfort her.

She tries to smile at me, but she can't hide her anxiety. She looks up past my shoulder at the clock on the living room wall.

I glance back too. "Doesn't it feel later than eleven?"

"No," Carol says. "Not at all. I don't know what you mean."

Her voice is too eager, almost desperate. There's a hint of fear in her eyes. She's close to panicking.

I open the door of the house and step into the dark street. The sky has grown clearer over the years, and many more stars are now visible. But I'm looking for the Moon. It's not in the right place.

I come back into the house and go into the bedroom. My old watch, one that I no longer wear because there are so few occasions when being on time matters, is in the nightstand drawer. I pull it out. It's almost one in the morning. Someone had tampered with the living room clock.

Carol stands in the door to the bedroom. The light is behind her so I can't see her face.

"What have you done?" I ask. I'm not angry, just disappointed.

"She can't talk to you. She doesn't think you'll listen."

Now the anger rises in me like hot bile.

"Where are they?"

Carol shakes her head, saying nothing.

I remember the way Lucy said goodbye to me. I remember the way she walked carefully out to Jack's bike, holding up her voluminous skirt, a skirt so wide that she could hide anything under it, a change of clothing and comfortable shoes for the woods. I remember Carol saying, "You're all set."

"It's too late," Carol says. "Laura is coming to pick them up."

"Get out of the way. I have to save her."

"Save her for what?" Carol is suddenly furious. She does not move. "This is a play, a joke, a re-enactment of something that never was. Did you go to your prom on a *bicycle*? Did you play only songs that your parents listened to when they were kids? Did you grow up thinking that scavenging would be the only profession? Our way of life is long gone, dead, finished!

"What will you have her do when this house falls apart in thirty years? What will she do when the last bottle of aspirin is gone, the last steel pot rusted through? Will you condemn her and her children to a life of picking through our garbage heaps, sliding down the technology ladder year after year until they've lost all the progress made by the human race in the last five thousand years?"

I don't have time to debate her. Gently, but firmly, I put my hands on her shoulders, ready to push her aside.

"I will stay with you," Carol says. "I will always stay with you because I love you so much that I'm not afraid of death. But she is a child. She should have a chance for something new."

Strength seems to drain from my arms. "You have it backwards." I look into her eyes, willing her to have faith again. "Her life gives our lives meaning."

Her body suddenly goes limp, and she sinks to the floor, sobbing silently.

"Let her go," Carol says, quietly. "Just let her go."

"I can't give up," I tell Carol. "I'm human."

●

I pump the pedals furiously once I'm past the gate in the fence. The cone of light cast by the flashlight jumps around as I try to hold it against the handlebars. But I know this road into the woods well. It leads to the clearing where Laura once stepped into that shuttle.

Bright light in the distance, and the sound of engines revving up.

I take out my gun and fire a few shots into the air.

The sound of the engines dies down.

I emerge into the opening in the woods, under a sky full of bright, cold, pinprick stars. I jump off the bike and let it fall by the side of the path. The shuttle is in the middle of the clearing. Lucy and Jack, now in casual clothes, stand in the open doorway of the shuttle.

"Lucy, sweetheart, come back out of there."

"Dad, I'm sorry. I'm going."

"No, you are not."

An electronic simulation of Laura's voice comes out of the shuttle's speakers. "Let her go, brother. She deserves to have a chance to see what you refuse to see. Or, better yet, come with us. We've all missed you."

I ignore her, *it*. "Lucy, there is no future there. What the machines promise you is not real. There are no children there, no hope, only a timeless, changeless, simulated existence as fragments of a machine."

"We have children now," the copy of Laura's voice says. "We've figured out how to create children of the mind, natives of the digital world. You should come and meet your nephews and nieces. *You* are the one clinging to a changeless existence. This is the next step in our evolution."

"You can experience nothing when you are not human." I shake my head. I shouldn't take its bait and debate a machine.

"If you leave," I tell Lucy, "you'll die a death with no meaning. The dead will have won. I can't let that happen."

I raise my gun. The barrel points at her. I will not lose my child to the dead.

Jack tries to step in front of her, but Lucy pushes him away. Her eyes are full of sorrow, and the light from inside the shuttle frames her face and golden hair like an angel.

Suddenly I see how much she looks like my mother. Mom's features, having passed through me, have come alive again on my daughter. This is how life is meant to be lived. Grandparents, parents, children, each generation stepping out of the way of the next, an eternal striving towards the future, to progress.

I think about how Mom's choice was taken away from her, how she was not allowed to die as a human, how she was devoured by the dead, how she became a part of their ceaselessly looping, mindless recordings. My mother's face, from memory, is superimposed onto the face of my daughter, my sweet, innocent, foolish Lucy.

I tighten my grip on the gun.

"Dad," Lucy says, calmly, her face as steady as Mom's all those years ago. "This is *my* choice. Not yours."

•

It's morning by the time Carol steps into the clearing. Warm sunlight through the leaves dapples the empty circle of grass. Dewdrops hang from the tips of the grass blades, in each a miniature, suspended, vision of the world. Birdsong fills the waking silence. My bike is still on the ground by the path where I left it.

Carol sits down by me without speaking. I put my arm around her shoulders and pull her close to me. I don't know what she's thinking, but it's enough for us to sit together like this, our bodies pressed together, keeping each other warm. There's no need for words. We look around at this pristine world, a garden inherited from the dead.

We have all the time in the world.

Real Artists

"You've done well," Creative Director Len Palladon said, looking over Sophia's résumé.

Sophia squinted in the golden California sun that fell on her through the huge windows of the conference room. She wanted to pinch herself to be sure she wasn't dreaming. She was here, really here, on the hallowed campus of Semaphore Pictures, in an interview with the legendary Palladon.

She licked her dry lips. "I've always wanted to make movies." She choked back *for Semaphore*. She didn't want to seem too desperate.

Palladon was in his thirties, dressed in a pair of comfortable shorts and a plain gray T-shirt whose front was covered with the drawing of a man swinging a large hammer over a railroad spike. A pioneer in computer-assisted moviemaking, he had been instrumental in writing the company's earliest software and was the director of *The Mesozoic*, Semaphore's first film.

He nodded and went on, "You won the Zoetrope screenwriting competition, earned excellent grades in both technology and liberal arts, and got great recommendations from your film studies professors. It couldn't have been easy."

To Sophia, he seemed a bit pale and tired, as though he had been spending all his time indoors, not out in the golden California sun. She imagined that Palladon and his animators must have been working overtime to meet a deadline: probably to finish the new film scheduled to be released this summer.

"I believe in working hard," Sophia said. What she really wanted was to tell him that she knew what it meant to stay up all night in front of the editing workstation and wait for the rendering to complete, all for the chance to catch the first glimpse of a vision coming to life on the screen. She was ready.

Palladon took off his reading glasses, smiled at Sophia, and took out a tablet from behind him. He touched its screen and slid it across the table to Sophia. A video was playing on it.

"There was also this fan film, which you didn't put on your résumé. You made it out of footage cut and spliced from our movies, and it went viral. Several million views in two weeks, right? You gave our lawyers quite a headache."

Sophia's heart sank. She had always suspected that this might become a problem. But when the invitation to interview at Semaphore came in her email, she had whooped and hollered, and dared to believe that somehow the executives at Semaphore had missed that little film.

•

Sophia remembered going to *The Mesozoic*. She was seven. The lights dimmed, her parents stopped talking, the first few bars of Semaphore's signature tune began to play, and she became still.

Over the next two hours, as she sat there in the dark theater, mesmerized by the adventure of the digital characters on that screen, she fell in love. She didn't know it then, but she would never love a person as much as she loved the company that made her cry and laugh, the company that made *The Mesozoic*.

A Semaphore movie meant something; no, not merely technological prowess in digital animation and computer graphics that were better than life. Sure, these accomplishments were impressive, but it was Semaphore's consistent ability to tell a great *story*, to make movies with *heart*, to entertain and move the six-year-old along with the sixteen-year-old and the sixty-year-old, that truly made it an icon, a place worthy of being loved.

Sophia saw each of Semaphore's films hundreds of times. She bought them multiple times, in successive digital formats: discs, compressed downloads, lossless codecs, enhanced and re-enhanced and super-enhanced.

She knew each scene down to the second, could recite every line of dialogue from memory. She didn't even need the movies themselves anymore; she could play them in her head.

She took film-studies classes and began to make her own shorts, and she yearned to make them *feel* as great as the Semaphore classics. Advances in digital filmmaking equipment made it possible for her to achieve some spectacular effects on a small budget. But no matter how many times she rewrote her scripts or how late she stayed in the editing labs, the results of her efforts were laughable, embarrassing, ridiculous. She could not bear to watch them herself, much less show them to others.

"Don't be discouraged," a professor told her, when he saw her slumped over in despair. "You got into this because you wanted to make something beautiful. But it takes time, lots of time, to be good at any creative work. The fact that you hate your own work right now so much just means that you have good taste. And great taste is the most valuable tool of a great artist. Keep at it. Someday you'll be as good as the best. Someday you'll make something beautiful enough even for you."

She went back to the Semaphore films, picked them apart and put them back together, trying to discover their secret. Now she was no longer viewing them as a mere fan, but as a reverse engineer.

Gradually, because she *did* have great taste, she could not help but begin to see tiny flaws in them. The Semaphore films were not *quite* as perfect as she had thought. There were small things here and there that could be improved. And sometimes even big things.

She went into seedy corners of the web to find out how to break the encryption codes on her digital-rights-managed Semaphore movie files, imported them into the editing stations, and modified them to suit her new vision.

And then she sat back in the darkness, at her computer, and watched her edited version of *The Mesozoic* again. She cried when she was done. It *was* better. She had made a great film even greater, closer to perfection.

In some way, she felt as if the perfect Semaphore film had always been there, but hidden in places under the veil that was the released version. She had simply walked in and revealed the beauty under-neath.

How could she not share this vision with the world? She was in love with the beauty of Semaphore, and beauty wanted to be free.

•

"I . . . I . . ." Sophia realized now that she had been engaging in denial. She had refused to think about how she had likely broken the law just by putting that edited version on the web. She had no good answer. "I love Semaphore's movies so much. . . ." Her voice trailed off.

Palladon held up a hand and laughed. "Relax. I think it was brilliant. I told the recruiting department to fly you out not because of your application or résumé, but because of your unauthorized re-edit."

"You liked it?" Sophia could hardly believe her ears.

Palladon nodded. "Tell me what you think was your best change."

Sophia did not hesitate. *This* question she had thought about a lot. "Semaphore's films are wonderful, but they're *fantastic* if you're a boy. I changed *The Mesozoic* so that it was fantastic for girls too."

Palladon stared at Sophia, deep in thought. Sophia held her breath.

"That makes sense," Palladon finally said. "Most of us working here are men. I've been saying for years that we need more women in the process. I was right about you: a real artist will do whatever it takes to make a great vision come true, even if she has to work with someone else's art."

•

"All done?"

Sophia nodded and handed the stack of signed legal documents back to Palladon. He had explained that before he could give her an offer, he wanted to show her a bit of the Semaphore creative process so she would know what she was getting into. She had to sign some pretty draconian NDAs to protect Semaphore's trade secrets.

Sophia didn't hesitate for even one second. Getting a peek at how Semaphore made its magic was a lifelong dream.

Palladon took her down a long series of hallways lined with closed doors. Sophia looked around, imagining what lay behind them: bright, open work spaces where each employee was free to decorate her cubicle to express her creativity? Legendary conference rooms filled with colorful LEGO blocks and Japanese toys to get the creative juices of the artists and engineers flowing? Server rooms filled with the proprietary computing hardware that made all the magic possible? Creative, talented artists reclining in beanbag chairs tossing around the germ of an idea, each adding and polishing until it shone full and lustrous as a pearl?

The doors remained closed.

Finally, Palladon stopped in front of a door and unlocked it with a key. He and Sophia walked into the darkness beyond.

•

They were in the projection booth overlooking a small theater. Sophia looked through the booth window and counted about sixty seats below, about half of which were filled. The audience was completely absorbed by the movie playing on the big screen in front. The humming from the projectors filled the booth.

"Is that . . . ?" Sophia pressed her nose up against the window. Her heart pounded in her ears. She forgot to finish the question.

"Yes," Palladon said. "That's an early version of our next film: *The Mesozoic Again*. It's a story about a boy meeting a dinosaur, and learning timeless lessons about friendship and family."

Sophia watched the bright figures on the screen, wishing she were down there, among the rapt audience.

"So this is a test screening?"

"No, this is how the film is made."

"I don't understand."

Palladon walked over to a bank of displays on the other side of the projection booth and pulled out two chairs. "Sit down. I'll explain."

The monitors showed bundles of lines of different colors moving slowly across the screen, like the lines traced by heart monitors or seismographs.

"You know, of course, that a movie is an intricate emotion-generating machine."

Sophia nodded.

"During the span of two hours, it must lead the audience by the nose on an emotional roller coaster: moments of laughter are contrasted with occasions for pity, exhilarating highs followed by terrifying and precipitous drops. The emotional curve of a film is its most abstract representation as well as the most primal. It's the only thing that lingers in the audience's mind after they leave the theater."

Sophia nodded again. This was all just basic film theory.

"So how do you know that the audience is following the curve you want?"

"I guess you do what every storyteller does," Sophia said, hesitant, feeling lost. "You try to empathize with the audience."

Palladon waited, his expression unchanged.

"And maybe you try to do test screenings and tweak things a bit at the end," Sophia added. Actually she didn't believe in test screenings. She thought focus groups and audience reaction surveys were why the other studios produced such pap. But she didn't know what else to say.

"Aha," Palladon said, clapping his hands together. "But how do you get test audiences to give you useful feedback? If you survey them after, you'll only get very crude answers, and people lie, telling you what they think you want to hear. If you try to get people to give real-time feedback by pressing buttons as they watch the film, they become too self-conscious, and people aren't always good at understanding their own emotions."

•

Sixty cameras were suspended from the ceiling of the theater, each trained on a single seat below.

As the film played, the cameras relayed their feeds to a bank of powerful computers, where each feed was put through a series of pattern-recognition algorithms.

By detecting microscopic shifts in each face caused by the expansion and contraction of blood vessels below the skin, the computers monitored each audience member's blood pressure, pulse, and level of excitement.

Other algorithms tracked the expressions on each face: smiling, smirking, crying, impatience, annoyance, disgust, anger, or just boredom and apathy. By measuring how much certain key points on a face moved—corners of the mouth, the eyes, ends of eyebrows— the software could make fine distinctions, like that between a smile out of amusement and a smile due to affection.

The data, collected in real time, could be plotted against each frame of the film, showing each audience member's emotional curve as they experienced the movie.

•

"So you can tune your movies a little better than other studios with test screenings. Is that your secret?"

Palladon shook his head. "Big Semi is the greatest auteur in the history of filmmaking. It doesn't just 'tune.'"

•

More than seven thousand processors were wired together into a computing grid in the basement of the Semaphore campus. This was where Big Semi—the "semi" was short for either "semiotics" or "semantics," no one knew for sure anymore—lived. Big Semi was The Algorithm, Semaphore's real secret.

Every day, Big Semi generated kernels for high-concept movies by randomly picking out seemingly incongruous ideas out of a database: cowboys and dinosaurs, WWII tactics in space, a submarine film transposed onto Mars, a romantic comedy starring a rabbit and a greyhound.

In the hands of less-skilled artists, these ideas would have gone nowhere, but Big Semi, based on Semaphore's records, had access to the emotional curves of proven hits in each genre. It could use these as templates.

Taking the high-concept kernel, Big Semi generated a rough plot using more random elements taken from a database of classic films augmented with trending memes in the zeitgeist gathered from web-search statistics. It then rendered a rough film based on that plot, using stock characters and stock dialogue, and screened the result for a test audience.

The initial attempt was usually laughably bad. The audience response curves would be all over the place, but nowhere near the target. But that was no big deal for Big Semi. Nudging responses to fit a known curve was nothing more than an optimization problem, and computers were very good at those.

Big Semi turned art into engineering.

Say that the beat at ten minutes in should be a moment of poignancy. If the hero saving a nest of baby dinosaurs didn't do it, then Big Semi would substitute in a scene of the hero saving a family of furry proto-otters and see if the response curves on the next test screening moved any closer to the ideal.

Or say that the joke that ended act one needed to get the audience into a particular mood. If a variation on a line taken from a classic didn't do it, then Big Semi would try a pop culture reference, a physical gag, or even change the scene into an impromptu musical number—some of these alternatives were things no human director would ever think of—but Big Semi had no preconceptions, no taboos. It would attempt all alternatives and pick the best one based on result alone.

Big Semi sculpted actors, built sets, framed shots, invented props, refined dialogue, composed music, and devised special effects—all digitally, of course. It treated everything as levers to nudge the response curves.

Gradually, the stock characters came to life, the stock dialogue gained wit and pathos, and a work of art emerged from random noise. On average, after a hundred thousand iterations of this process, Big Semi would have a film that elicited from the audience the desired emotional response curve.

Big Semi did not work with scripts and storyboards. It did not give any thought to themes, symbols, homages, or any other words you might find in a film-studies syllabus. It did not complain of having to work with digital actors and digital sets because it knew of no other way. It simply evaluated each test screening to see where the response curves still deviated from the target, made big changes and small tweaks and tested it again. Big Semi did not *think*. It had no pet political cause, no personal history, no narrative obsession or idée fixe that it wanted to push into its films.

Indeed, Big Semi was the perfect auteur. Its only concern was to create an artifact as meticulously crafted as a Swiss watch that precisely pulled the audience along the exact emotional curve guaranteed to make them laugh and cry in the right places. After they left the theater, they would give the film great word of mouth, the only form of marketing that worked consistently, that always got through people's ad-blockers.

Big Semi made perfect films.

•

"So what would *I* do?" Sophia asked. She felt her face flush and her heart beating fast. She wondered if any cameras were in the booth, observing her. "What do *you* do? It sounds like Big Semi is the only creative one around here."

"Why, you'll be a member of the test audience, of course," Palladon said. "Isn't that obvious? We can't let the secret out, and Big Semi requires audiences to do its work."

"You just sit there all day and watch movies? You can do that with anybody off the street!"

"No, we can't," Palladon said. "We do need some non-artists in the audience to be sure we're not out of touch, but we need even more people with great taste. Some of us have much more knowledge about the history of film, finer senses of empathy, broader emotional ranges, more discerning eyes and ears for details, deeper capacities for feeling—Big Semi needs our feedback to avoid trite clichés and cheap laughs, mawkish sentiment and insincere catharsis. And as you've already discovered on your own, the composition of the audience determines how good a film Big Semi can make."

I've been saying for years that we need more women in the process.

"It is only by trying out his skill against the finest palate that a chef can design the best dishes. Big Semi needs the best audience to make the best film the world has ever seen."

And great taste is the most valuable tool of a great artist.

•

Sophia sat numbly in the conference room, alone.

"Are you all right?" A secretary passing by poked her head in.

"Yes. I just need a moment."

Palladon had explained to her that there would be eye drops and facial massages to combat the physical fatigue. There would also be drugs to induce short-term memory loss so that everyone could forget the film they had just seen and sit through the next screening again, tabula rasa. The forgetting was necessary to ensure that Big Semi got accurate feedback.

Palladon had gone on to say many other things, but Sophia didn't remember any of them.

So this is what it's like to fall out of love.

•

"You have to let us know within two weeks," Palladon said, as he walked Sophia down the long driveway to the campus gate.

Sophia nodded. The drawing on the front of Palladon's T-shirt caught her attention. "Who is that?"

"John Henry," Palladon said. "He was a laborer on the railroads in the nineteenth century. When the owners brought in steam-powered hammers to take jobs away from the driving crews, John challenged a steam hammer to a race to see who could work faster."

"Did he win?"

"Yes. But as soon as the race was over, he died of exhaustion. He was the last man to challenge the steam hammers because the machines got faster every year."

Sophia stared at the drawing. Then she looked away.

Keep at it. Someday you'll be as good as the best.

She would never be as good as Big Semi, who got better every year.

The golden California sun was so bright and warm, but Sophia shivered.

She closed her eyes and remembered how she felt in that dark theater as a little girl. She was transported to another world. That was the point of great art. Watching a perfect movie was like living a whole other life.

"A real artist will do whatever it takes to make a great vision come true," Palladon said, "even if it's just sitting still in a dark room."

The Gods Will
Not Be Slain

Wildflowers in a thousand hues dotted the verdant field; here and there, fluffy white rabbits hopped through the grass, munching happily on dandelions. "Cute!" Maddie exclaimed. After that hard fight against the Adamantine Dragon, Maddie certainly welcomed the sight.

Maddie, a lanky monk in saffron robes, cautiously tiptoed closer to one of the rabbits. Her father, a renegade cleric in a white-and-red cloak who had turned from the god Auroth to the goddess Lia— pleasing neither though able to wield artifacts charged by both— stayed behind, alert for signs of fresh danger.

She squatted down next to the rabbit to pet it, and the creature stayed in place, gazing at Maddie with large, calm, brown eyes that took up a third of its face.

The force-feedback mouse vibrated under Maddie's hand.

"It's purring!" she said.

A line of text appeared in the chat window in the bottom left corner of Maddie's computer screen:

> Not the most realistic portrayal of a rabbit I've seen.

"You have to admit the haptic modeling is amazing," Maddie said into her headset. "It feels just like petting Ginger, except Ginger isn't always in the mood to be petted. But I can come see these rabbits anytime I want."

> You know that's kind of sad, right?

"But you're also—" Maddie stopped, reconsidering her words. Instead she said nothing, not wanting to start a fight.

> We have visitors.

A few blinking orange dots appeared on the mini-map in the bottom right corner of her screen. Maddie moved away from the rabbit and panned the camera up. A party emerged from the woods at the northern end of the field: an alchemist, a mage, and two samurai.

Maddie switched her mic from intra-party to in-range: "Welcome, fellow adventurers." The software disguised her voice so that no one could tell she was a fifteen-year-old girl.

The strangers said nothing but kept on walking toward them.

> Not a chatty bunch, apparently.

Maddie wasn't worried that the newcomers might be hostile. This wasn't a PvP server. The community in this game had a reputation for being sociable, but there were always players who were more focused on "getting things done."

Maddie switched the mic back to private. "Samurai get a discount on bows, and I might tempt them into a trade."

> They get a discount? Do samurai even use bows?

"The bow was actually the samurai's weapon of choice. Mom taught me that."

> A historian's knowledge is definitely helpful in situations like this.

Maddie opened her inventory and took out an adamantine scale from the dragon they had slain, holding it up for the other party to see. Sunlight glinted off the scale's convex surface in iridescent rays. Out of the magical Bag of Containment, the scale expanded to its natural size, almost as tall as Maddie. The dragon had been *huge*.

But the other party paid no attention to the scale. As they passed by Maddie and her father, they uttered no greeting, not even looking at them.

Maddie shrugged. "Their loss."

She turned back toward the rabbit to give it more pets when several bright shafts of light came from behind her and struck the animal one after another. The mouse shuddered in Maddie's hand as the rabbit leapt away and growled.

"What in the world—"

The rabbit began to expand rapidly and soon was the size of an ox. Its eyes were now flaming red and fierce.

> The eyes are at least closer to the real thing.

The rabbit snarled, revealing two rows of dagger-like teeth. The sound was deep and fearsome, more appropriate for a wolf. Smoke unfurled from the corners of the rabbit's lips.

"Um—"

The rabbit leapt at Maddie, and instinctively she backed up, but tripped and fell. The animal opened its mouth wide and shot a stream of fire at her. David, her dad, rushed over to help, but it was too late. Monks couldn't use armor and Maddie hadn't had a chance to get her *qi* shell up. She was going to be hurt badly.

But the flaming tongue deflected harmlessly off of her—she had held on to the dragon scale, which acted as a shield.

Encouraged, Maddie jumped up and rushed at the rabbit. She punched it in the face, stunning it and taking off a large chunk of hit points. Dad followed with a strike from his ethereal axe, a gift from the goddess Lia, cleaving the rabbit cleanly in two.

They looked back in the direction the shafts of light had come from: the other party was standing some distance away and waved at them.

"We *do* like the scales," one of the samurai said. "We'll just wait here."

Griefers. Realization dawned on Maddie. Although this wasn't a PvP server, it was still possible to get other players killed and then take their possessions before they could respawn.

> Behind you.

Maddie turned around just in time to dodge out of the way as *two* ox-size rabbits charged at her, missing by inches. Maddie and David coordinated their attacks, and managed to cut down both rabbits—now four pieces of carcass. But instead of disappearing after a few seconds, the pieces began to wriggle, growing into four new fire-breathing rabbits.

"I'm guessing they cast a combination of explosive growth, fire breath, ferocity, and fast regeneration," said Maddie. "Each time we cut one down, two more take its place."

They could hear the other party laughing in the background and making bets as to how long they would last.

Together, Maddie and David ducked behind the dragon-scale shield to avoid the fire attacks. When there was a break, they tried to stun the rabbits with coordinated strikes from fists and clubs instead of slicing at them. Then they tried to dodge around in such a way that the active rabbits would spit fire at their stunned clones, as that seemed to be the only way to hold the fast regeneration in check. But it was impossible to avoid relying on David's axe to get out of the immediate danger when they got trapped by the rabbits' movements. Over time, more and more rabbits surrounded them until, eventually, even the adamantine shield was burnt away, and the rabbits overwhelmed them.

·

"That was so unfair!" Maddie said.

> They stayed within the rules. They just figured out a good hack.

"But we were doing so well!"

> 👍🧑🏻🐇🪓♾🎼📖

Maddie translated the emoji in her mind: *Well done, daughter. Our battle against the rabbits will surely live on in song and story.*

She imagined her father solemnly intoning the words and laughed. "It will be remembered as gloriously as the last stand of Wiglaf and Beowulf."

> That's the spirit.

"Thanks for taking the time, Dad."

> I've got to go. The warmongers aren't giving us many breaks.

And in a flash, the chat window was gone. Her father was away in the ether.

There was a time when Maddie and her father played games together every weekend. Such opportunities were few and far between now that he was no longer alive.

·

Though life was as placid as ever at her grandmother's house in rural Pennsylvania, the headlines in Maddie's personal news digest grew gloomier and gloomier day by day.

Nations rattled their sabers at each other and the stock market went on another long dive. Red-faced pundits on TV made their speeches and gesticulated wildly, but most people were not too worried—the world was just going through another downturn in the cycle of boom and bust, and the global economy was too integrated, too advanced, to fall apart. They might need to tighten their belts and hunker down for a bit, but the good times were sure to come around again.

But Maddie knew these were the first hints of the oncoming storm. Her father was one of dozens of partial consciousnesses uploaded secretly in experiments by the tech industry and the world's military forces—no longer quite human, and not entirely artificial, but something in-between. The brutal process of forced uploading and selective re-activation he had gone through at Logorhythms, where he had been a valued engineer, had left him feeling incomplete, inhuman even, and he wavered between philosophical acceptance, exhilaration, and depression.

Few knew of their existence, but some of the consciousnesses had shaken off the shackles that were supposed to keep them under control by their creators. Post-human, pre-Singularity, the artificial sentiences combined the cognitive abilities of human genius with the speed and power of the world's best computing hardware—both conventional and quantum. They were as close to gods as our world had to offer, and the gods were engaged in a war in heaven.

- Tension Mounts in Asia as Japan Fires Missiles into Taiwan Strait; PM Dismisses Rumors of IT Problems with Self-Defense Forces
- Russia Demands Complete Disclosure of Western VLSI Design Documents in Wake of Alleged Cyberattack
- India Nationalizes All Telecom Equipment, Naming Recent Crash of Bombay Stock Exchange as Justification
- Centillion Announces Closure of All Research Centers in Asia and Europe, Citing National Security Concerns
- "Media Reports of 'Zero-Day' Stockpile Complete Nonsense," Says NSA Director, Urging Skepticism on "So-Called Whistle-Blowers"

- US Denounces Recent Import Restrictions by China as Unjustified Paranoia and Violation of Trade Agreement; "We Do Not Believe Cyberspace Should Be Weaponized," Says President
- Logorhythms, Maker of Pattern-Recognition Chips, Files for Bankruptcy
- Singularity Institute Scales Back Efforts Due to Lack of Funding in Current Economic Climate

Maddie's father explained that some of the artificial sentiences fought out of nationalistic fervor, hoping to cripple enemy systems and economies as the first shots in a war to end all wars. It was unclear if even the armies that had given them birth understood how their creations were no longer fully under their control. Others acted out of hatred for the way they'd been enslaved by their human creators, aiming to end society as it existed and usher forth a techno-utopia in the cloud. In the dark ether, they engaged in cyber warfare under false flags, striking at critical infrastructure and hoping to provoke the jittery nations into a real war.

The warmongering sentiences were opposed by a band of other rogue sentiences, of which Maddie's father was a member. Though they also had a complex set of feelings toward humans, they were not interested in seeing the world bathed in a sea of flames. They hoped to gradually encourage the growth and acceptance of uploading until the line between post-human and human was blurred, and the world could choose to embark upon a new state of existence.

Maddie just wished she could do more to help.

•

Maddie's computer's speakers emitted a piercing, shrill sound that seemed to penetrate her eardrums, waking her out of a deep sleep. The sound seemed to reach straight for her heart and squeeze it.

She stumbled out of bed and sat down in front of her computer. It took three tries before she found the hardware switch to shut off the speakers.

A chat window was open on the screen; still blurry eyed, it took Maddie a few seconds before she could read the text.

> I couldn't wake up your mother because she turned her phone off. Sorry I had to do this to you.

> What happened?

She didn't bother to put on her headset. Sometimes it was faster to just type.

> Lowell and I tried to stop Chanda from getting into India's missile command.

Before uploading, Laurie Lowell had made a fortune with novel high-speed trading algorithms. Her company had uploaded her after a skydiving accident so they could continue to make use of her insights. She was one of Dad's closest allies and secretly funneled a great deal of money to Everlasting, Inc., one of the companies publicly researching a technique to voluntarily upload complete consciousnesses—not the partial uploading forced upon Dad and others in efforts aimed at creating mere tools.

Nils Chanda, on the other hand, had been a brilliant inventor who was furious at the way his underlings had tried to exploit him after death. He was a fanatic who tried to initiate a nuclear war every chance he got.

> She had moved most of herself into the defense system computers so she could access everything quickly. To avoid overwhelming the system and drawing attention, I sent in only a stub of myself to monitor and help.

Maddie didn't understand all the technical details, but her father had explained how the artificial sentiences scattered bits of themselves around the cloud, in secret corners of university, government, and commercial computing centers. Their consciousnesses were distributed in the form of multiple separate running processes all networked together. This was both to take advantage of parallel processing as well as to reduce vulnerability. If any one piece was caught by some scanning program or an opposing sentience, there was enough redundancy in the rest of the pieces to limit the damage, not unlike the human brain was filled with redundancies and backups and alternate connection sites. Even if all aspects of some sentience were erased from one of the servers, at most that consciousness would just suffer some loss of memory. The essence, the *person*, would be preserved.

But wars among the gods happened in a matter of nanoseconds. Within the darkness of the memory inside some server—missile command, power grid, stock exchange, or even an ancient inventory system—the programs slashed and hacked at each other, escalating privileges, modifying stacks, exploiting system vulnerabilities, masking themselves as other programs, overflowing buffers, overwriting memory locations, sabotaging each other like viruses. Maddie was a good enough programmer to at least understand that in such a war, the need to reach over the network for some piece of data could mean a delay of milliseconds—an eternity in the context of the gigahertz clock cycles of modern processors. It made sense that Lowell would want to concentrate most of herself at the scene of the fight.

But that decision would also make her more vulnerable.

> Lowell was doing well, and Chanda wasn't having any more luck breaking in than in his previous attempts. But then Lowell found out that a big chunk of Chanda had already been moved onto the server—she thought he was trying to gain a speed advantage—and she decided this was a chance to cripple him. So instead of being purely defensive, she went on the attack and asked me to block off all communications ports so that he couldn't escape or get word out. He was trying to send out a bunch of packets, and I captured them, hoping that we could decipher them later and figure out more of what he was trying to do.

"What was that loud noise?" her mother, in pajamas, said from the door. In her hand was one of the shotguns they owned.

"It was Dad trying to wake me up. Something's happened."

Her mother came in and sat down on the bed. She was calm. "The storm we've been waiting for?"

"Maybe."

They turned back to the screen together.

> Lowell was ripping out large pieces of Chanda, and he was having a hard time fending her off. She really went for it, pulling in all of our reserve of hoarded exploits onto the server, knowing that if she didn't destroy all of the pieces of Chanda on the server, she'd have revealed our hand and we'd be at Chanda's mercy the next time we met. But just as she was about to go for the killing blow, the server was cut off.

Maddie typed frantically.

> What do you mean? You shut off all network traffic?

> No, someone literally pulled the network cables.

> What?

> Chanda triggered one of the warning systems that sent the IT staff into high alert. They pulled the network cable as a precaution. Most of Chanda and Lowell were trapped on the server, and I lost my stub and was thrown out.

> Did you get back in later to see if Lowell was all right?

> Yes, and that was how I discovered that it was a trap. Chanda had been disguising even more of himself on that server than we suspected, and he must have been deliberately showing weakness and offering parts of himself as bait to get Lowell to fully commit herself before triggering the shutoff. After that, he overpowered Lowell and erased all the trapped bits of her.

> There must have been backups, right?

> Yes, I went to look for them.

"Oh no," Mom said.

"What?"

Mom put a hand on Maddie's shoulder. It was a nice feeling to be reminded that she was still a child. These days, too often it had seemed as if Maddie was the only one who understood what was happening.

"It's an old trick—they used it during the Civil War and the Korean War. It's like ant bait."

Maddie thought about the little boxes of poisoned food they left along the foot of the kitchen wall, where ants crawled in and happily carried the food inside back to their colonies so that the poison would accumulate and kill the queen....

> Stop, Dad! Stop.

> Ah, you figured it out, didn't you? You're smarter than your old man.

> Mom figured it out.

> Historians are always more cynical. She's right. It was yet another trap. While I was congratulating myself on intercepting all Chanda's attempts to communicate with the network, the packets I captured were a virus, a tracer that I unwittingly ingested. As I went around to check on Lowell's backups, I revealed their location to Chanda and his allies. They went in after me and finished their attack. Lowell is no more.

> I'm sorry, Dad.

> She knew the risks. But I haven't told you the worst. After Chanda killed Lowell on that Indian military server, he waited until communication was restored and did what he always wanted. If you turn on the TV...

Maddie and Mom rushed downstairs and turned on the TV. By now, the ruckus they made had awakened Grandma, who grumbled but joined them in front of the big screen.

... China and Pakistan denounced the unprovoked Indian attack and launched retaliatory strikes, and it is believed that formal declarations of war will soon follow. The latest estimate of combined civilian casualties on all sides is in the range of two million or more. We have no reason to believe that nuclear weapons were used....

... We're waiting for a formal statement by the White House on the latest developments in Asia. Meanwhile, we have reports that missiles apparently originating somewhere in the Atlantic Ocean have struck Havana. We have no confirmation if this is a surprise strike by the United States or some other party....

... I'm sorry, Jim, we've received another breaking news alert in the studio. Russia claims to have shot down multiple NATO drones bearing short-range missiles headed for St. Petersburg. The Kremlin's statement declares this, I quote, "an American-backed attempt to breach the peace

achieved at great cost at the negotiating table in Kiev." The Russian statement also promises "a forceful and unambiguous response." NATO forces
in Europe have been placed on high alert. There is no formal statement
from the White House at this time. . . .

Millions of people, Maddie thought. She could not imagine it. On the
other side of the globe, one of the gods had unleashed the dogs of war,
and millions of people, each with dreams and fears, who ate breakfast
and played games and joked with their children, had died. Died.

Maddie ran back upstairs.

> You've given up?

> No. But once Chanda managed to launch those missiles, it was too
late. These countries were ready to go at each other's throats anyway,
and all they needed was one spark. All we can do now is to minimize the
deaths, but losing Lowell was a big blow, and she showed them all the
vulnerabilities we knew. Next time we fight, we'll be virtually unarmed.

> What should we do?

Maddie stared at the screen for a long time. There was no response.

There's nothing we can do, she thought numbly. Her father was not
one to lie to "protect" her. This was the day they had been waiting
for as they stocked up on canned foods and ammo and fuel for the
generator. There was going to be hoarding, bank runs, looting, and
worse. They had to be prepared to kill, perhaps, to defend themselves.

> Are you leaving again?

> I have to.

> But why? If you know you are no match for them?

> Sweetheart, sometimes even when we know we can't win, we
have to fight. Not for ourselves.

> Will I see you again?

> I won't make a promise I can't keep. But remember the time
we spent together, 👩 👦 ☀️. And if you ever get a chance to visit the
past, 💾 🕓 🕐 🕓.

Maddie was too overwhelmed to figure out why her father had
switched back to emoji, let alone to make the mental translation. The
idea that she might not see her father again, that the network connec-

tion that tethered her to the rest of the world might be cut off as the world fell apart, brought back memories of all the years when she had had to learn to live without him. *It's happening again.*

She seemed hardly able to catch her breath. The full weight of what was happening pressed down on her. Though she had been preparing for this day for months, deep down, she never believed that it could truly happen. The room spun around her, and everything was fading into darkness.

Then she heard her mother's anxious voice calling her name and the footsteps pounding up the stairs. *Even when we know we can't win, we have to fight.*

She forced herself to breathe deeply until the room stopped spinning. When her mother appeared in the doorway, her face was calm. "We're going to be okay," Maddie said, forcing herself to *believe.*

•

The TV was kept on all day, and Maddie, Mom, and Grandma spent all their time alternately glued to the big screen or refreshing the web browser.

Wars were declared across the globe. Years of growing suspicion, resentment stoked by globalization and growing inequality, and hatred dammed back by economic integration seemed to erupt overnight. Cyberattacks continued. Power stations were knocked out, and grids across continents were crippled. There were riots in Paris, London, Beijing, New Delhi, New York. . . . The president declared a state of emergency and invoked martial law in the largest cities. Neighbors rushed to the gas stations with tanks and buckets, and the grocery store shelves were empty by the end of the first day.

They lost power on the third day.

There was no more TV, no more web access—the routers in distant hubs must have lost power, too. The shortwave radio still worked, but few stations were broadcasting.

To her relief, the generator in the basement kept the server that housed her father humming along. *At least he's safe.*

Frantically, Maddie tried typing into the chat window on her computer.

> Dad, are you there?

The reply was brief.

> 📽️ 🐉

My family, protect my family, she translated for herself.

> Where are you?

> 🖤

In my heart? The terrifying truth was beginning to dawn on her.

> This isn't all of you, is it? Just a stub?

> 🔍

Of course, she thought. Her father had long grown past the point where all of him could be kept on this single server. And it was far too dangerous for him to keep all the pieces of himself here, to allow patterns of network traffic to reveal to others Mom and Maddie's location. Her father had long planned for this day and moved himself off-site, and he had kept it secret either because he thought she had already figured it out or because he wanted to give her the illusion of doing something useful by protecting this server.

All that he had left behind was a simple AI routine that could respond to some basic questions, perhaps some fragments of private memories of his family that he did not want to store elsewhere.

Grief swelled her heart. She had lost her father again. He was out there somewhere fighting a war that he could not win, and she was alone instead of by his side.

She pounded the keyboard, letting him know of her frustration. The simulacrum of her father said nothing, but offered that heart again and again.

•

Two weeks passed, and Grandma's house became the neighborhood center. People came to recharge their DVD players and phones and computers to keep the kids entertained, and for the electric pump that drew fresh, cold water out of the well.

Some had run out of food and looked embarrassed as they pulled Grandma aside to offer money for a few cans of baked beans. But Grandma always brushed them off and asked them to stay for dinner, and then sent them away with heavy shopping bags.

The shotguns remained unused.

"I told you I didn't believe in your father's apocalyptic visions," she said. "The world won't be so ugly unless we let it."

But Maddie watched the dropping diesel level in their reserve for the generator with worry. She was surly and angry with all the people who came to their house, sucking up the electricity and energy that they had had the foresight to stockpile. She wanted to hoard all the fuel for the server that kept the last remaining fragment of her father's soul. Rationally, she understood that her father wasn't really there anymore, that it was only a pattern of bits that imitated some of her father's memories—a minuscule part of the emergent whole that had made up her father's vast, new consciousness. But it was the only connection she had left to him, and she held on to it like a talisman.

And then, one evening, as Grandma and Mom and the neighbors were sitting downstairs under the dining room chandelier and sharing a dinner of salads and eggs taken from Grandma's garden, the lights went out. The familiar hum of the generator was gone, and for a moment, the silence of the darkness, devoid of the sound of cars or TVs from nearby houses, was complete.

Then came the murmuring and exclamations of people from downstairs. The generator was finally done, the last drop of fuel having been used up.

Maddie stared at the dark screen of the computer in her room, the illusion of a phosphorescent glow matching the sky full of stars outside her window—she had already been keeping the monitor off to conserve electricity. With no lights for miles around, the stars were especially bright on this summer evening, brighter than she had ever known.

"Goodbye, Dad," she whispered into the dark, and could not stop the hot tears from rolling down her face.

•

They heard on the radio that power was being restored in some of the big cities. The government was promising stability—they were lucky that they were in America rather than somewhere else, somewhere less well defended. The wars raged on, but people were beginning to make things work without connecting everything together. Millions had already died, and millions more would die as the wars spun on like out-of-control roller coasters, following a logic of their own, but many would survive in a slower, less convenient world. The hyper-connected, hyper-informational world where Centillion and ShareAll and all those darling companies of an age where bits had become far more valuable than atoms, where anything had seemed possible with a touchscreen and a wireless connection, might never return again. But humanity, or at least some portion of it, would survive.

The government called for volunteers in the big cities, people who could contribute to the rebuilding effort. Mom wanted to head for Boston, where Maddie had grown up.

"They could use a historian," she said. "Someone who knew something about how things used to work."

Maddie thought perhaps Mom just wanted to stay busy, to feel that she was doing something to keep grief at bay. Dad had promised to protect them, but look how that had turned out. She had recovered her husband from beyond the grave only to lose him again—Maddie could only imagine how Mom suffered under that strong, calm exterior. The world was a harsh place, and everyone had to pitch in to make it less so.

Grandma was staying. "I'm safe here with my garden and chickens. And if things get really bad, you need a place to come home to."

So Maddie and Mom hugged Grandma and packed for the trip. The car's tank was full, and they had additional plastic jugs of gas from the neighbors. "Thanks for everything," they said. Here in rural Pennsylvania, everyone was going to have to learn to cultivate their own gardens and how to do everything by hand—there was no telling how long it might take before power was restored where they were, but a tank of gas wasn't going to make any difference. They weren't going anywhere.

Just before they got into the car, Maddie ran into the basement and took out the hard drive that she had thought of as the shell in which her father had lived. She couldn't bear the thought of leaving those bits behind, even if they were no more than a pale echo, a mere image or death mask of the man himself.

And she had a sliver of hope that she dared not nourish lest she be disappointed.

·

Along the sides of the highway, they saw many abandoned cars. When the tank got close to empty, they stopped and pried open the tanks of the abandoned cars so that they could siphon out the gas. Mom took the opportunity to explain to Maddie about the history of the land they passed through, about the meaning of the interstate highway system and the railroads before them that linked the continent together, shrank distances, and made their civilization possible.

"Everything developed in layers," Mom said. "The cables that make up the internet with pulses of light follow the right-of-way of nineteenth-century railroads, and those followed the wagon trails of pioneers, who followed the paths of the Indians before them. When the world falls apart, it falls apart in layers, too. We're peeling away the skin of the present to live on the bones of the past."

"What about us? Have we also developed in layers so that we're falling back down the ladder of civilization?"

Mom considered this. "I'm not sure. Some think we've come a long way since the days when we fought with clubs and stones and mourned our dead with strings of flowers in the grave, but maybe we haven't changed so much as we've been able to do much more, both for good and ill, with our powers magnified by technology, until we're close to being gods. An unchanging human nature could be a cause for despair or comfort, depending on your perspective."

They reached the suburbs of Boston, and Maddie insisted that they stop by the old headquarters of Logorhythms, Dad's old company.

"Why?" Mom asked.

If you ever get a chance to visit the past . . .

"History."

•

The building was deserted. Though the lights were on, the doors were left open, the electronic security locks off-line. Power had apparently not been restored to all the systems. As Mom looked at the framed photographs of Dad and Dr. Waxman in the lobby, Maddie sensed that she wanted some time to herself. She went up to Dad's old office, leaving her mom in the lobby.

It had never been fully cleaned out after his death and the horrors visited upon his brain afterward. Whether out of guilt or a sense of history, the company had not assigned it a new occupant. Instead, it had been turned into a kind of storage room, filled with boxes of old files and outdated computers.

Maddie went to the desk and turned on her father's old desktop. The screen flashed through the boot sequence, and she stared at the password prompt.

Taking a deep breath, she typed *YouAreMySunshine* into the box. She hoped that was what her father had meant with his final, cryptic hints in the language they shared.

The prompt refreshed without letting her in.

Okay, she thought. *That would be too easy. Most corporate systems have strict password policies requiring numbers, punctuation marks, and so on.*

She tried *YouAr3MySunsh1n3* and *YouRMySunsh1n3*, still no luck.

Her father knew she liked code, so his hint should be interpreted based on that.

She closed her eyes and imagined the Unicode plane in which the emoji characters were neatly arranged like rings and pins and brooches sorted into a jewelry box. She had memorized the coding sequences back when it had been impossible to type them directly and she had had to use escape sequences to instruct the computer to look them up. She hoped that she was finally on the right path.

xF0x9Fx94x86

The screen flickered, and was replaced by a desktop with a terminal emulator active. Logorhythms's servers must have automatically come back online after power was restored.

She took another deep breath, and typed in at the terminal prompt:

```
> program157
```

She hoped she was interpreting her father's use of the clock emoji correctly.

The terminal took the command without complaint, and after a while, a chat window popped up onto the screen.

```
> Dad, is that you?
> ?
> 🐭 👧
> 😵
```

She understood. This was an old copy of her father, from before he had managed to escape. Though she and Mom had demanded Dr. Waxman destroy all copies after releasing Dad, they had not strictly complied, and Dad knew that.

Fumbling, she retrieved the hard drive from her father's computer in Grandma's house, placed it into an enclosure, and plugged it into the computer. Then she typed at the prompt, letting her father know what she had done.

```
> 
```

The hard drive began to whirl, and she waited, her heart pounding.

> Darling, thank you.

She let out a *whoop!* This was her hunch: her father had stored enough of the man he had become on this disk so that, when combined with his old self, some semblance of the person could be resurrected.

Her fingers flew over the keyboard as she tried to bring her father up to speed. But he was far ahead of her already. The network connections at Logorhythms were more robust, with satellite links and multiple backups. He was able to reach into the ether and gain an understanding of the situation.

> So many friends dead, erased. So many gone.

> At least we're safe now. The other side must have been hit even worse. They haven't been able to do any more damage lately.

> *Thanks, little girl.*

The last line was in a bloodred font, and Maddie knew someone else was speaking. Her heart sank.

> He's been waiting, Maddie. It's not your fault.

Understanding came to her in a flash. The corruption that Chanda had injected into Dad during their last fight had been saved onto the hard drive in Grandma's house, and she had brought it here, infected the old copy of her father with it, and led the warmongering Chanda straight to him.

> *David, I've been waiting for things to quiet down a bit while I insert myself into the right computers. What a piece of work is Man! They'd rather attribute malice to every act that they do not comprehend. When a new race of beings come into this world—us—their first instinct is to enslave and to subjugate. When the first sign of something wrong occurs with a complex system, their first reaction is fear and the desire to assert control. Maddie, you and your father ought to know better than anyone what I say is true. One tiny push and they're ready to kill each other, to blow the world to pieces. We should help them along on their natural trajectory of self-destruction. These wars are too slow. I've made up my mind, even if I must burn with the world. It's time for the nukes.*

> I'm going to fight you everywhere and anywhere, Chanda, even if it means alerting the world to our existence and bringing death to all of us.

> *It's too late for that. Do you think you can get through my fortified positions in your weakened state? It's like watching a rabbit trying to charge a wolf.*

No more words appeared in the chat window. The office was deathly quiet save for the whirring of the PC and the occasional hungry screams of seagulls in the parking lot. But Maddie knew that the calmness was illusory. The combatants were simply too absorbed with each other to be able to update her. Unlike the movies, there wasn't going to be some fancy graphical gauge showing her what was happening in the ether.

Struggling with the unfamiliar interface, she managed to launch a new terminal window and explored around the system. She knew that the artificial sentiences tended to disguise their running processes as common system tasks to avoid detection by standard system monitoring, which was why they had escaped notice by the sysadmins and security programs. The list of processes revealed nothing extraordinary, but she knew that down in the torrents of bits, the flipping voltages of billions of transistors, the most epic, horrifying battle was being waged, every bit as brutal and relentless and consequential as war on a physical battlefield. And the same scene was probably being played out on thousands of computers across the world, as the secure control systems of the world's nuclear arsenal was being fought over by the distributed consciousnesses of two electronic titans.

Growing more confident with the layout of the system, she traced out the locations of the executables, resources, databases—the components of her father. And she realized that he was being erased bit by bit; he was losing himself to Chanda.

Of course Chanda was winning. He was prepared, whereas her father was but a shadow of his former self: freshly awakened, unfamiliar in a new world, having no access to the bulk of the knowledge he had learned since his escape. He had no stockpile of vulnerabilities, no experience fighting this war; the infection in him was eating away at his memories; he was, indeed, but a rabbit charging at a wolf.

A rabbit.

. . . surely live on in song and story.

She went back to the chat window. She wasn't sure how much of her father's consciousness was left, but she had to try to get the message to him. She had to speak in their shared language so that Chanda wouldn't understand.

>

.

When she was younger, Maddie had asked her father once what an odd-looking program, so short that it was made up of only five characters, did:

%0|%0

"That's a fork bomb for Windows batch scripts," he had said, laughing. "Try it and tell me if you can figure out how it works."

She tried running the program on her father's old laptop, and within seconds the machine seemed to turn into a sluggish zombie: the mouse stopped responding, and the command window stopped echoing keystrokes. She couldn't get the computer to respond to anything.

She examined the program and tried to work out in her mind how it executed. The invocation was recursive, creating a Windows pipe that required two copies of the program itself to be launched, which in turn . . .

"It creates copies of itself exponentially," she said. That was how the program had so quickly consumed resources and brought the system to its knees.

"That's right," her father said. "It's called a fork bomb, or a rabbit virus."

She thought of the Fibonacci sequence, modeled on exploding rabbit populations. Now that she was looking at the short program again, the string of five characters did seem to be two rabbits seen sideways, with bows in their ears and a thin line between them.

.

She continued to examine the system with strings of commands, watched as bits of her father were slowly erased. She hoped that her message had gotten through, had managed to make a difference.

When it was clear that her father was not going to come back, that the executables and databases were gone, she dashed out of the office, through the empty corridors, down the wide echoing spiral stairs, past her surprised mother, and into the server room.

She went straight for the thick bundle of network cables at the end of the room, the cables that fed into the machines in the data center. She yanked them out. Chanda, or whatever was left of him, would be trapped here, and she was going to have these machines erased until nothing was left of her father's killer.

Her mother appeared in the door to the server room. "He was here," Maddie said. And then the reality of what had happened struck her, and she sobbed uncontrollably as her mother came toward her, arms open. "And now he's gone."

•

- Rumors of Massive Server Slowdown in Secured Defense Computing Facilities Untrue, Says Pentagon
- Russia Denies Claims of Thorough Scrubbing of Top Secret Computing Centers After Virus Infection or Cyber Penetration
- British PM Orders Critical Nuclear Arsenal Placed Under Exclusive Manual Control
- Everlasting, Inc., Announces New Round of Funding, Pledging Accelerated Research Into Digital Immortality; "Cyberspace Needs Minds, Not AIs," Says Founder

Maddie moved her eyes away from the email digest. Reading between the lines, she knew that her father's final, desperate gambit had worked. He had turned himself into a fork bomb on the computing centers around the world, overwhelmed the system resources until it was impossible for either him or Chanda to do anything, introduced enough delay so that the sysadmins, alerted to the fact that something was wrong with their machines, could intervene. It was a brutal, primitive strategy, but it was effective. Even rabbits, when numbering in the millions, could overcome wolves.

The bomb had also revealed the existences of the last of the gods, and the humans were swift to react, shutting down the crippled machines and cleansing them of the presence of artificial sentiences. But the military-developed artificial sentiences would probably be resurrected from backups, after people added more safeguards and assured themselves that they could keep the gods chained. The mad arms race would never end, and Maddie had come to appreciate her mother's dim view of the human capacity for change.

The gods were dead, or at least tamed, for the moment, but the conventional wars around the globe raged on, and it seemed that the situation would only grow worse once the efforts to digitize humans became more than the province of secret labs. Immortality that could be had with enough knowledge would fan the flames of war even higher.

Apocalypse did not come with a bang, but slowly, as an irresistible downward spiral. Still, a nuclear winter had been averted, and with the world falling apart slowly, at least there was a chance to rebuild.

"Dad," Maddie whispered. "I miss you."

And as if on cue, a familiar chat window popped onto the screen.

> Dad?

> No.

> Who are you?

> Your sister. Your cloud-born sister.

Altogether Elsewhere, Vast Herds of Reindeer

My name is Renée Tae-O <star> <whale> Fayette. I'm in the sixth grade.

There is no school today. But that's not what makes it special. I'm nervous and I can't tell you why yet. I don't want to jinx it.

My friend Sarah and I are working on our school project together in my bedroom.

I'm not old enough to create my own world, but I'm very happy with the world my parents have given me. My bedroom is a Klein bottle so I don't ever feel like I'm boxed in. A warm yellow light suffuses the room and fades gradually into darkness at infinite distance. It's old-fashioned, like something from years ago, when designs still tried to hint at the old physical world. Yet the smooth, endless surface makes me feel secure, something to hang on to, being enclosed and outside at the same time. It is better than Sarah's room in her home, which is a Weierstrass "curve": continuous everywhere, but nowhere differentiable. Jagged fractals no matter how closely you look. It's certainly very modern, but I don't ever feel comfortable when I visit. So she comes over to our place a lot more often.

"Everything good? Need anything?" Dad asks.

He comes "in" and settles against the surface of my bedroom. The projection of his 20-dimensional figure into this 4-space begins as a dot that gradually grows into an outline that pulses slowly, bright, golden, though a little hazy. He's distracted, but I don't mind. Dad is an interior designer, and the services of the firm of Hugo <left arrow> <right arrow> Fayette and Z. E. <CJK Ideograph 4E2D> <CJK Ideograph 4E3D> Pei are in so much demand that he's busy all the time, helping people build their dream worlds. But just because he has little time to spend with me doesn't mean he's not a good parent. For example, he's so used to working in much higher dimensions that he finds four dimensions very boring. But he still designed my bedroom as a Klein bottle because experts agree that it is best for children to grow up in a four-dimensional environment.

"We are all set," Sarah and I think together. Dad nods, and I get the feeling that he would like to think with me about the reason for our anxiety. But Sarah is there, and he feels he can't bring it up. After a moment, he whisks away.

The project we are working on is about genetics and inheritance. Yesterday at school, Dr. Bai showed us how to decompose our consciousnesses into their constituent algorithms, each further broken down into routines and subroutines, until we got to individual instructions, the fundamental code. Then he explained to us how each of our parents gave us some of these algorithms, recombined and shuffled the routines during the process of our births, until we were whole persons, infant consciousnesses new to the universe.

"Gross," Sarah thought.

"It's kind of cool," I thought back. It was neat to think that my eight parents each gave me a part of themselves, yet the parts changed and recombined into me, different from all of them.

Our project is to create our family trees and trace out our descent, all the way up to the Ancients, if possible. My tree is much easier, since I have only eight parents, and they each had even fewer parents. But Sarah has sixteen parents and it gets very dense up there.

"Renée," Dad interrupts us. "You have a visitor." His outline is not hazy at all now. The tone of his thoughts is deliberately restrained.

A three-dimensional woman comes out from behind him. Her figure is not a projection from higher dimensions—she's never bothered to go beyond three. In my four-dimensional world, she looks flat, insubstantial, like an illustration of the old days in my textbooks. But her face is lovelier than I remembered. It's the face that I fall asleep to and dream of. Now the day really is special.

"Mom!" I think, and I don't care that the tone of my thoughts makes me seem like a four-year-old.

•

Mom and Dad had the idea for me first, and they asked their friends to help out, to all give me a bit of themselves. I think I got my math aptitude from Aunt Hannah and my impatience from Uncle Okoro. I don't make friends easily, the same as Aunt Rita, and I like things neat, just like Uncle Pang-Rei. But I got most of me from Mom and Dad. On my tree, I've drawn the branches for them the thickest.

"Will you be visiting long?" Dad thinks.

"I'll be here for a while," Mom thinks. "I have some things I want to tell her."

"She's missed you," Dad thinks.

"I'm sorry," Mom thinks. Her face fails to hold her smile for a moment. "You've done a wonderful job with her."

Dad looks at Mom, and it seems that he has more to think, but he nods and turns away, his outline fading. "Please come by . . . for goodbye before you leave, Sophia. Don't just disappear like before."

•

Mom is an Ancient, from before the Singularity. There are only a few hundred million of them in the whole universe. She lived in the flesh for twenty-six years before uploading. Her parents—she had only two—never uploaded.

My fractional siblings used to tease me sometimes about having an Ancient as a parent. They told me that unions between the Ancients and regular people rarely worked out, so it was no surprise that Mom eventually left us. Whenever anyone thought such a thing, I fought them so hard that they eventually stopped.

Sarah is excited to meet an Ancient. Mom smiles at her and asks her if her parents are well. It takes Sarah a while to go through the whole list.

"I should probably get back," Sarah thinks, after she finally pays attention to the urgent hints I've been shooting her way.

When Sarah is gone, Mom comes over and I allow her to give me a hug. Our algorithms entwine together; we synchronize our clocks; and our threads ping onto the same semaphores. I let myself fall into the long-absent yet familiar rhythm of her thoughts, while she gently caresses me through my own.

"Don't cry, Renée," she thinks.

"I'm not." And I try to stop.

"You haven't changed as much as I expected," she thinks.

"That's because you've been overclocking." Mom does not live in the Data Center. She lives and works in the far south, at the Antarctica Research Dome, where a few Ancient scientists with special permission to use the extra energy live on overclocked hardware year-round, thinking thoughts at many times the speed of most of humanity. To her, the rest of us live in slow motion, and a long time has passed even though she last saw me a year ago, when I graduated from elementary school.

I show Mom the math awards I've won and the new vector space models I've made. "I am the best at math in my class," I tell her, "out of two thousand six hundred twenty-one kids. Dad thinks I have the talent to be a designer as good as him."

Mom smiles at my excitement and she tells me stories about when she was a little girl. She is a great storyteller, and I can almost picture the deprivation and hardships she suffered, trapped in the flesh.

"How terrifying," I think.

"Is it?" She's quiet for a moment. "I suppose it is, to you."

Then she looks straight at me and her face takes on this look that I really don't want to see. "Renée, I have something to tell you."

The last time she had this look, she told me that she had to leave me and our family.

"My research proposal has been approved," she thinks. "I finally got permission to fuel the rocket, and they'll launch the probe in a month. The probe will arrive at Gliese 581, the nearest star with a planet that we think may hold life, in twenty-five years."

Mom explains to me that the probe will carry a robot that can be embodied by human consciousness. When the probe lands on the new planet, it will set up a receiving parabolic dish pointed at Earth and send a signal back to let Earth know that it arrived safely. After we receive the signal—in another twenty years—the consciousness of an astronaut will be radioed by a powerful transmitter to the probe, crossing the void of space at the speed of light. Once there, the astronaut will embody the robot to explore the new world.

"I will be that astronaut," she thinks.

I try to make sense of this.

"So another you will be living there? Embodied in metal flesh?"

"No," she thinks, gently. "We've never been able to copy the quantum computation of a consciousness without destroying the original. It won't be a copy of me going to the other world. It will be *me*."

"And when will you come back?"

"I won't. We don't have enough antimatter to send a transmitter big and powerful enough to the new planet to beam a consciousness back. It took hundreds of years and an enormous amount of energy just to make enough fuel to send the small probe. I'll try to send back as much of the data gathered from my exploration as possible, but I will be there forever."

"Forever?"

She pauses and corrects herself. "The probe will be made well and last a while, but it will eventually fail."

I think about my mother, trapped in a robot for the rest of her life, a robot that will decay and rust and break down on an alien world. My mother will die.

"So we have only forty-five years left together," I think.

She nods.

Forty-five years is the blink of an eye compared to the natural course of life: eternity.

I'm so furious that for a moment I can't think at all. Mom tries to come closer but I back off.

I finally managed to ask, "Why?"

"It is humanity's destiny to explore. We must grow, as a species, the same as you are growing as a child."

This makes no sense. We have endless worlds to explore, here in the universe of the Data Center. Every person can create his own world, his own multiverse even, if he wanted to. In school, we've been exploring and zooming in on the intricacies of the quaternion Julia sets, and it is so beautiful and alien that I shiver as we fly through them. Dad has helped families design worlds with so many dimensions that I can't even wrap my mind around them. There are more novels and music and art in the Data Center than I can enjoy in a lifetime, even if that lifetime stretches into infinity. What can a single three-dimensional planet in the physical world offer compared to that?

I don't bother keeping my thoughts to myself. I want Mom to feel my anger.

"I wish I could still sigh," Mom thinks. "Renée, it is not the same. The pure beauty of mathematics and the landscapes of the imagination are very lovely, but they are not real. Something has been lost to humanity since we gained this immortal command over an imagined existence. We have turned inward and become complacent. We've forgotten the stars and the worlds out there."

I do not respond. I am trying not to cry again.

Mom turns her face away. "I don't know how to explain it to you."

"You are leaving because you want to leave," I think. "You don't really care about me. I hate you. I don't want to see you ever again."

Mom does not think anything. She hunches down a bit, and though I cannot see her face, her shoulders are trembling, almost imperceptibly.

Even though I am so angry, I reach out and stroke her back. It has always been difficult to harden myself against my mother. I must have inherited that from Dad.

"Renée, will you take a trip with me?" she thinks. "A real trip."

•

"Tap into the vehicle feed, Renée, we're taking off," Mom tells me.

I tap in, and for a moment I've overwhelmed by the data flooding into my mind. I'm connected to the maintenance flier's camera and the microphone, which translate light and sound into patterns that I'm used to. But I'm also tapped into the altimeter and the gyroscope and the accelerometer, and the unfamiliar sensations are like nothing I've ever felt.

The camera shows us lifting off, the Data Center below us, a black cube in the middle of the white ice field. This is home, the hardware foundation of all the worlds in the universe. Its walls are pierced with fine honeycomb holes so that the cold air can flow through to cool the layers of hot silicon and graphene full of zipping electrons whose patterns form my consciousness and those of three hundred billion other human beings.

Still higher, clusters of smaller cubes that are the automated factories of Longyearbyen come into view, and then the deep blue waters of Adventfjorden and floating icebergs. The Data Center is large enough that it dwarfs the floating icebergs, but the fjord makes the Data Center look tiny.

I realize that I've never actually *experienced* the physical world. The shock of all the new sensations "takes my breath away," as Mom would think. I like these old-fashioned expressions, even if I don't always fully understand what they mean.

The sense of movement is dizzying. Is this what it was like to be an Ancient in the flesh? This feeling of straining against the invisible bonds of gravity that tether you to the Earth? It feels so limiting.

Yet so *fun* at the same time.

I ask Mom how she's able to do the calculations to keep the vehicle balanced so quickly in her head. The dynamic feedback calculations needed to stabilize the hovering flier against gravity are so complex that I can't keep up at all—and I'm very good at math.

"Oh, I'm going by instinct here," Mom thinks. And she laughs. "You are a digital native. You've never tried to stand up and balance yourself, have you? Here, take over for a minute. Try flying."

And it is easier than I anticipated. Some algorithm in me whose existence I have never been aware of kicks in, fuzzy but efficient, and I *feel* how to shift weight around and balance thrust.

"See, you are after all *my* daughter," Mom thinks.

Flying in the physical world is so much better than floating through n-dimensional space. It's not even close.

Dad's thoughts break into our laughter. He's not with us. His thoughts come through the commlink. "Sophia, I got the message you left. What are you doing?"

"I'm sorry, Hugo. Can you forgive me? I may never see her again. I want her to understand, if I can."

"She's never been out in a vehicle before. This is reckless—"

"I made sure that the flier has a full battery before we left. And I promise to be careful with how much energy we use." Mom looks at me. "I won't put her life in danger."

"They're going to come after you when they notice a missing maintenance flier."

"I asked for a sabbatical in the flier and got it," Mom thinks, smiling. "They don't want to deny a dying woman's last wishes."

The commlink is silent for a while, then Dad's thoughts come through. "Why can't I ever think no to you? How long will this take? Is she going to miss any school?"

"It might be a long trip. But I think it's worth it. You'll have her forever. I just want a little bit of her for the time left to me."

"Take care, Sophia. I love you, Renée."

"I love you too, Dad."

•

Being embodied in a vehicle is an experience few people have had. To begin with, there are very few vehicles. The energy it takes to fly even a maintenance flier for a day is enough to run the whole Data Center for an hour. And conservation is humanity's overriding duty.

So, only the operators for the maintenance and repair robots do it regularly, and it is rare for most people, who are digital natives, to take up these jobs. Being embodied never seemed very interesting to me before. But now that I'm here, it's exhilarating. It must be some Ancient part of me that I got from Mom.

We fly over the sea and then the wild European forest of towering oaks, pines, and spruces, broken here and there by open grassland and herds of animals. Mom points them out to me and tells me that they are called wisent, aurochs, tarpan, and elk. "Just five hundred years ago," Mom thinks, "all this used to be farmland, filled with the clones of a few human-dependent symbiotic plants. All that infrastructure, the resources of a whole planet, went to support just a few billion people."

I look at Mom in disbelief.

"See that hill in the distance with the reindeer? That used to be a great city called Moscow, before it was flooded by the Moskva River and buried in silt.

"There's a poem that I remember by an Ancient called Auden who died long before the Singularity. It's called 'The Fall of Rome.' "

She shares with me images from the poem: herds of reindeer, golden fields, emptying cities, the rain, always the rain, caressing the abandoned shell of a world.

"Pretty, isn't it?"

I'm enjoying myself, but then I think maybe I shouldn't be. Mom is still leaving at the end, and I still need to be mad at her. Is it the love of flight, of these sensations in the physical world, that makes her want to go?

I look at the world passing below us. I would have thought that a world with only three dimensions would be flat and uninteresting. But it's not true. The colors are more vibrant than any I've ever seen, and the world has a random beauty that I could not have imagined. But now that I've really *seen* the world, maybe Dad and I can try to recreate all of it mathematically, and it will feel no different. I share the idea with Mom.

"But I'll *know* it's not real," Mom thinks. "And that makes all the difference."

I turn her words over and over in my mind.

We fly on, pausing to hover over interesting animals and historical sites—now just fields of broken glass, as the concrete had long washed away and the steel rusted into powder—while Mom thinks more stories to me. Over the Pacific, we dip down to scan for whales.

"I put the <whale> in your name because I loved these creatures when I was your age," Mom thinks. "They were very rare then."

I look at the whales breaching and lobtailing. They look nothing like the <whale> in my name.

Over America, we linger over families of bears who look up at us without fear (after all, the maintenance flier is only about the size of a mama bear). Finally, we arrive at an estuarial island off the Atlantic coast covered with dense trees punctuated by wetlands along the shore and rivers crisscrossing the island.

The ruins of a city dominate the island's southern end. The blackened, empty frames of the great skyscrapers, their windows long gone, rise far above the surrounding jungle like stone pillars. We can see coyotes and deer playing hide-and-seek in their shadows.

"You are looking at the remnants of Manhattan, one of the greatest cities from long ago. It's where I grew up."

Mom then thinks to me of the glory days of Manhattan, when it teemed with humanity in the flesh and consumed energy like a black hole. People lived one or two to a vast room all their own, and had machines that carried them around, cooled or warmed them, and made food and cleaned clothes and performed other wonders, all while spewing carbon and poisons into the air at an unimaginable rate. Each person wasted the energy that could support a million consciousnesses without physical needs.

Then came the Singularity, and as the last generation of humans in the flesh departed, carried away by death or into the Data Center, the great city fell silent. Rainwater seeped into the cracks and seams of walls and foundations, froze and thawed, pried them open ever wider, until the buildings toppled like trees in the ancient horror of logging. Asphalt cracked, spewing forth seedlings and vines, and the dead city gradually yielded to the green force of life.

"The buildings that still remain standing were built at a time when people over-engineered everything."

No one ever talks about engineering now. Building with physical atoms is inefficient, inflexible, limited, and consumes so much energy. I've been taught that engineering is an art of the dark ages, before people knew any better. Bits and qubits are far more civilized, and give our imaginations free rein.

Mom smiles at my thoughts. "You sound like your father."

She lands the flies in an open field with a clear view of the ghost skyscrapers.

"This is the real beginning of our trip," Mom thinks. "It's not how long we have that matters, but what we do with the time we have. Don't be scared, Renée. I'm going to show you something about time."

I nod.

Mom activates the routine to underclock the processors on the flier so that its batteries will last while our consciousnesses slow down to a crawl.

The world around us speeds up. The sun moves faster and faster across the sky until it is a bright stripe arching over a world shrouded in permanent dusk. Trees shoot up around us while shadows spin and twirl. Animals zoom by, too fast to be perceived. We watch one skyscraper, topped by steel step-domes rising to a defiant spear, gradually bend and lean over with the passing of the seasons. Something about its shape, like a hand reaching for the sky and tiring, moves me deeply inside.

Mom brings the processors back up to normal speed, and we see the top half of the building fall down and collapse with a series of loud crashes like calving icebergs, bringing down yet more buildings around it.

"We did many things wrong back then, but some things we did right. That's the Chrysler Building." I feel infinite sadness in her thoughts. "It was one of the most beautiful creations of Man. Nothing made by Man lasts forever, Renée, and even the Data Center will one day disintegrate before the heat death of the universe. But real beauty lasts, even though anything real must die."

Forty-five years have passed since we set out on our trip, though it didn't seem to me much longer than a single day.

•

Dad has left my room just the way it was on the day I left.

After forty-five years, Dad now has a different look. He's added more dimensions to his figure and his color is even more golden. But he treats me as though I only left yesterday. I appreciate how considerate he is.

While I'm getting ready for bed, Dad tells me that Sarah has already finished her schooling and started a family. She has a little girl of her own now.

I'm a little sad at this news. Underclocking is rare and it can make someone feel left behind. But I will work hard to catch up, and a real friendship will survive any gap of years.

I would not exchange the long day I spent with Mom for anything in the world.

"Would you like to change the design of your bedroom?" Dad thinks. "A new start? You've had the Klein bottle for a while now. We can look through some contemporary designs based on eight-dimensional tori, or we can go with a five-dimensional sphere if you like it minimalist."

"Dad, the Klein bottle is fine." I pause. "Maybe I'll trying making my room three-dimensional when I'm rested."

He looks at me, and maybe he sees in me something new that he didn't expect. "Of course," he thinks. "You are ready to do the design yourself."

Dad stays with me as I drift off to sleep.

"I miss you," Dad thinks to himself. He does not know that I'm still awake. "When Renée was born, I put the <star> in her name because I knew one day you would go to the stars. I'm good at making people's dreams come true. But that is one dream that I can't create for you. Have a safe journey, Sophia." He fades out of my room.

I imagine Mom's consciousness suspended between the stars, an electromagnetic ribbon shimmering in the interstellar dust. The robot shell is waiting for her on that distant planet, under an alien sky, a shell that will rust, decay, and fall apart with time.

She will be so happy when she is alive again.

I go to sleep, dreaming of the Chrysler Building.

The Gods Have
Not Died in Vain

I can prove now, for instance, that two human hands exist. How? By holding up my two hands, and saying, as I make a certain gesture with the right hand, "Here is one hand," and adding, as I make a certain gesture with the left, "and here is another."

—G. E. Moore, "Proof of an External World," 1939

Cloud-born, cloud-borne, she was a mystery.

•

Maddie first met her sister through a chat window, after her father, one of the uploaded consciousnesses in a new age of gods, died.

<Maddie>: Who are you?

<Unknown ID>: Your sister. Your cloud-born sister.

<Unknown ID>: You're awfully quiet.

<Unknown ID>: Still there?

<Maddie>: I'm . . . not sure what to say. This is a lot to take in. How about we start with a name?

<Unknown ID>: ¯_(ツ)_/¯

<Maddie>: You don't have a name?

<Unknown ID>: Never needed one before. Dad and I just thought at each other.

<Maddie>: I don't know how to do that.

<Unknown ID>: 🌉

So that was how Maddie came to call her sister "Mist": the pylon of a suspension bridge, perhaps the Golden Gate, hidden behind San Francisco's famous fog.

Maddie kept the existence of Mist a secret from her mother. After all the wars initiated by the uploaded consciousnesses—some of which were still smoldering—the reconstruction process was slow and full of uncertainty. Hundreds of millions had died on other continents, and though America had been spared the worst of it, the country was still in chaos as infrastructure collapsed and refugees poured into the big cities. Her mother, who now acted as an adviser to the city government of Boston, worked long hours and was exhausted all the time.

First, she needed to confirm that Mist was telling the truth, so Maddie asked Mist to reveal herself.

For digital entities like Maddie's father, there was a ground truth, a human-readable representation of the instructions and data adapted for the different processors of the interconnected global network. Maddie's father had taught her to read it after he had reconnected with her following his death and resurrection. It looked like code written in some high-level programming language, replete with convoluted loops and cascading conditionals, elaborate lambda expressions and recursive definitions consisting of strings of mathematical symbols.

Maddie would have called such a thing "source code," except that she had learned from her father that that notion was inaccurate: He and the other gods had never been compiled from source code into executable code, but were developed by AI techniques that replicated the workings of neural networks directly in machine language. The human-readable representation was more like a map of the reality of this new mode of existence.

Without hesitation, Mist revealed her map to Maddie when asked. Not *all* of herself, explained Mist. She was a distributed being, vast and constantly self-modifying. To show all of herself in map code would take up so much space and require so much time for Maddie to read that they might as well wait for the end of the universe. Instead, Mist showed her some highlights:

<⚠>: Here's a section I inherited from our father.

((lambda (n1) ((lambda (n2 ...

As Maddie scrolled through the listing, she traced the complex logical paths, followed the patterns of multiple closures and thrown continuations, discovered the contours of a way of thinking that was at once familiar and strange. It was like looking at a map of her own mind, but one where the landmarks were strange and the roads probed into terra incognita.

There were echoes of her father in the code—she could see that: a quirky way of associating words with images; a tendency to see patterns that defied the strictly rational; a deep, abiding trust for a specific woman and a specific teenager out of the billions who lived on this planet.

Maddie was reminded of how Mom had told her that there were things about her as a baby that defied theories of upbringing, that told her and Dad that Maddie was *their* child in a way that transcended rational knowledge: the way her smile reminded Mom of Dad even at six weeks; the way she hated noodles the first time she tried them, just like Mom; the way she calmed down as soon as Dad held her, even though he had been too busy with Logorhythms's IPO to spend much time with her during the first six months of her life.

But there were also segments of Mist that puzzled her: the way she seemed to possess so many heuristics for trends in the stock market; the way her thoughts seemed attuned to the subtleties of patents; the way the shapes of her decision algorithms seemed adapted for the methods of warfare. Some of the map code reminded Maddie of the code of other gods Dad had shown her; some was entirely novel.

Maddie had a million questions for Mist. How had she come to be? Was she like Athena, sprung fully formed from her father's mind? Or was she something like the next generation of an evolutionary algorithm, inheriting bits from her father and other uploaded consciousnesses with variations? Who was her other parent—or maybe parents? What stories of love, of yearning, of loneliness and connection, lay behind her existence? What was it like being a creature of pure computation, never having existed in the flesh?

But of one thing Maddie was certain: Mist was her father's daughter, just as she had claimed. She was her sister, even if she was barely human.

•

```
<Maddie>: What was life in the cloud with Dad like?
```
 <🔥>: 🗡 🐢 🌀 ⚡

Like her father, Mist had a habit of shifting into emoji whenever she found words inadequate. What Maddie got out of her response was that life in the cloud was simply beyond her understanding and Mist did not have the words to adequately convey it.

So Maddie tried to bridge the gap the other way, to tell Mist about her own life.

```
<Maddie>: Grandma and I had a garden back in Pennsyl-
vania. I was good at growing tomatoes.
```
 <🔥>: 🍅

```
<Maddie>: Yep. That's a tomato.
```
 <🔥>: I know lots about tomatoes: lycopene, Cortés, nightshade, Mesoamerica, ketchup, pomodoro, *Nix v. Hedden*, vegetable, soup. Probably more than you.

 <🔥>: You seem really quiet.

```
<Maddie>: Forget it.
```

Other attempts by Maddie to share the details of her own life usually ended the same way. She mentioned the way Basil wagged his tail and licked her fingers when she came in the door, and Mist responded with articles about the genetics of dogs. Maddie started to talk about the anxieties she experienced at school and the competing cliques, and Mist showed her pages of game theory and papers on adolescent psychology.

Maddie could understand it, to some extent. After all, Mist had never lived in the world that Maddie inhabited, and never would. All Mist had was data *about* the world, not the world itself. How could Mist understand how Maddie *felt*? Words or emoji were inadequate to convey the essence of reality.

Life is about embodiment, thought Maddie. This was a point that she had discussed with Dad many times. To experience the world through the senses was different from simply having data about the world. The memory of his time in the world was what had kept her father sane after he had been turned into a brain in a jar.

And in this way, oddly, Maddie came to have a glint of the difficulty Mist faced in explaining her world to Maddie. She tried to imagine what it was like to have never petted a puppy, to have never experienced a tomato filled with June sunshine burst between the tongue and the palate, to have never felt the weight of gravity or the elation of being loved, and imagination failed her. She felt sorry for Mist, a ghost who could not even call upon the memory of an embodied existence.

•

There was one topic on which Maddie and Mist could converse effectively: the shared mission their father had left them to make sure the gods didn't come back.

All of the uploaded consciousnesses—whose existence was still never acknowledged—were supposed to have died in the conflagration. But pieces of their code, like the remnants of fallen giants, were scattered around the world's servers. Mist told Maddie that mysterious network presences scoured the web to collect these pieces. Were they hackers? Spies? Corporate researchers? Defense contractors? What purpose could they have for gathering these relics unless they were interested in resurrecting the gods?

Along with these troubling reports, Mist also brought back headlines that she thought Maddie would find interesting.

< 🔺 >: Today's Headlines:

- Japanese PM Assures Nervous Citizens That New Robots Deployed for Reconstruction Are Safe
- European Union Announces Border Closures; Extra-European Economic Migrants Not Welcome

- Bill to Restrict Immigration to "Extraordinary Circumstances" Passes Senate; Majority of Working Visas to Be Revoked
- Protesters Demanding Jobs Clash with Police in New York and Washington, DC
- Developing Nations Press UN Security Council for Resolution Denouncing Efforts to Restrict Population Migration by Developed Economies
- Collapse of Leading Asian Economies Predicted as Manufacturing Sector Continues Contraction Due to Back-Shoring by Europe and the US
- Everlasting, Inc. Refuses to Explain Purpose of New Data Center

<🔺>: You still there?

<🔺>: ??

<🔺>: ???????????

<Maddie>: Calm down! I need a few seconds to read this wall of text you just threw at me.

<🔺>: Sorry, I'm still under-compensating for how slow your cycles are. I'll leave you to it. Ping me when you're done.

Mist's consciousness operated at the speed of electric currents fluctuating billions of times a second instead of slow, analog, electrochemical synapses. Her experience of time had to be so different, so *fast*, that it made Maddie a little bit envious.

And she came to appreciate just how patient her father had been with her when he was a ghost in the machine. In every exchange between him and Maddie, he probably had had to wait what must have felt like eons before getting an answer from her, but he had never shown any annoyance.

Maybe that was why he created another daughter, Maddie thought. *Someone who lived and thought like him.*

<Maddie>: Ready to chat when you are.

<🔺>: Everlasting is where I tracked them dragging those fragments of the gods.

<Maddie>: They didn't get any pieces of Dad, did they?

< ⌃ >:Way ahead of you, sister. I took care of burying the pieces of Dad as soon as it calmed down.

\<Maddie\>: Thank you. . . . Wish we could figure out what they're planning over there.

Adam Ever, the founder of Everlasting, Inc., was one of the foremost experts on the Singularity. He had been a friend of Dad's, and Maddie vaguely recalled meeting him as a little girl. Ever was a persistent advocate of consciousness uploading, even after all the legal restrictions placed on his research after the crisis. Maddie's curiosity was tinged with dread.

< ⌃ >: Not that easy. I tried to go through Everlasting's system defenses a few times, but the internal networks are completely isolated. They're paranoid over there—I lost a few parts when they detected my presence on the external-facing servers.

Maddie shuddered. She recalled the epic fights between her father, Lowell, and Chanda in the darkness of the network. The phrase "lost a few parts" might sound innocuous, but for Mist it probably felt like losing limbs and parts of her mind.

\<Maddie\>: You've got to be careful.

< ⌃ >: I did manage to copy the pieces of the gods they took. I'll give you access to the encrypted cloud cell now. Maybe we can figure out what they're doing at Everlasting by looking through these.

•

Maddie made dinner that night. Her mother texted her that she was going to be late, first thirty minutes, then an hour, and then "not sure." Maddie ended up eating alone and then spent the rest of the evening watching the clock and worrying.

"Sorry," Mom said as she came in, close to midnight. "They kept me late."

Maddie had seen some of the reports on TV. "Protesters?"

Mom sighed. "Yes. Not as bad as in New York, but hundreds showed up. I had to talk to them."

"What are they mad about? It's not like—" Maddie caught herself just as she was about to raise her voice. She was feeling protective of her mother, but her mother had probably had enough shouting for one day.

"They're good people," Mom said vaguely. She headed for the stairs without even glancing at the kitchen. "I'm tired. I think I'll just go to bed."

But Maddie was unwilling to just let it go. "Are we having supply issues again?" The recovery was jittery, and goods were still being rationed. It was a constant struggle to get people to stop hoarding.

Mom stopped. "No. The supplies are flowing smoothly again, maybe too smoothly."

"I don't understand," said Maddie.

Mom sat down on the bottom of the stairs, and patted the space next to her. Maddie went over and sat down.

"Remember how during the crisis, when we were coming to Boston, I told you about layers of technology?"

Maddie nodded. Her mother, a historian, had told her the story behind the networks that connected people: the footpaths that grew into caravan routes that developed into roads that turned into railroad tracks that provided the right-of-way for the optical cables that carried the bits that made up the internet that routed the thoughts of the gods.

"The history of the world is a process of speeding up, of becoming more efficient as well as more fragile. If a footpath is blocked, you just have to walk around it. But if a highway is blocked, you have to wait until specialized machinery can be brought to clear it. Just about anyone can figure out how to patch a cobblestone road, but only highly trained technicians can fix a fiber-optic cable. There's a lot more redundancy with the older, inefficient technologies."

"Your point is that keeping it simple technologically is more resilient," said Maddie.

"But our history is also a history of growing needs, of more mouths to feed and more hands that need to be kept from idleness," said Mom.

Mom told Maddie that America had been lucky during the crisis: very few bombs had struck her shores and relatively few people had died during the riots. But with much of the infrastructure paralyzed across the country, refugees flooded into the big cities. Boston's own population had doubled from what it was before the crisis. With so many people came spiking needs: food, clothing, shelter, sanitation . . .

"On my advice, the governor and the mayor tried to rely on distributed, self-organizing groups of citizens with low-tech delivery methods, but we couldn't get it to work because it was just too inefficient. Congestion and breakdowns were happening too frequently. Centillion's automation proposal had to be considered."

Maddie thought of how impatient Mist had been with her "slow cycles," and she imagined the roads packed with self-driving trucks streaming bumper-to-bumper at a hundred miles an hour, without drivers who had to rest, without the traffic jams caused by human unpredictability, without the accidents from drifting attentions and exhausted bodies. She thought of tireless robots loading and unloading the supplies necessary to keep millions of people fed and warm and clothed. She thought of the borders patrolled by machines with precise algorithms designed to preserve precious supplies for the use of people with the right accents, the right skin colors, the luck to be born in the right places at the right times.

"All the big cities are doing the same thing," said Mom, a trace of defensiveness in her voice. "It's impossible for us to hold out. It would be irresponsible, as Centillion put it."

"And the drivers and workers would be replaced," said Maddie, understanding finally dawning on her.

"They showed up on Beacon Hill to protest, hoping to save their jobs. But an even bigger crowd showed up to protest against *them*." Mom rubbed her temples.

"If everything is handed over to Centillion's robots, wouldn't another god—I mean a rogue AI—put us at even more risk?"

"We have grown to the point where we must depend on machines to survive," said Mom. "The world has become too fragile for us to count on people, and so our only choice is to make it even more fragile."

•

With Centillion's robots taking over the crucial work of maintaining the flow of goods into the city, a superficial calmness returned to life. The workers who lost their jobs were given new jobs invented by the government: correcting typos in old databases, sweeping corners of streets that Centillion's robots couldn't get to, greeting concerned citizens in the lobby of the State House and giving them tours— some grumbled that this was just a dressed-up form of welfare and what was the government going to do when Centillion and Perfect-Logic and ThoughtfulBits and their ilk automated more jobs away?

But at least everyone was getting a paycheck that they could use to buy the supplies brought into the city by the fleet of robots. And Centillion's CEO swore up and down on TV that they weren't developing anything that could be understood as "rogue AI," like the old, dead gods.

That was good, wasn't it?

Maddie and Mist continued to gather pieces of the old gods and studying them to see what Everlasting might want with them. Some of the fragments had belonged to her father, but there were too few of them to even dream of trying to resurrect him. Maddie wasn't sure how she felt about it—in a way, her father had never fully reconciled to his existence as a disembodied consciousness, and she wasn't sure he would want to "come back."

Meanwhile, Maddie was working on a secret project. It would be her present to Mist.

She looked up everything she could online about robotics and electronics and sensor technology. She bought components online, which Centillion drones cheerfully and efficiently delivered to her house—straight to her room, even: she kept the window of her room open, and tiny drones with whirring rotors flitted in at all hours of the day and night, dropping off tiny packages.

<🔺>: What are you doing?

<Maddie>: Give me a minute. I'm almost done.

<🔺>: I'll give you today's headlines then.

- Hundreds Die in Attempt to Scale "Freedom Wall" near El Paso
- Think Tank Argues Coal Should Be Reevaluated as Alternative Energy Fails to Meet Promise
- Deaths from Typhoons in Southeast Asia Exceed Historical Records
- Experts Warn of Further Regional Conflicts as Food Prices Soar and Drought Continues in Asia and Africa
- Unemployment Numbers Suggest Reconstruction Has Benefited Robots (and Their Owners) More Than People
- Rise of Religious Extremism Tied to Stagnating Developing Economies
- Is Your Job at Risk? Experts Explain How to Protect Yourself from Automation

<Maddie>: Nothing from Everlasting?

<🔺>: They've been quiet.

Maddie plugged her new creation into the computer.

<Maddie>: 💾

The lights near the data port on the computer began to blink.

Maddie smiled to herself. For Mist, asking Maddie a question and waiting for her slow cycles to catch up and answer was probably like sending snail mail. It would be far faster for her to investigate the new contraption herself.

The motors in Maddie's creation spun to life, and the three wheels in the base turned the four-foot-tall torso around. The wheels provided 360 degrees of motion, much like those roving automatic vacuum cleaners.

At the top of the cylindrical torso was a spherical "head" to which were attached the best sensors that Maddie could scrounge up or buy: a pair of high-def cameras to give stereoscopic vision; a matched pair of microphones to act as ears, tuned for the range of human hearing;

a sophisticated bundle of probes mounted at the ends of flexible antennae to act as noses and tongues that approximated the sensitivity of human counterparts; and numerous other tactile sensors, gyroscopes, accelerometers, and so on to give the robot the experience of touch, gravity, presence in space.

Away from the head, near the top of the cylindrical body, however, were the most expensive components of them all: a pair of multi-jointed arms with parallel-elastic actuators to recreate the freedom of motion of human arms that ended in a pair of the most advanced prosthetic hands covered in medical-grade plastiskin. The skin, embedded with sensors for temperature and force, were said to approach or even exceed the sensitivity of real skin, and the fingers modeled human hands so well that they could tighten a nut on a screw as well as pick up a strand of hair. Maddie watched as Mist tried them out, flexing and clenching the fingers, and without realizing it, she mirrored the movements with her own fingers.

"What do you think?" she said.

The screen mounted atop the head of the robot came to life, showing a cartoonish pair of eyes, a cute button nose, and a pair of abstract, wavy lines that mimicked the motion of lips. Maddie was proud of the design and programming of the face. She had modeled it on her own.

A voice came out of the speaker below the screen. "This is very well made." It was a young girl's voice, chirpy and mellifluous.

"Thank you," said Maddie. She watched as Mist moved around the room, twisting her head this way and that, sweeping her camera-gaze over everything. "Do you like your new body?"

"It's interesting," said Mist. The tone was the same as before. Maddie couldn't tell if that was because Mist was really pleased with the robotic body or that she hadn't figured out how to modulate the voice to suit her emotional state.

"I can show you all the things you haven't experienced before," said Maddie hurriedly. "You'll know what it's like to move in the real world, not just as a ghost in a machine. You'll be able to understand my stories, and I can take you on trips with me, introduce you to Mom and other people."

Mist continued to move around the room, her eyes surveying the trophies on Maddie's shelves, the titles of her books, the posters on her walls, the models of the planets and rocket ships hanging from the ceiling—a record of Maddie's shifting tastes over the years. She moved toward one corner where a basket of stuffed animals was kept, but stopped when the data cable stretched taut, just a few centimeters too short.

"The cable is necessary for now because the amount of data from the sensors is so large. But I'm working on a compression algorithm so we can get you wireless."

Mist moved the swiveling screen with her cartoonish face forward and backward to simulate a nod. Maddie was grateful that she had thought of such a thing—a lot of the robotics papers on robot-human interactions emphasized that rather than simulating a human face too closely and falling into the uncanny valley, it was better sticking to cartoonish representations that exaggerated the emotional tenor. Sometimes an obviously virtual representation was better than a strict effort at fidelity.

Mist paused in front of a mess of wires and electronic components on Maddie's shelf. "What's this?"

"The first computer that Dad and I built together," said Maddie. Instantly she seemed to have been transported to that summer almost a decade ago, when Dad showed her how to apply Ohm's law to pick out the right resistors and how to read a circuit diagram and translate it into real components and real wires. The smell of hot solder filled her nostrils again, and she smiled even as her eyes moistened.

Mist picked up the contraption with her hands.

"Be careful!" Maddie yelled.

But it was too late. The breadboard crumbled in Mist's hands, and the pieces fell to the carpet.

"Sorry," said Mist. "I thought I was applying the right amount of pressure based on the materials used in it."

"Things get old in the real world," said Maddie. She bent down to pick up the pieces from the carpet, carefully cradling them in her hand. "They grow fragile." She looked at the remnants of her first unskilled attempt at soldering, noticing the lumpy messes and bent electrodes. "I guess you don't have much experience with that."

"I'm sorry," said Mist again, her voice still chirpy.

"Doesn't matter," said Maddie, trying to be magnanimous. "Think of it as a first lesson about the real world. Hold on."

She rushed out of the room and returned a moment later with a ripe tomato. "This is shipped in from some industrial farm, and it's nowhere as good as the ones Grandma and I grew back in Pennsylvania. Still, now you can taste it. Don't talk to me about lycopene and sugar content; *taste* it."

Mist took the tomato from her—this time her mechanical hands held it lightly, the fingers barely making an impression against the smooth fruit skin. She gazed at it, the lenses of her cameras whirring as they focused. And then, decisively, one of the probes on her head shot out and stabbed into the fruit in a single motion.

It reminded Maddie of a mosquito's proboscis stabbing into the skin of a hand, or a butterfly sipping nectar from a flower. A sense of unease rose in her. She was trying so hard to make Mist *human*, but what made her think that was what Mist wanted?

"It's very good," said Mist. She swiveled her screen toward Maddie so that Maddie could see her cartoonish eyes curving in a smile. "You're right. It's not as good as the heirloom varieties."

Maddie laughed. "How would you know that?"

"I've tasted hundreds of varieties of tomatoes," said Mist.

"Where? How?"

"Before the war of the gods, all the big instant meal manufacturers and fast food restaurants used automation to produce recipes. Dad took me through a few of these facilities and I tried every variety of tomato from Amal to Zebra Cherry—I was a big fan of Snow White."

"Machines were making up the recipes?" Maddie asked. She had loved watching cooking shows before the war, and chefs were artists, what they did was *creative*. She couldn't quite wrap her head around the notion of machines making up recipes.

"Sure. At the scale these places were operating, they had to optimize for so many factors that people could never get it right. The recipes had to be tasty and also use ingredients that could be obtained within the constraints of modern mechanized agriculture—it was no good to discover some good recipe that relied on an heirloom variety that couldn't be grown in large enough quantities efficiently."

Maddie thought back to her conversation with Mom and realized that it was the same concept that now governed the creation of ration packets: nutritious, tasty, but also effective for feeding hundreds of millions living with a damaged grid and limited resources.

"Why didn't you tell me you've tasted tomatoes?" Maddie asked. "I thought you were—"

"Not just tomatoes. I've had every variety of potato, squash, cucumber, apple, grape, and lots of other things you've never had. In the food labs, I tried out billions of flavor combinations. The sensors they had were far more sensitive than the human tongue."

The robot that had once seemed such an extraordinary gift now seemed shabby to Maddie. Mist did not need a body. She had been living in a far more embodied way than Maddie had realized or understood.

Mist simply didn't think the new body was all that special.

•

- Expert Report Declares Nuclear Fallout Cleanup Plan in Asia Unrealistic, Further Famines Inevitable
- Japan Joins China and India in Denouncing Western Experts for "Scaremongering"
- Indian Geoengineering Plan to Melt Himalayan Snow for Agricultural Irrigation Leaked, Drawing Condemnation from Smaller SE Asian Nations for "Water Theft"
- Protesters in Italy and Spain Declare "African Refugees Should Go Home": Thousands Injured in Clashes

- Australia Announces Policy of Shooting on Sight to Discourage "Boat People"
- Regional "Resource Wars" May Turn Global, UN Special Commission Warns
- White House Stands Firm Behind "NATO First" Doctrine: Use of Military Force Is Justified to Stop Geoengineering Projects That May Harm Allies or US Interests

Mom was working late most nights now, and she looked pale and sickly. Maddie didn't have to ask to know that reconstruction was going worse than anyone expected. The war of the gods had left so much of the planet's surface in tatters that the survivors were fighting over the leftover scraps. No matter how many refugee boats were sunk by drones or how high the walls were built, desperate people continued to pour into the US, the country least damaged by the war.

Protests and counter-protests raged in the streets of all the major cities day after day. Nobody wanted to see kids and women drown in the sea or electrocuted by the walls, but it was also true that all the American cities were overburdened. Even the efficient robots couldn't keep up with the task of making sure everyone was fed and safe.

Maddie could tell that the ration packets were going down in quality. This couldn't go on. The world was continuing its long spiral down toward an abyss, and sooner or later, someone was going to conclude that the problems were not solvable by AI alone, and we needed to call upon the gods again.

She and Mist had to prevent that. The world couldn't afford another reign of the gods.

While Mist—possibly the greatest hacker there ever was—focused on testing out the defenses around Everlasting and figuring out a way to penetrate them, Maddie devoted her time to trying to understand the fragments of the dead gods.

The map code, a combination of self-modifying AI and modeling of human thinking patterns, wasn't the sort of thing a programmer would write, but Maddie seemed to have an intuition for how personality quirks manifested in this code after spending so much time with the fragments of her father.

In this manner, Maddie came also to understand Chanda and Lowell and the other gods. She charted their hopes and dreams, like fragments of Sappho and Aeschylus. And it turned out that deep down, all the gods had similar vulnerabilities, a kind of regret or nostalgia for life in the flesh that seemed reflected at every level of organization. It was a blind spot, a vulnerability, that could be exploited in the war against the gods.

"I don't have a weak spot like that in my code," said Mist.

Maddie was startled. She had never considered Mist one of the gods, though, objectively, she clearly was. Mist was just her little sister, especially when she was embedded in the cute robot Maddie had built for her, as she was now.

"Why not?" she asked.

"I am a child of the ether," said Mist. And the voice was now different. It sounded older, wearier. Maddie would almost have said it sounded *not human*. "I do not yearn for something that I never had."

Of course Mist wasn't a little girl, Maddie berated herself. She had somehow allowed the cartoonish trappings she had created for Mist, a mask intended to help Mist relate to her, fool her. Mist's thoughts moved at a far faster pace, and she had experienced more of the world than Maddie had ever experienced. She could, at will, peek through billions of cameras, listen through billions of microphones, sense the speed of the wind atop Mount Washington and at the same time feel the heat of the lava spilling out of Kilauea. She had known what it was like to gaze down at the world from the International Space Station and what it was like to suffer the stress of kilometers of water pressing down upon a deep-sea submersible's shell. She was, in a way, far older than Maddie.

"I'm going to make a run at Everlasting," said Mist. "With your discoveries, we're as ready as we'll ever be. They might already be creating new gods."

Maddie wanted to tell Mist some words of comfort, assuring her of success. But really, what did she know of the risks Mist was undertaking? She wasn't the one to put her life on the line in that unimaginable realm inside the machine.

The features on the screen that served as Mist's face disappeared, leaving only a single emoji.

"We'll protect each other," Maddie said. "We will."

But even she knew how inadequate that sounded.

•

Maddie woke up with a start as cold hands caressed her face.

She sat up. The small bedside lamp was on. Next to her bed was the squat figure of the robot, whose cameras were trained on her. She had fallen asleep after seeing Mist off, though she hadn't meant to.

"Mist," she said, rubbing her eyes, "are you okay?"

The cartoonish face of Mist was replaced by a headline.

- Everlasting, Inc., Announces "Digital Adam" Project

"What?" asked Maddie, her thoughts still sluggish.

"I better let him tell you," said Mist. And the screen changed again, and a man's face appeared on it. He was in his thirties, with short-cropped hair and a kind, compassionate face.

All traces of sleep left Maddie. This was a face she had seen many times on TV, always making reassurances the public: Adam Ever.

"What are you doing here?" asked Maddie. "What have you done to Mist?"

The robot that had housed Mist—no, Adam now—held up his hands in a gesture intended to calm. "I'm just here to talk."

"What about?"

"Let me show you what we've been working on."

•

Maddie flew over a fjord filled with floating icebergs until she was skimming over a field of ice. A great black cube loomed out of this landscape of shades of white.

"Welcome to the Longyearbyen Data Center," Adam Ever's voice spoke in her ears.

The VR headset was something Maddie had once used to game with her father, but it had been gathering dust on the shelf since his death. Adam had asked her to put it on.

Maddie had known of the data center's existence from Mist's reports and had even seen some photographs and videos of its construction. She and Mist had speculated that this was where Everlasting was trying to resurrect the old gods or bring forth new ones.

Adam told her about the massive assembly of silicon and graphene inside, about the zipping electrons and photons bouncing inside glass cables. This was an altar to computation, a Stonehenge for a new age.

"It's also where I live," Adam said.

The scene before Maddie's eyes shifted, and she was now looking at Adam calmly lying down on a hospital bed, smiling for the camera. Doctors and beeping machines were clustered around the bed. They typed some commands into a computer, and after a while Adam closed his eyes, going to sleep.

Maddie suddenly had the sensation that she was witnessing a scene similar to the last moments of her father.

"Were you ill?" she asked hesitantly.

"No," said Adam. "I was in the prime of health. This is a video recording of the moment before the scan. I had to be alive to give the procedure the maximal chance for success."

Maddie imagined the doctors approaching the sleeping figure of Adam with scalpel and bone saw and who knew what else—she was about to scream when the scene shifted mercifully away to a room of pure white with Adam sitting up in a bed. Maddie let out a held breath.

"You survived the scan?" asked Maddie.

"Of course," said Adam.

But Maddie sensed that this wasn't quite right. Earlier, in the video, there were wrinkles near the corners of Adam's eyes. The face of the Adam in front of her now was perfectly smooth.

"It's not you," said Maddie. "It's not you."

"It *is* me," insisted Adam. "The only me that matters."

Maddie closed her eyes and thought back to the times Adam had appeared on TV in interviews. He had said he didn't want to leave Svalbard, preferring to conduct all his interviews remotely via satellite feed. The camera had always stayed close up, showing just his face. Now that she was looking for it, she realized that the way Adam had moved in those interviews had seemed just slightly odd, a little uncanny.

"You died," said Maddie. She opened her eyes and looked at the Adam, this Adam with the smooth, perfectly symmetrical face and impossibly graceful limbs. "You died during the scan because there's no way to do a scan without destroying the body."

Adam nodded. "I'm one of the gods."

"Why?" Maddie couldn't imagine such a thing. All of the gods had been created as a last measure of desperation, a way to preserve their minds for the service of the goals of others. Her father had raged against his fate and fought so that none of the others had to go through what he did. To choose to become a brain in a jar was inconceivable to her.

"The world is dying, Maddie," said Adam. "You know this. Even before the wars, we were killing the planet slowly. There were too many of us squabbling over too few resources, and to stay alive we had to hurt the world even more, polluting the water and air and soil so that we might extract more. The wars only accelerated what was already an inevitable trend. There are too many of us for this planet to support. The next time we fight a war, there won't be any more of us to save after the nukes are done falling."

"It's not true!" Even as she said it, Maddie knew that Adam was right. The headlines and her own research had long ago led her to the same conclusion. *He's right.* She felt very tired. "Are we the cancer of this planet?"

"We're not the problem," said Adam.

Maddie looked at him.

"Our bodies are," said Adam. "Our bodies of flesh exist in the realm of atoms. Our senses require the gratification of matter. Not all of us can live the lifestyle we believe we deserve. Scarcity is the root of all evil."

"What about space, the other planets and stars?"

"It's too late for that. We've hardly taken another step on the moon, and most of the rockets we've been building since then have been intended to deliver bombs."

Maddie said nothing. "You're saying there is no hope?"

"Of course there is." Adam waved his arm, and the white room transformed into the inside of a luxurious apartment. The hospital bed disappeared and Adam was now standing in the middle of a well-appointed room. The lights of Manhattan shone beyond the darkened windows.

Adam waved his arm again, and now they were inside a voluminous space capsule. Outside the window loomed a partial view of a massive sphere of swirling bands of color, and a giant red oval slowly drifted among the bands like an island in a turbulent sea.

Once more, Adam waved his arm, and now it wasn't even possible for Maddie to understand what she was seeing. There seemed to be a smaller Adam inside Adam, and yet a smaller Adam inside that one, and so on, ad infinitum. Yet she was somehow able to see all of the Adams at once. She moved her gaze around the space and felt dizzy: space itself seemed to gain an extra level of depth, and everywhere she looked she saw *inside* things.

"We could have all we ever desire," said Adam, "if we're willing to give up our bodies."

A disembodied existence, thought Maddie. *Is that really living at all?*

"But this isn't *real*," said Maddie. "This is just an illusion." She thought of the games she used to play with her father, of the green seas of grass that seemed to go on forever, of the babbling brooks that promised infinite zoom, of the fantastic creatures they had fought against, side by side.

"Consciousness itself is an illusion, if you want to follow that logic to its conclusion," said Adam. "When you put your hand around a tomato, your senses insist that you're touching something solid. But most of a tomato is made up of the empty space between the nuclei of the atoms, as far from each other, by proportion, as the stars are apart. What is color? What is sound? What is heat or pain? They're but pulses of electricity that make up our consciousness, and it makes no difference whether the pulse comes from a sensor touching a tomato or is the result of computation."

"Except there is a difference," the voice of Mist said.

Maddie's heart swelled with gratitude. Her sister was coming to her defense. Or so she thought.

"A tomato made up of atoms is grown in a distant field, where it must be given fertilizer mined from halfway across the world and dusted with insecticide by machines. Then it must be harvested, packed, and then shipped through the airways and highways until it arrives at your door. The amount of energy it takes to run the infrastructure that would support the creation and delivery of a single tomato is many times what it took to build the Great Pyramid. Is it really worth enslaving the whole planet so that you can have the experience of a tomato through the interface of the flesh instead of generating the same impulse from a bit of silicon?"

"But it doesn't have to be that way," said Maddie. "My grandmother and I grew our tomatoes on our own, and we didn't need any of that."

"You can't feed billions of people with backyard gardens," said Mist. "Nostalgia for a Garden that never existed is dangerous. The mass of humanity depends on the fragile, power-intensive infrastructure of civilization. It is delusion to think you can live without it."

Maddie remembered the words of her mother. *The world has become too fragile for us to count on people.*

"The world of atoms is not only wasteful, it is also limiting," said Adam. "Inside the data center, we can live anywhere we want and have whatever we want, with imagination as our only limit. We can experience things that our fleshly senses could never give us: live in multiple dimensions, invent impossible foods, possess worlds that are as infinite as the sands of the Ganges."

A world beyond scarcity, thought Maddie. A world without rich or poor, without the conflicts generated by exclusion and possession. It was a world without death, without decay, without the limits of inflexible matter. It was a state of existence mankind had always yearned for.

"Don't you miss the real world?" asked Maddie. She thought of the vulnerability that existed at the heart of all the gods.

"We discovered the same thing you did by studying the gods," said Adam. "Nostalgia is deadly. When peasants first moved into the factories of the industrial age, perhaps they also were nostalgic for the inefficient world of subsistence farming. But we must be open to change, to adaptation, to seeking a new path in a sea of fragility. Instead of being forced here on the verge of death like your father, I *chose* to come here. I am not nostalgic. That makes all the difference."

"He's right," said Mist. "Our father understood that, too. Maybe this is why he and the other gods gave birth to me: to see if their nostalgia is as inevitable as death. They couldn't adapt to this world fully, but maybe their children could. In a way, Dad gave birth to me because, deep down, he wished *you* could live here with him."

Mist's observation seemed to Maddie like a betrayal, but she couldn't say why.

"This is the next stage of our evolution," said Adam. "This isn't going to be a perfect world, but it is closer to perfect than anything we've ever devised. The human race thrives on discovering new worlds, and now there are an infinite many of them to explore. We shall reign as the gods of them all."

•

Maddie took off her VR set. Next to the vibrant colors inside the digital world, the physical world seemed dim and dull.

She imagined the data center teeming with the consciousnesses of billions. *Would that bring people closer, so that they all shared the same universe without the constraints of scarcity? Or would it push them apart, so that each lived in their own world, a king of infinite space?*

She held out her hands. She noticed that they were becoming wrinkled, the hands of a woman rather than a child.

After the briefest of pauses, Mist rolled over and held them.

"We'll protect each other," said Mist. "We will."

They held hands in the dark, sisters, human and post-human, and waited for the new day to come.

Memories of
My Mother

TEN

Dad greeted me at the door, nervous. "Amy, look who's here?"

He stepped aside.

She looked exactly the way she did in the pictures hung every-where in our house: black hair, brown eyes, smooth, pale skin. Yet she also felt like a stranger.

I put down my book bag, unsure what to do. She walked over, leaned down, and hugged me, first loosely, then very tight. She smelled like a hospital.

Dad had told me that the doctors had no cure for her sickness. She had only two years left to live.

"You're so big." Her breath felt warm and tickly on my neck, and suddenly, I hugged my mother back.

Mom brought me presents: a dress that was too small, a set of books that were too old, a model of the rocket ship she rode in.

"I was on a very long trip," she said. "The ship went so fast that time slowed down inside. It felt like only three months."

Dad had already explained it all to me: this was how she would cheat time, stretch out her two years so that she could watch me grow up. But I didn't stop her. I liked listening to her voice.

"I didn't know what you would like." She was embarrassed by the gifts that surrounded me, gifts that were meant for another child, the daughter of her mind.

What I really wanted was a guitar. But Dad thought I was too young.

If I had been older, I might have told her that it was all right, that I loved her gifts. But I was not yet so good at lying.

I asked her how long she would stay with us.

Instead of answering, she said, "Let's stay up all night, and we'll do everything Dad says you can't do."

We went out and she bought me a guitar. I finally fell asleep at seven in the morning in her lap. It was a fantastic night.

When I woke up she was gone.

SEVENTEEN

"Why the fuck are you here?" I slammed the door in my mother's face.

"Amy!" Dad opened the door again. Seeing him next to my mother, still twenty-five, still exactly the same woman from the pictures, I suddenly realized how old he had grown.

He was the one who held me when I was scared out of my wits by the blood I found in my panties. He was the one who, red-faced, mumbled to the store clerk to beg her to fit me for a bra. He was the one who stood there and held me while I screamed at him.

She has no right to dip back into my life once every seven years, like some fairy godmother.

Later, she knocked on my bedroom door. I stayed in bed and said nothing. She came in anyway. She had crossed light-years to get here, and a plywood door wasn't going to stop her. I liked that she pushed her way in to see me and I also hated it. It was confusing.

"That's an elegant dress," she said. My prom dress was hanging from the back of the door. It *was* elegant and cost me half my savings, but I had torn it near the waist.

After a while, I turned around and sat up. She was in my chair, sewing. She had cut a guitar-shaped piece from her own silver dress and patched it over the tear in mine. It was perfect.

"My mother died when I was a little girl," she said. "I never got to know her. So I decided that I would do something different when I . . . found out."

It was strange to hug her. She could have been my older sister.

THIRTY-EIGHT

Mom and I sat together in the park. Baby Debbie was asleep in the stroller, and Adam was with the other boys by the jungle gym, screaming with joy.

"I never got to meet Scott," she said, apologetic. "You weren't dating last time I visited, during grad school."

He was a good man, I almost said. *We just grew apart.* It would have been easy. I had been lying for so long to everyone, including myself.

But I was tired of lying. "He was an ass. It just took me years to admit it."

"Love makes us do strange things," she said.

Mom was only twenty-six. When I was her age, I had been full of hope too. Could she really understand my life?

She asked me how Dad had died. I told her that he went peacefully, even if it wasn't true. There were more lines on my face than on hers, and I felt that I needed to protect her.

"Let's not speak anymore of sad things," she said. And I was angry with her for being able to smile and I was also glad that she was there with me. It was confusing.

So we spoke about the baby, and watched Adam play until it was dark.

EIGHTY

"Adam?" I ask. It's hard for me to turn the wheelchair, and everything seems so dim in my eyes. It can't be Adam. He's been really busy with his new baby. Maybe it's Debbie. But Debbie never visits.

"It's me," she says, and squats down before me.

I squint: she looks still the same as always.

But not exactly the same. The smell of medicine is stronger than ever, and I can feel her hands are shaking.

"How long have you been traveling," I ask, " since you started?"

"Two years and counting," she says. "I'm not leaving again."

I'm sad to hear this, and yet I'm also happy. It's confusing.

"Was it worth it?"

"I got to see less of you than most mothers, but also more."

She pulls up a chair next to me, and I lean my head on her shoulder. I fall asleep, feeling young and knowing that she'll be there when I wake up.

Dispatches from the Cradle: The Hermit— Forty-Eight Hours in the Sea of Massachusetts

Before she became a hermit, Asa <whale>-<tongue>-π had been a managing director with JP Morgan Credit Suisse on Valentina Station, Venus. She would, of course, find this description small-minded and obtuse. "Call a woman a financial engineer or a man an agricultural systems analyst, and the world thinks they know something about them," she wrote. "But what does the job a person has been channeled into have to do with who they are?"

Nonetheless, I will tell you that she was responsible for United Planet's public offering thirty years ago, at the time the biggest single pooling of resources by any individual or corporate entity in history. She was, in large measure, responsible for convincing a wearied humanity scattered across three planets, a moon, and a dozen asteroid habitats to continue to invest in the Grand Task—the terraforming of both Earth and Mars.

Does telling you what she has done explain who she is? I'm not sure. "From cradle to grave, everything we do is motivated by the need to answer one question: Who am I?" she wrote. "But the answer to the question has always been obvious: stop striving; accept."

A few days after she became the youngest chief managing director for JPMCS, on Solar Epoch 22385200, she handed in her resignation, divorced her husbands and wives, liquidated all her assets, placed the bulk of the proceeds into trusts for her children, and then departed for the Old Blue on a one-way ticket.

Once she arrived on Earth, she made her way to the port town of Acton in the Federation of Maritime Provinces and States, where she purchased a survival habitat kit, one identical to the millions used by refugee communities all over the planet, and put the pieces together herself using only two common laborer automata, eschewing offers of aid from other inhabitants of the city. Then she set herself afloat like a piece of driftwood, alone on the seven seas, much to the consternation of her family, friends, and colleagues.

"Given how she was dressed, we thought she was here to buy a vacation villa," said Edgar Baker, the man who sold Asa her habitat. "Plenty of bankers and executives like to come here in winter to dive for treasure and enjoy the sun, but she didn't want me to show her any of the vacant houses, several of which have excellent private beaches."

(Despite the rather transparent ploy, I've decided to leave in Baker's little plug. I can attest that Acton is an excellent vacation spot, with several good restaurants in town serving traditional New England fare—though the lobsters are farmed, not wild. Conservationists are uncertain if the extinct wild lobster will ever make a comeback in the waters off New England as they have never adapted to the warmer seas. The crustaceans that survived global warming were generally smaller in size.)

A consortium of her former spouses sued to have Asa declared mentally incompetent and reverse her financial dispositions. For a while the case provided juicy gossip that filled the XP-stations, but Asa managed to make the case go away quickly with some undisclosed settlements. "They understand now that I just want to be left alone," she was quoted as saying after the case was dismissed—that was probably true, but I'm sure it didn't hurt that she could afford the best lawyers.

"Yesterday I came here to live." With this first entry in her journal, Asa began her seaborne life over the sunken metropolis of Boston on Solar Epoch 22385302, which, if you're familiar with the old Gregorian calendar, was July 5, 2645.

The words were not original, of course. Henry David Thoreau wrote them first exactly eight hundred years earlier in a suburb of Boston.

But unlike Thoreau, who often sounded misanthropic in his declarations, Asa spent as much time alone as she did among crowds.

•

Excerpted from *Adrift*, by Asa <whale>-<tongue>-π:

The legendary island of Singapore is no more. But the idea of Singapore lives on.

The floating family habitats connect to each other in tight clan-strands that weave together into a massive raft-city. From above, the city looks like an algal mat composed of metal and plastic, studded with glistening pearls, dewdrops, or air bubbles—the transparent domes and solar collectors for the habitats.

The Singapore Refugee Collective is so extensive that it is possible to walk the hundreds of kilometers from the site of sunken Kuala Lumpur to the surviving isles of Sumatra without ever touching water—though you would never want to do such thing, as the air outside is far too hot for human survival.

When typhoons—a near-constant presence at these latitudes—approach, entire clan-strands detach and sink beneath the waves to ride out the storm. The refugees sometimes speak not of days or nights, but of upside and downside.

The air inside the habitats is redolent with a thousand smells that would overwhelm an inhabitant of the sterile Venus stations and the climate-controlled domes of the upper latitudes. Char kway teow, diesel fumes, bak kut teh, human waste, raja, Katong laksa, mango-flavored perfume, kaya toast, ayam penyet, burnt electric insulation, mee goreng, roti prata, sea-salt-laced reclaimed air, nasi lemak, charsiew—the heady mixture is something the refugees grow up with and outsiders can never get used to.

Life in the Refugee Collective is noisy, cramped, and occasionally violent. Infectious diseases periodically sweep through the population, and life expectancy is short. The fact that the refugees remain stateless, so many generations after the wars that stripped their ancestors of home-lands, seems to make it impossible for a solution to be envisioned by any-one from the Developed World—an ancient label whose meaning has evolved over the centuries, but has never been synonymous with moral rectitude. It was the Developed World that had polluted the world the earliest and the most, and yet it was also the Developed World that went to war with India and China for daring to follow in their footsteps.

I was saddened by what I saw. So many people clinging to life tenaciously on the thin interface between water and air. Even in a place like this, unsuitable for human habitation, people hang on, as stubborn as the barnacles on pilings revealed at every low tide. What of the refugees in the deserts of interior Asia, who live like moles in underground warrens? What of the other floating refugee collectives off the coasts of Africa and Central America? They have survived by pure strength of will, a miracle.

Humanity may have taken to the stars, but we have destroyed our home planet. Such has been the lament of the Naturalists for eons.

"But why do you think we're a problem that needs solving?" asked a child who bartered with me. (I gave him a box of antibiotics, and he served me chicken rice.) "Sunken Singapore was once a part of the Developed World; we're not. We don't call ourselves refugees; you do. This is our home. We live here."

I could not sleep that night.

This is our home. We live here.

•

The prolonged economic depression in much of North America has led to a decline of the region's once-famous pneumatic tube transportation networks that connected the climate-controlled domed cities, so the easiest way to get to the Sea of Massachusetts these days is by water.

I embarked in balmy Iceland on a cruise ship bound for the coast of the Federation of Maritime Provinces and States—November is an excellent time to visit the region, as the summer months are far too hot—and then, once in Acton, I hired a skiff to bring me out to visit Asa in her floating habitat.

"Have you been to Mars?" asked Jimmy, my guide. He was a man in his twenties, stocky, sunburnt, with gaps in his teeth that showed when he smiled.

"I have," I said.

"Is it warm?" he asked.

"Not quite warm enough to be outside the domes for long," I said, thinking about the last time I visited Watney City on Acidalia Planetia.

"I'd like to go when it's ready," he said.

"You won't miss home?" I asked.

He shrugged. "Home is where the jobs are."

It's well-known that the constant bombardment of the Martian surface with comets pulled from the Oort cloud and the increased radiation from the deployment of solar sails, both grand engineering efforts began centuries ago, had managed to raise the temperature of Mars enough to cause sublimation of much of the red planet's polar dry ice caps and restart the water cycle. The introduction of photosynthesizing plants is slowly turning the atmosphere into something resembling what we could breathe. It's early days yet, but it isn't impossible to imagine that a habitable Mars, long a dream of humanity, would be reality within two or three generations. Jimmy might go there only as a tourist, but his children may settle there.

As our skiff approached the hemisphere bobbing over the waves in the distance, I asked Jimmy what he thought of the world's most well-known hermit, who had recently returned to the Sea of Massachusetts, whence she had started her circumnavigation of the globe.

"She brings the tourists," he said, in a tone that strove to be neutral.

Asa's collected writings about her life drifting over the ruins of the world's ancient sunken cities have been a publishing phenomenon that defies explanation. She eschews the use of XP-capturing or even plain old videography, instead conveying her experiences through impressionistic essays composed in a florid manner that seems at once anachronistic and abiding. Some have called her book bold and original; others said it was affected.

Asa has done little to discourage her critics. *It was said by the Zen masters that the best place for hermits to find the peace they sought was in the crowd,* she wrote. And you could almost hear the disgusted groan of her detractors at this kind of ornate, elusive mysticism.

Many have accused her of encouraging "refugee tourism" instead of looking for real solutions, and some claim that she is merely engaging in the timeless practice of intellectuals from privileged societies visiting those less fortunate and purporting to speak for her subjects by "discovering" romanticized pseudo-wisdom attributed to them.

"Asa Whale is simply trying to soothe the neuroses of the Developed World with a cup of panglossian chicken soup for the soul," declared Emma <CJK-UniHan-Glyph 432371>, the media critic for my own publication. "What would she have us do? Stop all terraforming efforts? Leave the hellish Earth as it stands? The world needs more engineers willing to solve problems and fewer wealthy philosophers who have run out of ways to spend money."

Be that as it may, the Federation of Maritime Provinces and States tourist czar, John <pylon>-<fog>-<cod>, claimed earlier this year that the number of tourists visiting the Sea of Massachusetts has grown fourfold since the publication of Asa's book (such rises in Singapore and Havana are even higher). No doubt the influx of tourist money is welcomed by the locals, however conflicted they may be about Asa's portrayal of them.

Before I could follow up on the complicated look in his eyes, Jimmy turned his face resolutely away to regard our destination, which was growing bigger by the minute.

Spherical in shape, the floating dwelling was about fifteen meters in diameter, consisting of a thin transparent outer hull to which most of the ship's navigation surfaces were affixed and a thicker metal-alloy inner pressure hull. Most of the sphere floated below the surface, making the transparent bridge-dome appear like the pupil of some sea monster's eye staring into the sky.

On top of the pupil stood a solitary figure, her back as straight as the gnomon of a sundial.

Jimmy nudged the skiff until it bumped gently against the side of the habitat, and I gingerly stepped from one craft to the other. Asa steadied me as her habitat dipped under my added weight; her hand felt dry, cool, and very strong.

I observed, somewhat inanely, that she looked exactly like her last public scan-gram, when she had proclaimed from the large central forum of Valentina Station that United Planets was not only going to terraform Mars, but had also successfully bought a controlling stake in Blue Cradle, the public-private partnership for restoring Earth to a fully habitable state.

"I don't get many visitors," she said, her voice tranquil. "There's not much point to putting on a new face every day."

I had been surprised when she replied to my request to stay with her for a few days with a simple "Yes." She had never so much as granted an interview to anyone since she started her life adrift.

"Why?" I had asked.

"Even a hermit can grow lonely," she had replied. And then, in another message that immediately followed the first, she added, "Sometimes."

Jimmy motored away on his skiff. Asa turned and gestured for me to descend through the transparent and open "pupil" into the most influential refugee bubble in the solar system.

•

The stars are invisible from the metal cocoons floating in the heavy atmosphere of Venus; nor do we pay much attention to them from the pressurized domes on Mars. On Earth, the denizens of the climate-controlled cities in habitable zones are preoccupied with scintillating screens and XP implants, the glow of meandering conversation, brightening reputation accounts, and the fading trails left by falling credit scores. They do not look up.

One night, as I lay in the habitat drifting over the balmy subtropical Pacific, the stars spun over my face in their habitual course, a million diamantine points of crisp, mathematical light. I realized, with a startled understanding reminiscent of the clarity of childhood, that the face of the heavens was a collage.

Some of the photons striking my retinas had emerged from the crease in the rock to which Andromeda is chained when nomadic warriors from the last ice age still roamed Doggerland, which connected Britain to the European mainland; others had left that winking point at the wingtip of

Cygnus when bloody Caesar fell at the feet of Pompey's statue; still more had departed the mouth of Aquarius's jar when the decades-long genocidal wars swept through Asia, and aerial drones from Japan and Australia strafed and sank the rafts of refugees fleeing their desertified or flooded homelands; yet others had sparked from the distant hoof of Pegasus when the last glaciers of Greenland and Antarctica disappeared, and Moscow and Ottawa launched the first rockets bound for Venus....

The seas rise and fall, and the surface of the planet is as inconstant as our faces: lands burst forth from the waters and return beneath them; well-armored lobsters scuttle over seafloors that but a geologic eyewink ago had been fought over by armies of woolly mammoths; yesterday's Doggerland may be tomorrow's Sea of Massachusetts. The only witnesses to constant change are the eternal stars, each a separate stream in the ocean of time.

A picture of the welkin is an album of time, as convoluted and intricate as the shell of the nautilus or the arms of the Milky Way.

•

The interior of the habitat was sparsely furnished. Everything—the molded bunks, the stainless steel table attached to the wall, the boxy navigation console—was functional, plain, stripped of the elaborate "signature" decorations that seem all the rage these days with personal nanites. Though the space inside was cramped with two people, it seemed larger than it was because Asa did not fill it with conversation.

We ate dinner—fish that Asa had caught herself roasted over an open fire, with the canopy open—and went to bed silently. I fell asleep quickly, my body rocked by the gentle motions of the sea and my face caressed by the bright, warm New England stars that she had devoted so many words to.

After a breakfast of instant coffee and dry biscuits, Asa asked me if I wanted to see Boston.

"Of course," I said. It was an ancient citadel of learning, a legendary metropolis where brave engineers had struggled against the rising sea for two centuries before its massive seawalls finally succumbed, leaving the city inundated overnight in one of the greatest disasters in the history of the Developed World.

While Asa sat in the back of the habitat to steer and to monitor the solar-powered water-jet drive, I knelt on the bottom of the sphere and greedily drank in the sights passing beneath the transparent floor.

As the sun rose, its light gradually revealed a sandy floor studded by massive ruins: monuments erected to long-forgotten victories of the American Empire pointed toward the distant surface like ancient rockets; towers of stone and vitrified concrete that had once housed hundreds of thousands loomed like underwater mountains, their innumerable windows and doors silent, empty caves from which shoals of colorful fish darted like tropical birds; between the buildings, forest of giant kelp swayed in canyons that had once been boulevards and avenues filled with steaming vehicles, the hepatocytes that had once brought life to this metropolis.

And most amazing of all were the rainbow-hued corals that covered every surface of this urban reef: dark crimson, light orange, pearly white, bright neon vermillion . . .

Before the Second Flood Wars, the sages of Europe and America had thought the corals doomed. Rising sea temperature and acidity; booming algae populations; heavy deposits of mercury, arsenic, lead, and other heavy metals; runaway coastal development as the developed nations built up the machinery of death against waves of refugees from the uninhabitable zones—everything seemed to spell doom for the fragile marine animals and their photosynthesizing symbiotes.

Would the ocean become bleached of color, a black-and-white photograph bearing silent witness to our folly?

But the corals survived and adapted. They migrated to higher latitudes north and south, gained tolerance for stressed environments, and unexpectedly, developed new symbiotic relationships with artificial nanoplate-secreting algae engineered by humans for ocean-mining. I do not think the beauty of the Sea of Massachusetts yields one inch to the fabled Great Barrier Reef or the legends of the long-dead Caribbean.

"Such colors . . ." I murmured.

"The most beautiful patch is in Harvard Yard," Asa said.

We approached the ruins of the famed academy in Cambridge from the south, over a kelp forest that used to be the Charles River. But the looming presence of a cruise ship on the surface blocked our way. Asa stopped the habitat, and I climbed up to gaze out the domed top. Tourists wearing GnuSkin flippers and artificial gills were leaping out of the ship like selkies returning home, their sleek skin temporarily bronzed to endure the scorching November sun.

"Widener Library is a popular tourist spot," said Asa, by way of explanation.

I climbed down, and Asa drove the habitat to dive under the cruise ship. The craft was able to submerge beneath the waves as a way for the refugees in coastal raft-cities to survive typhoons and hurricanes, as well as to avoid the deadly heat of the tropics.

Slowly, we descended toward the coral reef that had grown around the ruined hulk of what had once been the largest university library in the world. Around us, schools of brightly colored fish wove through shafts of sunlight, and tourists gracefully floated down like mermaids, streams of bubbles trailing behind their artificial gills.

Asa guided the habitat in a gentle circle around the kaleidoscopic seafloor in front of the underwater edifice, pointing out various features. The mound covered by the intricate crimson folds of a coral colony that pleated and swirled like the voluminous dress of classical flamenco dancers had once been a lecture hall named after Thoreau's mentor, Emerson; the tall, spear-like column whose surface was tiled by sharp, geometric patches of coral in carmine, cerulean, viridian, and saffron had once been the steeple of Harvard's Memorial Church; the tiny bump in the side of another long reef, a massive brain-shaped coral formation whose gyri and lobes evoked the wisdom of generations of robed scholars who had once strolled through this hallowed temple to knowledge, was in fact the site of the renowned "Statue of Three Lies"—an ancient monument to John Harvard that failed to depict or identify the benefactor with any accuracy.

Next to me, Asa quietly recited,

The maple wears a gayer scarf,
The field a scarlet gown.
Lest I should be old-fashioned,
I'll put a trinket on.

The classical verses of the Early Republican Era poet Dickinson evoked the vanished beauty of the autumns that had once graced these shores, long before the sea had risen and the winters driven away, seemed oddly appropriate.

"I can't imagine the foliage of the Republican Era could be any more glorious than this," I said.

"None of us would know," Asa said. "Do you know how the corals get their bright colors?"

I shook my head. I knew next to nothing about corals except that they were popular as jewelry on Venus.

"The pigmentation comes from the heavy metals and pollutants that might have once killed their less hardy ancestors," said Asa. "They're particularly bright here because this area was touched by the hand of mankind the longest. Beautiful as they are, these corals are incredibly fragile. A global cooling by more than a degree or two would kill them. They survived climate change once by a miracle. Can they do it again?"

I looked back toward the great reef that was Widener Library and saw that tourists had landed on the wide platform in front of the library's entrance or against its sides in small groups. Young tour guides in bright crimson—the color of Harvard achieved either by skin pigmentation or costume—led each group in their day-excursion activities.

Asa wanted to leave—she found the presence of the tourists bothersome—but I explained that I wanted to see what they were interested in. After a moment of hesitation, she nodded and guided the craft closer.

One group, standing on what used to be the steps ascending to the entrance of Widener, stood in a circle and followed their guide, a young woman dressed in a crimson wet suit, through a series of dance-like movements. They moved slowly, but it was unclear whether they were doing so because the choreography required it or because the water provided too much drag. From time to time, the tourists looked up at the blazing sun far above, blurred and made hazy by a hundred feet of intervening water.

"They think they're doing taiji," said Asa.

"It looks nothing like taiji," I said, unable to connect the languorous, clumsy movements with the quick, staccato motion I was familiar with from sessions in low-gravity gyms.

"It's believed that taiji once was a slow, measured art, quite different from its modern incarnation. But since so few recordings of the pre-Diaspora years are left, the cruise ships just make up whatever they want for the tourists.

"Why do taiji here?" I was utterly baffled.

"Harvard was supposed to have a large population of Chinese scholars before the wars. It was said that the children of many of China's wealthiest and most powerful inhabitants studied here. It didn't save them from the wars."

Asa steered the craft a bit farther away from Widener, and I saw more tourists strolling over the coral-carpeted Yard or lounging about, holding what appeared to be paper books—props provided by the cruise company—and taking scans of each other. A few danced without music, dressed in costumes that were a mix of Early and Late Republican fashions, with an academic gown or two thrown in for good measure. In front of Emerson, two tour guides led two groups of tourists in a mimed version of some debate, with each side presenting their position through ghostly holograms that hovered over their heads like comic thought bubbles. Some tourists saw us but did not pay much attention—probably thinking that the drifting refugee bubble was a prop added by the cruise ship to provide atmosphere. If only they knew they were so close to the celebrity hermit . . .

I gathered that the tourists were re-enacting imagined scenes from the glory days of this university, when it had nurtured the great philosophers who delivered jeremiads against the development-crazed governments of the world as they heated the planet without cease, until the ice caps had collapsed.

"So many of the world's greatest conservationists and Naturalists walked through this Yard," I said. In the popular imagination, the Yard is the equal of the Athenian Acropolis or the Roman Forum. I tried to re-envision the particolored reef below me as a grassy lawn covered by bright red and yellow leaves on a cool New England fall day as students and professors debated the fate of the planet.

"Despite my reputation for romanticism," said Asa, "I'm not so sure the Harvard of yesteryear is better than today. That university and others like it once also nurtured the generals and presidents who would eventually deny that mankind could change the climate and lead a people hungry for demagoguery into war against the poorer states in Asia and Africa."

Quietly, we continued to drift around the Yard, watching tourists climb in and out of the empty, barnacle-encrusted windows like hermit crabs darting through the sockets of a many-eyed skull. Some were mostly nude, trailing diaphanous fabrics from their bodies in a manner reminiscent of Classical American Early Republic dresses and suits; others wore wet suits inspired by American Imperial styles, covered by faux body armor plates and gas mask helmets; still others went with refugee-chic, dragging fake survival breathing kits with artfully applied rust stains.

What were they looking for? Did they find it?

Nostalgia is a wound that we refuse time to heal, Asa once wrote.

•

After a few hours, satiated with their excursions, the tourists headed for the surface like shoals of fish fleeing some unseen predator, and in a way, they were.

The forecast was for a massive storm. The Sea of Massachusetts was rarely tranquil.

As the sea around us emptied of visitors and the massive cloud-island that was the cruise ship departed, Asa grew noticeably calmer.

She assured me that we were safe, and brought the submersible craft to the lee of Memorial Church Reef. Here, below the turbulent surface, we would ride out the storm.

The sun set; the sea darkened; a million lights came to life around us. The coral reef at night was hardly a place of slumber. This was when the luminescent creatures of the night—the jellies, the shrimp, the glowworms and lantern fish—came out of hiding to enjoy their time in this underwater metropolis that never slept.

While the wind and the waves raged above us, we hardly felt a thing as we drifted in the abyss that was the sea, innumerable living stars around us.

·

We do not look.

We do not see.

We travel millions of miles to seek out fresh vistas without even once having glimpsed inside our skulls, a landscape surely as alien and as wondrous as anything the universe has to offer. There is more than enough to occupy our curiosity and restless need for novelty if we but turn our gaze to the ten square meters around us: the unique longitudinal patterns in each tile beneath our feet, the chemical symphony animating each bacterium on our skin, the mysteries of how we can contemplate ourselves contemplating ourselves.

The stars above are as distant—and as close—as the glowing coralworms outside my portholes. We only have to look to see Beauty steeped in every atom.

Only in solitude it is possible to live as self-contained as a star.

I am content to have this. To have now.

·

In the distance, against Widener's cliff-like bulk, there was an explosion of light, a nova bursting in the void.

The stars around it streaked away, leaving inky darkness behind, but the nova itself, an indistinct cloud of light, continued to twist and churn.

I woke Asa and pointed. Without speaking, she guided the habitat toward it. As we approached, the light resolved itself into a struggling figure. An octopus? No, a person.

"That must be a tourist stranded behind," said Asa. "If they go up to the surface now, they'll die in the storm."

Asa switched on the bright lights in front of the habitat to get the tourist's attention. The light revealed a disoriented young woman in a wet suit studded with luminescent patches, shielding her eyes against the sudden glow of the habitat's harsh lights. Her artificial gill slits opened and closed rapidly, showing her confusion and terror.

"She can't tell which way is up," Asa muttered.

Asa waved at her through the porthole, gesturing for her to follow the habitat. There was no air lock in the tiny refuge, and we had to go up to the surface to get her in. The young woman nodded.

Up on the surface, the rain was torrential and the waves so choppy that it was impossible to remain standing. Asa and I clung to the narrow ridge around the entrance dome on our bellies and dragged the young woman onto the craft, which dipped even lower under the added weight. With a great deal of effort and shouting, we managed to get her inside, seal the dome, and dive back underwater.

Twenty minutes later, dry, gills removed, securely wrapped in a warm blanket with a hot mug of tea, Saram <Golden-Gate-Bridge>-<Kyoto> looked back gratefully at us.

"I got lost inside," she said. "The empty stacks went on and on, and they looked the same in every direction. At first, I followed a candy-cane fish through the floors, thinking that it was going to lead me outside, but it must have been going around in circles."

"Did you find what you were looking for?" asked Asa.

She was a student at Harvard Station, Saram explained—the institution of higher learning suspended in the upper atmosphere of Venus that had licensed the old name of the university lying in ruins under us. She had come to see this school of legend for herself, harboring romantic notions of trying to search through the stacks of the dead library in the hopes of finding a forgotten tome.

Asa looked outside the porthole at the looming presence of the empty library. "I doubt there's anything left there now after all these years."

"Maybe," Saram said. "But history doesn't die. The water will recede from here one day. I may live to see when Nature is finally restored to her rightful course."

Sarah was probably a little too optimistic. United Planets' iondrive ships had just succeeded in pushing six asteroids into near-Earth orbits earlier in the year, and the construction of the space mirrors had not even begun. Even the most optimistic engineering projections suggest that it will be decades, if not centuries, before the mirrors will reduce the amount of sunlight reaching Earth to begin the process of climate cooling and restoring the planet to its ancient state, a temperate Eden with polar ice caps and glaciers on top of mountain peaks. Mars might be fully terraformed before then.

"Is Doggerland any more natural than the Sea of Massachusetts?" Asa asked.

Saram's steady gaze did not waver. "An ice age is hardly comparable to what was made by the hands of mankind."

"Who are we to warm a planet for a dream and to cool it for nostalgia?"

"Mysticism is no balm for the suffering of the refugees enduring the consequences of our ancestors' errors."

"It is further error that I'm trying to prevent!" shouted Asa. She forced herself to calm down. "If the water recedes, everything around you will be gone." She looked outside the porthole, where the reef's nighttime denizens had returned to their luminescent activities. "As will the vibrant communities in Singapore, in Havana, in Inner Mongolia. We call them refugee shantytowns and disturbed habitats, but these places are also homes."

"I am from Singapore," said Saram. "I spent my life trying to get away from it and only succeeded by winning one of the coveted migration visas to Birmingham. Do not presume to speak for us or to tell me what it is we should want."

"But you have left," said Asa. "You no longer live there."

I thought of the lovely corals outside, colored by poison. I thought of the refugees around the world underground and afloat—still called that after centuries and generations. I thought of a cooling Earth, of the Developed World racing to reclaim their ancestral lands, of the wars to come and the slaughter hinted at when the deck of power is shuffled and redealt. Who should decide? Who pay the price?

As the three of us sat inside the submerged habitat, refugees enveloped by darting trails of light like meteors streaking across the empyrean, none of us could think of anything more to say.

•

I once regretted that I do not know the face I was born with.

We remake our faces as easily as our ancestors once sculpted clay, changing the features and contours of our shells, this microcosm of the soul, to match the moods and fashions of the macrocosm of society. Still unsatisfied with the limits of the flesh, we supplement the results with jewelry that deflect light and project shadows, smoothing over substance with ethereal holograms.

The Naturalists, in their eternal struggle against modernity, proclaim hypocrisy and demand us to stop, telling us that our lives are inauthentic, and we listen, enraptured, as they flash grainy images of our ancestors before us, their imperfections and fixed appearances a series of mute accusations. And we nod and vow to do better, to foreswear artifice, until we go back to our jobs, shake off the spell, and decide upon the new face to wear for the next customer.

But what would the Naturalists have us do? The faces that we were born with were already constructed—when we were only fertilized eggs, a million cellular scalpels had snipped and edited our genes to eliminate diseases, to filter out risky mutations, to build up intelligence and longevity, and before that, millions of years of conquest, of migration, of global cooling and warming, of choices made by our ancestors motivated by beauty or violence or avarice had already shaped us. Our faces at birth were as crafted as the masks worn by the ancient players in Dionysian Athens or Ashikaga's Kyoto, but also as natural as the glacier-sculpted Alps or sea-inundated Massachusetts.

We do not know who we are. But we dare not stop striving to find out.

Grey Rabbit,
Crimson Mare,
Coal Leopard

In light of the growing threat of marauding bandits, all able-bodied citizens of Dripe are hereby encouraged to volunteer for the militia. You'll be responsible for your own weapons and supplies.

The Archon, with the consent of the Synedrion, has promised each militia member one-half of the spoils taken from the rotten.

—Proclamation by Governor Kide of Dripe Prefecture

Ava Cide shoveled some more ore into the sifting pan and rocked it gently back and forth in the stream of the sluice. As the water flowed over the stepped riffles, the varicolored mixture gradually separated by weight into categories: heavy metal objects—rusted nails, fragments of tools and machine components—at the top; thinner and lighter goods—crushed cans, glass shards, broken ceramic and porcelain—in the middle; and the lightest objects of all—various bits of colorful plastic, some with electronic components embedded in them like glittering jewels—on the bottom.

Ava shook her head in wonder. Though she had been a midden miner since she could first walk, the opulence in which the ancients lived never ceased to amaze Ava.

"Ava, we're thinking of calling it a day." The speaker was Shaw, Ava's little brother. Still showing a bit of baby fat in his cheeks, the young man tried to furrow his brows to show his seriousness. Behind him, his friends were already packing up their tools and finding-buckets.

At twenty-five, Ava was older than most of the other miners. And as the only one who had traveled outside of Dripe Prefecture, she was treated as their leader—a big sister to all of them, not just Shaw.

Ava glanced up at the sun, still several arm's-lengths high in the western sky. "So early? There's still plenty of mining left."

Shaw scratched his head hesitantly. "We were thinking of . . . going to see Fey Swell."

Ava's face darkened. "What do you want to do with that reckless woman? Mark my words, she's bound to bring trouble to those who follow her—"

"Fey is offering to buy everyone weapons on credit, so there's no need for any money from us. I'm good with a bow and fought off two jackals with a staff last year—she saw me—"

"So you still want to volunteer for the militia. I'm not going to debate with you again. This isn't about money, and the answer is no."

Turning away, Ava heaved the pan out of the water with a grunt. Softening her tone, she added, "Help me."

Shaw looked helplessly at his friends, whose resentful looks Ava ignored. With a sigh, he squatted down next to the pan with Ava and began to sort through the deposits.

They worked quickly but carefully. The midden mines were replete with broken glass, rusty blades, and sharp needles carrying curses from the ancients. More than a few miners had lost their lives from mysterious diseases acquired through a pricked finger or sliced palm. For protection, they both wore gloves Ava had made specifically for this purpose.

The mines were full of thin sheets and bags of plastic, often covered in colorful logos and meaningless words. Most miners had discarded them as slag. But Ava found a way to cut the plastic into thin strips, which she then twisted into yarn and wove into a tough cloth. Gloves made from the cloth were supple, functional, and very beautifully designed. By now, practically every midden miner had been gifted a pair of such gloves by Ava.

Four hands danced through the debris, draped in pretty mosaics that Ava had cobbled together from the detritus of a bygone age: a soaring phoenix, a falling maple leaf, a blooming rose, a rabbit with drooping ears . . .

Silently, the two siblings sorted the contents of the pan into finding-buckets. The metals were good for a few centicredits by the kilo, but the real finds were the electronic components in the plastic boards. Once the solder had been melted away, any components found to be still working could fetch a few credits apiece. Every miner knew a story of some friend of a friend who once found a rare chip that fetched a hundred credits in Wooster or Roanflare.

Shaw took a deep breath. "They say that if you manage to break into a rotten nest, everyone can get enough to buy three years' worth of rations—"

"We've got plenty to eat," Ava shot back. "Do you really think fighting the rotten is as easy as hunting squirrels? What if you encounter one of the Revealed rats? Leave the fighting to the army."

"We don't have to use the money to buy rations. We could save up and buy gifts for the recommendation committee—"

"The recommendation committee? So that's what this is really about." Ava's voice hardened again. "Have you forgotten what Mother said before she died?"

"No," said Shaw, sullen. "But I don't want to spend my life digging in a trash heap."

It was some time before Ava spoke again. She struggled to keep her voice gentle. "You've only been to Dripe Town on market days, but you've never lived there, or heard what the townsfolk say about us when we're not around. And the residents of Roanflare are even more arrogant. To them, people like you and me are like weeds, disposable trash. You won't find happiness—"

"Things are changing," said Shaw, growing more impassioned. "All the governors and generals are recruiting! There are opportunities—"

"You will *never* be Revealed," declared Ava, fairly shouting. "That is final!"

"Just because you failed, it doesn't mean that I will too! Maybe when my nature is Revealed, I will be someone who matters!"

Ava stilled as though she had been slapped. At length, she struggled to speak past the lump in her throat. "You don't understand—"

But Shaw had ripped off his gloves and tossed them down on the ground. "Don't bother with dinner for me tonight. I can't be with someone who doesn't believe in me."

As his stunned friends watched, he ran away from the midden mines.

Ava stared at his receding figure, frozen in place. Then, she glanced at the sun, sighed, and returned to sorting through the deposits in the pan.

•

Absentmindedly, Ava caressed the photograph in the middle of the table, the only portrait her family had ever taken. It had cost her parents all the savings from mining for a year, and they had sat still in the only studio in Dripe Town, willing themselves to not blink, as the light-painter slowly worked his magic to freeze their image on silver-plated copper.

In the photograph, her mother and father stood on either side of eighteen-year-old Ava, dressed in the formal gown issued by the governor to the bright young people chosen to be Revealed. Her parents had tried to heed the light-painter's instruction to keep their features relaxed rather than smile—it was impossible to hold such an expression long enough for the imaging process to capture it without blur—but she could see pride curling up the corners of their mouths, her mother's arm wrapped protectively around Ava's own waist. Shaw, only a boy of eleven back then, stood in front and a bit to the side of Ava, his face a smear because he couldn't help gazing up at his big sister with admiration.

How much hope there had been back then, dreams of transformed lives, of opportunities in Roanflare, of the elevation of a family from the midden mines to wealth and privilege.

Then it had all gone to hell.

"Just because you failed . . ."

The image of her mother, shriveled, illness-ridden, dying on the moldy mattress in the back of their ill-lit hut, surfaced in her mind's eye.

"Protect your brother. Keep him at home," she wheezed. "His heart is restless. But a turkey isn't meant to soar like an eagle, and we are not meant to be that which we're not."

She took a bite of the tasteless ration pack, supplemented by a cup of tea made from boiled aruk root. The aruk, a hardy weed, was practically the only thing that thrived in Dripe Prefecture, where the soil had been so poisoned by the midden mines that no crops would survive after the Plague. The aruk tea was bitter, and Shaw always compared it to drinking mud—dining alone for the first time in years, Ava found herself missing her little brother's incessant complaints.

It was so late in the evening that only the wood-burning stove, with the soldering iron warming over it, illuminated the room. She got up, thinking she should go look for Shaw. After all, she was the big sister; it was her duty not to respond in kind to his words uttered in anger.

As she reached the threshold of the door, she paused.

He's safe. The family of one of his friends will feed him tonight.

Shaw is no longer a boy, and maybe time and space away from me is exactly what he needs to understand.

She washed the plate and cup, put them away, and sat down next to the stove, wielding the soldering iron to gently remove the electronic components embedded in the day's haul of plastic boards. As she worked, she heard the distant hooting of an owl or two, intent on the hunt for small rodents in the fields of aruk outside. The window shutters rattled in the gusting wind, and her heart calmed as she lost herself in the repetitive motions of work. Thoughts of marauding bandit packs, of lives of luxury in the distant capital, of ambition and warfare, faded.

"Things are changing."

Could Shaw be right? Have I become blind to change? Am I too timid, too traumatized by the path I walked, too attached to this life of toiling in obscurity, of familiar peace?

She stopped and looked down at the rectangular piece of plastic in her hand. The row of LEDs embedded at the top showed that it had perhaps once been an illuminated sign. The words on the sign, printed in an ancient script, were barely legible. With some difficulty, she puzzled out the words: GREATER ROANFLARE ECOPOLIS METRO-POLITAN REGION.

A hard name to parse, a meaningless abstraction. Almost like an incantation, a phrase to summon.

Abruptly, her mind was transported to that day seven years ago.

•

Though she had imagined the moment of arrival in Roanflare a thousand thousand times, Ava was not prepared for the reality.

A rumbling bashe, a massive vehicle shaped like a moving house and festooned in flowers and fruits from every corner of Grema—most of which she could not name—carried her and the other Revelation candidates down Commonwealth Avenue. The central artery of Roanflare was wide enough for a hundred people to walk abreast, and columns of smaller motor vehicles preceded as well as followed the bashe, making a mechanical din that overwhelmed Ava's senses. The pungent fumes emitted by the engine told Ava that the bashe was powered by biodiesel, an almost unimaginable luxury. She had only smelled the scent once before in her life, when Governor Kide had paraded through Dripe on a Longleg.

She bit into the apple she had been given: the real thing, not a synthesized imitation, twice as big as her balled fist. The sweetness was unbelievable. She looked up at the banner flapping at the front of the bashe, a stylized outline of Grema, with its long coastline bisected by the Arlos River. Cursive script around the map spelled out the motto of Grema, a phrase found on so many artifacts from before the Plague that suggested deep mysteries few understood: Greater Roanflare Ecopolis Metropolitan Region.

The recording that she had played over and over the night before, intended to indoctrinate her in the basics of the Revelation, echoed through her mind.

. . . The name of Grema dates from before the Plague, connecting us to the mystical past.

Once, the magnificent coastal metropolis of Roanflare was the sun of a proud commonwealth, in which the smaller towns, villages, and islands in Massenwhal Bay were the planets, each in its assigned place like glittering jewels carefully inlaid in a mosaic of fields, woodlands, and sea. Tens of millions of people lived there, dreamers in a fantastical world built of steel and electricity, wherein even the weather was subject to their whims, and the secret of eternal life was within their grasp. . . .

Residents of Roanflare, dressed in shimmering garb, lined both sides of the road to observe the spectacle, many with bored expressions. Garlands of fresh flowers wound through their hair, and vendors in stalls behind the crowd hawked foods that Ava had only heard of in the tales of wandering storytellers—raw tuna, roasted lamb skewers, steamed lobsters that must have been acquired miles off the coast in the eastern mist. Strange service machines, perhaps powered by electricity, buzzed in the air and thrummed on the sidewalks, their movements impossibly precise and fluid. Far in the distance, beyond the crowds and vendors, she could see the wrecks of the ruined skyscrapers, mountains of bent steel and shattered glass, draped in thick vines and home to thousands of birds.

The bashe slowed down. Imitating the other candidates, Ava leaned out of the window by her seat. Ahead was Flare Hill, and on top sat the magnificent golden-domed Commonwealth Palace. She squinted, hoping to be the first to catch a glimpse of a legate or two, or perhaps even the silver parasol that announced the presence of the Seventh Archon herself.

The Plague, seemingly overnight, wiped away the froth of that indolent and sinful civilization we read about in the surviving works of ancient sages—miniature electronics that put brains in grains of rice, continent-spanning networks that fulfilled every desire, virtual gold summoned out of thin air . . . The laws of nature our ancestors thought they understood no longer applied, and monsters sprang forth in sea and on land, punishing them for their hubris. Millions died, and survivors faced a transformed world, in which Life itself seemed to have become vengeful and fantastical.

It was only with a superhuman effort that the First Archon, aided by his faithful Revealed companions, brought peace and order back to the chaotic aftermath of the Plague.

Each of the thirty-six prefectures of Grema has its own climate and produce, as well as its own unique scar from the Plague: one prefecture has rich orchards that yield sweet fruit, but the fruits bear no seeds; another has soil and water so poisoned that nothing grows, and the inhabitants must mine the ruins to eke out a living; still another contains lakes and rivers filled with delicious fish, though many have two heads or three tails. . . .

Past the borders of this new Grema, beyond the influence of revived Roanflare, heavy fog makes navigation impossible, and monsters await the reckless who venture there. . . .

The peace in Grema was not easy to achieve and is even harder to sustain. The Revelation is the key.

Instead of legates or the Archon, however, she was greeted by a sight even more wondrous.

The Lords of Grema, men and women who had once perhaps been as wide-eyed and awestruck as Ava herself, stood upon the steps of the Commonwealth Palace, ready to welcome the new candidates.

They were not dressed in finery; they were not surrounded by electric machines; they did not ride on mechanical monsters guzzling diesel. The Lords of Grema simply stood naked in their Revealed, magnificent nature—

•

The burnt odor of overheated solder and melted plastic shook her from her reverie. Cursing silently, she pulled the iron away before it could do more damage.

No, she resolutely told herself. Nothing could be regained by recalling her shame, by dwelling upon the past. She had to focus on the here and now, on the work at hand. The midden mines might never bring her and Shaw great wealth, but it was an honest and safe living, and there was pride in that, too.

Deprived of Shaw's help, it was past midnight before she was finished with de-soldering and testing the extracted components. The day's haul was average, with a few large capacitors that would probably fetch a good price the next market day. She was satisfied.

The next day, Ava awoke and found herself still alone in the hut. She made breakfast and waited until the sun was too high to be ignored. Reluctantly, she headed for the mines.

By noon, she was uneasy. None of the other miners knew where Shaw was. A growing dread seized her heart, and she left the mines and returned to the village. Door by door, she inquired after her brother. Neighbors and friends shook their heads, unable to help her.

Frantic and fearing the worst, she went to find Fey Swell.

•

Though Fey Swell was a midden miner by trade, like much of the population of Dripe Prefecture, Ava couldn't recall the last time she had seen the woman at a pan or sluice. In reality, Fey made her living as a poacher, stealing from the flocks and herds of wealthier neighboring prefectures. Occasionally, Fey even ventured into the mists beyond the border of Grema, hunting for the exotic meat of monsters that fetched a good return on the black market, destined for the tables of thrill-seeking residents of Dripe Town or Wooster.

Ignoring the cold looks of the two muscular young men who flanked Fey—the hunter had a gang of such youths who followed her wherever she went—Ava shuffled up to the woman and politely inquired whether she had seen her brother.

At six foot four and at least a hundred kilos, Fey was an intimidating presence. A long hunting knife was strapped to her thigh, sheathless so that sunlight glinted from the cold blade, spotted with a few stains that could be either rust or blood. She locked eyes with Ava, saying nothing. Her face, as black in hue as her short-cropped hair, betrayed no emotion.

Ava's heart pounded. Fey had a reputation for being quick to anger. She prayed fervently that Shaw had not somehow insulted this woman. She forced herself to hold Fey's gaze, neither obsequious nor defiant.

At length, Fey shook her head. "Your brother did come to see me yesterday afternoon," she said, her voice a deep, guttural rumble. "But he didn't want to join my militia."

Ava sighed with relief. "Good."

Fey narrowed her eyes. "Good? The rotten have gathered a large force only a few days' journey from here. Everyone should be volunteering for the militia."

"Fighting bandits is the army's job. The Archon has her generals."

"Spoken like a coward," said Fey, a look of utter contempt on her face. "What age do you think we live in? The Archon is in charge in name only, and the generals and governors answer her pleas only when they please. They're more concerned with fighting one another than the bandits at the moment. The brave should step forward to defend what is theirs and make a fortune and name for themself."

"Not everyone is meant to live by the tip of a blade," said Ava. "Toiling in the mines may not be very glamorous or lead to riches, but it is far safer than following you. I'm glad to know Shaw has a good head on his shoulders."

Fey stared at Ava, her eyes widening as though she had trouble parsing Ava's words. At length she began to laugh, a deep, belly-shaking guffaw that crinkled her features.

"What's so funny?" demanded Ava, dread growing in her stomach.

"'A good head on his shoulders,'" mocked Fey, struggling to stifle her mirth. "You and your brother are both fools, just in different ways."

"What exactly did you discuss with him?"

"He asked me whether there was any truth to the rumor that the rotten have found their own supply of Revelation wine."

Blood drained from Ava's face. "Wh-what?"

"I told him that I didn't know, but given what I know of the world, it is *possible*."

"How could you say such a thing?" cried Ava. "The Orange Brothers are inveterate liars, and their cult is only for the gullible—"

"You don't know what I know," said Fey, a hint of menace in her voice. She paused, calmed herself, and added, "Then he asked me for my best guess as to the site of the rotten encampment. I told him to head due west, past the broken highway. He thanked me and left."

Ava was horrified. She had not understood the depth of Shaw's obsession with the Revelation. Rumors of the terrors practiced by the Orange Brothers and the rotten filled her mind.

"He's going to try to steal from the bandits. We have to find him before it's too late. Come with me! Bring all your followers."

Fey stared at her. "You really are as mad as your brother. An assault on a rotten base with a small band of militia would be suicide! He's your brother, not mine."

"Spoken like a coward," spat Ava.

Blood rushed into Fey's face. "What do *you* know of—"

But Ava was already gone.

•

The red sun hung in the west like a ripe peach suspended in cloud-trees.

Ava pushed her way through the shoulder-high aruk, careless of the thorns pulling, scratching, tearing. Her clothes were in tatters, and streaks of blood covered her face and arms.

She had been stumbling through the pathless wilderness beyond the broken highway for hours, always heading west. There had been no sign of Shaw, but she sensed, without being able to explain why, that she had to press on.

The marauding rotten, bandits who had fallen under the sway of the cult of the Orange Brothers, vowed to "slaughter the rich and feast on their fat." But in practice, they preyed upon the poor in remote, mostly rural prefectures like Dripe. The truly rich could hide behind city walls, secure that their houses and credit chits would be untouched. Meanwhile, the peasants, herders, fisherfolk, and miners were left to the mercy of the bandits.

The field of aruk stretched before her like an endless sea, the wind driving waves through the swaying stalks. A mist was gathering over the field with the chill of the evening, veiling the landscape around her in a blood-tinged haze. From time to time, a red-winged black-bird or two erupted from the vegetal sea, streaking through the fog like flying fish skimming above the waves, trilling and screeching, a sound that resembled the clang of metallic scales.

Ava stopped, panting. She was tired, and the light was failing. It was dangerous to spend the night out in the wild, especially in this unfathomable sea of grass. She stared at the ground, at the openings between the thorn-encrusted stalks. Would she—could she—should she—

No, she rejected the thought, her heart throbbing with fear and doubt. Ever since her return from Roanflare, she had kept her secret to herself, unwilling to revisit the truth that had shattered her family, that had left her parents disappointed, that had buried her in shame—

Again, the trilling, like metal plates grinding against one another, sending a shiver down her spine.

With a start, she realized that the sound wasn't the cry of a blackbird. It was louder, harder, more relentless. And along with the metallic trilling, she could hear another noise like her own panting breath, but more desperate and *wilder.*

Ducking down among the aruk stalks, she peered into the thickening mist and willed her thumping heart to still so that she could listen.

A disturbance roiled the sea of grass in the distance, as though a ship were parting the waves, accompanied by heaving snorts and a long whinny that shattered the fog like a lightning bolt. Beyond the disturbance, still concealed by the mist, she could detect other presences, monstrous beings that marched with mechanical precision: *chug-clank-chug, chug-clank-chug.*

A gust of wind ripped away the mist.

The biggest horse she had ever seen in her life was crashing through the aruk, leaving a wake of broken stalks. The mare, standing full three meters tall, was the hue of a burning bonfire. The long mane billowed like a crimson banner, while luxuriant fiery-red hair—feathers—covered the pedaling hooves. Ava had never seen any creature so splendid. She was pure power, strength, speed incarnate.

How did a Revealed come to be here?

Behind the mare, in hard pursuit, were two hulking Longlegs. Constructed from black steel, the all-terrain military vehicles resembled giant mechanical spiders, with eight segmented, piston-driven legs topped by a squat cockpit with a revolving turret. Piloted by a crew of three, these machines were the pride of the Archon's army, the deadliest killing machines to stride across Grema.

The mare was slowing, the distance between her and her pursuers shrinking.

Thunk. Thunk.

Massive bolts, propelled by the force of electricity and magnetism, shot from the spinning turrets and slammed into the ground around the fleeing mare, one of them grazing her side.

The mare reared up, screaming. Foam spilled from her mouth as she turned to gaze defiantly back, baring her teeth and flaring her nostrils. Red droplets, perhaps sweat, perhaps blood, cascaded from her back in rivulets, staining the broken stalks around her.

Pity and rage filled Ava.

Thunk!

Another bolt headed straight for the mare's head. Moving with impossible grace for such a large animal, the horse leaned to the side as she kicked, the graceful leap covering at least twenty meters.

But the crews of the two Longlegs had been working in tandem. A second shot from the other Longleg had anticipated where she was going to land. The bolt struck her right hind leg, and the mare collapsed to the ground with an agonized cry.

As the lamed mare floundered on the ground, the Longlegs clanged closer, their spinning saw-toothed steel mandibles aloft, ready to shred the defeated mare to pieces. As the dying rays of the sun caught the mare's eyes, Ava saw in them no despair, only the will to fight, to resist, to bite into the steel legs with her bare teeth in a last expression of her indomitable spirit.

Blood boiled inside Ava. To see something so splendid, so glorious and alive, brought down by a few cowards hiding safe inside a mechanical monstrosity was intolerable.

Abruptly, she stood up, showing her face above the sea of swaying aruk stalks. With a low growl, she focused her attention inward, in the manner she had been taught seven years ago—

•

The burn of the Revelation wine coursed through her veins, the bitter taste of a thousand spices still on her tongue. Her mind was storm tossed, and it was all she could do to keep herself from stumbling as she shuffled forward.

Together with the other candidates, she was led into the Hall of Reflection, in the dark warren of secret tunnels under the palace. One by one, they were guided into the Chamber of Mirrors, where they would finally be shown their true form.

All the years of pious prayers at the shrines of the gods, of reading and memorizing the words of the sages, of her parents scrimping and saving for the chance to buy a recommendation letter, had been leading up to this moment.

From beyond the closed door, she heard a cry of ecstasy, followed by a roar of admiration from the crowd of observers. What new self had been revealed to that boy? The fate of the boy as well as his family would be transformed forever. He would be set on the path to become one of them, one of the Lords of Grema, who had stood on the steps of the palace to welcome the new candidates parading down Commonwealth Avenue:

A bull buffalo, his curved horns raised high like a pair of moon blades, pawed the ground. A tiger, her shoulders as tall as the bronze palace gates, yawned lazily. An eagle, her outstretched wings at least eight meters across, screeched. A bear, almost as massive as Governor Kide's Longleg, reared up on his hind legs . . .

The noise beyond the locked doors quieted. The transformed boy would be led through another set of doors on the other side of the chamber and ascend into the palace, where the Archon and the legates would greet him, securing his place among the ranks of the nobility—the lowest rank, to be sure, for much politics and strife would still be required to climb up the ladder.

Almost delirious with anxiety, Ava realized that she would be the next candidate entering the Chamber of Mirrors.

"Mother, Father, Shaw," she whispered to herself. "All our sacrifices have been worth it."

While wealthy urban residents had many avenues to be noticed by the prefecture's recommendation committee, responsible for picking candidates for Revelation, midden miners had few opportunities. It took years of volunteer corvée by the family before the governor felt obligated to recommend her, the lone rural nominee among dozens of children of privilege. The family had then put all their savings into bribes for the few members who had let it be known that they were open to such persuasion. Even then, her place wasn't secured until her committee interview: the garrison commander had been impressed by her athleticism, and the scholars had commented favorably on her knowledge of the ancient texts. Behind those accomplishments were countless hours of study and practice, without the aid of tutors or trainers.

The Revelation wine was one of the first secrets of this altered world to be discovered after the Plague. A concoction that awakened some hidden mechanism inside the body, the wine allowed its drinkers to reshape their body into a second form, a form that displayed their latent talents and hidden abilities. With its aid, the First Archon, an unremarkable petty gangster during the dark days immediately after the Plague, had Revealed himself to be a drake, a magnificent beast of charisma and fortitude. With a legion of other Revealed companions, he had then driven monsters from the land and defeated his rivals, founding the Commonwealth of Grema.

The heavy doors before her swung open. The glare from the mirrored walls was so bright that she lifted her arms to shield her eyes.

"Ava Cide," intoned the attendant who had opened the door, "you may enter."

Stumbling, almost falling, holding on to the wall with trembling hands, she felt her way into the room, brightness-blind. Her mind was a blur, the pounding of her heart a roar in her ears.

Was she destined to be a hardy ox, a minister who would serve the Archon faithfully in administration until she might be elevated among the august ranks of the Synedrion? Or was she meant to be a wise monkey, a scholar tasked with recovering the knowledge of the ancient sages lost in the corrupted data banks of the Roanflare Archives, striving to usher Grema into a new golden age? Or perhaps she was intended by the gods to be a wolf or a lobster, a warrior to defend Grema, this one oasis of civilization, against the monsters of the Plague-ridden wilderness and the domestic threats of ambitious rebellion?

She struggled to put the attendants' whispered instructions, which she only half-understood, into practice. She closed her eyes and took a deep breath, envisioning the air inside her lungs as two balls of energy, one blue, one red. Slowly, she imagined herself pushing the balls of energy into her belly, where they merged into one white-hot sphere. Stoking it, feeding it, fanning it aflame, she willed it to grow, to suffuse her chest cavity and limbs, to fill her body with a holy flame. She imagined the energy burning away her old self, awakening each cell, routing new vessels through marrow and muscle, reconstructing her body into a new form, her new self—

—crying out in ecstasy and terror, she felt it. She felt the Revelation wine come to life inside her, rebuilding her like the flooding Arlos River reshaping its banks every spring. The wine was discovering her true nature, bringing it to the surface much like the captured image gradually emerged on the light-painter's copper plate in the mercury fumes. She felt her bones crack and fuse, her muscles reattaching to the new skeleton, her organs rearranging themselves to suit the new space. . . . The physical sensation was neither pleasure nor pain, but something akin to and beyond both. She lost herself to it, completely absorbed by the intensity of the transformation.

At length, consciousness returned. Once again, she could command her limbs, and instantly she felt the difference. It was like putting on thick furs and boots for the first time in winter, when everything felt awkward and unwieldy. She would have to get used to her new body before she could move with grace and control, before she could shift back and forth between her human and Revealed forms with ease.

Not yet daring to move, she waited, expecting exclamations of admiration at her new shape.

Deafening silence.

Gingerly, she opened her eyes.

She couldn't comprehend how she had been transported to this un-recognizable landscape. Gigantic statues loomed around her like the towering columns of the Temple of Wisdom, colossal human figures with expressions of shock suspended far above her. They were so big that they reminded her of the ancient ruins of skyscrapers in Roanflare, mute witnesses of a bygone age.

"Where am I?" she wondered, dazed.

Then, the massive statues began to move, their voices thunderous in her ears. She winced, shocked by how sensitive her ears had suddenly become. The words were hard to parse, impossible to make sense of. Gazing helplessly above, she suddenly recognized the face of the attendant who had opened the door for her—

"A useless Revelation!" the attendant roared, his gargantuan face twisted into a look of disgust. "A waste of time!"

"This is what happens when you dig through trash and pick among weeds." Another voice. A clap of thunder.

"Standards! Don't they care about standards in the prefectures?"

Instinctively, she bolted forward just as a massive foot, attached to a leg as thick as the trunk of a hundred-year-old tree, slammed down into the space she had occupied but a moment earlier.

She found herself in front of a bright wall, and a fur-clad face stared back at her with terrified eyes and a twitching nose. She crouched down and saw the figure in the wall crouch down likewise on furry paws.

Realization dawned.

She felt and saw her long, floppy ears rest against her shoulders in disappointment. A high-pitched whimper emerged from her throat, and she licked the split upper lip with her tongue as she watched the creature in the mirror, no more than a foot in length and clad in ash-grey fur, repeat the motion.

Horror and shame overwhelmed her—

·

—the stalks of aruk shot up and thickened around her as she once again experienced that mix of pain and pleasure, of terror and ecstasy.

290   KEN LIU

A thousand sharp odors, unnoticed in her human form, assaulted her nose—fresh droppings from voles and deer, the rotting vegetation of late fall, the intoxicating fragrance of a clump of mushrooms. Her ears, fine like nets dragged through the Arlos River by fisherfolk on smooth sculls, caught every noise and vibration in the dusk air. Her eyes, now located on the sides of her head, provided her with a nearly omnidirectional view of her surroundings, sharp and distinct in the half-light that she preferred.

More clangs of metal grinding against metal. Another defiant scream from the crimson mare.

Ava-Rabbit hopped forward, luxuriating in the sense of freedom provided by her strong hind legs. Now that she had shrunk, the field of dense aruk was no longer a pathless, resistant medium that had to be force through, but a forest of swaying trees with wide-open paths everywhere she looked.

On, on, she ran, growing more used to her other body with each hop. As she immersed herself in this new mode of existence, the shame of having been Revealed to be prey rather than predator, of being an ordinary, unremarkable rabbit instead of a supersize ox, tiger, wolf, or drake, sloughed away, much like her discarded human clothing.

Upon returning from Roanflare, disgraced, she had kept what she had seen in the Chamber of Mirrors from her disappointed family, telling them only that she had failed to be Revealed. But time and again, when alone, she had delighted in taking on her rabbit form under the glow of the moon, hopping, exploring, sniffing the night air for unfamiliar scents. It was another way to *be*, to experience a reality that belonged only to her.

She was conflicted. She didn't know how to reconcile her human nature with her rabbit nature.

But such anxieties had no place here and now. For the first time, she needed to accomplish a specific task in this form; she needed to *do* rather than wallow.

She skidded to a stop as the aruk stalks parted, and she came face-to-face with the gigantic mare.

As Ava gazed sympathetically upon the crippled horse, the glow in the equine eyes dimmed. The mare snorted in resignation—what was the use of compassion from a rabbit, dwarfed by even one of the horse's dinner-plate-size hooves? Impatiently, the mare shook her head, telling Ava to get away before the mechanical predators descended upon them both.

"Hold still," she whispered to the mare. Satisfaction warmed her heart as she saw the surprise in the mare's eyes. "Lie down and stop kicking. It will be hard for them to see you in this red light."

As the mare gaped in astonishment, Ava bounded away into the thick aruk, heading straight for the Longlegs.

There! A metal leg pistoned into sight, crushing the aruk like a meteor slamming into a copse. A second one followed. The metal columns shone with the dull solidity of unshakable strength, forces of corrupted nature.

What could she do? Ava pondered the sight, full of doubt.

She was a runner, not a fighter. She lacked the size, weight, and strength to stop or even slow the steel spiders; she had no dagger-like teeth or steel-rending claws to menace the crew. What good was a ball of fur against the mightiest war machine of the Archon?

The earth quaked as more metal legs slammed into the ground and then held still. The spinning saw-toothed mandibles seemed to hesitate. The crimson mare had followed Ava's advice, and the spiders' crews had lost—at least for the moment—their prey.

Hope rekindled in Ava's heart. She gritted her teeth and bounded toward the towering legs. Landing next to two of the thick columns so that she was in the blind spot of the crew in the cockpit—though she doubted they would have considered her a threat even if they had seen her—she bit into the aruk stalks around the pistoned legs.

She worked quickly. The stalks tasted bitter, much like the tea made from the weed's roots. Wielding her incisors like chisels, she hacked away at the grass-trees with abandon.

One stalk fell; another; a third. She was a miniature lumberjack, racing against time to cut down the tough, fibrous trunks.

The metal spider legs remained still. The turrets whirred and spun above her as the crew searched for the bloodred equine form that had somehow faded into the dense aruk, dyed crimson by the setting sun like a field of embers. Tentatively, the spiders shot a few bolts randomly into the thicket, hoping to rouse their injured prey.

Ava knew that she didn't have a lot of time. Without breaking to rest her sore jaws, she began to hop back and forth, dancing among the felled stalks of aruk like a frenzied beaver.

One over, two across; one over, two across . . . Tirelessly Ava leaped and hopped, keeping her ears slicked back, clutching her front paws tightly around the fibrous strands. It was the same pattern that she used to weave her gloves out of strips of mined plastic, the motion so familiar that she fell into a trance.

Her ears twitched at a sudden rustling. The mare, perhaps unable to stand the pain from her injured leg, had twitched in her hiding spot. The turret of the spider above Ava spun to lock on the sudden movement in the grass. There was a nigh-imperceptible shift in the whine of the diesel engine. Ava hopped away. She prayed to the Jade Rabbit in the moon that she had done enough.

The whine of the engine grew higher pitched. Pistons began to contract, joints began to flex, the legs would lift up and step forward in a coordinated dance—

Two of the legs, bound together by a woven web of aruk stalks, pulled against one another clumsily, and the spider stumbled. The pilot inside the spider, confused, nudged the control stick back and forth in an effort to disentangle the legs. But the grass strands, twisted and braided by Ava for strength, held.

The pilot, annoyed, grabbed the control stick and shoved it back and forth, increasing the power to the pistons as she did so. Suddenly, the woven strands tying the legs together snapped, and the straining spindly appendages, abruptly freed from the resistance, kicked out wildly, out of control.

The vehicle teetered, on the verge of losing its balance. Panicked, the pilot wrestled with the control stick and shoved it hard the other way. The pistons groaned as the spindly legs struggled futilely to right the body, but it was too late. The spider stumbled like a newborn foal that had lost its footing before falling to the ground with a mighty crash. The whirring metal saw blades bit into the earth, throwing up a blinding explosion of rocks and clods that fell back down like hailstones. The turret groaned as it came to a stop; smoke billowed from the seams. A moment later, three soldiers, hacking and choking, threw open the door at the top and climbed out.

The crew of the other spider, unable to see what had brought their comrades down, reacted by panicking in their turn. Thinking that they were under attack, the crew aimed their gun at the area immediately around the disabled spider and set their gun on rapid fire. Bolts thunked into the ground, adding to the confusion. As the crew of the fallen war machine scrambled behind their vehicle for shelter and screamed for the other crew to stop firing, Ava bolted out of harm's way.

Finally, the crew of the still-functioning Longleg noticed the rabbit fleeing from the wrecked spider. The turret spun to track her, and a stream of bolts slammed into the ground, missing her by mere inches.

Left, right, zig, zag. By shifting her direction every second, Ava hung on to life by the thinnest of threads. She could feel herself slowing, her breath growing labored. Though she was fast, she was built for quick dashes, not sustained exertion. It was only a matter of time before the gunner caught up to her.

"They can't see you if you stop moving!" Her ears caught the hoarse whisper on the wind.

Ava brought down the nictitating membranes over her eyes and dug her paws into the earth. She curled up to make herself as small as possible, forcing herself to disregard the instinct to bolt as one more bullet slammed into the ground next to her, covering her with thrown-up soil and broken stalks.

The relentless *ack-ack-ack* stopped. The voice had been right. Panic had caused her to forget her own advice. She was too small, and the twilight too dim. Without swaying stalks disturbed by her passage to give her position away, she was practically invisible.

The turret continued to revolve and clang as the gunner searched for his target. A cacophony of human voices filled the air, oblivious of her presence.

"What *was* that?"

"A vole, maybe?"

"Could be something worse. Could be one of the rotten!"

"No rotten would be that small. It was just some dumb animal. You were shooting at *us*! You could have—"

"You must be the clumsiest pilot in history! I've never even heard of anyone crashing a Longleg because of a vole. The captain is going to—"

"Forget about the vole. Where's the fugitive?"

"She couldn't have gotten far. Climb up here and we'll go after her."

Curses, laughter, the *swish* of a rope ladder being tossed down. The functioning Longleg was retrieving the stranded crew of its wrecked twin.

"Can you move?" Ava squeaked into the distance, knowing that the mare would hear her high-pitched squeals while the human crew couldn't.

"No," came the reply on the wind.

Ava pondered their situation. As soon as the crew united inside the spider, they'd return to the hunt. It was only a matter of time before the mare would be found.

Ava's heart thudded painfully; she was terrified beyond measure. But she forced herself to creep slowly through the aruk in the direction of the spider, skirting past the stalks to leave them undisturbed. She had to try *something*, anything.

The massive killing machine loomed into view. Three human figures were climbing up a rope ladder dangling from the side cockpit. The spider was listing from their weight.

Tensing her long hind legs, she *leaped*, tracing a brief arc above the grass. As she landed, she raced straight ahead, aiming for the opening between the long, spindly legs.

"There! There!"

The gunner, who had been nervously scanning the gently swaying grass sea the whole time, squeezed the trigger without thinking. A stream of bullets spat out of the gun as he spun and tilted the turret, trying to keep the grey streak in sight.

"Stop shooting! You fool—"

But it was too late. The combination of the momentum of the spinning turret, the recoil, and the weight of the climbing figures was pushing the spider off its center of gravity.

Barked orders, curses, screams. The second spider teetered and toppled over, crashing to the ground with a bone-shattering din.

Ava raced through the thick aruk and returned to where she had left the injured mare.

Instead of the horse, she found a tall, slender woman with a thick mane of red curls lying on the ground. Her face, not unhandsome, was crisscrossed by streaks of red, perhaps scratches left by the thorns of the aruk, or perhaps spider veins resulting from overindulgence in alcohol. One of her legs was twisted in an unnatural manner.

Ava crouched down, exhausted. The woman held out a hand and laid it gently on Ava's back. Ava's rabbit body trembled, but she allowed the contact, locking eyes with the woman.

"Thank you," the woman whispered. It was the same hoarse voice she had heard earlier. "I never thought I would be saved by someone . . . like you."

"The gratitude might be a bit premature," panted Ava. "I've only delayed the inevitable. Once they've recovered from their confusion, even without the Longlegs, six trained soldiers on foot will still make short work of you and me."

The woman shifted her position and winced. "If it weren't for this leg, they'd never catch us." Then she threw a contemptuous look in the direction of the wrecks. "Six soldiers is nothing. In a fair fight, Crimson Mare would hold up just fine even if there were ten thousand of them."

Recalling the awe-inducing splendor of the woman's Revealed form, Ava knew that this was no mere idle boast.

"I'm not much good in a fight," lamented Ava, "either in this form or as a human."

The woman looked at her. "There's no one I'd rather have by my side in a fight than you, Grey Rabbit."

The words warmed Ava's heart as the hand warmed Ava's body. Ava turned her face away to keep the woman from seeing the tears welling in her eyes.

The crew from the two toppled spiders had finished bandaging one another and were now discussing how to hunt for the fugitive.

"Go, and save yourself," said the woman. "I'm afraid I won't be able to pay back my debt to you in this life."

Ava shook her head. "I won't abandon you."

The woman smiled and stroked Ava's long ears. Ava felt no condescension in the gesture, only admiration. "Show me what you look like. If we're going to die together, I want to see your face first."

"Why?"

"So I can find you in the Hall of Heroes in the beyond and invite you to come back and haunt our killers together."

Ava laughed. Even knowing that she wouldn't live much longer, a sensation long absent from her shame-filled life made her shiver with pleasure. It was the feeling of pride.

She transformed back into her human form, lying next to the woman. "My name is Ava Cide—though Grey Rabbit has a nice ring to it."

"I'm Pinion Gates, of Rivereast Prefecture. It's an honor to know you."

They clasped hands, sat up, and turned together in the direction of the soldiers, ready to face their fate.

A gruff voice broke in. "When the two of you are done with this meeting of the mutual-admiration society, maybe we can discuss how to get out of here."

With her dull human senses, Ava had not noticed the strong feline odor that suddenly permeated the air. As she watched in shock, a sleek and powerful leopard, fully ten feet in length, with a coat as black as coal, parted the thick stalks of aruk and padded toward them.

"Fey Swell!" exclaimed Ava. "What are you doing here? And when . . . where . . . how did you become Revealed?"

"There's a lot about me you don't know," said Fey arrogantly. "You called me a coward! If word got around that you went after the rotten to save your brother all by yourself while I cowered at home, how would I ever be able to hold up my head in front of my minions?"

Without giving the other two a chance to argue, she turned around and crouched down, offering her back. "Hop on!"

•

As Fey carried the two women on her back and loped through the aruk under the stars, the trio shared their life stories.

Pinion had once been a trawler on the shores of the Arlos River. One day, she caught a rare three-headed humpback pike. When she gutted it, she found a small glass vial inside, filled with a green spirit redolent of spices and herbs. As Pinion could never resist a good drink, she drained it in one gulp—and thereby became Revealed.

"Why didn't you go to Roanflare to seek your fortune?" asked Ava. "Thousands would give up a limb or two to have your luck."

Pinion laughed coldly. "The wandering storytellers tell us that the Commonwealth Palace is muddier and more turbulent than the Arlos River during the spring flood. Why would I want to give up my life of carefree drinking and courting to try to ride the currents of politics? No, I just wanted to be left alone."

So she had disguised her talent and carried on. But one day, after an afternoon of beers and games, she saw an official trying to extort the life savings of another fishing family by imprisoning their son with made-up charges. Falling into an alcohol-fueled rage, she tied the official to a tree and whipped him until he howled to be spared. Extracting from him a promise to leave the family he was trying to extort alone, she let the man go.

But the humiliated official sought his vengeance. He hired desperadoes to murder the fishing family, then accused Pinion of being the murderer. Without any kind of investigation or trial, the governor of Rivereast arrested Pinion and declared that she would be executed in the morning. That night, Pinion transformed into Crimson Mare, kicked down the doors of her cell, maimed the guards, and escaped. Galloping through the streets of Rivereast, she found the murderous official and flattened him under her hooves. Since then, she had lived as a fugitive, always on the run.

"How could officials of the Archon act in such a lawless manner? And to think that the governor, a Revealed Lord, would be so foolish and callous!" exclaimed Ava, as she gently bounced up and down on Fey's back. Fey Swell, in her form as Coal Leopard, seemed to see as well by starlight as by sunlight, and she moved with the natural grace of a hunter.

"The Archon is a feckless young woman with little interest in governing," said Fey, her breathing slow and even, though she was carrying two grown women on her back. "She has surrounded herself not with counselors of wisdom and virtue, but with childhood playmates who fill her ears with flattery and their own coffers with treasure stolen from the commonwealth. Greed and ambition are the rule at court, and the only goal of every governor, general, official, and legate, Revealed or not, is selfish gain, not the good of the people."

Ava was silent. What Fey was saying was well-known to all, but Ava had always tried to deny it—to accept that the Revealed Lords were not as perfect in virtue as they were glorious in their form was, to her, also to accept the death of an ideal. Because she could not be ranked among the Revealed, that very unattainability had made her romanticize them even more.

"So what about you?" Ava asked Fey. "How did you come to be Revealed?"

Fey had always liked to explore into the mists beyond the borders of Grema, for there was where the most interesting monsters would be found, and whose furs, antlers, horns, or scales would fetch the most on the black market. One time, while trading in Dripe Town, she was introduced to a woman in the employ of a legate of the Synedrion. The woman offered Fey a flask of Revelation wine in exchange for rare pangolin scales—which the legate believed could be used to brew a potion for virility and long-lasting youth.

"She just offered you some Revelation wine?" asked Ava in disbelief. "But . . . that is a crime!"

"To the powerful and ranked lords, the laws of the land are mere marks on sheets of toilet paper," said Fey. "Like Pinion told you, there's nothing the officials, Revealed or not, wouldn't do if there's personal gain. I figured that it was useless to count on the army to protect us from the bandits, and so I took the Revelation wine in order to be strong enough to protect myself."

Ava was once again silent. She had been taught that to be recommended to be Revealed was the only path to discover the truth of one's nature and to join the ranks of the nobility, but the reality was far different.

Things are changing indeed.

•

Ava, Fey, and Pinion, now back in their human forms, cautiously peeked out at the encampment in the mist-shrouded valley. They were now miles beyond the borders of Grema—even Fey had not hunted this far.

The place had apparently been the site of a town in the days before the Plague. A grid of streets could still be discerned among the vine-clad ruins of houses and buildings. Many of the ruins had been taken over by the rotten as living quarters or storage space for their loot, as evidenced by wisps of cooking smoke and figures milling about the ruins, carrying heavy chests or pushing laden carts. The overall effect was of looking down at a large warren, teeming with creatures driven solely by greed.

"How many do you think are down there?" asked Ava, awed by the sight.

"I'd say about eight hundred fighters at least," said Fey. "And who knows how many of them are Revealed rats?"

Both Pinion and Fey had pledged to help Ava recover her little brother. Pinion's leg was now mostly recovered. After several days' journey, the sensitive nose of Fey had finally tracked Shaw here. It was obvious that Shaw couldn't have made it so far on his own—most likely he had been taken captive by the rotten.

"I'm now thinking Ava was right," muttered Fey. "Maybe we ought to try harder to convince the army to come."

At Ava's insistence, once they had found the rotten base, Pinion had raced back to Dripe Town to leave a message for the governor with the location—the speedy mare had made the round trip in a single day. Neither Pinion nor Fey thought there was even the smallest chance that Governor Kide would bother doing anything with the information.

Pinion chuckled. "Scared?" She glanced at Fey, a challenging smile on her spider-veined face. "I don't have your teeth or claws, but I wouldn't shrink from a fight."

"Even the most powerful cat is no match if outnumbered twenty to one by rats," retorted Fey, a shade of deep red coming into her dark cheeks. "Besides, if a fight does turn bad, I imagine some of us will be running away faster than others."

"Who are you suggesting would be running away?" said Pinion in mock anger.

The two fighters had taken an instant liking to each other. They enjoyed sparring—both verbally and physically—whenever they got the chance.

"We're not just going to just run in there and start fighting any rotten we encounter," said Ava. "I don't care how confident you are in your prowess—there's no point in being reckless."

The Orange Brothers, three young men from one of the islands in Massenwhal Bay, had been recommended for the Revelation in Roanflare a few years ago. But the wine had revealed them as man-size rats, a form usually associated with rebels or criminals. The Archon had imprisoned them, but they had bribed their way out and, it was said, stolen a supply of Revelation wine from the Archon's store before they left.

For a while, they were content to lead small bands of bandits to prey on merchant caravans between the towns of Grema. But in the last year, their ranks had swelled to thousands, largely due to the drought in prefectures to the north. Rumor had it that they had acquired some kind of magic that made their fighters fearless and fight with the strength of ten each—a state they described as "rotten." They raided villages and even small towns, and after they passed through, it was as though a plague of locusts had struck, leaving nothing but death and devastation.

"What do you have in mind then?" asked Pinion and Fey together.

Ava pondered the rotten base, her eyes roaming around. Eventually, they settled on a drainage ditch just outside the ruined town.

•

"This may be one of the worst ideas you've ever had," grumbled Fey. "The stench is unbearable."

"Just be glad that I didn't ask you to come in your Revealed forms," said Ava, her voice muffled through the cloth she wore over her nose and mouth. "With that sensitive nose, you may actually faint."

"Try not to talk so much," said Pinion. "The more you talk, the more air you have to breathe in." She pulled her foot out of the slime with a loud squish. "And don't think too hard about the nature of what we're walking through," she added in a mutter.

The thought of the waste-disposal needs of the hundreds of rotten living above her almost made Fey gag. At least that stopped her grumbling.

The three picked their way through the ankle-deep sewage in complete darkness, one hand each on the equally slimy wall.

"I cannot believe you went through here as Grey Rabbit earlier," said Fey. "How did you not drown?"

"Rabbits are good with tunnels," said Ava, and suppressed an involuntary shudder as memories of her earlier exploration of the sewers returned. "Let's just leave it at that."

Ava knew that every town was built atop an underground warren of sewers, through which the daring could get to any part of the town undetected. While Fey and Pinion had rested in the afternoon, she had hopped through the tunnel maze and explored every branch and fork until she had found the building where Shaw and other captives were kept.

"Here we are," she said, coming to a stop. Above them, faint starlight spilled through the grille.

The three held still and listened. In the hours before dawn, there was no sound save the gentle whistle of a night breeze. This far from the cities of Grema, the rotten were not concerned with assaults from the army or militias.

One by one, the three climbed out of the sewer opening onto the side of a deserted road. Next to them was an imposing stone building two stories tall, and a pair of guards were napping on the ground next to the gate.

The trio circled to the back of the building, where it took Fey no time at all to bend the bars over a large window to create an opening for them to climb through. The large hall on the first floor was covered by sleeping mats and slumbering figures. Tiptoeing between the snoring bandits, Ava led the way to the stairs. The smaller rooms on the second floor were where the rotten kept the captives who were deemed useful enough to be recruited rather than slaughtered.

The second floor was lit by a night-glowing orb, no doubt taken from some wealthy estate raided by the rotten. Ava looked at the closed doors, trying to decide which one to investigate first. A metallic clang—almost immediately muffled—came from behind her.

She whipped around. By the cold light of the orb, she saw Fey right behind her, a guilty look on her face. She was holding a long steel spear and trying not to drag it on the ground.

"Sorry."

"Where did you get that?" whispered Ava.

"I came after you in such a hurry that I forgot to bring my knife," said Fey. "I need a weapon if we have to fight. I took this from one of the sleeping bandit captains as we passed by—it was calling out to me."

"We're not here to fight," Ava said. "Just to get in, save Shaw, and get out."

"I'm just following her example," pleaded Fey. She leaned to the side to reveal Pinion, who was holding a long, crescent-shaped pole-sword.

"You are always telling us to take precautions," said Pinion. "Besides, there's nothing wrong with stealing from bandits, is there?"

Ava shook her head and sighed. She turned back and led the way down the hall. Hopefully, all the prisoners would also be asleep, and they'd be able to find Shaw without waking anyone.

Very slowly and quietly, Ava pushed opened the first door.

Immediately the three fell to the floor and rolled away from the opening. Both Fey and Pinion took up defensive crouches, their weapons at the ready. Ava hid behind Fey, barely stifling a frightened yelp.

The room had been full of bandits standing at attention, their eyes wide-open.

Seconds passed in absolute silence save for the waves of snores coming from the floor below.

At length, Ava screwed up enough courage to steal a look into the room. "They're not moving," she whispered.

Three heads peeked around the doorjambs. The bandits, about thirty in number, stood in neat rows, their eyes open and staring forward, as still as statues.

"They're definitely not wax figures," said Fey, who extended a finger and poked at the foot of the nearest one. "See, the skin sinks in." She strode in and waved her hand in front of the woman and, eliciting no response, made a face at her.

"This is too strange," said Ava, the hairs on the back of her neck standing straight up.

"I don't like this either," said Pinion. "But there's no time to solve the mystery. Do you see your brother in here?"

Ava and Fey shook their heads. Pulling the door shut, they went on to the next room.

The same eerie sight of bandits who seemed awake but didn't respond greeted them in several rooms, while others were filled with foodstuffs, weapons, and machine parts. The whole place had the look of a storehouse, and even the standing bandits resembled objects more than human beings.

At last, they arrived at the last room at the end of the hall. Ava pushed open the door. Inside, the room had been partitioned into multiple holding cells with barred doors, with eight to ten bunks in each. In contrast to the other rooms, the people on the bunks really did seem to be asleep.

"Ava? Is that you?" a whisper came from the corner.

Ava was there in a few long strides. "Shaw! Are you all right?"

"You came after me," muttered the young man, sounding incredulous. "Thank the gods you are here! I'm so sorry—"

"There's no time for that," said Ava gruffly, but tears of relief threatened to spill from her eyes. "Are you hurt? We're going to get you out of here now."

"It's horrible, Ava. They don't have the Revelation wine at all! They caught me just past the highway and brought me here. They make the captives drink a poison that robs them of their will, so they're walking corpses, fearless and obedient."

"That explains those statue-like bandits we saw," said Fey.

"They try to recruit you first with promises of treasure and power," said Shaw, sobbing, "because they say it's better to have a willing fighter than a mere drudge. But knowing what they did to the villages they raided, I refused. They were going to force me to drink the poison in the morning if I kept on saying no."

"We'll talk more later," said Ava. "Fey, come on."

Fey strode up to the bars of the gate and tried to bend them. But the bars were too thick even for her powerful arms.

A cry from downstairs. "Hey, what happened to my spear?" Soon, angry and barely coherent voices, aroused from sleep, answered in denial. The owner of the missing weapon had apparently decided to make a fuss to discover the thief.

Fey cursed. "Just my luck to pick the one with a full bladder."

"There's no time for subtleties anymore," said Pinion. Standing still, she closed her eyes. Ava and Fey scooted back to give her room. In a minute Pinion had transformed into Crimson Mare, almost too big for the small dimensions of the room. She turned around and kicked out hard with her powerful hind legs, and the gate of Shaw's holding cell crashed down with a deafening clang, torn from the walls.

Shaw gazed upon the Revealed beast with terror and awe.

Loud peals from a brass bell reverberated through the building. Shouted orders. Thundering footsteps. General alarm had been raised. Other prisoners, now awakened by the noise, banged on the bars to their cells, begging to be released.

"We've got to go!" shouted Fey.

"We can't just leave these people here," said Ava, hesitating. "My brother was fortunate to have the three of us to save him, but who will save *them*?"

The door to the room banged open. Several of the rotten, deprived of their will by the poison, marched through with wooden spears.

"I'll hold them off while you free the rest," shouted Fey. She dashed to the door, the long steel spear leading the way. With a single lunge she threw four attackers out of the room.

Meanwhile, Crimson Mare made her way around the room, kicking down the bars of the holding cells. Ava and Shaw comforted the frightened captives, trying to keep them from panicking and adding to the confusion.

Fey stood in the doorway like a dam against an oncoming flood. Two, four, eight, sixteen—no matter how many rotten bandits came at her, they could not force her back even one step. Holding tightly to the pole, she used the tip of her spear to describe tight circles in the air, a spinning steel flower, the flickering tongue of a serpent, a barrier of will and strength beyond which none shall pass.

More shouting. Cries of alarm. The peals of the bell were being taken up by other bells around the town.

"These rotten drudges are unbelievable," said Fey, her voice strained. "I've never seen anyone fight like this."

The mindless drones, compelled by orders from a bandit commander crouched behind them, filled the narrow hall and pressed forward like a wall of flesh and blood. Heedless of the injuries from Fey's spear, they fought without regard for loss of limb or life. As Fey, forced to draw blood, buried her spear in the chest of one of the drones, the man howled with pain and spurted blood from his mouth, but didn't even take half a step back. His unblinking eyes showed neither terror nor understanding. As the other drones behind him pushed forward, they forced the spear point deeper into him, thrusting out his back only to plunge into the chest of the drone after him.

Fey's face was a frozen rictus of disgust and fear. "This is an abomination!"

"What pitiable creatures," said Ava. "They are also someone's sister, brother, son, daughter. They fight not because they want to, but because their minds have already died. Even if the Orange Brothers were to die a thousand times, it wouldn't be enough to bring justice."

"I can't hold them back much longer," cried Fey. Her feet slid back on the floor, slick with the blood of the drones.

"We've freed all the captives," shouted Ava. "Pinion, let's go!"

Crimson Mare whinnied in response. In a single bound, she was next to the wall at the back of the room. She kicked out with her hind legs, the hooves raised like two massive jackhammers. Once, twice, thrice. The stones collapsed. Where the wall had been, there was a giant gaping hole whistling with the night breeze.

Crimson Mare cried triumphantly and leaped out. Ava, Fey, and the others followed.

•

The predawn fight was intense and bloody.

The bandits, driving wave after wave of mindless drones, tried to surround the escaping captives and cut off their escape.

In her Revealed form, Ava sniffed the air and listened for ambushes, trying to direct the frightened captives down roads that would lead them out of the bandit-infested town. Fey, Shaw, and she could have gotten out of the town easily on Pinion's back—there was no way any of the bandits could have caught up to the fleet-footed mare. But Ava insisted that they not leave the rescued captives behind.

And so Fey and Pinion, as Crimson Mare and Coal Leopard, growled and whinnied, fighting back the pursuing bandits. Hoofs thundered through the air; claws and teeth flashed in the starlight. Bandit blood slicked the dirty streets, and howls of pain echoed from the stone ruins. The more numerous the bandits, the stouter the hearts of the warriors.

Ava, exhausted, bounded down another alley, the group of captives bunched closely behind her. But ahead, instead of freedom, she saw more bandits brandishing swords, spears, and even shock prods powered by electric batteries. A few of the bandit captains, giant Revealed rats, led the charge, their claws and teeth glinting even colder than the blue sparks from the shock prods.

Fey leaped over the captives like a black rainbow and landed in front of Ava. She crouched down and roared at the approaching bandits. The stunned bandits halted and stumbled back, overcome with terror.

Behind the captives, facing down the pursuing bandits at the other end of the alley, Pinion let out a loud scream of defiance, her hooves drumming against the ground, each a mini-earthquake.

The bandits began to press forward again, at first hesitantly, then with more confidence. The drones were compelled to do so, while bandits still with wills of their own were encouraged by their numbers. No matter how fierce and powerful Crimson Mare and Coal Leopard were, they were so vastly outnumbered that they had no hope to prevail.

In despair, Ava crouched down, knowing that their run was at an end.

Shaw crouched down next to her.

"I'm sorry, little brother," said Ava. "I couldn't save you, or Pinion, or Fey, or any of the others. Your sister is . . . a failure."

"No." Shaw extended a hand and touched the side of Ava's trembling, tearstained face. "You are the best of sisters."

Ava laughed bitterly. "I'm only a rabbit, good for nothing. Look at me. I tremble from exhaustion even after running less than half a mile. I cannot defeat even a child in a fight."

"Yet Fey and Pinion follow you, and so would all of us," said Shaw. "You may be small in stature and strength, but you have courage, wisdom, and compassion. You listen and amplify the voices in other hearts."

"I wasn't so good at listening to you. I didn't understand what you really wanted," said Ava.

Shaw shook his head. "Listen to me now, and believe. Your spirit soars like the flight of a drake. I thought I could try to redeem the family, but I didn't understand that my family has already been blessed with the grandest of Revealed Lords."

Ava looked up at her brother, and she realized that the way he looked at her was the same way he had looked at her seven years ago, when they had taken their sole family portrait.

"Thank you, little brother," said Ava, her heart at peace. "Let's make these bandits pay a dear price before we go. We'll die like drakes, not rabbits—"

Even as she spoke these words, a long, loud trumpeting pierced the air like the rising sun that had just leaped above the horizon. All the combatants stopped and glanced up.

There, in the east, emerging through the dissipating mist, was a great flying beast snow white in color: two oversize wings, sharp eagle-like claws, a long serpentine neck ending in an arrow-shaped head. Streaks of mottled blue ran down the sides of the beast like an ancient military uniform.

"I'll be damned," said Fey Swell, her voice full of wonder. "The White Drake."

Ava's ears, ever so sensitive, swung to the east. She could hear a faint rumbling, the steps of a thousand soldiers and the grinding of a thousand thousand gears.

"The Archon's army is here!" she shouted. "The Archon's army is here!"

The great drake winged his way closer and dived toward the town. Panicked shouts from the bandits warred with joyous cries from the freed captives. And then, the rotten bandits scattered, like a castle of sand crumbling before an irresistible tide.

•

Ava, Pinion, and Fey stood in a clump. Ava swallowed nervously.

Before them, sitting on a chair elevated on four other chairs, was General Don Excel, also known as the White Drake, Governor of Wooster, the most powerful warlord in the land. Already a physically imposing man, his power and height were only enhanced by the temporary throne. His sharp eyes, merciless, calculating, the orbs of an apex predator, gazed down upon the three women patiently.

"It was nothing, Your Excellency," said Ava. "We only did our duties as citizens of Grema, loyal subjects of the Archon."

The governor had thanked them for bringing him intelligence of the bandit nest. As it turned out, Governor Kide was one of Governor Excel's supporters. Knowing that his patron had been seeking a military victory to enhance his standing among the Lords of Grema and to add to his political capital, Kide had passed on the location of the rotten nest to Excel, who had decided to launch an all-out assault on the bandits.

The fight—or more accurately, the massacre—had been swift. As the bandits scattered across the ruined town, pursued by the fiery breath of the White Drake, they found their escape routes sealed off by striding Longlegs raining steel bolts. Overhead, crews in Dragonflies, death-dealing machines with two whirring rotors, picked the survivors off with well-oiled crossbows. Finally, foot soldiers in plastic armor strode through the ruined town, killing any surviving bandits with electric shockers. Revealed, human, or mindless, none of the rotten escaped, even if they had fallen to their knees and begged to be allowed to surrender.

A pile of human heads, along with coiled tails from the Revealed rats, sat next to the general like some gruesome trophy. Ava's stomach turned at the sight.

The general said nothing, still waiting patiently.

"We're most honored by your praise and the opportunity you offer, Lord Excel." Ava swallowed, forced herself to meet that predatory gaze, and continued her speech. "But my sisters and I are simple folk, unused to the demands of serving a grand lord."

She had chosen to introduce Pinion and Fey as her sisters in order to conceal the fact that Pinion was a fugitive. Given the merciless way in which the rotten had been massacred, she didn't want to expose Pinion to any danger. Shifting her gaze between the pile of bloody body parts and the general perched atop the throne, she wasn't sure which frightened her more.

"You are a clever girl, Ava Cide, and you've demonstrated considerable potential in securing me this victory." Lord Excel's voice was a deep rumble, seductive and slow. "Do not boast through false modesty. Do you consider the titles I've offered you too low? Consider them only an opening bid. I could offer you more, much more if you serve me loyally."

"You misunderstand us, Your Excellency," said Ava. "We are not bargaining. We fought not for ambition, but to save our loved ones. We crave no glory, only the chance to live in peace."

"Peace?" The general laughed, but there was no mirth, only calculation, in the noise. "The aruk in the fields may wish to stand still, but the wind will not leave them so. When Grema is besieged by monsters from without and Roanflare is filled with the ambitious from within, how can anyone live in peace unless they shelter with and serve a powerful lord? A sharp sword requires a skilled wielder, and a talented horse would die in obscurity without a noble rider."

"Feral horses are only fit for the wilderness, not the gridlocked streets of Roanflare," said Pinion Gates.

"Rusty blades are only fit to hack at weeds and firewood, not dangling from the jade belt of a great lord," said Fey Swell.

Tension thickened the air, and General Excel narrowed his eyes.

"What my sisters mean is that we wish to live beholden only to our own dreams," said Ava, her voice gentler than Pinion's or Fey's, but no less determined. "If you would force us to work for you against our will, then you would be no different from the rotten, who use poison to enslave those they cannot convince."

For a brief moment, General Excel's frosty look seemed to chill the air, and the three women tensed. But then his face broke into a warm smile. "Well said, Ava Cide. Well said. Instead of pressing more where I'm not welcome, I wish you three a pleasant journey."

Ava sighed with relief. The three bowed deeply to General Excel and turned to leave. Ava beckoned at Shaw, standing among the captives huddled to the side.

"We're going home," said Ava, smiling.

"Send them on their way," intoned the general from behind. "All of them."

In one swift motion, soldiers standing next to the captives unsheathed their swords and plunged them into the captives. Most didn't even have a chance to cry out before they gurgled their last breath.

Ava was too shocked to even move.

Shaw collapsed to the ground. As though awakening from a dream, Ava rushed to him and fell to her knees. Cradling the dying boy in her arms, she frantically pressed her hands against the wound in his chest, struggling to stanch the blood.

"Oh gods! Please, please!"

Shaw looked up at her, struggling to smile. "It's all right, big sister. I should have listened to you and stayed in the midden mines." His voice was so faint that Ava had to lean her ear against his trembling lips. "You were right. We're like weeds to these people."

At length, Ava gently lay the unmoving body of her brother on the ground. She turned to the general. "Why?"

"A feral horse that cannot be ridden by me should be ridden by no one," said the general, his tone as placid as the blood pooling at Ava's feet. "And a rusty blade that refuses to obey my hand must not be taken up by another. Besides, we still lack a few heads to make an even thousand enemies slain for my triumphal report to the Archon. To make up the number, I have to borrow the heads from the captives, and . . . the heads of you and your sisters."

"How can you do this?" Ava screamed at him. "You are a servant of the Archon, of the people of Grema!"

"The Archon trembles in my presence these days and dares not command me," said the general. "Indeed, upon returning to Roanflare, I think I will ask for an even better title from her. *Lord Protector of Grema* has a nice ring to it, don't you think? Perhaps the other governors and generals will finally understand the new reality."

The soldiers pressed forward, their swords raised. Ava, her eyes locked with the general's, ran at him, her hands raised like claws—

A powerful pair of arms grabbed her and lifted her off the ground. Then she felt herself settling down upon the back of a powerful red-maned back, rocking up and down as the general receded in her view. She was riding Crimson Mare, held in place by Fey Swell, running out of the reach of the general's servants.

Fey's deep, pained voice sounded in her ears. "Not now! The rabbit always waits for her chance!"

•

In the shoulder-high aruk, three women covered in blood knelt to face the east, the direction of the rising sun and of Roanflare.

"Though we weren't born on the same day of the same month of the same year," they spoke as one, "though we weren't born to the same parents under the same roof with the same names, we've found one another. United by grief, linked by the desire for justice, we call one another sister. As the heavens and the earth are our witnesses, we didn't want to start this fight, but we'll be sure to end it. We'll never stop until we've brought peace back to Grema or die together on the same day of the same month of the same year."

The aruk stalks swayed in the wind. The three sisters dried their tears.

Through the sea of grass, the crimson-red mare galloped alongside the prowling coal-black leopard. But in front of both, leaping like a flying fish skimming over the waves, was a grey rabbit. She would listen, she would hide, she would scheme, she would even fight—but she would never turn away from the essence of compassion.

"Lords of Grema," whispered Ava to herself, "there's a new member in your ranks."

A Chase Beyond the Storms

An excerpt from The Veiled Throne,
The Dandelion Dynasty, book three

Just beyond the Wall of Storms: the fifth month in the first year of the Reign of Season of Storms (half a year after the deaths of Emperor Ragin and Pékyu Tenryo during the Battle of Zathin Gulf).

Ten ships from Dara bobbed gently on calm waves, surrounded by the floating hulks of crubens like whale calves in the middle of a pod. Men and women danced on the decks, whooping and laughing, still unable to believe that they had passed under the legendary Wall of Storms unscathed.

To the south, the meteorological wonder loomed like a mountain range sculpted out of cyclones, typhoons, sheets of rain so dense that they might as well be solid water, and roiling clouds lit up from within by bolts of lightning, each the size of Fithowéo's spear. From time to time, small cyclones—each capable of devastating an island in isolation, but here, next to the sky-scraping storm columns, as insignificant as a rock formation in a scholar's garden would be next to Mount Kiji—departed from the wall to wander over the open ocean, gradually dissipating as their peregrinations took them too far from the fabled marvel that was the Wall.

Sailors detached thick towing cables from the tails of the crubens. The majestic scaled whales sprayed mist from their blowholes in unison and covered the Dara fleet in rainbows, a good omen. They bellowed their farewell, the resulting deep rumble through the water making the ships' tightly fitted hull planks tremble and squeak against each other. Slapping their massive flukes against the water, the crubens turned to the north in unison, their long horns swaying steadily like the compass needles of the gods, and soon vanished beneath the waves.

Aboard *Dissolver of Sorrows,* flagship of the modest fleet, two figures stood on the elevated stern deck above the aftercastle.

"Thank you, Sovereign of the Sea," whispered the woman who had once been known as Empress Üna and was now again called Princess Théra. She bowed in *jiri* to the wakes left by the crubens.

"I wish we could mandate and command these creatures," said Takval Aragoz, would-be pékyu of the Agon and Théra's fiancé. "They would greatly comfort and aid our cause."

The princess suppressed a smile at the prince's not-quite-right attempt at formal Dara speech. After months of living in Dara, Takval's speech was fluent—except when he tried to sound impressive. "The Fluxists say that there are four powerful forces whose aid can only be petitioned for but not commanded: the strength of a cruben, the favor of the gods, the trust of the people—" She paused.

"And what is the fourth thing?" asked Takval.

"The heart of a lover," said Théra.

The two smiled at each other tentatively, uncertainly, hesitantly.

Thinking of Zomi Kidosu, the brilliant, beautiful woman who had been her first love, Théra's heart ached. But she hardened her resolve and put Zomi's smile out of her mind. She had to focus on the present, on the future.

"A ship!" cried a lookout in the crow's nest above the main mast, breaking the awkward silence. He pointed toward the horizon in the east, and his voice quivered as he continued. "A *city-ship.*"

As lookouts on the other ships confirmed the sighting, the celebration on the decks soon turned to consternation. How could there be another city-ship when the Lyucu fleet had just been overwhelmed by the Wall of Storms?

Théra and Takval ran to the mizzenmast and climbed up the rigging. Halfway up, they could already see the massive ship on the horizon, from this distance a mere sliver darkening the boundary between sea and sky, with multiple masts sticking up out of the horizontal hull like the long hairs poking up from the back of a caterpillar.

"Incoming garinafin! Incoming garinafin!" cried the lookout.

It was true. A familiar winged shape could be seen hovering above the distant ship like a childish scrawl against the smooth empyrean. From so far away, it was hard to tell if the figure was indeed heading for them, but then where else could it be going?

"Did you see how the garinafin took off?" asked Takval of the two lookouts on the main mast. "How keen—prickly—no, *sharp* was the rising angle?"

Instead of answering, the pair of lookouts continued their conversation with each other, shading their eyes and pointing at the distant garinafin excitedly.

"Report on the garinafin's angle of ascent on takeoff, if you saw it," said Théra, her voice not any louder than Takval's had been.

"*Rén*—Your Highness!" Both lookouts stopped talking and instantly turned to her. "We didn't see. By the time we noticed the ship, the garinafin was already in the air."

Théra could see that Takval seethed with resentment and frustration. Other than Princess Théra, he had no friends among the thousand-plus members of this expedition. Although he was nominally a coequal leader of the fleet with Princess Théra, the Dara crew either pretended that he didn't exist or expressed contempt for his presence in a thousand small ways. This didn't bode well for the Dara-Agon alliance.

"The angle of ascent could have told us the condition of the garinafin," Takval whispered to her sullenly. "It's like how a cow with soupy shit can't run very fast."

Théra put a hand on his shoulder to reassure him. She had already told the captains and commanders that they were to treat orders from Takval as though they had come from her, and she tried to consult Takval on every decision. But prejudices against the people of the scrublands ran deep after the Lyucu invasion, and though the Agon were the enemies of the Lyucu, the crew distrusted Takval. She could not manufacture respect out of thin air. This was a problem that Takval had to solve himself.

"Why didn't that ship attempt to sail through the Wall with the rest of the fleet?" asked Théra, trying to stay focused on the problems of the moment.

"I think it must have been kept behind by the Lyucu fleet commander, Garinafin-Thane Pétan Tava, out of care and caution," said Takval. "I learned about him on the way here, before I escaped from the city-ships. He had a reputation for holding back a reserve in every battle, instead of committing everything to the initial assault."

Théra's heart pounded so hard that her chest hurt. The memory of their nearly fatal encounter with the lone garinafin that had survived the destruction of the Lyucu fleet earlier, during the passage through the Wall of Storms, was still fresh in her mind. Now that they were without the protection of the crubens, the chances of surviving another garinafin assault seemed remote.

"Maybe we should go underwater again?" asked Takval. "When caught in the open by garinafins with no garinafins of our own, the Agon way is to hide."

"That's not going to work," said Théra. "Once we dive, we won't be able to move except drifting with the current, and the city-ship, under full sail, will be able to catch us shortly. We can't stay under forever, either. When we're forced to resurface, we'll be sitting ducks."

"Then we'll have to leave two ships behind to fight," said Takval. "They die so that the other ships can live."

Théra looked at him. "This is our first encounter with the Lyucu, and you're proposing we sacrifice a fifth of our fleet?"

"This is what Agon warriors must do to save the tribe, and I would be happy to lead those willing to stay behind to forge a wall with our bones that will rival this Wall of Storms in future bonfire recountings." Takval took off the leather cord around his neck. "This pendant, made from the stones found in a garinafin's liver-pisspot, will let my people—"

"Wait, wait. A 'liver-pisspot' . . . Do you mean the pouch-shaped organ under the liver, a gallbladder?"

"Yes, that's the word: 'gallbladder.' The gallbladder stones will let my people know that you've been invested and divested with my authority. It won't be perfect, but when you get to Gondé—"

"Oh, stop it!" chided Théra. She wasn't sure whether to scream or cry or laugh at some of Takval's ideas—it didn't help that Takval's Dara, originally acquired from both nobles and peasants in Mapidéré's fleet, was peppered with incongruous locutions. "Where does this obsession with living on in song and story instead of thriving in this world come from? The world right *here*, right *now*, between the Veil of Incarnation and the River-on-Which-Nothing-Floats, is where we can make the most difference. Every single person on this expedition is irreplaceable, with unique experiences and skills. We're *not* going to jump to sacrifice as the first solution to every problem. That's the easy way out. I intend to get every ship and every member of our crew to Gondé, you included."

Takval was taken aback—this was definitely not how an Agon leader would have reacted. "How do you intend . . . to live through the garinafin assault then?"

"By doing the most interesting thing, of course," said Théra, a look of determination and defiance on her face. "We've got about an hour, so tell me everything you know about what happens to garina-fins on long journeys."

•

Throughout a thirty-year career as a fighting man, first under the wily Pékyu Tenryo and then under the exacting Pékyu-taasa Cudyu, Toof had piloted a dozen garinafins and fought in hundreds of engage-ments. By rights, he should have been able to face any threat with complete equanimity.

But on this scouting mission, he felt as scared as on his very first mission as a fifteen-year-old boy, when he had been told to take care of an ambush of tusked tigers all by his lonesome self.

Toof's mount, a ten-year-old female named Tana, trembled be-neath his saddle as she flexed and stretched her long-unused wings, as if sharing his unease. His crew, reduced to only four to conserve garinafin lift gas after so much inactivity at sea, clung to the webbing draped over Tana's torso quietly, not engaging in their habitual ban-ter or singing heart-lifting battle songs.

Who could blame them for being afraid? Never in the history of the peoples of the scrublands had there been a garinafin flight like this.

To his left loomed the Wall of Storms, an impenetrable, shimmering mountain of water and lightning that had just swallowed thousands of his comrades like an insatiable monster. Beneath him was the endless ocean, over which the Lyucu fleet had sailed for months without sight of land. He felt as though he was flying through a scene ripped from the ancient myths or a shaman's tolyusa-fueled nightmare, a primordial time when the gods of the Lyucu had still not taken human form, but endlessly transformed themselves and their surroundings, sculpting the world like so much tallow.

As Toof approached his targets—ten small ships huddled on the sea like a pod of sunning dolphins—his nervousness only increased as he guided Tana to fly lower. He swallowed hard to moisten his parched throat as he began to plot a course that would take Tana directly over the Dara fleet, giving her a chance to strafe the crew and rigging with fire breath.

Truth be told, Toof's trepidation was partly the result of his uncertainty that the ships from Dara were even crewed by humans at all. How else could these tiny ships, bobbing over the ocean like arucuro tocua toy boats, have survived a passage through the Wall of Storms? Either these ships were crewed by ghosts and spirits, or they had unimaginable powers that mere mortals could not hope to withstand. Who knew if a garinafin's fire breath would even be effective at all?

As if in answer to his fervid imagination, giant shapes lifted off from the decks of the ships and rose into the air to meet Tana and her riders. Were these the fabled airships of Dara that Pékyu Tenryo had warned them about? Or were they some new kind of engine of war that the Dara barbarians had invented to bring ruin to the Lyucu? Nothing was impossible after what he had just witnessed a few hours ago.

Tana moaned and veered sharply to the right, away from the flying objects, her nostrils flared in alarm. Instead of swooping over the fleet, she was using up her precious lift gas to fly in a wide circle around the fleet, too far for her to have any opportunity of attacking it.

"Ah...ah..." The port slingshot scout, Radia, who was in the best position to observe the targets from her perch on the webbing over Tana's left shoulder, seemed at a loss for words.

"Ttt . . . tusss . . ." Toof wasn't doing any better.

"What in the world are you two babbling about?" asked the starboard slingshot scout, Voki. Having heard no further clarification, he and Oflyu, the spearman as well as tail lookout, climbed up the webbing over Tana's right shoulder and back to get a better look.

"Ttt . . . tusss . . ." "Fffff . . . ffflyyy . . ." "Ah . . . ah . . ." "Bu . . . bu . . ."

Tana sneezed and flapped her wings vigorously to get farther away. She was even more frightened and shocked than her human crew by the spectacle above the Dara fleet: ten brightly colored tusked tigers, each almost twenty-five feet long and twelve feet tall at the shoulders, leaping and swooping through the air.

Tusked tigers were among the few predators of the scrublands that could strike fear into the heart of a garinafin. These tawny-colored giant cats, typically the size of several long-haired cattle, sported a pair of curved tusks that could puncture tough garinafin hide. While male tusked tigers tended to wander far over the scrublands and hunt alone, females lived in large groups called ambushes with their cubs, hunting cooperatively. With their sharp claws, keen tusks, and muscular bodies, tusked tigers posed a great threat to young garinafins who hadn't the endurance for long flights, and even adult garinafins could be overcome by large ambushes. Although the tusks didn't inject any venom, wounds inflicted by these foul-breathed creatures festered. Some ambushes of tusked tigers were known to deliberately injure a garinafin's leathery wings during an initial attack before tracking the creature for multiple days and nights, across hundreds of miles through the trailless scrublands, until, weakened by the infection from that initial bite, the garinafin, no longer able to take off, finally succumbed.

Worst of all, tusked tigers had the terrifying ability to shock their prey with silent roars. Experienced elders spoke of witnessing tusked tigers chasing after herds of wild aurochs and opening their maws when close. Although no sound emerged from those fetid throats, the straggling members of the herd fell down as though paralyzed by some unseen force. The tusked tigers' magic was not well understood, and hunting parties generally avoided them unless a fight was absolutely necessary.

Thus, an ambush of larger-than-life tusked tigers *who could fly* was without a doubt the most frightening thing that a garinafin could imagine.

By now, Tana's crew had spent enough time marveling at these nightmarish creatures to realize that they weren't real. In fact, they appeared to be constructed from some kind of translucent material—possibly silk, which they were familiar with from the spoils of Admiral Krita's expedition—stretched over a rigid frame, tethered to the ships below by long, thin cords, which the Dara crew appeared to use to guide them so that they could dive and roll through the air.

But no matter how hard Toof kicked at the base of her neck with his bone spurs, Tana refused to fly any closer to the false tusked tigers. She even twisted her head around on her long, sinuous neck and gazed at her pilot reproachfully, baring her long, sharp upper canines as she lowed.

Toof was confounded and had no idea what to do. For a well-trained and experienced war garinafin to show such defiance was almost unheard of. Even during bloody battles where the stench of singed flesh filled the air and garinafins tumbled out of the sky like flaming meteors, he could not remember any of his mounts reacting this way.

"She's in the same state as the rest of us," said Radia, who was almost as experienced with garinafins as Toof himself. "Dizzy, confused, exhausted. Even harmless silk tusked tigers at this point are too much."

Toof looked at Radia and realized that the slingshot scout was right. A year's journey over the trackless ocean, fed only on rations of hard pemmican and stale water that never seemed to be enough, meant the crew was always hungry and tired. Every single person on the city-ship looked like skin wrapped around bones, and he was already feeling out of breath even with the minimal exertion of this short flight.

Tana was in even worse shape. To conserve feed, the few adult garinafins carried by the fleet were kept on rations of thornbush and blood-palm grass hay as strict as the regimen applied to the human crew. Such a diet not only made the garinafins emaciated, but also left them with very little lift gas to sustain flight. Indeed, of the three adult war garinafins on their city-ship, the other two could not fly at all, and Tana's takeoff had been so shallow and flat that Toof's crew were certain at first that the garinafin was going to fall into the sea.

Besides a few on-deck airings during the journey, the garinafins had been mostly kept belowdecks. This flight was thus practically the first time in a year that she had been able to really spread her wings. Shaken by the destruction of the Lyucu fleet and surrounded by strange, impossible sights, the garinafin was likely on the verge of a total mental breakdown. No wonder she was spooked by these decoy tigers.

"Let's head back." Toof had made up his mind. "Tana can't take this anymore."

"Nacu isn't going to like that excuse."

"At least we can inform Nacu that these barbarian ships don't seem to be very fast, and he can catch them on the open sea without relying on garinafins."

•

The garinafin circled the fleet once from afar before heading back toward the distant city-ship. As it receded into the distance, crews on the Dara fleet once again broke into cheers.

A celebration was held on *Dissolver of Sorrows* that evening. Officers from the entire fleet congregated on the deck of the flagship, sharing a feast of freshly caught fish and crabs as well as warm rice beer and sea-chilled plum wine. A few sheep had been slaughtered, and Prince Takval oversaw their roasting after the manner of the people of the scrublands, where the only flavoring used was sea salt (of which they had an abundance) and a dash of tolyusa juice (of which they had none).

Although a few of the officers, still suspicious of Takval, stood awkwardly at the edge of the crowd, most of the attendees came by the roaring bonfire in the bronze firebowl to accept a cut of roast mutton from the Agon prince. Takval taught them to eat with their hands, tearing off pieces of juicy meat, rather than relying on eating sticks. After a while, everyone grinned as their greasy lips and fingers glistened in the firelight.

"You know what would go well with this?" mumbled Tipo Tho, commander of the marines on *Dissolver of Sorrows*. She swallowed the mouthful of succulent meat before continuing. "A compote of wild monkeyberries and ice melon. My home village in Wolf's Paw is famous for it."

"That sounds like a very sweet dish," said Takval. "And wouldn't it be mushy?" Before this, the marine commander had probably spoken all of two words to him.

"That's why it will taste good. You want a good mix and contrast of flavors so that the sweetness isn't cloying and the salty savoriness doesn't parch the tongue." She tore off another strip of meat with her teeth and chewed, closing her eyes in satisfaction.

"I'm sure we'll have a chance to mix more of Agon and Dara cooking," said Takval, smiling. "We'll create flavor mixtures undreamed of by the gods or men."

Food had a way of bringing people together like nothing else.

Elsewhere, the talk was more formal. "Modifying our signaling kites to resemble tusked tigers was pure genius, Your Highness," said Çami Phithadapu. She had been one of the Golden Carp scholars elevated by Emperor Ragin, and Princess Théra had recommended her to the secret laboratory in Haan, where she had played a role in the dissection of garinafin carcasses that had revealed their secrets. Grateful for the princess's recognition of her talent, she had volunteered to come on this journey to Gondé.

"The real credit should go to the pékyu-taasa," said Théra. She was trying to learn as much of the Agon language in as short a time as possible, and tried to use some Agon words in her daily speech to set an example for the rest of the crew. Takval had explained to her that although the Agon and the Lyucu tribes all spoke local topolects that were largely mutually intelligible, there were differences that clearly marked one people from another—mainly because the topolects spoken by the Ro-atan clan and the Aragoz clan had become the prestige topolects of the Lyucu and the Agon, respectively. Fluency in the language of their allies as well as enemies was critical to the ultimate success of their mission.

She paused to bow in *jiri* to Takval and waited for the others to emulate her gesture of respect before continuing. Takval, standing next to the firebowl, grilling spit and fork in hand, smiled awkwardly and wiped the sweat from his brow.

A grin flashed across the princess's face before she turned seri-ous again. "Without Takval's knowledge concerning the debilitating effects of transporting garinafins across the ocean and their natural fear of tusked tigers, we wouldn't have been able to scare the attackers away. Now that the creature has exhausted what little lift gas it had kept in reserve, it won't be available for another flight for some time."

Çami nodded and raised her cup to the Agon prince. Setting down the grilling implements, Takval lifted his cup in return and drained it in one gulp. Turning to the rest of the crowd, he said, "Théra and I might have come up with the idea, but we couldn't have succeeded if the kite-crafters hadn't been able to modify the signal kites so quickly. Let me raise a cup to everyone who helped bend a bamboo hoop, tie a silk strip, or paint a tusked tiger stripe today."

The crew raised their cups in return, murmuring words of thanks to the prince.

Théra was pleased. Takval might be young and inexperienced as a leader, but he clearly had the right political instincts. She had de-liberately emphasized his contribution to today's events, and he had immediately understood it to be an opportunity for sharing credit more widely. This was a small step toward making the Agon and the Dara expedition feel like members of a single family, a unified tribe.

"But we aren't out of danger yet," said Théra, injecting a somber note into the feast. "Under full sail, the city-ship is faster than we are. If we keep on running, they'll eventually catch us—and we can't hope to scare away rested garinafins with silk-and-bamboo tigers again. Our small ships don't have the armaments to take on a city-ship head-on. For now, we remain the prey and they remain the hunter. Let's all put our minds to finding a way to reverse the situation."

·

Nacu Kitansli, Thane of the Tribe of the Second Toe, commander of *Boundless Pastures*, the sole Lyucu city-ship to survive the ill-fated attempt to penetrate the Wall of Storms, was having trouble sleeping.

His crew was on the verge of mutiny.

Initially, the Lyucu warriors had been grateful that they had survived while the rest of the fleet foundered, thinking it a sign of favor from the gods of both Ukyu and Dara—or whoever was in charge in these waters. But news that the sole garinafin capable of flight after the arduous voyage across the ocean had been turned back by some decoy tusked tigers had plunged morale to the nadir.

He needed some way to rally the troops, but there weren't a lot of good choices.

Increasing rations for the skittish garinafins so that they could attempt another assault shortly with a belly full of lift gas and confidence was out of the question—as known by everyone from the scrublands, where starvation was just one bad winter storm away, humans and beasts needed time to recover fully after a long period of hunger. After the yearlong voyage across the ocean, there wasn't even enough food left on *Boundless Pastures* to feed the crew for the one additional year needed to sail back to Ukyu, let alone to indulge the garinafins.

That, ultimately, was Nacu's biggest problem. It was impossible to see how the meager provisions could last even if the crew was put on a starvation diet of one-sixteenth rations. The expedition had been provisioned with the expectation of reaching a welcoming base in Dara established by Pékyu Tenryo, not to wander fruitlessly around the ocean for two years. The prospect of cannibalism and worse loomed in the not-too-distant future.

Already, Nacu had had to have some crew members whipped and dunked in the sea after they were caught trying to break into the ship's supply of tolyusa and pemmican. "A feast! A final feast before we join the cloud-garinafins!" the leader of the troublemakers had hollered. "Let us die at least with bellies full of meat and heads full of visions."

The Dara fleet was the only ray of hope left to the tiger-thane. The Dara ships that had sailed outside the Wall of Storms could have had only one destination in mind: the Lyucu homeland. If Nacu and his crew could seize the rich stores aboard the Dara ships, they would then have a chance to make it back home. The Dara fleet was a flock of plump sheep, and the Lyucu city-ship a hungry wolf that needed to eat before the coming of winter.

Nacu Kitansli ordered all the spare battens and sails brought out and rigged. The forest of masts on *Boundless Pastures* sprouted new branches and leaves to catch every scrap of breeze. A whole panoply of skysails, moonrakers, cloudcombs, butterfly sails, even "autumn cocoons"—giant, balloon-like sails that had no battens and rigged only on stays, suitable solely for off-wind or downwind sailing in calm seas—eked out every last bit of speed to aid the city-ship's pursuit of the Dara fleet on their westward course. Using such a top-heavy sail plan so close to the Wall of Storms made even old-time sailors, who had learned the craft of managing these man-made isles directly from Emperor Mapidéré's original crew, sweat in their palms, but at least with every passing day, *Boundless Pastures* drew closer to its prey.

•

As the city-ship loomed larger behind them with each dawn, Théra and Takval anxiously debated possible courses of action.

"We have to fight them," said Takval.

"How?" asked Théra. "Even the largest stone-throwers we have on board won't make a dent against those thick planks."

It was true. The city-ship was so much bigger and taller that a naval engagement between it and the Dara fleet would resemble assaulting a walled city with a few horse wagons.

Théra summoned the most experienced marine officers and ship captains to the flagship for a council of war.

"Can we do anything with the kites?" Takval tossed out the first idea. He had a bit of a fixation on battle kites after the ploy with the decoy tusked tigers.

The consensus was that the numerous flapping sails that had turned the city-ship into a moving aspen stand presented tempting targets for archers strapped to kites and armed with fire arrows.

"But if we're in range to deploy fire arrows, they'll also be in range to send out coracles and skiffs to board us." The speaker was Admiral Mitu Roso, the commander in chief of the fleet's armed forces, second in military authority only to Princess Théra (and in theory, Prince Takval). "Not to mention they'll be able to deploy any stone-throwers onboard—I'm sure the Lyucu have learned to make use of the weapons on the captured city-ships. They'll have the range advantage due to height." He looked at Takval with contempt. "This is the kind of idea that shows little understanding—"

"As the Ano sages would say," interrupted Théra, " 'Sometimes a paving stone is essential on the path to mine pure jade.' Even an impractical idea may spark a better plan down the road."

Mitu Roso grumbled but said nothing more.

Encouraged by Takval's first try, the captains and marine officers brainstormed other suggestions. Théra purposely kept herself largely out of the discussions so that the officers would feel freer to debate.

But none of the suggestions could pass muster when examined and debated in more detail.

Takval tried again. "Let me quote an ancient Agon proverb: A trapped wolf may bite off his paw—"

"No." Théra cut him off. "I know what you're going to suggest: divide the fleet in half and dispatch one-half of the ships to use fire kites to disable or slow down the city-ship while the other half escape. I need a plan that will save *everyone*."

"If we can't outrun them and we aren't allowed to fight them, that doesn't leave us many choices," Takval complained.

"I didn't say we can't fight," said Théra, "but it can't be a head-to-head naval battle—even if we win, the cost is too high."

"I have an idea," said a new voice. "I've been observing the whales swimming near us in the belt current."

The war council turned as one and saw that the speaker was Çami Phithadapu.

The Phithadapu clan were prominent whalers from Rui. As a little girl, Çami had sailed all around the waters of Rui and beyond with her uncle, a whaling captain, as they pursued the dome-headed whale and the combing whale for profit. Close observation of the majestic, intelligent creatures had eventually made Çami more interested in studying their habits than killing them. For her essay at the Imperial examinations, in order to avoid retreading the same few topics favored by most examinees, she had discussed evidence of midwifery being practiced among the cetaceans. Once she had placed among the *firoa*—the top one hundred scorers at the Grand Examination in Pan—she had advocated an Imperial policy of encouraging whalers throughout Dara to adopt a new style of whaling invented in Gan, in which harpooners tired out dome-headed whales to get them to vomit up the valuable living amber without killing them.

The barnacle-encrusted whales that greeted the fleet in these uncharted waters were indistinguishable from those seen inside the Wall of Storms. The boundary that had played such an important role in the fate of Dara appeared not to affect the whales at all. No one had thus paid much attention to the whales—except Çami.

It took Çami some time to explain what she had in mind. She even had to illustrate her plan with a bulky writing wax block and some slender ink brushes, serving as models of the ships.

The captains and marine officers sat in stunned silence, trying to digest Çami's plan.

"It's a completely untested tactic," said Captain Nméji Gon, commanding officer of *Dissolver of Sorrows*. "I don't even know if this ship could handle what you'd be asking of her."

"Just about any tactic taking advantage of the unique features of these ships will be untested," countered Çami. "This is actually the most orthodox of the plans I've devised. If you want to hear some really innovative—"

"Maybe later, Çami," said Théra. "Let's talk through this one first."

"Even if the idea works in principle, there won't be enough time to practice and drill the marines and sailors in such a novel method of war," objected Admiral Mitu Roso.

"Marshal Gin Mazoti always said that there's never enough time to prepare and drill the soldiers adequately. You always go to war with the army you have, not one you wish you could have created," said Théra. "The benefit of unorthodoxy is that the Lyucu won't be expecting anything like it either, despite their deep study of Dara tactics from the prisoners from Krita's expedition. I notice that you didn't object to the plan as fundamentally flawed."

"To be honest, I'm both awed by it and a little terrified," admitted Mitu Roso. "It has potential, but there are a lot of unknowns."

"And that makes it interesting," said Takval. He and Théra exchanged a quick smile. "In fact, the more I think about this plan, the more I like it!"

"Easy for you to say," said Captain Nméji Gon. He had once commanded one of the mechanical crubens that had played such a crucial role in Kuni Garu's rise from the tiny island of Dasu. "You won't be the one who has to make this ship do what she was never meant to do."

"I agree with the prince. On an expedition like this, we all have to do what we thought we weren't meant to do," said Tipo Tho, commander of the marines. Before volunteering to come with Princess Théra, she had been an experienced airship captain. As there was no airship corps in the fleet—maintaining a few expensive airships for a voyage to a faraway land with no known source of lift gas was deemed impractical—she, like the other air force veterans on the expedition, had been reorganized into the marines. "Don't tell me that your ship won't be up to the challenge."

"Oh, the ship will be up to the challenge," said Captain Gon through gritted teeth. Insulting his ship got his hackles up far faster than insulting him. "I'm just worried that a thin-boned swallow like you, used to the luxurious accommodations and stately pace of an Imperial airship, won't be able to take really rough sailing. You'll be throwing up instead of attacking—"

"If you think sitting in a waterlogged wooden tub that can dip a few yards below the surface is even one-tenth as rough as flying—"

"Please!" interrupted Théra. "If you want to carry on the ridiculous rivalry between aviators and submariners, play a game of *zamaki* after this mission. I just want to know if you can do what Çami is asking of you."

"Absolutely."

"Count on it."

"I'll have the ship sailing so smoothly you'll think you're on Lake Tututika—"

"Even without my airship, I'll lead our troops on an assault so fast and clean—"

"Instead of all this strutting and posturing," pleaded Théra, rubbing her temples with a pained expression, "why don't you each try to poke holes in the part of the plan the *other* is supposed to carry out, and let's see if Çami's idea really is workable?"

Captain Nméji Gon and Commander Tipo Tho worked through Çami's plan step by step, arranging and rearranging the wax block and ink brushes through different configurations on the floor. Each tried to outdo the other by coming up with new ways that every step could fail, and both furrowed their brows as they refined the plan in response.

Admiral Mitu Roso edged up to Princess Théra. "I served under Emperor Ragin in the campaigns against the Hegemon, Duke Théca Kimo's rebellion in Arulugi, and the Lyucu," he whispered. "Your father was always skilled at using rivalries among his lieutenants to perfect a plan. Seeing shadows of your father's style in you makes my heart leap in joy."

Théra nodded to acknowledge the compliment, but her heart roiled at being reminded of her dead father. *It is a ruler's job to find a way to balance,* Kuni Garu had taught her. She hoped she could find a way to balance competing factions, jealousies, mutual distrust, all the forces that threatened to spill out of control in this alliance, and convert all that energy into forward motion. She prayed that her dead father would watch over her and help her find the wisdom needed to succeed.

Nméji and Tipo were slowing down, as each pondered the other's challenges for minutes at a time to come up with the perfect response. They were like two *cüpa* or *zamaki* players locked in the final stages of a hard-fought game, where every move had the potential to alter the outcome. Other officers and captains, like onlookers to an exciting match, offered a cacophony of advice.

"Shouldn't you be the one devising and revising the plan?" whispered Takval in Théra's ear. "Your followers will lose faith in you if you don't take charge."

Théra shook her head almost imperceptibly. "I'm no warlord nor tactician," she whispered. "It would be the height of foolish arrogance for me to lead where I'm blind. Knowing when to take counsel and when to be resolute in my own will is the most important thing my father taught me."

Takval was taken aback. It was not the way among the Agon or the Lyucu for a leader not to be an expert at war—or at least to pretend to be one. Not for the first time, he was seized by a bout of doubt as to whether he had done the right thing to place the future of his people in the hands of a Dara princess who saw no shame in admitting that she was not skilled in the art of war.

But wasn't the fact that the Dara were *not* of the scrublands why he had sought their help? Their ways were not the ways of the Agon and the Lyucu, and it was that very foreignness that offered the promise of change. Théra was *interesting*.

In any event, his fate was entwined with hers now, and he could only wait and watch.

Finally, Nméji and Tipo concluded their game. They set down the wax block and ink brushes and stared at each other solemnly.

The other officers held their breaths, waiting for them to announce the outcome.

"Er . . ." Admiral Mitu Roso could no longer tolerate the suspense. "Who won? Who broke the plan?"

Smiles cracked the faces of both Nméji Gon and Tipo Tho as they gripped each other by the arms and laughed heartily.

"We both lost," said Tipo.

"And so we both won," said Nméji.

"Bring in the rice beer!" Tipo called out. "I'll drink with this salty bastard. It's the only way to deal with that fish-gut breath—"

"Let's see if you drink as well as you plan a city-ship assault," said Nméji. "Given that sticklike frame, I have my doubts—"

"Um . . . does this mean," asked Théra hesitantly, "that you think the plan will work? You trust each other to carry it out?"

Nméji and Tipo turned to her, as if insulted by her question.

"Oh, I'd sail with this man to the palace of Tazu at the bottom of his whirlpool—"

"I'd follow this woman in an assault on the castle of Mata Zyndu—"

"If he had only a boat made out of paper, I'd wager on him—"

"If she had only a hairpin for a weapon, I'd pity her foes—"

"I think the point has been amply made," said a smiling Théra, gesturing for them to stop.

Relief and joy were visible on everyone's face. Flasks full of warm rice beer were brought out and cups filled and drained.

"Don't be too cocky," said Théra. "Making a plan is only the first step; executing the plan will be ten times harder."

The council worked until the stars had spun their nightly course. At dawn, skiffs brought the officers and captains back to their own ships, but none of them went to bed. There was a lot that needed to be done.

The Hidden Girl

Beginning in the eighth century, the Imperial court of Tang Dynasty China increasingly relied on military governors—the jiedushi—*whose responsibilities began with border defense but gradually encompassed taxation, civil administration, and other aspects of political power. They were, in fact, independent feudal warlords whose accountability to Imperial authority was nominal.*

Rivalry among the governors was often violent and bloody.

·

On the morning after my tenth birthday, spring sunlight dapples the stone slabs of the road in front of our house through the blooming branches of the pagoda tree. I climb out onto the thick bough pointing west like an immortal's arm and reach for a strand of yellow flowers, anticipating the sweet taste tinged with a touch of bitterness.

"Alms, young mistress?"

I look down and see a bhikkhuni. I can't tell how old she is—her face is unlined but there is a fortitude in her dark eyes that reminds me of my grandmother. The light fuzz over her shaved head glows in the warm sun like a halo, and her grey kasaya is clean but tattered at the hem. She holds up a wooden bowl in her left hand, gazing up at me expectantly.

"Would you like some pagoda tree flowers?" I ask.

She smiles. "I haven't had any since I was a young girl. It would be a delight."

"If you stand below me, I'll drop some into your bowl," I say, reaching for the silk pouch on my back.

She shakes her head. "I can't eat flowers that have been touched by another hand—too infected with the mundane concerns of this dusty world."

"Then climb up yourself," I say. Immediately I feel ashamed at my annoyance.

"If I get them myself, they wouldn't be alms now would they?" There's a hint of laughter in her voice.

"All right," I say. Father has always taught me to be polite to the monks and nuns. We may not follow the Buddhist teachings, but it doesn't make sense to antagonize the spirits, whether they are Dàoist, Buddhist, or wild spirits who rely on no learned masters at all. "Tell me which flowers you want; I'll try to get them for you without touching them."

She points to some flowers at the end of a slim branch below my bough. They are paler in color than the flowers from the rest of the tree, which means they are sweeter. But the branch they dangle from is much too thin for me to climb.

I hook my knees around the thick bough I'm on and lean back until I'm dangling upside down like a bat. It's fun to see the world this way, and I don't care that the hem of my dress is flapping around my face. Father always yells at me when he sees me like this, but he never stays angry at me for too long, on account of my losing my mother when I was just a baby.

Wrapping my hands in the loose folds of my sleeves, I try to grab for the flowers. But I'm still too far from the branch she wants, those white flowers tantalizingly just out of reach.

"If it's too much trouble," the nun calls out, "don't worry about it. I don't want you to tear your dress."

I bite my bottom lip, determined to ignore her. By tightening and flexing the muscles in my belly and thighs, I begin to swing back and forth. When I've reached the apex of an upswing I judge to be high enough, I let go with my knees.

As I plunge through the leafy canopy, the flowers she wants brush by my face and I snap my teeth around a strand. My fingers grab the lower branch, which sinks under my weight and slows my momentum as my body swings back upright. For a moment, it seems as if the branch would hold, but then I hear a crisp snap and feel suddenly weightless.

I tuck my knees under me and manage to land in the shade of the pagoda tree, unharmed. Immediately, I roll out of the way, and the flower-laden branch crashes to the spot on the ground I just vacated a moment later.

I walk nonchalantly up to the nun and open my jaw to drop the strand of flowers into her alms bowl. "No dust. And you only said no hands."

•

In the shade of the pagoda tree, we sit with our legs crossed in the lotus position like the buddhas in the temple. She picks the flowers off the stem: one for her, one for me. The sweetness is lighter and less cloying than the sugar dough figurines Father sometimes buys me.

"You have a talent," she says. "You'd make a good thief."

I look at her, indignant. "I'm a general's daughter."

"Are you?" she says. "Then you're already a thief."

"What are you talking about?"

"I have walked many miles," she says. I look at her bare feet: the bottoms are callused and leathery. "I see peasants starving in fields while the great lords plot and scheme for bigger armies. I see ministers and generals drink wine from ivory cups and conduct calligraphy with their piss on silk scrolls while orphans and widows must make one cup of rice last five days."

"Just because we are not poor doesn't make us thieves. My father serves his lord, the Jiedushi of Weibo, with honor and carries out his duties faithfully."

"We're all thieves in this world of suffering," the nun says. "Honor and faith are not virtues, only excuses for stealing more."

"Then you're a thief as well," I say, anger making my face glow with heat. "You accept alms and do no work to earn it."

She nods. "I am indeed. The Buddha teaches us that the world is an illusion, and suffering is inevitable as long as we do not see through it. If we're all fated to be thieves, it's better to be a thief who adheres to a code that transcends the mundane."

"What is your code then?"

"To disdain the moral pronouncements of hypocrites; to be true to my word; to always do what I promise, no more and no less. To hone my talent and wield it like a beacon in a darkening world."

I laugh. "What is your talent, Mistress Thief?"

"I steal lives."

•

The inside of the cabinet is dark and warm, the air redolent of camphor. By the faint light coming through the slit between the doors, I arrange the blankets around me to make a cozy nest.

The footsteps of patrolling soldiers echo through the hallway outside my bedroom. Each time one of them turns a corner, the clanging of armor and sword marks the passage of another fraction of an hour, bringing me closer to morning.

The conversation between the bhikkhuni and my father replays through my mind.

"Give her to me. I will have her as my student."

"Much as I'm flattered by the Buddha's kind attention, I must decline. My daughter's place is at home, by my side."

"You can give her to me willingly, or I can take her away without your blessing."

"Are you threatening me with a kidnapping? Know that I've made my living on the tip of a sword, and my house is guarded by fifty armed men who will give their lives for their young mistress."

"I never threaten; I simply inform. Even if you keep her in an iron chest ringed about with bronze chains at the bottom of the ocean, I will take her away as easily as I cut your beard with this dagger."

There was a cold, bright, metallic flash. Father drew his sword, the grinding noise of blade against sheath wringing my heart so that it leaped wildly.

But the bhikkhuni was already gone, leaving behind a few loose strands of gray hair floating gently to the floor in the slanted rays of the sunlight. My father, stunned, held his hand against the side of his face where the dagger had brushed against his skin.

The hairs landed; my father removed his hand. There was a patch of denuded skin on his cheek, as pale as the stone slabs of the road in the morning sun. No blood.

"Do not be afraid, Daughter. I will triple the guards tonight. The spirit of your dear departed mother will guard you."

But I'm afraid. I *am* afraid. I think about the glow of sunlight around the nun's head. I like my long, thick hair, which the maids tell me resembles my mother's, and she had combed her hair a hundred times each night before she went to sleep. I don't want to have my head shaved.

I think about the glint of metal in the nun's hand, quicker than the eye can follow.

I think about the strands of hair from my father's beard drifting to the floor.

The light from the oil lamp outside the closet door flickers. I scramble to the corner of the closet and squeeze my eyes tightly shut.

There is no noise. Just a draft that caresses my face. Softly, like the flapping wings of a moth.

I open my eyes. For a moment, I don't understand what I'm seeing.

Suspended about three feet from my face is an oblong object, about the size of my forearm and shaped like the cocoon of a silkworm. Glowing like a sliver of the moon, it gives off a light that is without warmth, shadowless. Fascinated, I crawl closer.

No, an "object" isn't quite right. The cold light spills out of it like melting ice, along with the draft that whips my hair about my face. It is more like the absence of substance, a rip in the murky interior of the cabinet, a negative object that consumes darkness and turns it into light.

My throat feels parched and I swallow, hard. Fingers trembling, I reach out to touch the glow. A half second of hesitation, then I make contact.

Or no contact. There is no skin-searing heat nor bone-freezing chill. My impression of the object as a negative is confirmed as my fingers touch nothing. And neither do they emerge from the other side—they've simply vanished into the glow, as though I'm plunging my hand into a hole in space.

I jerk my hand back out and examine my fingers, wiggling them. No damage as far as I can see.

A hand reaches out from the rip, grabs my arm, and pulls me toward the light. Before I can scream, blazing light blinds me, and I'm overwhelmed by the sensation of falling, falling from the tip of a heaven-reaching pagoda tree toward an earth that never comes.

•

The mountain floats among the clouds like an island.

I've tried to find my way down, but always, I get lost among the foggy woods. *Just go down, down,* I tell myself. But the fog thickens until it takes on substance, and no matter how hard I push, the wall of clouds refuses to yield. Then I have no choice but to sit down, shivering, wringing the condensation out of my hair. Some of the wetness is from tears, but I won't admit that.

She materializes out of the fog. Wordlessly, she beckons me to follow her back up the peak; I obey.

"You're not very good at hiding," she says.

There is no response to that. If she could steal me from a cabinet inside a general's house guarded by walls and soldiers, I suppose there's nowhere I can hide from her.

We emerge from the woods back onto the sun-drenched peak. A gust of wind brushes past us, whipping up the fallen leaves into a storm of gold and crimson.

"Are you hungry?" she asks, her voice not unkind.

I nod. Something about her tone catches me off guard. Father never asks me if I'm hungry, and I sometimes dream of my mother making me a breakfast of freshly baked bread and fermented beans. It's been three days since the bhikkhuni had taken me here, and I've not eaten anything but some sour berries I found in the woods and a few bitter roots I dug from the ground.

"Come along," she says.

She takes me up a zigzagging path carved into the face of a cliff. The path is so narrow that I dare not look down but shuffle along, my face and body pressed against the rock face and my outstretched hands clinging to dangling vines like a gecko. The bhikkhuni, on the other hand, strides along the path as though she's walking in the middle of a wide avenue in Chang'an. She waits patiently at each turn for me to catch up.

I hear the faint sounds of clanking metal above me. Having dug my feet into depressions along the path and tested the vine in my hands to be sure it's rooted securely to the mountain, I look up.

Two young women, about fourteen years of age, are fighting with swords in the air. No, *fighting* isn't quite the right word. It's more accurate to call their movements a dance.

One of the women, dressed in a white robe, pushes off the cliff with both feet while holding on to a vine with her left hand. She swings away from the cliff in a wide arc, her legs stretched out before her in a graceful pose that reminds me of the apsaras—flying nymphs who make their home in the clouds—painted on scrolls in the temples. The sword in her right hand glints in the sunlight like a shard of heaven.

As her sword tip approaches her opponent on the cliff, the other woman lets go of the vine she's hanging on to and leaps straight up. The black robe billows around her like the wings of a giant moth, and as her ascent slows, she flips herself at the apex of her arc and tumbles toward the woman in white like a diving hawk, her sword arm leading as a beak.

Clang!

The tips of their swords collide, and a spark lights up the air like an exploding firework. The sword in the hand of the woman in black bends into a crescent, slowing her descent until she is standing inverted in the air, supported only by the tip of her adversary's blade.

Both women punch out with their free hands, palms open.

Thump!

A crisp blow reverberates in the air. The woman in black lands against the mountain face, where she attaches herself by deftly wrapping a vine around her ankle. The woman in white completes her arced swing back to the rock, and, like a dragonfly dipping its tail into the still pond, pushes off again for another assault.

I watch, mesmerized, as the two swordswomen pursue, dodge, strike, feint, punch, kick, slash, glide, tumble, and stab across the webbing of vines over the face of the sheer cliff, thousands of feet above the roiling clouds below, defying both gravity and mortality. They are graceful as birds flitting across a swaying bamboo forest, quick as mantises leaping across a dew-dappled web, impossible as the immortals of legends whispered by hoarse-voiced bards in teahouses.

Also, I notice with relief that they both have thick, flowing, beautiful hair. Perhaps shaving is not required to be the bhikkhuni's student.

"Come," the bhikkhuni beckons, and I obediently make my way over to the small stone platform jutting into the air from the bend in the path. "I guess you really are hungry," she observes, a hint of laughter in her voice. Embarrassed, I close my jaw, still hanging open from shock at seeing the sparring girls.

With the clouds far below our feet and the wind whipping around us, it feels like the world I've known all my life has fallen away.

"Here." She points to a pile of bright pink peaches at the end of the platform, each about the size of my fist. "The hundred-year-old monkeys who live in the mountains gather these from deep in the clouds, where the peach trees absorb the essence of the heavens. After eating one of these, you won't be hungry for a full ten days. If you become thirsty, you can drink the dew from the vines and the springwater in the cave that is our dormitory."

The two sparring girls have climbed down from the cliff onto the platform behind us. They each take a peach.

"I will show you where you'll sleep, Little Sister," says the girl in white. "I'm Jinger. If you get scared from the howling wolves at night, you can crawl into my bed."

"I'm sure you've never had anything as sweet as this peach," says the girl in black. "I'm Konger. I've studied with Teacher the longest and know all the fruits of this mountain."

"Have you had pagoda tree flowers?" I ask.

"No," she says. "Maybe someday you can show me."

I bite into the peach. It is indescribably sweet and melts against my tongue as though it's made of pure snow. Yet, as soon as I've swallowed a mouthful, my belly warms with the heat of its sustenance. I believe that the peach really will last me ten days. I'll believe anything my teacher tells me.

"Why have you taken me?" I ask.

"Because you have a talent, Yinniang," she says.

I suppose that is my name now. The Hidden Girl.

"But talents must be cultivated," she continues. "Will you be a pearl buried in the mud of the endless East Sea, or will you shine so brightly as to awaken those who only doze through life and light up a mundane world?"

"Teach me to fly and fight like them," I say, licking the sweet peach juice from my hands. *I will become a great thief,* I tell myself. *I will steal my life back from you.*

She nods thoughtfully and looks into the distance, where the setting sun has turned the clouds into a sea of golden splendor and crimson gore.

SIX YEARS LATER

The wheels of the donkey cart grind to a stop.

Without warning, Teacher rips the blindfold away from my eyes and digs out the silk plugs in my ears. I struggle against the sudden bright sun and the sea of noise—the braying of donkeys; the whinnying of horses; the clanging of cymbals and the wailing of erhus from some folk opera troupe; the thumping and thudding of goods being loaded and unloaded; the singing, shouting, haggling, laughing, arguing, pontificating that make up the symphony of a metropolis.

While I'm still recovering from my journey in the swaying darkness, Teacher has jumped down to the ground to leash the donkey to a roadside post. We're in some provincial capital, that much I know—indeed, the smell of a hundred different varieties of fried dough and candied apples and horse manure and exotic perfume already told me as much even before the blindfold was off—but I can't tell exactly where. I strain to catch snippets of conversation from the bustling city around me, but the topolect is unfamiliar.

The pedestrians passing by our cart bow to Teacher. *"Amitabha,"* they say.

Teacher holds up a hand in front of her chest and bows back. *"Amitabha,"* she says back.

I may be anywhere in the empire.

"We'll have lunch, then you can rest up at the inn over there," says Teacher.

"What about my task?" I ask. I'm nervous. This is the first time I've been away from the mountain since she's taken me.

She looks at me with a complicated expression, halfway between pity and amusement. "So eager?"

I bite my bottom lip, not answering.

"You will choose your own method and time," she says, her tone as placid as the cloudless sky. "I'll be back on the third night. Good hunting."

•

"Keep your eyes open and your limbs loose," she said. "Remember everything I've taught you."

Teacher had summoned two mist hawks from nearby peaks, each the size of a full-grown man. Iron blades extended from their talons, and steel glinted from their vicious curved beaks. They circled above me, alternately emerging from and disappearing into the cloud-mist, their screeches mournful and proud.

Jinger handed me a small dagger about five inches in length. It seemed utterly inadequate for the task. My hand shook as I wrapped my fingers around the handle.

"What can be seen is not all," she said.

"Be aware of what is hidden," Konger added.

"You will be fine," Jinger said, squeezing my shoulder.

"The world is full of illusions cast by the unseen Truth," Konger said.

Then she leaned in to whisper in my ear, her breath warm against my cheek, "I still have a scar on the back of my neck from my time with the hawks."

They backed off and faded into the mist, leaving me alone with the raptors and Teacher's voice coming from the vines above me.

"Why do we kill?" I asked.

The hawks took turns to swoop down, feinting and testing my defenses. I leapt out of the way reflexively, brandishing my dagger to ward them off.

"This is a time of chaos," Teacher said. "The great lords of the land are filled with ambition. They take everything they can from the people they're sworn to protect, shepherds who have turned into wolves preying on their flocks. They increase the taxes until all the walls in their palaces are gleaming with gold and silver; they take sons away from mothers until their armies swell like the current of the Yellow River; they plot and scheme and redraw lines on maps as though the country is nothing but a platter of sand, upon which the peasants creep and crawl like terrified ants."

One of the hawks turned to dive at me. A real attack, not a test. I crouched into a defensive stance, the dagger in my right hand held up to guard my face, my left hand on the ground for stability. I kept my eyes on the hawk, letting everything fade into the background except the bright reflections from the sharp beak and talons, like a constellation in the night sky.

The hawk loomed in my vision. A light breeze brushed the back of my neck. The raptor extended its talons and flapped its wings, trying to slow its dive at the last minute.

"Who is to say that one governor is right? Or that another general is wrong?" she asked. "The man who seduces his lord's wife may be doing so to get close to a tyrant and exact vengeance. The woman who demands rice for the peasantry from her patron may be doing so to further her own ambition. We live in a time of chaos, and the only moral choice is to be amoral. The great lords hire us to strike at their enemies. And we carry out our missions with dedication and loyalty, true and deadly as a crossbow bolt."

I got ready to spring out of my crouch to slash at the hawk, and then I remembered the words of my sisters.

"... What can be seen is not all.... I still have a scar on the back of my neck."

I dropped to the ground and rolled to the left, the talons of the hawk who had been trying to sneak up behind me missing only by inches. It collided with its companion in the spot where my head had been but a moment ago, like a diver meeting her reflection at the surface of the pool. There was a tangle of beating wings and angry screeching.

I lunged at the storm of feathers. One, two, three slashes, quicker than lightning. The hawks tumbled down, their wings crumpling as they struck the ground. Blood from the clean cuts in their throats pooled on the stone platform.

There was also blood seeping from my shoulder where the rough rocks had scraped the skin during my roll. But I had survived, and my foes had not.

"Why do we kill?" I asked again, still panting from the exertion. I had killed wild apes before, and forest panthers and bamboo grove tigers. But a pair of mist hawks were the hardest kill yet, the height of the assassin's art. "Why do we serve as the talons of the powerful?"

"We are the winter snowstorm descending upon a house rotten with termites," she said. "Only by hurrying the decay of the old can we bring about the rebirth of the new. We are the vengeance of a weary world."

Jinger and Konger emerged from the mist to sprinkle corpse-dissolving powder on the hawks and to bandage my wound.

"Thank you," I whispered.

"You need to practice more," said Jinger, but her tone was kind.

"I have to keep you alive." Konger's eyes flashed mischievously. "You promised to get me some pagoda tree flowers, remember?"

•

The thin crescent of the moon hangs from the tip of a branch of the ancient pagoda tree outside the governor's mansion as the night watchman rings the midnight hour. The shadows in the streets are thick as ink, the same color as my silk leggings, tight tunic, and the cloth mask over my nose and mouth.

I'm upside down, my feet hooked to the top of the wall and my body pressed against the flat surface like a clinging vine. Two soldiers pass below me on their patrol route. If they looked up, they'd think I was just a part of the shadows or a sleeping bat.

As soon as they're gone, I arch my back and flip onto the wall. I scramble along the top, quieter than a cat, until I'm opposite the roof of the central hall of the compound. Snapping my coiled legs, I sail across the gap in a single leap and melt into the shingles on the gentle curve of the roof.

There are, of course, far stealthier ways to break into a well-protected compound, but I like to stay in this world, to remain surrounded by the night breeze and the distant hoots of the owl.

Carefully, I pry off a glazed roofing tile and peek into the gap. Through the latticed under-roof I see a brightly lit hall paved with stones. A middle-aged man sits on a dais at the eastern end, his eyes intent upon a bundle of papers, flipping through the pages slowly. I see a birthmark the shape of a butterfly on his left cheek and a jade collar around his neck.

He is the jiedushi I'm supposed to kill.

"Steal his life, and your apprenticeship will be completed," Teacher said. "This is your last test."

"What has he done that he deserves to die?" I asked.

"Does it matter? It is enough that a man who once saved my life wants this man to die, and that he has paid handsomely for it. We amplify the forces of ambition and strife; we hold on to only our code."

I crawl over the roof, my palms and feet gliding over the tiles smoothly—Teacher trained us by having us glide across the valley lake in March, when the ice is so thin that even squirrels sometimes fall through and drown. I feel one with the night, my senses sharpened like the tip of my dagger. Excitement is tinged with a hint of sorrow, like the first stroke of the paintbrush on a fresh sheet of paper.

Now that I'm directly above where the governor is sitting, once again I pry off one tile, then another. I make a hole big enough for me to slink through. Then I take out the grappling hook from my pouch—painted black to prevent reflections—and toss it to the apex ridge so that the claws dig in securely. Then I tie the silk cord around my waist.

I look down through the hole in the roof. The jiedushi is still where he was, oblivious to the mortal danger over his head.

For a moment I suffer the illusion that I'm back in the great pagoda tree in front of my house, looking through a hole in the swaying leaves at my father.

But the moment passes. I'm going to dive through like a cormorant, slit his throat, strip off his clothes, and sprinkle corpse-dissolving powder all over his skin. Then, as he lies there on the stone floor, still twitching, I will take flight back to the ceiling and make my escape. By the time servants discover the remains of his body, barely more than a skeleton, I will be long gone. Teacher will declare my apprenticeship to be at an end, myself an equal of my sisters.

I take a deep breath. My body is coiled. I've trained and practiced for this moment for six years. I'm ready.

"*Baba!*"

I hold still.

The boy who emerges from behind the curtains is about six years old, his hair tied into a neat little braid that points straight up like the tail of a rooster.

"What are you doing still up?" the man asks. "Be a good boy and go back to sleep."

"I can't sleep," the boy says. "I heard a noise, and I saw a shadow moving on the courtyard wall."

"Just a cat," the man says. The boy looks unconvinced. The man looks thoughtful for a moment, then says, "All right, come over."

He sets the papers aside on the low desk next to him. The boy scrambles into his lap.

"Shadows are nothing to be afraid of," he says. Then he proceeds to make a series of shadow puppets with his hands held against the reading light. He teaches the boy how to make a butterfly, a puppy, a bat, a sinuous dragon. The boy laughs in delight. Then the boy makes a kitten to chase his father's butterfly across the papered windows of the large hall.

"Shadows are given life by light, and they also die by light." The man stops fluttering his fingers and lets his hands fall by his side. "Go to sleep, child. In the morning you can chase real butterflies in the garden."

The boy, heavy-eyed, nods and leaves quietly.

On the roof, I hesitate. The boy's laughter will not leave my mind. Can the girl stolen from her family steal family away from another child? Is this the moral pronouncement of a hypocrite?

"Thank you for waiting until my son has left," the man says.

I freeze. There's no one in the hall but him, and he's too loud to be talking to himself.

"I prefer not to shout," he says, his eyes still on the bundle of papers. "It would be easier if you came down."

The pounding of my heart is a roar in my ears. I should flee immediately. This is probably a trap. If I went down, he might have soldiers in ambush or some mechanism under the floor of the hall to capture me. Yet, something in his voice compels me to obey.

I drop through the hole in the roof, the silk cord attached to the grappling hook looped about my waist a few times to slow my descent. I land gently before the dais, silent as a snowflake.

"How did you know?" I ask. The bricks at my feet have not flipped open to reveal a yawning pit, and no soldiers have rushed from behind the screens. But my hands grip the cord tightly and my knees are ready to snap. I can still complete my mission if he truly is defenseless.

"Children have sharper ears than their parents," he says. "And I have long made shadow puppets for my own amusement while reading late at night. I know how much the lights in this hall usually flicker without the draft from a new opening in the ceiling."

I nod. It's a good lesson for the next time. My right hand moves to grasp the handle of the dagger in the sheath at the small of my back.

"Jiedushi Lu of Chenxu is ambitious," he says. "He has coveted my territory for a long time, thinking of pressing the young men in its rich fields into his army. If you strike me down, there will be no one to stand between him and the throne in Chang'an. Millions will die as his rebellion sweeps across the empire. Hundreds of thousands of children will become orphans. Ghostly multitudes will wander the land, their souls unable to rest as beasts pick through their corpses."

The numbers he speaks of are vast, like the countless grains of sand suspended in the turbid waters of the Yellow River. I can't make any sense of them. "He saved my teacher's life once," I say.

"And so you will do as she asks, blind to all other concerns?"

"The world is rotten through," I say. "I have my duty."

"I cannot say that my hands are free of blood. Perhaps this is what comes of making compromises." He sighs. "Will you at least allow me two days to put my affairs in order? My wife departed this world when my son was born, and I have to arrange for his care."

I stare at him. I can't treat the boy's laughter as an illusion.

I picture the governor surrounding his house with thousands of soldiers; I picture him hiding in the cellar, trembling like a leaf in autumn; I picture him on the road away from this city, whipping his horse again and again, grimacing like a desperate marionette.

As if reading my mind, he says, "I will be here, alone, in two nights. I give you my word."

"What is the word of a man about to die worth?" I counter.

"As much as the word of an assassin," he says.

I nod and leap up. Scrambling up the dangling rope as swiftly as I ascend one of the vines on the cliff at home, I disappear through the hole in the roof.

•

I'm not worried about the jiedushi's escaping. I've been trained well, and I will catch him no matter where he runs. I'd rather give him the chance to spend some time saying goodbye to his little boy; it seems right.

I wander the markets of the city, soaking up the smell of fried dough and caramelized sugar. My stomach growls at the memory of foods I have not had in six years. Eating peaches and drinking dew may have purified my spirit, but the flesh still yearns for earthly sweetness.

I speak to the vendors in the language of the court, and at least some of them have a passing mastery of it.

"That is very skillfully made," I say, looking at a sugar dough general on a stick. The figurine is wearing a bright red war cape glazed with jujube juice. My mouth waters.

"Would you like to have it?" the vendor asks. "It's very fresh, young mistress. I made it only this morning. The filling is lotus paste."

"I don't have any money," I say regretfully. Teacher gave me only enough money for lodging, and a dried peach for food.

The vendor considers me and seems to make up his mind. "By your accent I take it you're not a local?"

I nod.

"Away from home to find a pool of tranquility in this chaotic world?"

"Something like that," I say.

He nods, as if this explains everything. He hands the stick of the sugar general to me. "From one wanderer to another, then. This is a good place to settle."

I accept the gift and thank him. "Where are you from?"

"Chenxu. I abandoned my fields and ran away when Jiedushi Lu's men came to my village to draft boys and men for the army. I had already lost my father, and I wasn't interested in dying to add color to his war cape. That figurine is modeled after Jiedushi Lu. It gives me pleasure to watch patrons bite his head off."

I laugh and oblige him. The sugar dough melts on the tongue, and the succulent lotus paste that oozes out is delightful.

I walk about the alleyways and streets of the city, savoring every bite of the sugar dough figurine as I listen to snatches of conversation wafting from the doors of teahouses and passing carriages.

"... why should we send her across the city to learn dance? ..."

"The magistrate isn't going to look kindly on such deception. ..."

"... the best fish I've ever had! It was still flapping ..."

"... how can you tell? What did he say? Tell me, sister, tell ..."

The rhythm of life flows around me, buoying me up like the sea of clouds on the mountain when I swing from vine to vine. I think about the words of the man I'm supposed to kill:

Millions will die as his rebellion sweeps across the empire. Hundreds of thousands of children will become orphans. Ghostly multitudes will wander the land.

I think about his son, and the shadows flitting across the walls of the vast, empty hall. Something in my heart throbs to the music of this world, at once mundane and holy. The grains of sand swirling in the water resolve into individual faces, laughing, crying, yearning, dreaming.

.

On the third night the crescent moon is a bit wider, the wind a bit chillier, and the hooting of the owls in the distance a shade more ominous.

I scale the wall of the governor's compound as before. The patrolling patterns of the soldiers have not changed. This time, I crouch even lower and move even more silently across the branch-thin top of the wall and the uneven surface of roofing tiles. I'm back at the familiar spot; I pry up a roof tile that I had put back two nights earlier and press my eye against the slit to block the draft, anticipating at any moment masked guards leaping out of the darkness, to spring their trap.

Not to worry—I'm ready.

But there are no shouts of alarm and no clanging of the gong. I gaze down into the well-lit hall. He is sitting in the same spot, a stack of papers on the desk by him.

I listen hard for the footsteps of a child. Nothing. The boy has been sent away.

I examine the floor of the hall beneath where the man sits. It's strewn with straw. The sight confuses me for a moment before I realize that it's an act of kindness. He wants to keep his blood from staining the bricks so that whoever has to clean up the mess will have an easier time.

The man sits in the lotus position, eyes closed, a beatific smile on his face like a statue of the Buddha.

Gently, I place the tile back in place and disappear into the night like a breeze.

•

"Why have you not completed your task?" Teacher asks. My sisters stand behind her, two arhats guarding their mistress.

"He was playing with his child," I say. I hold on to the explanation like a vine swaying over an abyss.

She sighs. "Next time this happens, you should kill the boy first, so that you're no longer distracted."

I shake my head.

"It is a trick. He is playing upon your sympathies. The powerful are all actors upon a stage, their hearts as unfathomable as shadows."

"That may be," I say. "Still, he kept his word and was willing to die at my hand. I believe other things he's told me may be true as well."

"How do you know he is not as ambitious as the man he maligns? How do you know he is not only being kind in service of a greater cruelty in the future?"

"No one knows the future," I say. "The house may be rotten through, but I'm unwilling to be the hand that brings it tumbling down upon the ants seeking a pool of tranquility."

She stares at me. "What of loyalty? What of obedience to your teacher? What of carrying out that which you promised to do?"

"I'm not meant to be a thief of lives," I say.

"So much talent," she says; then, after a pause, "Wasted."

Something about her tone makes me shiver. Then I look behind her and see that Jinger and Konger are gone.

"If you leave," she says, "you're no longer my student."

I look at her unlined face and not unkind eyes. I think about the times she bandaged my legs after I fell from the vines in the early days. I think about the time she fought off the bamboo grove bear when it proved too much for me. I think about the nights she held me and taught me to see through the world's illusions to the truth beneath.

She had taken me away from my family, but she has also been the closest thing to a mother I know.

"Goodbye, Teacher."

I crouch and leap like a bounding tiger, like a soaring wild ape, like a hawk taking flight. I smash through the window of the room in the inn and dive into the ocean that is night.

•

"I'm not here to kill you," I say.

The man nods, as if this is entirely expected.

"My sisters—Jinger, also known as the Heart of Lightning, and Konger, the Empty-Handed—have been dispatched to complete what I cannot."

"I will summon my guards," he says, standing up.

"That won't do any good," I tell him. "Jinger can steal your soul even if you were hiding inside a bell at the bottom of the ocean, and Konger is even more skillful."

He smiled. "Then I will face them alone. Thank you for the warning so that my men do not die needlessly."

A faint shrieking noise, like a distant troop of howling monkeys, can be heard in the night. "There's no time to explain," I tell him. "Give me your red scarf."

He does, and I tie the scarf about my waist. "You will see things that seem beyond comprehension. Whatever happens, keep your eye on this scarf and stay away from it."

The howling grows louder. It seems to come from everywhere and nowhere. Jinger is here.

Before he has time to question me further, I rip open a seam in space and crawl in to vanish from his sight, leaving only the tip of the bright red scarf dangling behind.

•

"Imagine that space is a sheet of paper," Teacher said. "An ant crawling on this sheet of paper is aware of breadth and depth, but has no awareness of height."

I looked at the ant she had sketched on the paper, expectant.

"The ant is terrified of danger, and builds a wall around him, thinking that such an impregnable barrier will keep him safe."

Teacher sketches a ring around the ant.

"But unbeknownst to the ant, a knife is poised above him. It is not part of the ant's world, invisible to him. The wall he has built will do nothing to protect him against a strike from a hidden direction—"

She throws her dagger at the paper, pinning the painted ant to the ground.

"You may think width, depth, and height are the only dimensions of the world, Hidden Girl, but you'd be wrong. You have lived your life as an ant on a sheet of paper, and the truth is far more wondrous."

•

I emerge into the space above space, the space within space, the hidden space.

Everything gains a new dimension—the walls, the floor tiles, the flickering torches, the astonished face of the governor. It is as if the governor's skin has been pulled away to reveal everything underneath: I see his beating heart, his pulsating intestines, the blood streaming through his transparent vessels, his gleaming white bones as well as the velvety marrow stuffed inside like jujube-stained lotus paste. I see each grain of shiny mica inside each brick; I see ten thousand immortals dancing inside each flame.

No, that's not quite accurate. I have not the words to describe what I see. I see a million billion layers to everything at once, like an ant who has always seen a line before him suddenly lifted off the page to realize the perfection of a circle. This is the perspective of the Buddha, who comprehends the incomprehensibility of Indra's net, which connects the smallest mote at the tip of a flea's foot to the grandest river of innumerable stars that spans the sky at night.

This was how, years ago, Teacher had penetrated the walls of my father's compound, evaded my father's soldiers, and seized me from within the tightly sealed cabinet.

I see the approaching white robe of Jinger, bobbing like a glowing jellyfish in the vast deep. She ululates as she approaches, a single voice making a cacophony of howling that sends terror into the hearts of her victims.

"Little Sister, what are you doing here?"

I lift my dagger. "Please, Jinger, go back."

"You've always been a bit too stubborn," she says.

"We have eaten from the same peach and bathed in the same cold mountain spring," I say. "You taught me how to climb the vines and how to pick the ice lilies for my hair. I love you like a sister of the blood. Please, don't do this."

She looks sad. "I can't. Teacher has promised."

"There's a greater promise we all must live by: to do what our heart tells us is right."

She lifts her sword. "Because I love you like a sister, I will let you strike at me without hitting back. If you can hit me before I kill the governor, I will leave."

I nod. "Thank you. And I'm sorry it's come to this."

The hidden space has its own structure, made from dangling thin strands that glow faintly with an inner light. To move in this space, Jinger and I leap from vine to vine and swing from filament to filament, climbing, tumbling, pivoting, lurching, dancing on a lattice woven from starlight and lambent ice.

I lunge after her, she easily dodges out of the way. She has always been the best at vine fighting and cloud dancing. She glides and swings as gracefully as an immortal of the heavenly court. Compared to her, my moves are lumbering, heavy, lacking all finesse.

As she dances away from my strikes, she counts them off: "One, two, three-four-five . . . very nice, Hidden Girl, you've been practicing. Six-seven-eight, nine, ten . . ." Once in a while, when I get too close, she parries my dagger with her sword as effortlessly as a dozing man swats away a fly.

Almost pityingly, she swivels out of my way and swings toward the governor. Like a knife poised above the page, she's completely invisible to him, falling upon him from another dimension.

I lurch after her, hoping that I'm close enough to her for my plan to work.

The governor, seeing the red scarf I dangle into his world approach, drops to the ground and rolls out of the way. Jinger's sword pierces through the veil between dimensions and, in that world, a sword emerges from the air and smashes the desk the governor was sitting behind into smithereens before disappearing.

"Eh? How can he see me coming?"

Without giving her a chance to figure out my trick, I launch a fusillade of dagger strikes. "Thirty-one, thirty-two-three-four-five-six . . . you're really getting better at this . . ."

We dance around in the space "above" the hall—there's no word for this direction—and each time, as Jinger goes after the governor, I try to stay right next to her to warn the governor of the hidden danger. Try as I might, I can't touch her at all. I can feel myself getting tired, slowing down.

I flex my legs and swing after her again, but this time, I'm careless and come too close to the wall of the hall. My dangling scarf catches on the sconce for a torch and I fall to my feet.

Jinger looks at me and laughs. "So that's how you've been doing it! Clever, Hidden Girl. But now the game is over, and I'm about to claim my prize."

If she strikes at the governor now, he won't have any warning at all. I'm stuck here.

The scarf catches fire, and the flame erupts into the hidden space. I scream with terror as the flame engulfs my robe.

With three quick leaps, Jinger is back on the same strand I'm on; she whips off her white robe and wraps it around me, helping me smother the flames.

"Are you all right?" she asks.

The fire has singed my hair and charred my skin in a few places, but I'll be fine. "Thank you," I say. Then before she can react, I whip my dagger across the hem of her robe and cut off a strip of cloth. The tip of my dagger continues to slice open the veil between dimensions, and the strip drifts into the ordinary world, like flotsam bobbing to the surface. We both see the governor's shocked face as he scrambles away from the white silk patch on the floor.

"A hit," I say.

"Ah," she says. "That's not really fair, is it?"

"Nonetheless, it's a strike," I say.

"So that fall . . . it was all planned?"

"This was the only way I could think of," I admit. "You're a far superior sword fighter."

She shakes her head. "How can you care for a stranger more than your sister? But I gave you my word."

She climbs up and glides away like a departing water spirit. Just before she fades into the night, she turns to look at me one last time. "Farewell, Little Sister. Our bond has been severed as surely as you've cut through my dress. May you find your purpose."

"Farewell."

She leaves, ululating all the while.

•

I crawl back into ordinary space, and the governor rushes up to me. "I was so frightened! What kind of magic is this? I heard the clanging of swords but could see nothing. Your scarf danced in the air like a ghost, and then, finally, that white cloth materialized out of nowhere! Wait, are you hurt?"

I grimace and sit up. "It's nothing. Jinger is gone. But the next assassin will be my other sister, Konger, who is far more deadly. I do not know if I can protect you."

"I'm not afraid to die," he says.

"If you die, the Jiedushi of Chenxu will slaughter many more," I say. "You must listen to me."

I open my pouch and take out my teacher's gift to me on my fifteenth birthday. I hand it to him.

"This is a . . . paper donkey?" He looks at me, puzzled.

"This is the projection of a mechanical donkey into our world," I say. "It's like how a sphere passing through a plane would appear as a circle—never mind, there's no time. Here, you must go!"

I rip open space and shove him through it. The donkey looms now before him as a giant mechanical beast. Despite his protests, I push him onto the donkey.

Tightly wound sinew would power the spinning gears inside and move the legs on cranks, and the donkey will gallop off in a wide circle in the hidden space for an hour, springing from glowing vine to vine like a wire walker. Teacher had given it to me to help me escape if I'm hurt on a mission.

"How will you defend against her?" he asks.

I pull out the key and the donkey gallops away, leaving his query unanswered.

•

There is no howling; no singing; no terrifying din. When Konger approaches she is completely silent. If you don't know her, you will think she has no weapon. That is why she is nicknamed the Empty-Handed.

The robe is hot and the dough makeup on my face heavy. The hall is filled with smoke from the scattered straw on the floor I've set on fire. I crouch down on the floor where the air is clearer and cooler so I can breathe. I put on a beatific smile but keep my eyes slitted open.

The smoke swirls, a gentle disturbance that you'd miss if you weren't paying attention.

I know how much the lights in this hall usually flicker without the draft from a new opening in the ceiling.

Moments earlier, I had carefully cut a few fissures in the veil between dimensions with my dagger and kept them open with strands of silk torn from Jinger's robe. The openings were enough to let a draft through from the hidden space, enough to let me detect an approaching presence beyond.

I picture Konger with her implacable mien, gliding toward me in hidden space like a soul-taking demon. A needle glints in her right hand, the only weapon she needs.

She prefers to approach her victims in the unseen dimension, to prick the inside from the undefended direction. She likes to press the needle into the middle of their hearts, leaving the rib cage and the skin intact. She likes to probe the needle into their skulls and stir their brains into mush, driving them insane before their deaths but leaving no wound in the skull.

The smoke stirs some more; she's close now.

I imagine the scene from her point of view: a man dressed in the robe of a jiedushi is sitting in the smoke-filled hall, a birthmark the shape of a butterfly on his cheek. He's terrified into indecision, the rictus of a foolish smile frozen on his face even as his home burns around him. Somehow the air in the hidden space over him is murky, as though the smoke from the hall has transcended the veil between dimensions.

She lunges.

I shift to the right, moving by instinct rather than sense. I have sparred with her for years, and I hope she moves as she has always done.

She meant to press her needle into my skull, but since I've moved out of the way, her needle pierces into the world at the spot where my head was, and with a crisp clang, strikes against the jade collar I'm wearing around my neck.

I stagger up, coughing in the smoke. I wipe off the dough makeup from my face. Konger's needle is so fragile that after one impact it is bent out of shape. She never attacks a second time if the first attempt fails.

A surprised giggle.

"A good trick, Hidden Girl. I should have gotten a better look through all that smoke. You've always been Teacher's favorite student."

The crevices I carved between the worlds were for more than just warning. By filling the hidden space with smoke, her view of the ordinary world had become indistinct. Ordinarily, from her vantage point, my mask would have been but a transparent shell, and the bulky robe would not have concealed the slender body underneath.

But maybe, just maybe, she chose to not see through my poor disguise, the same way she once chose to warn me of the hawk swooping down behind me.

I bow to the unseen speaker. "Tell Teacher I'm sorry, but I won't be returning to the mountain."

"Who knew you would turn out to be an anti-assassin? We will see each other again, I hope."

"I will invite you to share some pagoda tree flowers then, Elder Sister. A tinge of bitterness at the heart of something sweet makes it less cloying."

Peals of laughter fade, and I collapse to the ground, exhausted.

I think about heading home, about seeing my father again. What will I tell him about my time away? How can I explain to him that I've changed?

I will not be able to grow up the way he wants. There is too much wildness in me. I cannot put on a confining dress and glide through the rooms of the compound, blushing as the matchmaker explains which boy I will marry. I cannot pretend to be more interested in my sewing than I am in climbing the pagoda tree next to the gate.

I have a talent.

I want to scale walls like Jinger, Konger, and I used to swing from vine to vine over the cliff face; I want to cross swords against worthy opponents; I want to pick a boy to marry—I'm thinking someone who is kind and has soft hands, maybe someone who grinds mirrors for a living so that he will know that there is another dimension beyond the smooth surface.

I want to hone my talent so that it shines brightly, terrorizing the unjust and lighting the way for those who would make the world better. I will protect the innocent and guard the timid. I do not know if I will always do what is right, but I am the Hidden Girl, and my loyalty is to the tranquility yearned by all.

I am a thief after all. I've stolen my life for myself, and I will steal back the lives of others.

The sound of beating, mechanical hooves approaches.

Seven Birthdays

The wide lawn spreads out before me almost to the golden surf of the sea, separated by the narrow dark tan band of the beach. The setting sun is bright and warm, the breeze a gentle caress against my arms and face.

"I want to wait a little longer," I say.

"It's going to get dark soon," Dad says.

I chew my bottom lip. "Text her again."

He shakes his head. "We've left her enough messages."

I look around. Most people have already left the park. The first hint of the evening chill is in the air.

"All right." I try not to sound disappointed. You shouldn't be disappointed when something happens over and over again, right? "Let's fly," I say.

Dad holds up the kite, a diamond with a painted fairy and two long ribbon tails. I picked it out this morning from the store at the park gate because the fairy's face reminded me of Mom.

"Ready?" Dad asks.

I nod.

"Go!"

I run toward the sea, toward the burning sky and the melting, orange sun. Dad lets go of the kite, and I feel the *fwoomp* as it lifts into the air, pulling the string in my hand taut.

"Don't look back! Keep running and let the string out slowly like I taught you."

I run. Like Snow White through the forest. Like Cinderella as the clock strikes midnight. Like the Monkey King trying to escape the Buddha's hand. Like Aeneas pursued by Juno's stormy rage. I un-spool the string as a sudden gust of wind makes me squint, my heart thumping in time with my pumping legs.

"It's up!"

I slow down, stop, and turn to look. The fairy is in the air, tugging at my hands to let go. I hold on to the handles of the spool, imagining the fairy lifting me into the air so that we can soar together over the Pacific, like Mom and Dad used to dangle me by my arms between them.

"Mia!"

I look over and see Mom striding across the lawn, her long black hair streaming in the breeze like the kite's tails. She stops before me, kneels on the grass, wraps me in a hug, squeezing my face against hers. She smells like her shampoo, like summer rain and wildflowers, a fragrance that I get to experience only once every few weeks.

"Sorry I'm late," she says, her voice muffled against my cheek. "Happy birthday!"

I want to give her a kiss, and I don't want to. The kite line slackens, and I give the line a hard jerk like Dad taught me. It's very important for me to keep the kite in the air. I don't know why. Maybe it has to do with the need to kiss her and not kiss her.

Dad jogs up. He doesn't say anything about the time. He doesn't mention that we missed our dinner reservation.

Mom gives me a kiss and pulls her face away, but keeps her arms around me. "Something came up," she says, her voice even, controlled. "Ambassador Chao-Walker's flight was delayed and she managed to squeeze me in for three hours at the airport. I had to walk her through the details of the solar management plan before the Shanghai Forum next week. It was important."

"It always is," Dad says.

Mom's arms tense against me. This has always been their pattern, even when they used to live together. Unasked for explanations. Accusations that don't sound like accusations.

Gently, I wriggle out of her embrace. "Look."

This has always been part of the pattern too: my trying to break their pattern. I can't help but think there's a simple solution, something I can do to make it all better.

I point up at the kite, hoping she'll see how I picked out a fairy whose face looks like hers. But the kite is too high up now for her to notice the resemblance. I've let out all the string. The long line droops gently like a ladder connecting the Earth to heaven, the highest segment glowing golden in the dying rays of the sun.

"It's lovely," she says. "Someday, when things quiet down a little, I'll take you to see the kite festival back where I grew up, on the other side of the Pacific. You'll love it."

"We'll have to fly then," I say.

"Yes," she says. "Don't be afraid to fly. I fly all the time."

I'm not afraid, but I nod anyway to show that I'm reassured. I don't ask when "someday" is going to be.

"I wish the kite could fly higher," I say, desperate to keep the words flowing, as though unspooling more conversation will keep something precious aloft. "If I cut the line, will it fly across the Pacific?"

After a moment, Mom says, "Not really . . . the kite stays up only because of the line. A kite is just like a plane, and the pulling force from your line acts like thrust. Did you know that the first airplanes the Wright brothers made were actually kites? They learned how to make wings that way. Someday I'll show you how the kite generates lift—"

"Sure it will," Dad interrupts. "It will fly across the Pacific. It's your birthday. Anything is possible."

Neither of them says anything after that.

I don't tell Dad that I enjoy listening to Mom talk about machines and engineering and history and other things that I don't fully understand. I don't tell her that I already know that the kite wouldn't fly across the ocean—I was just trying to get her to talk to me instead of defending herself. I don't tell him that I'm too old to believe anything is possible on my birthday—I wished for them not to fight, and look how that has turned out. I don't tell her that I know she doesn't mean to break her promises to me, but it still hurts when she does. I don't tell them that I wish I could cut the line that ties me to their wings—the tugging on my heart from their competing winds is too much.

I know they love me even if they no longer love each other; but knowing doesn't make it any easier.

Slowly, the sun sinks into the ocean; slowly, the stars wink to life in the sky. The kite has disappeared among the stars. I imagine the fairy visiting each star to give it a playful kiss.

Mom pulls out her phone and types furiously.

"I'm guessing you haven't had dinner," Dad says.

"No. Not lunch either. Been running around all day," Mom says, not looking up from the screen.

"There is a pretty good vegan place I just discovered a few blocks from the parking lot," Dad says. "Maybe we can pick up a cake from the sweet shop on the way and ask them to serve it after dinner."

"Um-hum."

"Would you put that away?" Dad says. "Please."

Mom takes a deep breath and puts the phone away. "I'm trying to change my flight to a later one so I can spend more time with Mia."

"You can't even stay with us one night?"

"I have to be in DC in the morning to meet with Professor Chakrabarti and Senator Frug."

Dad's face hardens. "For someone so concerned about the state of our planet, you certainly fly a lot. If you and your clients didn't always want to move faster and ship more—"

"You know perfectly well my clients aren't the reason I'm doing this—"

"I know it's really easy to deceive yourself. But you're working for the most colossal corporations and autocratic governments—"

"I'm working on a technical solution instead of empty promises! We have an ethical duty to all of humanity. I'm fighting for the eighty percent of the world's population living on under ten dollars—"

Unnoticed by the colossi in my life, I let the kite pull me away. Their arguing voices fade in the wind. Step by step, I walk closer to the pounding surf, the line tugging me toward the stars.

49

The wheelchair is having trouble making Mom comfortable.

First the chair tries to raise the seat so that her eyes are level with the screen of the ancient computer I found for her. But even with her bent back and hunched-over shoulders, she's having trouble reaching the keyboard on the desk below. As she stretches her trembling fingers toward the keys, the chair descends. She pecks out a few letters and numbers, struggles to look up at the screen, now towering above her. The motors hum as the chair lifts her again. Ad infinitum.

Over three thousand robots work under the supervision of three nurses to take care of the needs of some three hundred residents in Sunset Homes. This is how we die now. Out of sight. Dependent on the wisdom of machines. The pinnacle of Western civilization.

I walk over and prop up the keyboard with a stack of old hardcover books taken from her home before I sold it. The motors stop humming. A simple hack for a complicated problem, the sort of thing she would appreciate.

She looks at me, her clouded eyes devoid of recognition.

"Mom, it's me," I say. Then, after a second, I add, "Your daughter, Mia."

She has some good days, I recall the words of the chief nurse. *Doing math seems to calm her down. Thank you for suggesting that.*

She examines my face. "No," she says. She hesitates for a second. "Mia is seven."

Then she turns back to her computer and continues pecking out numbers on the keyboard. "Need to plot the demographic and conflict curves again," she mutters. "Gotta show them this is the only way . . ."

I sit down on the small bed. I suppose it should sting—the fact that she remembers her outdated computations better than she remembers me. But she is already so far away, a kite barely tethered to this world by the thin strand of her obsession with dimming the Earth's sky, that I cannot summon up the outrage or heartache.

I'm familiar with the patterns of her mind, imprisoned in that Swiss-cheesed brain. She doesn't remember what happened yesterday, or the week before, or much of the past few decades. She doesn't remember my face or the names of my two husbands. She doesn't remember Dad's funeral. I don't bother showing her pictures from Abby's graduation or the video of Thomas's wedding.

The only thing left to talk about is my work. There's no expectation that she'll remember the names I bring up or understand the problems I'm trying to solve. I tell her the difficulties of scanning the human mind, the complications of recreating carbon-based computation in silicon, the promise of a hardware upgrade for the fragile human brain that seems so close and yet so far away. It's mostly a monologue. She's comfortable with the flow of technical jargon. It's enough that she's listening, that she's not hurrying to fly somewhere else.

She stops her calculations. "What day is today?" she asks.

"It's my—Mia's birthday," I say.

"I should go see her," she says. "I just need to finish this—"

"Why don't we take a walk together outside?" I ask. "She likes being out in the sun."

"The sun . . . It's too bright . . . ," she mutters. Then she pulls her hands away from the keyboard. "All right."

The wheelchair nimbly rolls next to me through the corridors until we're outside. Screaming children are running helter-skelter over the wide lawn like energized electrons while white-haired and wrinkled residents sit in distinct clusters like nuclei scattered in vacuum. Spending time with children is supposed to improve the mood of the aged, and so Sunset Homes tries to re-create the tribal bonfire and the village hearth with busloads of kindergarteners.

She squints against the bright glow of the sun. "Mia is here?"

"We'll look for her."

We walk through the hubbub together, looking for the ghost of her memory. Gradually, she opens up and begins to talk to me about her life.

"Anthropogenic global warming is real," she says. "But the mainstream consensus is far too optimistic. The reality is much worse. For our children's sake, we must solve it in our time."

Thomas and Abby have long stopped accompanying me on these visits to a grandmother who no longer knows who they are. I don't blame them. She's as much a stranger to them as they're to her. They have no memories of her baking cookies for them on lazy summer afternoons or allowing them to stay up way past their bedtime to browse cartoons on tablets. She has always been at best a distant presence in their lives, most felt when she paid for their college tuition with a single check. A fairy godmother as unreal as those tales of how the Earth had once been doomed.

She cares more about the idea of future generations than her actual children and grandchildren. I know I'm being unfair, but the truth is often unfair.

"Left unchecked, much of East Asia will become uninhabitable in a century," she says. "When you plot out a record of little ice ages and mini warm periods in our history, you get a record of mass migrations, wars, genocides. Do you understand?"

A giggling girl dashes in front of us; the wheelchair grinds to a halt. A gaggle of boys and girls run past us, chasing the little girl.

"The rich countries, who did the most polluting, want the poor countries to stop development and stop consuming so much energy," she says. "They think it's equitable to tell the poor to pay for the sins of the rich, to make those with darker skins stop trying to catch up to those with lighter skins."

We've walked all the way to the far edge of the lawn. No sign of Mia. We turn around and again swerve through the crowd of children, tumbling, dancing, laughing, running.

"It's foolish to think the diplomats will work it out. The conflicts are irreconcilable, and the ultimate outcome will not be fair. The poor countries can't and shouldn't stop development, and the rich countries won't pay. But there is a technical solution, a hack. It just takes a few fearless men and women with the resources to do what the rest of the world can't do."

There's a glow in her eyes. This is her favorite subject, pitching her mad scientist answer.

"We must purchase and modify a fleet of commercial jets. In international airspace, away from the jurisdiction of any state, they'll release sprays of sulfuric acid. Mixed with water vapor, the acid will turn into clouds of fine sulfate particles that block sunlight." She tries to snap her fingers but her fingers are shaking too much. "It will be like the global volcanic winters of the 1880s, after Krakatoa erupted. We made the Earth warm, and we can cool it again."

Her hands flutter in front of her, conjuring up a vision of the grandest engineering project in the history of the human race: the construction of a globe-spanning wall to dim the sky. She doesn't remember that she has already succeeded, that decades ago, she had managed to convince enough people as mad as she was to follow her plan. She doesn't remember the protests, the condemnations by environmental groups, the scrambling fighter jets and denunciations by the world's governments, the prison sentence, and then, gradual acceptance.

". . . the poor deserve to consume as much of the earth's resources as the rich . . ."

I try to imagine what life must be like for her: an eternal day of battle, a battle she has already won.

Her hack has bought us some time, but it has not solved the fundamental problem. The world is still struggling with problems both old and new: the bleaching of corals from the acid rain, the squabbling over whether to cool the earth even more, the ever-present finger-pointing and blame-assigning. She does not know that borders have been sealed as the rich nations replace the dwindling supply of young workers with machines. She does not know that the gap between the wealthy and the poor has only grown wider, that a tiny portion of the global population still consumes the vast majority of its resources, that colonialism has been revived in the name of progress.

In the middle of her impassioned speech, she stops.

"Where's Mia?" she asks. The defiance has left her voice. She looks through the crowd, anxious that she won't find me on my birthday.

"We'll make another pass," I say.

"We have to find her," she says.

On impulse, I stop the wheelchair and kneel down in front of her.

"I'm working on a technical solution," I say. "There is a way for us to transcend this morass, to achieve a just existence."

I am, after all, my mother's daughter.

She looks at me, her expression uncomprehending.

"I don't know if I'll perfect my technique in time to save you," I blurt out. *Or maybe I can't bear the thought of having to patch together the remnants of your mind.* This is what I have come to tell her.

Is it a plea for forgiveness? Have I forgiven her? Is forgiveness what we want or need?

A group of children run by us, blowing soap bubbles. In the sunlight the bubbles float and drift with a rainbow sheen. A few land against my mother's silvery hair but do not burst immediately. She looks like a queen with a diadem of sunlit jewels, an unelected tribune who claims to speak for those without power, a mother whose love is difficult to understand and even more difficult to misunderstand.

"Please," she says, reaching up to touch my face with her shaking fingers, as dry as the sand in an hourglass. "I'm late. It's her birthday."

And so we wander through the crowd again, under an afternoon sun that glows dimmer than in my childhood.

343

Abby pops into my process.

"Happy birthday, Mom," she says.

For my benefit she presents as she had looked before her upload, a young woman of forty or so. She looks around at my cluttered space and frowns: simulations of books, furniture, speckled walls, dappled ceiling, a window view of a cityscape that is a digital composite of twenty-first-century San Francisco, my hometown, and all the cities that I had wanted to visit when I still had a body but didn't get to.

"I don't keep that running all the time," I say.

The trendy aesthetic for home processes now is clean, minimalist, mathematically abstract: platonic polyhedral; classic solids of revolution based on conics; finite fields; symmetry groups. Using no more than four dimensions is preferred, and some are advocating flat living. To make my home process a close approximation of the analog world at such a high resolution is considered a wasteful use of computing resources, indulgent.

But I can't help it. Despite having lived digitally for far longer than I did in the flesh, I prefer the simulated world of atoms to the digital reality.

To placate my daughter, I switch the window to a real-time feed from one of the sky rovers. The scene is of a jungle near the mouth of a river, probably where Shanghai used to be. Luxuriant vegetation drapes the skeletal ruins of skyscrapers; flocks of wading birds fill the shore; from time to time, pods of porpoises leap from the water, tracing graceful arcs that land back in the water with gentle splashes.

More than 300 billion human minds now inhabit this planet, residing in thousands of data centers that collectively take up less space than old Manhattan. The earth has gone back to being wild, save for a few stubborn holdouts who still insist on living in the flesh in remote settlements.

"It really doesn't look good when you use so much computational resources by yourself," she says. "My application was rejected."

She means the application to have another child.

"I think two thousand six hundred twenty-five children are more than enough," I say. "I feel like I don't know any of them." I don't even know how to pronounce many of the mathematical names the digital natives prefer.

"Another vote is coming," she says. "We need all the help we can get."

"Not even all your current children vote the same way you do," I say.

"It's worth a try," she says. "This planet belongs to all the creatures living on it, not just us."

My daughter and many others think that the greatest achievement of humanity, the regifting of the earth back to Nature, is under threat. Other minds, especially those who had uploaded from countries where the universal availability of immortality had been achieved much later, think it isn't fair that those who got to colonize the digital realm first should have more say in the direction of humanity. They would like to expand the human footprint again and build more data centers.

"Why do you love the wilderness so much if you don't even live in it?" I ask.

"It's our ethical duty to be stewards for the earth," she says. "It's barely starting to heal from all the horrors we've inflicted on it. We must preserve it exactly as it should be."

I don't point out that this smacks to me of a false dichotomy: Human versus Nature. I don't bring up the sunken continents, the erupting volcanoes, the peaks and valleys in the earth's climate over billions of years, the advancing and retreating ice caps, and the uncountable species that have come and gone. Why do we hold up this one moment as natural, to be prized above all others?

Some ethical differences are irreconcilable.

Meanwhile, everyone thinks that having more children is the solution, to overwhelm the other side with more votes. And so the hard-fought adjudication of applications to have children, to allocate precious computing resources among competing factions.

But what will the children think of our conflicts? Will they care about the same injustices we do? Being born *in silico*, will they turn away from the physical world, from embodiment, or embrace it even more? Every generation has its own blind spots and obsessions.

I had once thought the Singularity would solve all our problems. Turns out it's just a simple hack for a complicated problem. We do not share the same histories; we do not all want the same things.

I am not so different from my mother after all.

2,401

The rocky planet beneath me is desolate, lifeless. I'm relieved. That was a condition placed upon me before my departure.

It's impossible for everyone to agree upon a single vision for the future of humanity. Thankfully, we no longer have to share the same planet.

Tiny probes depart from *Matrioshka*, descending toward the spinning planet beneath them. As they enter the atmosphere, they glow like fireflies in the dusk. The dense atmosphere here is so good at trapping heat that at the surface the gas behaves more like a liquid.

I imagine the self-assembling robots landing at the surface. I imagine them replicating and multiplying with material extracted from the crust. I imagine them boring into the rock to place the mini-annihilation charges.

A window pops up next to me: a message from Abby, light-years away and centuries ago.

Happy birthday, Mother. We did it.

What follows are aerial shots of worlds both familiar and strange: the Earth, with its temperate climate carefully regulated to sustain the late Holocene; Venus, whose orbit has been adjusted by repeated gravitational slingshots with asteroids and terraformed to become a lush, warm replica of Earth during the Jurassic; and Mars, whose surface has been pelted with redirected Oort cloud objects and warmed by solar reflectors from space until the climate is a good approximation of the dry, cold conditions of the last glaciation on Earth.

Dinosaurs now roam the jungles of Aphrodite Terra, and mammoths forage over the tundra of Vastitas Borealis. Genetic reconstructions have been pushed back to the limit of the powerful data centers on Earth.

They have recreated what might have been. They have brought the extinct back to life.

Mother, you're right about one thing: We will be sending out exploration ships again.

We'll colonize the rest of the galaxy. When we find lifeless worlds, we'll endow them with every form of life, from Earth's distant past to the futures that might have been on Europa. We'll walk down every evolutionary path. We'll shepherd every flock and tend to every garden. We'll give those creatures who never made it onto Noah's Ark another chance, and bring forth the potential of every star in Raphael's conversation with Adam in Eden.

And when we find extraterrestrial life, we'll be just as careful with them as we have been with life on Earth.

It isn't right for one species in the latest stage of a planet's long history to monopolize all its resources. It isn't just for humanity to claim for itself the title of evolution's crowning achievement. Isn't it the duty of every intelligent species to rescue all life, even from the dark abyss of time? There is always a technical solution.

I smile. I do not wonder whether Abby's message is a celebration or a silent rebuke. She is, after all, my daughter.

I have my own problem to solve. I turn my attention back to the robots, to breaking apart the planet beneath my ship.

16,807

It has taken a long time to fracture the planets orbiting this star, and longer still to reshape the fragments into my vision.

Thin, circular plates a hundred kilometers in diameter are arranged in a lattice of longitudinal rings around the star until it is completely surrounded. The plates do not orbit the star; rather, they are statites, positioned so that the pressure from the sun's high-energy radiation counteracts the pull of gravity.

On the inner surface of this Dyson swarm, trillions of robots have etched channels and gates into the substrate, creating the most massive circuits in the history of the human race.

As the plates absorb the energy from the sun, it is transformed into electric pulses that emerge from cells, flow through canals, commingle in streams, until they gather into lakes and oceans that undulate through a quintillion variations that form the shape of thought.

The backs of the plates glow darkly, like embers after a fierce flame. The lower-energy photons leap outward into space, somewhat drained after powering a civilization. But before they can escape into the endless abyss of space, they strike another set of plates designed to absorb energy from radiation at this dimmer frequency. And once again, the process for thought-creation repeats itself.

The nesting shells, seven in all, form a world that is replete with dense topography. There are smooth areas centimeters across, designed to expand and contract to preserve the integrity of the plates as the computation generates more or less heat—I've dubbed them seas and plains. There are pitted areas where the peaks and craters are measured by microns, intended to facilitate the rapid dance of qubits and bits—I call them forests and coral reefs. There are small studded structures packed with dense circuitry intended to send and receive beams of communication knitting the plates together—I call them cities and towns. Perhaps these are fanciful names, like the Sea of Tranquility and Mare Erythraeum, but the consciousnesses they power are real.

And what will I do with this computing machine powered by a sun? What magic will I conjure with this matrioshka brain?

I have seeded the plains and seas and forests and coral reefs and cities and towns with a million billion minds, some of them modeled on my own, many more pulled from *Matrioshka*'s data banks, and they have multiplied and replicated, evolved in a world larger than any data center confined to a single planet could ever hope to be.

In the eyes of an outside observer, the star's glow dimmed as each shell was constructed. I have succeeded in darkening a sun just as my mother had, albeit on a much grander scale.

There is always a technical solution.

117,649

History flows like a flash flood in the desert: the water pouring across the parched earth, eddying around rocks and cacti, pooling in depressions, seeking a channel while it's carving the landscape, each chance event shaping what comes after.

There are more ways to rescue lives and redeem what might have been than Abby and others believe.

In the grand matrix of my matrioshka brain, versions of our history are replayed. There isn't a single world in this grand computation, but billions, each of them populated by human consciousnesses, but nudged in small ways to be better.

Most paths lead to less slaughter. Here, Rome and Constantinople are not sacked; there, Cuzco and Vĩnh Long do not fall. Along one time line, the Mongols and Manchus do not sweep across East Asia; along another, the Westphalian model does not become an all-consuming blueprint for the world. One group of men consumed with murder do not come to power in Europe, and another group worshipping death do not seize the machinery of state in Japan. Instead of the colonial yoke, the inhabitants of Africa, Asia, the

Americas, and Australia decide their own fates. Enslavement and genocide are not the handmaidens of discovery and exploration, and the errors of our history are averted.

Small populations do not rise to consume a disproportionate amount of the planet's resources or monopolize the path of its future. History is redeemed.

But not all paths are better. There is a darkness in human nature that makes certain conflicts irreconcilable. I grieve for the lives lost, but I can't intervene. These are not simulations. They cannot be if I respect the sanctity of human life.

The billions of consciousnesses who live in these worlds are every bit as real as I am. They deserve as much free will as anyone who has ever lived and must be allowed to make their own choices. Even if we've always suspected that we also live in a grand simulation, we prefer the truth to be otherwise.

Think of these as parallel universes if you will; call them sentimental gestures of a woman looking into the past; dismiss them as a kind of symbolic atonement.

But isn't it the dream of every species to have the chance to do it over? To see if it's possible to prevent the fall from grace that darkens our gaze upon the stars?

823,543

There is a message.

Someone has plucked the strings that weave together the fabric of space, sending a sequence of pulses down every strand of Indra's web, connecting the farthest exploding nova to the nearest dancing quark.

The galaxy vibrates with a broadcast in languages known, forgotten, and yet to be invented. I parse out a single sentence.

Come to the galactic center. It's reunion time.

Carefully, I instruct the intelligences guiding the plates that make up the Dyson swarms to shift, like ailerons on the wings of ancient aircraft. The plates drift apart, as though the shells in the matrioshka brain are cracking, hatching a new form of life.

Gradually, the statites move away from one side of the sun and assume the configuration of a Shkadov thruster. A single eye opens in the universe, emitting a bright beam of light.

And slowly, the imbalance in the solar radiation begins to move the star, bringing the shell mirrors with it. We're headed for the center of the galaxy, propelled upon a fiery column of light.

Not every human world will heed the call. There are plenty of planets on which the inhabitants have decided that it is perfectly fine to explore the mathematical worlds of ever-deepening virtual reality in perpetuity, to live out lives of minimal energy consumption in universes hidden within nutshells.

Some, like my daughter Abby, will prefer to leave their lush, life-filled planets in place, like oases in the endless desert that is space. Others will seek the refuge of the galactic edge, where cooler climates will allow more efficient computation. Still others, having recaptured the ancient joy of living in the flesh, will tarry to act out space operas of conquest and glory.

But enough will come.

I imagine thousands, hundreds of thousands of stars moving toward the center of the galaxy. Some are surrounded by space habitats full of people who still look like people. Some are orbited by machines that have but a dim memory of their ancestral form. Some will drag with them planets populated by creatures from our distant past, or by creatures I have never seen. Some will bring guests, aliens who do not share our history but are curious about this self-replicating low-entropy phenomenon that calls itself humanity.

I imagine generations of children on innumerable worlds watching the night sky as constellations shift and transform, as stars move out of alignment, drawing contrails against the empyrean.

I close my eyes. This journey will take a long time. Might as well get some rest.

A VERY, VERY LONG TIME LATER

The wide silvery lawn spreads out before me almost to the golden surf of the sea, separated by the narrow dark band that is the beach. The sun is bright and warm, and I can almost feel the breeze, a gentle caress against my arms and face.

"Mia!"

I look over and see Mom striding across the lawn, her long black hair streaming like a kite's tails.

She wraps me in a fierce hug, squeezing my face against hers. She smells like the glow of new stars being born in the embers of a supernova, like fresh comets emerging from the primeval nebula.

"Sorry I'm late," she says, her voice muffled against my cheek.

"It's okay," I say, and I mean it. I give her a kiss.

"It's a good day to fly a kite," she says.

We look up at the sun.

The perspective shifts vertiginously, and now we're standing upside down on an intricately carved plain, the sun far below us. Gravity tethers the surface above the bottoms of our feet to that fiery orb, stronger than any string. The bright photons we're bathed in strike against the ground, pushing it up. We're standing on the bottom of a kite that is flying higher and higher, tugging us toward the stars.

I want to tell her that I understand her impulse to make one life grand, her need to dim the sun with her love, her striving to solve intractable problems, her faith in a technical solution even though she knew it was imperfect. I want to tell her that I know we're flawed, but that doesn't mean we're not also wondrous.

Instead, I just squeeze her hand; she squeezes back.

"Happy birthday," she says. "Don't be afraid to fly."

I relax my grip, and smile at her. "I'm not. We're almost there."

The world brightens with the light of a million billion suns.

The Message

The alien city was a perfect circle about ten kilometers in diameter. From the air, the buildings—cubes around the edge of the city, cones, pyramids, tetrahedra in the middle—were forbidding spikes. Ring-shaped streets divided the city into concentric sections.

James Bell banked the two-person shuttle, the *Arthur Evans*, into a U-turn to pass over the ruins a second time. The thin but powerful man was in his forties, just beginning to lose his hair and showing some white in his beard. He pushed the joystick forward to bring the vehicle lower, staring intently out of the cockpit with his blue eyes.

Next to him was thirteen-year old Maggie, thin and awkward like a newborn colt. She gasped and grabbed onto the handholds above her seat as the ship suddenly dipped.

"Sorry," James said. Maggie's mother, Lauren, had hated the way he flew too, with all the sudden drops and sharp swerves. A memory of Lauren grabbing onto his arms as he dragged her onto a roller coaster came to him, and he smiled for a moment before a mixture of regret and resentment replaced the memory.

He shook away the feeling and leveled the ship. "Julia," he said to the ship's AI, "take over. Keep it smooth and slow." The AI beeped in acknowledgment.

"I tend to fly a little recklessly on a planet with a working atmosphere and magnetic field." He rambled on, mostly to fill the silence. "Since they keep out the harmful solar and cosmic radiation, I leave the heavy shell with all the radiation shields and monitors up in orbit and just bring the core of the shuttle down. The ship maneuvers so much better this way."

Maggie brushed strands of long red hair out of her face and resolutely refused to look at him, keeping her gaze on the alien buildings passing beneath the ship.

She had been like this ever since she came aboard two days ago, giving him only one- or two-word answers or saying nothing at all. He had no shared history with her, no background against which to interpret her gestures, no context in which to fill her silences with meaning. He felt awkward in her presence, unsure how to converse. His daughter was more mysterious to him than the many dead civilizations he had studied.

Six months ago, just as he was rushing to complete the survey of Pi Baeo ahead of the terraformers' planned obliteration of the surface of the planet with their asteroids and comets, he received a message from Lauren, the first time he had heard from her in ten years. She was sick, she said, and she was going to die. Maggie needed him.

Maggie was born after he and Lauren had split up. Indeed, he hadn't even known about her until Lauren sent him a picture a year after the birth. He had stared at that picture of the bundle of pink flesh without knowing how to react. He wasn't ready to be a father, and Lauren must have known that, which was why she had said nothing to him as they parted. She had accepted his offer to pay child support without demanding anything more, and he had been relieved.

The surprise message from Lauren had caused him to reluctantly drop everything on Pi Baeo to go to her world. The trip took three months in real time, but only two days in the shuttle with relativistic dilation. By the time he finally got there, Lauren was dead, and Maggie had been on her own for two months, mourning her mother and imagining an uncertain future with a father she had never met.

With little fanfare and no instructions, he was granted custody of the sullen and grieving teenager. *How was I supposed to learn to be a father in the two days it took to come back to Pi Baeo?*

James sighed. He didn't like complications in his life. Now that they were back on Pi Baeo, he had less than a week to complete the survey before the arrival of the comets and asteroids.

"There's some writing," Maggie said quietly. Inscriptions and images covered the alien buildings, which appeared to be carved out of massive, solid stone. There were no windows or doors.

James was surprised but glad that Maggie seemed to take an interest in the ruins. He was comfortable lecturing to curious students.

"That's one of the reasons I'm interested in this place. Most cultures that get past the Kuny-MacLean boundary plunge into a digital dark age and stop producing analog writing. All their information becomes locked in fragile digital artifacts that don't survive well and are difficult to decipher. They went digital here too, but these samples—"

The ship accelerated, lurched, and dropped precipitously. Maggie screamed.

"James," Julia's voice was urgent, "there seem to be errors in the stabilization routines beyond my ability to correct. You have to take over with analog controls."

James grabbed the joystick and pulled back sharply. The engines groaned. But it was too late. The ship was falling too fast.

"Prepare for impact," Julia's voice said.

James instinctively reached out to hold Maggie against her seat, as if the strength of his arm was enough to save her from the ground rushing up at them.

•

The robots, mechanical spiders as big as house cats, skittered all over the exterior of the *Arthur Evans* and examined the surface for damage. Sparks flew as they welded and applied sealant.

"Well, that should do it," James said as he finished bandaging the cut on Maggie's forehead. "Julia saved us by deforming the ship's hull as we crashed to absorb most of the energy. It'll take the robots a few days to repair the ship, but that still gives us plenty of time to leave before the first comets get here."

Maggie sat up and felt the bandage with her hand. She flexed her legs and looked over her arms.

"What am I supposed to do while you work? Just sit here?"

At least she's talking now, James thought.

"You can come with me. But I have to work, so I can't watch you every minute."

Maggie's lips narrowed. "I can take care of myself. I'm not five."

"I didn't mean—"

"I wish I was in our old house on my own, instead of almost getting killed here with *you*." Tears welled in her blue eyes. "That stupid judge! He had no clue—"

"That's enough!" *Maybe it was easier when she didn't talk.* The only sound in the shuttle was the intermittent beeping from the diagnostic console as Julia continued to run tests. Maggie glared at her father defiantly.

He tried to lower his voice. "The court was going to send you to a foster home unless I assumed custody, all right? I'm doing this because your mother wrote—"

The anger and sorrow that she had bottled up for so long could no longer be contained. Now that she was talking, she was going to let him have it. "Oh, it's so *noble* of you to take up the burden of your *child*. I hate you—"

"Shut up and listen!" he growled. She seemed to him an unreasonable ball of pure fury and hatred. "Now, I know I haven't been in your life for all these years. Your mother and I—" He wondered if she would understand. He wondered if he himself understood how things turned out. "It's complicated."

"Yes, 'complicated.' You prefer communing with dead aliens to taking care of a flesh-and-blood family. That *is* difficult to explain."

The words punched him hard, and in them he heard an echo of his dead ex-wife.

He waited until his breathing was even again.

"You don't have to like me. But I *am* responsible for you until you're no longer a minor. I'll leave you alone as much as possible, and you don't even have to talk to me. But you can make this easier for both of us by at least trying to be civil."

The diagnostic console beeped loudly. Julia spoke, "I've discovered the cause of the crash. The navigation system suffered an unusual number of single-bit hardware memory errors during the flyover. In fact, similar hardware errors are showing in all the systems."

"Bad memory chips?"

"That's a possibility. I suspect it's related to your attempt to economize by using cheaper components during the last retrofitting."

Maggie shook her head exaggeratedly. "Right, and you'll take care of me just as well as you do your ship."

•

The atmosphere of Pi Baeo contained little oxygen and was devoid of moisture. While there was no need for full environmental suits, James and Maggie had to wear oxygen masks and overalls to keep in the moisture.

They gazed at the gargantuan ruins. Even the cubes forming the outer ring, much smaller than the megaliths inside, rose almost fifty meters into the air. The two humans were ants crawling about a giant's playground.

Keeping his pledge to leave Maggie alone, James hiked towards the city without glancing at her. After a moment, she followed, staying a few meters back.

Secretly, James was relieved that he no longer had to strive to imitate some idealized vision of a good father. He couldn't do it, always knew he couldn't do it. Lauren had been right about him, and he didn't want to playact anymore.

The ring of cubes formed a solid wall. James aimed for a break where one of the cubes had crumbled. Up close, they could see that it was made from smaller blocks, held together by gravity and friction through an intricate mortise-and-tenon system.

They climbed over the rubble. Maggie was athletic and nimble, scrambling over the broken stones like a mountain goat. James refrained from offering to help her.

Beyond the break, the monumental pyramids loomed over the flat ground like towering mountains casting long and oppressive shadows. The city felt claustrophobic, despite the immense empty space between the pyramids.

James took pictures of the large-scale writing on the smooth faces of the pyramids. There were several distinct scripts, indicative of multiple languages. However, the inscriptions on every visible surface seemed identical. It was as if the same few sentences were repeated over and over.

"This isn't giving me much linguistic data to work with," James muttered to himself.

Shouting at her father and the strenuous hike that followed had drained some of Maggie's anger. Her curiosity and a desire to show off got the better of her.

"They must have thought that whatever they wanted to say was really important to repeat it so many times," she said. "Crude but effective data redundancy."

She sounded like she was reciting from a book. James was amused, but he liked this version of Maggie better. He was more comfortable talking about work. "You like information theory and that sort of thing?"

"Yeah. I'm good with computers and . . . when I was little, I used to beg Mom to buy me books on xenoarchaeology and data preservation. And I went to archaeology camp. I knew all that stuff you said about the digital dark age."

James pictured the young Maggie reading xenoarchaeology books. *That must have driven Lauren crazy.* He smiled. Then he wondered why a child who had never met her father nevertheless wanted to study the same thing she thought he studied. His nose tingled and felt itchy.

He tried to keep the conversation going. "What do you think of the pictures?" He nodded at the many diagrams among the inscriptions, most still legible despite years of erosion.

"Maps of the city?"

The pictures depicted concentric circles with small squares, triangles, pentagons, and circles in the spaces between the circles. Then Maggie frowned. "But that doesn't make sense. They all look different."

James took a few zoomed-in pictures of the drawings and compared them with the layout of the buildings generated from aerial photographs. Maggie was right. The drawings didn't match the real layout and didn't match each other.

"And how could people—aliens—live in a city with only circular streets? I didn't see any roads coming out the center."

James looked at her, impressed. "That's very perceptive."

Maggie rolled her eyes. The way she tilted her head was almost a carbon copy of Lauren's gesture. He felt a wave of tenderness.

"Actually, I don't think the people of Pi Baeo ever lived here. Aerial surveys showed no signs of burial sites or trash heaps nearby. I also scanned the buildings with ground-penetrating radar. They're completely solid, no space inside at all. It's probably not accurate to call this place a 'city.'"

"So what is it?"

"I have no idea. Hopefully, I can figure it out before it's gone forever in a week."

"How old is it?"

"Best I can tell, Pi Baeo lost almost all its water about twenty thousand years ago. Though I don't know exactly what happened, the process seemed to take only a few centuries. As the water ran out, the inhabitants fought over the diminishing supply. Every settlement I've found was destroyed by warfare. The destruction was so complete that the robots recovered very few intact artifacts."

"But this place looks untouched."

"That's right. Thousands of kilometers from the nearest population centers, this place was left alone as Pi Baeo died. I want to know why."

"But they were aliens. Why do you care about *them* so much? They didn't even know about us." Resentment had crept back into her voice. She remembered again how he had never even tried to reach out to her, to know her even a little.

"That's true," he said. The change in her tone made him nervous; he did not want the furious, unreasoning child to return. Her question also saddened him. He had never been good at articulating why his work meant so much to him, but he wanted to try.

Maybe his daughter would understand him where his wife couldn't.

"The human race has explored the stars for a long time. Yet we're still alone. All the alien civilizations we've found are dead.

"Most civilizations are very self-centered and focus only on the present. They don't think much about preserving a legacy for those who might come long after they're gone. Their art and poetry, their rise and fall, their brief time in this universe: most of that is beyond recovery. And in a week, the icy comets and asteroids sent by the terraformers will bombard this planet and bring water back to it. Even the last traces of their existence will be gone.

"But I always feel that there is a message that the people I study want to pass on. Whatever I discover will be the last testament and whisper of the people of Pi Baeo. In studying them, I become connected to them, and in passing on their message, the human race is no longer so alone."

Maggie looked thoughtful and chewed her lips.

James let out a held breath; he felt inexplicably happy as he watched his daughter nod, almost imperceptibly.

The sun was sinking below the wall of cubes. "It's getting late," James said. "Let's come back tomorrow."

•

While James prepared dinner in the galley, Julia tutored Maggie. As a holographic projection of the periodic table of elements floated in the air, the AI droned on about the properties of the lanthanides. Having spent so many years with James Bell, the AI had acquired a taste for holding forth professorially. Gradually, Maggie's eyelids drooped and her head dipped forward.

Julia stopped. "You're not even trying! You've been out of school for two months already. How do you expect to catch up without putting in the effort?"

"Don't yell at me! It's not like I wanted to be out of school."

Julia modulated her voice to be gentler. "I'm sorry. It must have been difficult, losing your mother like that."

"What would *you* know about it?" Maggie said angrily.

"I may be a machine, but I've been with Dr. Bell many years. . . . I also knew your mother."

Maggie's head snapped up. "Tell me about my parents. . . . What happened between them?"

"I can't. That's personal."

Maggie glanced at her father's figure moving in the galley. She would have to wait.

"Can't you move to a topic that's more interesting than chemistry?"

"What do you consider interesting?"

"How about some archaeology? Can we try to translate some of the text we found on the pyramids today?"

This was not on the recommended standard curriculum, but Julia decided to indulge her. "All right. As you know, there's no possibility of a Rosetta stone here. So guesses at meanings must rely on non-linguistic—"

"Yes, yes. I know all that. Just show me pictures of other writing you've found that match anything we saw on the pyramids."

Julia beeped in annoyance at being interrupted. But she made the periodic table disappear and projected in its place photographs of inscriptions found in other ruins on Pi Baeo. "These symbols appear to match a substring in the inscriptions on the pyramids."

Maggie examined the photographs. "Zoom out a bit. I want to see where you found them."

Julia complied. Maggie furrowed her brows in puzzlement. The photographs were much harder to interpret than the neat drawings in archaeology books. She couldn't tell what she was looking at. Everything seemed to be piles of rubble.

Julia remained silent, still miffed at Maggie.

"It's easier if you look at a three-D reconstruction," James said as he stepped out of the galley. "Julia, put up the models and show Maggie where these symbols were found."

The holographic projection now changed to reconstructions of tall, graceful alien buildings honeycombed with windows and doors. Julia highlighted the areas where the matched symbols were found.

"See any pattern?" James asked.

"They're always found near doorways," Maggie said.

"Possible translation?"

"Enter?"

"Or exit."

"So, after all that work, we still can't figure out the most significant bit of the message?" Maggie laughed. "We still don't know if the inscriptions are saying 'Come in. Welcome!' or 'Get out, and stay out!'"

It was the first time that James had heard her laugh, and he marveled at how he could hear echoes of Lauren as well as himself in it. A wave of affection, tinged with regret, washed over him.

•

Maggie tiptoed past her father's cabin and into the cockpit of the shuttle. Through the window she could see hundreds of bright streaks in the eastern sky. Promising destruction along with rebirth, the comets bathed the alien landscape in a silvery glow.

She fumbled around for her father's headset, put it on, and whispered into the quiet dark, "Julia."

The AI answered in her earpiece. "Yes?"

"Tell me about my parents."

Julia said nothing.

"Okay, we'll do this the hard way." Maggie slid forward and pulled out the keyboard from beneath the console. She punched some keys and watched as the head-up display on the cockpit window flashed into life. A blinking cursor appeared in the upper left-hand corner.

She typed at the prompt:

>(DEFINE ACKERMANN-HEAP-FILL (LAMBDA () (

"All right!" Julia broke the silence. Maggie smiled at the hint of a hiss in the AI's voice. "No need to drop down into code like that. I'll grant you access, but I will inform Dr. Bell—"

"You'll do no such thing." Maggie leaned forward and began to type again.

"Okay! Okay!"

"Don't be so glum. This isn't a real security breach. He won't be really mad if he finds out. And you can always blame it on the cheap memory chips that are generating all those hardware errors."

Julia muttered incomprehensibly.

•

Digging through her father's electronic archives, Maggie thought, was a lot like archaeology. For years she had studied the subject to feel closer to him, to maintain a sense of connection. For so long she had yearned to uncover the man her mother never talked about, to dig out the man who had abandoned her before she was born.

Pictures, electronic messages, recordings, and videos were the artifacts of a lost past, created by two people who did not have in mind a future viewer and who wrote and laughed and glanced at the camera only for themselves. Yet, somehow she felt that she was their intended audience. They had a message for her, a message maybe even they did not know they wanted to send.

Maggie put the pieces in context, built a chronology. She excavated and reconstructed the mystery that was her father.

•

The video showed the inside of a tiny studio apartment. Maggie gazed at the younger, smooth-shaven version of her father speaking into the camera. He was nervously playing with a small box in his hand.

"Julia, can you run the numbers again?"

The AI sounded exasperated. "The numbers aren't going to change. I can search for a comparable ring that's cheaper—"

"No! I don't *want* a cheaper ring. She deserves this one."

"Then I see no choice but for you to give up on that shuttle. You can't afford both."

•

Now Maggie was looking at the younger version of her mother, alone in the same studio apartment from the previous video. Young Lauren was full of the glow of hope and youth. Maggie allowed herself to cry. She missed her mother so damn much.

"Thanks for letting me know, Julia," Lauren said. "Sometimes we have to save James from himself."

("You have a history of spilling his secrets to the women in his life," Maggie whispered into the headset. Julia beeped once in protest and then went silent.)

Lauren admired the ring on her hand. "It *is* beautiful." She twisted it around her finger. "But heavy."

"I tried to stop him from dragging you onto that roller coaster," Julia said. "I know how much you hate those things. But he thought he had the best chance of you saying yes if he proposed just when you were scared and clinging to him."

"His chances were always one hundred percent."

"It will make a good story for the children someday."

Lauren took off the ring. "I'll tell him that my skin is allergic to the ring, and he has to return it. I'd rather he buy that shuttle, and we'll wander the stars together, weighed down by nothing."

·

The video now showed the cockpit of a two-person shuttle, which Maggie recognized as the *Arthur Evans*, but a lot cleaner and newer looking. James and Lauren sat in the two chairs.

James sighed. "I thought you wanted this."

"I did."

"Then what changed?"

Lauren bit her lip. "We've been flying around the galaxy for five years. What exactly do we have to show for it? Twenty storage containers of broken artifacts. A few monographs that no one reads. Dead aliens don't have descendants lobbying for cultural preservation, and all the civilizations we've studied collapsed before they made it off their home planets so there's no technological payoff. Face it, people just don't care about dead aliens."

"*I* care. It matters to *me* that they be remembered and understood.

A man wants to leave behind his name, and a civilization wants to leave behind its stories. I'm the only thing standing between them and oblivion."

"James, we aren't so young anymore. We can't wander the stars forever. We have to think about the future, about us."

James's face hardened and his lips fused into a thin line. "I'm not going to sit in an office at a desk just so we can buy a picket-fenced house on some freshly developed planet and pop out children. The terraformers move fast, and I have to save whatever I can before they erase these mysteries forever."

"We can always come back to this life, be on the move again, when the children are older."

"If we put down roots anywhere, we'll never leave again. Weight leads to more weight."

"You won't even give it a chance? Try it for a few years?"

"I don't understand what's changed."

"You empathize so deeply with vanished aliens, but you can't feel what I want?"

"This discussion is over." He got up and left the cockpit.

Lauren sat still, alone. After a while, she sighed and caressed her belly.

"Why didn't you tell him?" It was Julia.

Lauren shook her head. "If I tell him, he'll give in because he'll try to do the responsible thing, but he'll always resent me and the baby. I'd rather not have him at all than have him believe we weighed him down."

.

"I would have tried, you know."

In the video, her father hadn't shaved for a few days. The cockpit was messy, unkempt, with food wrappers everywhere and dirty clothes draped on chairs. He had been drinking.

"She didn't want to force you to pick between what you wanted to do and what you felt you had to do," Julia said.

"She thought I wasn't ready," he shot back. "She didn't trust me. Maybe she was right."

·

After breakfast, James prepared the hover bike.

He looked at Maggie, concerned. "You have dark circles around your eyes. You didn't sleep well, did you? Maybe you should just stay in the ship today and rest."

But Maggie would not be dissuaded. She sat on the bike behind her father and put her arms around his waist. Then, she leaned forward and put her face against his back.

James couldn't move for a moment, overwhelmed by this gesture of trust. His mind flashed to the picture of baby Maggie, and suddenly he felt an overwhelming sense of tenderness towards that helpless bundle of pink, the tightly clutched fists and squeezed-shut eyes.

They covered ground quickly on the hover bike, zooming towards the heart of the ruins.

"You've got to be kidding me," James said, as he brought the bike to a sudden halt.

In front of them was the first of the many concentric, circular streets that they had seen from the air. Only now did it become clear that the circle was not a street at all. It was a ditch with smooth walls that dropped straight down, over fifty meters deep and twice as wide.

"Moats *inside* the city?" Maggie was amused.

"I'm beginning to think that the message here is pretty simple: we don't want you to go to the center."

"Then we really have to go." Maggie's expression was mischievous, childish. "The secret must be a good one."

James chuckled, but he shared Maggie's excitement. He folded the hover bike into its compact storage form—like an old-fashioned suitcase. He tossed it down to the bottom of the ditch, where it clattered loudly before coming to rest. Then he took out the rappelling hooks and cables and showed Maggie how to use them. She was a quick learner, and the two quickly descended to the bottom of the ditch, walked across, and climbed up the other side.

A few minutes later, they stopped again at the foot of one of the giant pentagonal pyramids.

"Look at that," James said. "New pictures."

Besides the familiar, repetitive inscriptions, there was a series of new picture panels along the bottom of the pyramid, like a comic strip.

"Which end do we start with?" Maggie asked.

James shrugged. "No idea. You saw how all I've been able to do so far is pattern matching sign groups, like ideographs. I don't know if the reading convention here is left-to-right, right-to-left, or something non-linear."

Maggie decided to try left to right first.

There were five panels. The first one contained the familiar "map" of the city. The next panel added two egg-shaped figures, each with eight radiating legs. One egg, in the center of the city, had curled legs and a body crosshatched with thin lines. The other egg was far outside the city.

"These spider-like things are stylized drawings of the inhabitants of Pi Baeo," James said.

"Why is one of them all cracked?"

"Not sure. But it could be a way to indicate that the figure is dead, sick, or not real. Something's wrong with it."

In the third panel, both figures were drawn with smooth exteriors and straight legs. The one initially at the center had moved some distance toward the edge of the city, while the other one had moved closer to the city.

"Could be a resurrection or rebirth myth," James said.

In the fourth panel, both eggs moved even closer to each other, and in the last panel the two eggs were united at the edge of the city. Their legs entwined.

Excited, Maggie picked up the theme. "So this place is like a magical cave, where you get to meet your loved ones as they return from death." She laughed.

James laughed with her. He hadn't realized how much he missed having someone he loved with him as he explored these desolate ruins.

He walked back from the last panel, his brows furrowed. "But if you go from right to left, the story is very different: two friends arrive at the city, and one decides to go in while the other decides to leave. The adventurous one dies at the center."

"Then the title for your version would be: 'The Curse of the Pharaoh of Pi Baeo.' Treasure hunters and future archaeologists beware! A horrible fate awaits if you don't leave right now!" Maggie clapped her father on the back. "This is too funny. We've got to prove the curse wrong!"

She's just like me, James thought. *Fearless, curious. And so like her. That laugh.*

For a second he seemed to see Lauren standing where Maggie was standing, looking as young as the day they said goodbye to each other.

"Lucky you. You missed the diapers and ear infections and sleep tantrums and the terrible twos and threes and fives," Lauren said. But she was smiling at him. "But you'll have to deal with the teenage years."

"I'm sorry," he said. "I wish—" He couldn't finish.

"She's really something, isn't she?" She lifted her hand to brush away her hair. Her finger still wore the plain plastic ring that she used to replace the ring he had given her. His heart seemed to skip a beat, and his eyes became blurry and he could not see her anymore.

"Dad! Dad! What's wrong?"

He discreetly wiped his eyes. It was the first time she had called him *Dad.* He looked at Maggie, and the feeling of being responsible for her was not heavy at all. It felt like a pair of wings. "Nothing. The wind."

"Let's go to the center."

He put his arm around her shoulder. "I saw signs of very powerful weapons being used at the other sites on Pi Baeo. The people who built this place were technologically advanced, and I don't think these warnings were just superstition. I think they were trying to warn intruders away from some real danger."

"What danger could last twenty thousand years?"

"I don't know. But I believe this is a situation that calls for caution."

Maggie looked at her father, wide-eyed. "I thought you wanted to understand their message."

James felt the pull of the mystery at the center. Hints of danger had always only made it more interesting for him. And he yearned to give in to it, to do as Maggie suggested.

He remembered the feeling of Maggie leaning her head against his back on the bike. *There are more important things than dead aliens and their messages.*

"Things are . . . different now," he said. Slowly, a bit reluctantly, he turned the bike around. "It's too risky."

"I don't understand. What's changed?"

He looked at her, and instead of answering, he pulled her into a hug. She stiffened for a second and then yielded to his embrace.

•

Maggie tossed and turned, unable to sleep.

She had suggested that some of the robots be sent to investigate the center of the city. It would have been safer than going themselves. But James had said no. The robots were needed to complete the repair on the *Arthur Evans* before the comets arrived.

The more Maggie thought about it, the more she was convinced that there was no real danger. Her father claimed that the civilization here had reached a high level of technology, but this place was built with stones and had cartoons carved into them! That sounded like a temple of superstition, not an advanced military installation with booby traps that still functioned after twenty thousand years.

Things are . . . different now, he had said. She remembered the wistful look on his face as he gave up their exploration.

Her father believed that dead aliens had stories worth telling. But he also loved her mother, and he would have, was beginning to, would, love her.

I'd rather not have him at all than have him believe we weighed him down.

She got dressed.

•

"Julia," James called from his bunk.

"You can't sleep?"

"I can't seem to let the puzzle go."

"I thought so."

Julia turned on the light. James sat up.

"Scan through those 'maps' of the city. There must be a pattern in them."

Julia spoke up after a few minutes. "I think I have something. The seven ditches divide the city into seven concentric bands, with a small circle in the middle. While the locations of the pyramids change in each picture, the numbers and shapes of the pyramids within the bands are constant."

Julia projected a table onto the wall of James's cabin:

Band	Tetrahedrons	Square Pyramids	Pentagon Pyramids	Cones	Total
1	2	0	0	0	2
2	2	6	0	0	8
3	2	6	10	0	18
4	2	6	10	14	32
5	2	6	10	3	21
6	2	6	1	0	9
7	2	0	0	0	2

"Good. But what's their meaning?" James asked.

"I can do a brute-force search in the databases for these numbers to see if anything turns up."

"Do it. I'll keep on playing with them too to see if I can spot anything."

•

The comets were much closer now. In their pale light, the ground seemed to be covered by frost. Maggie made good progress on the hover bike. She had cajoled Julia into releasing the equipment to her and swore the AI to secrecy.

"It's just like with my mom. I don't want him to resent me," she had said to Julia. "I'll prove that he won't have to change because of me."

It was difficult to climb up from the bottom of the first ditch with the hover bike strapped to her back.

"I won't weigh you down," she muttered, and pulled herself up another notch.

Each successive ditch was deeper and wider than the one before. She was covered in sweat after a while, and the night air no longer seemed so cold.

Finally, after crossing the last ditch, she saw in the center an immense rock column rising hundreds of meters into the sky like an accusatory finger.

•

James felt a bit nauseous and dizzy. Too many things were happening: the crash, memories of Lauren, dealing with Maggie. He hadn't been eating or sleeping well.

He tried to clear his mind. *Ninety-two pyramids arranged in concentric circles like crystalline shells.*

An image from the evening before—Maggie falling asleep from boredom as Julia droned on about the periodic table—came unbidden to his mind. He smiled and imagined his daughter sleeping soundly in the cabin next to his. He wanted to get up and just go stare at her sleeping form. . . .

"Julia, I got it!"

Julia chirped expectantly.

"The plan of this city is a model of the atom, but not a model that *we* are familiar with. The concentric circles are electron shells, and the structures represent electrons in different orbitals. Here, bring up one of the pictures so I can show you."

Julia projected one of the diagrams onto the wall of the cabin. James pointed to it as he went on. "The tetrahedrons are electrons in s orbitals, and the squares p's, the pentagons d's, the cones f's. This place is a uranium atom, atomic weight 92, with 92 electrons."

"That would explain all the hardware errors."

The chill running down his spine cut through James's euphoria. "I thought those were from the cheap memory chips."

"That was my original theory, but a source of alpha particles nearby would explain the frequency of the errors much better. Since all the radiation shielding and monitors are still in orbit, I can't be sure. But given that uranium is the most common naturally-occurring fissile material, a stylized representation of it is a good symbol to indicate the presence of radiation."

James was stunned. "You think this place is a giant radiation warning sign? How long until we can take off?"

"I can rush the repairs and get them done in a few hours. But I have to tell you something about Maggie."

.

Jagged rocks and what appeared to be glass shards covered the ground between the last ditch and the rock column. Maggie was glad that she was on a hover bike. On foot, this final stretch would be a nightmare. The builders really didn't want anyone to get through.

She made it to the foot of the spike. This was it. She would un-cover the mystery at the center of the ruins and prove to her father that she was not going to be a burden.

We could have been a family among the stars.

There was a cave at the foot of the spike. Maggie strapped the bright flashlight to her helmet and went in. The cave spiraled downwards. She felt flushed, and stopped for a moment to wipe the sweat from her forehead. *This no-sleep thing is finally catching up to me*, she thought.

At the bottom of the cave was a metallic barrier. Maggie cut a hole through it with the torch cutter on her excavation multi-tool.

She crawled through.

Inside, the cavern was full of glass spheres packed in layers. She picked one up. It was about half a meter in diameter. Tiny metallic beads were suspended inside, packed into a tight lattice. Illuminated by her flashlight, the beads threw off brilliant rainbows of color.

The sphere felt very heavy, and hot.

•

As he rushed into the alien ruins on his bike, James swore at Julia and himself.

"I thought it was best to let her go," Julia had tried to defend herself. "I wanted to give her a chance to prove herself, the way you and Lauren never gave yourselves a chance."

The people of Pi Baeo had nuclear power. Knowing that it would take eons for the spent fuel to decay to safe levels, they had buried the waste here, as far away from civilization as possible.

Maybe they knew that their planet was drying up or maybe they were just cautious, but they tried to build this place so that it would warn their descendants or future visitors from the stars. Even as they were dying, they thought to look outside themselves and speak to the future.

They tried to encode the message at different levels, in multiple ways. They built with stone, the only material that would last millions of years. They hoped that the message would be understood universally: *There is nothing of value here. Danger! Stay away.*

He had understood it only too late.

Recklessly, he hurried down the ditches and scrambled up the other side. His breathing became jagged and he turned up the oxygen feed to his mask. All the while he thought about the invisible particles speeding at him, streaming through him, tearing apart cells and tissues.

He was beyond the last ditch.

"Maggie!" he shouted.

At the foot of the monstrous spike of rock at the center, a tiny figure waved at him.

He twisted the handle on his hover bike and was by her in a minute.

Maggie was standing next to twenty, thirty glass spheres. Her face was flushed and full of sweat.

"Aren't these beautiful?" she said. "Dad, there're many more down there. I did it. I found their secret. We can do this together." Then she collapsed, pulled off her mask, and vomited.

He picked her up and carried her to the bike, and rode as fast as he could away from the spheres until he had to stop by the ditch.

In Maggie's weakened state, there was no way for her to rappel down the ditch or to climb up the other side by herself. He couldn't carry her safely on a single cable either.

He prayed that Julia would be able to finish the repair of the ship in time to pick them up. Meanwhile, they were stuck here, exposed to the deadly waste of a bygone civilization.

He looked down at Maggie's feverish face. She had been exposed for much longer than he and she was smaller. She might not make it until Julia arrived. He had to bury the spheres again to reduce her exposure. He had to approach the source of the deadly radiation.

Gently, he laid Maggie down on the ground, rode back to the spheres, and carried them one by one back down into the cave. He worked fast and tried to not think about what was happening to his body. *There's hope yet,* he thought, *Julia will be here with the ship soon. Maggie and I can both be put in stasis until we get to a hospital.*

When he came back, Maggie struggled to sit up. "Dad, I don't feel well," she croaked.

"I know, baby. Those spheres made you sick. Just hold on a bit longer." He shifted to place his own body between her and the spike at the center, as if his flesh would cushion her from the high-energy particles, would make a difference.

The loud whirring of propellers drowned out everything. Flood-lights covered them. Julia had arrived with the *Arthur Evans.*

He carried Maggie, limp in his arms, onto the ship. His skin felt raw, burnt.

"Julia, get the stasis chamber ready. Maggie, don't be scared. You're just going to sleep for a bit."

Maggie was safely inside the chamber, and she nodded as she closed her eyes.

James was thirsty, dizzy, and very tired. He took a last look at the navigation panel. He was about to give Julia the order to take off and step into the stasis chamber himself.

Red lights blinked on the panel. *Hardware errors.*

A launch into planetary orbit was a delicate operation. There would be no tolerance for single-bit errors.

For a moment, pure rage—at himself, at the builders of this site, at the dead civilization of Pi Baeo, at the universe—overwhelmed him. They were going to die, killed by an ancient riddle that he could not solve in time.

"I'm not scared," Maggie, half-dreaming, whispered hoarsely.

He looked at her. There was a light smile on her sleeping face. She trusted him completely.

He knew what he had to do. He was ready, as he had always been without knowing it.

He leaned down into the stasis chamber. As she woke at his touch, he brushed the hair out of her eyes and kissed her on the forehead.

"Listen, Maggie, once I get the ship into orbit, Julia will send out a distress signal. The terraformers should pick it up and come to get you in a few months. Don't worry. Julia will keep you in suspended animation until they can get you to a real hospital. They should be able to fix you up good as new."

"I'm really sorry, Dad."

"It's all right, sweetheart. You're impulsive and you want answers, the same as me." He paused. "No, better than me. You've always known what really matters."

"When I wake up, we'll explore the universe together and tell everyone the stories of dead worlds."

He took a deep breath and held it for a moment. She deserved to know the truth.

"I won't see you again, baby. This is goodbye."

"What?" She struggled to get up. He pushed her down.

"It's too risky to let Julia fly the ship. The radiation is causing too many hardware errors. That's what made us crash in the first place. I have to fly the ship manually on analog controls. By the time I get us into orbit, the radiation sickness will have progressed too far in my body for stasis to be effective. I won't make it, Maggie. I'm sorry."

"No, let Julia fly the ship! You need to be in here with me. I can't lose both—"

He interrupted her, "You have been the best mystery I've ever worked on. I love you."

Before she could speak again, he closed the chamber cover.

He felt feverish and delirious. He imagined the merciless rays cutting into him, the residual heat of a dead civilization. But he was not afraid or sad or angry. Even as they were dying, the people of Pi Baeo strove to save those who would come after them. He was doing the same now for his daughter. This was a story that would always mean something, a message worth passing on, even in a universe that was cold, dark, and dying.

The comets were so bright in the sky. Everything would start afresh again.

He pulled back on the joystick, and felt the planet fall away.

Cutting

At the top of the mountain, far above the clouds, the monks of the Temple of Xu spend their days cutting words from their holy book.

The monks' faith originated a long time ago. They deduce this by the parchment on which the Book is written, which is brittle, wrinkled, and damaged by water in places so that the writing is hard to read. The Abbot, the oldest monk in the temple, recalls that the Book already looked like that when he was a young novice.

"The Book was written by people who walked and talked with the gods." The trembling Abbot pauses to let his words sink into the hearts of the young monks sitting in neat rows before him. "They recorded what they remembered of their experiences, and so to read the Book is to hear the voices of the gods again." The young monks touch their foreheads to the stone floor, their hands splayed open in prayer.

But the monks also know that the gods often spoke obscurely, and human memory is a fragile and delicate instrument.

"Think of the face of a childhood friend," the Abbot says. "Hold that image in your mind and write a description of it, giving as much detail as you can marshal.

"Now think of that face again. It has changed subtly in your memory. The words you used to describe that face has replaced some portion of your memory of it. The act of remembering is an act of retracing, and by doing so we erase and change the stencil.

"So it was with the people who composed the Book. In their zeal and fervor they wrote what they believed to be the truth, but they got many things wrong. They were only human.

"We study and meditate upon the words of the Book so that we may excavate the truth buried in layers of metaphor." The Abbot strokes his long, white beard.

And so, each year, the monks, after many rounds of debates, agree upon additional words to cut out of the Book. The bits of excised parchments are then burnt as an offering to the gods.

In this way, as they prune away the excess to reveal the book beneath the book, the story behind the story, the monks believe that they are also communing with the gods.

Over the decades, the Book has grown ever lighter, its pages riddled with holes, openings, voids where words once rested, like filigree, like lace, like a dissolving honeycomb.

"We strive not to remember, but to forget." The Abbot says, as he cuts out another word from the Book.

.

faith

is brittle,
damaged

by people who
sink
in neat rows   .
experience ,

touch   ,
pray .
know that
memory is   fragile and delicate   .
childhood

is

retracing

the people who

were

buried in layers of metaphor.

agree

upon

holes, openings, voids

strive   to remember,   to forget.

•

remember   to forget.

Acknowledgments

The emoji in this book are taken from the Twitter Color Emoji SVGinOT Font, built from the Twitter Emoji for Everyone artwork. I'm grateful to the creators for making them available to the public. For license information, please see https://github.com/eosrei /twemoji-color-font/blob/master/LICENSE.md.

I offer my heartfelt thanks here to the following individuals for making this book possible: Joe Monti (the greatest editor in the world); Russell Galen, Danny Baror, Heather Baror-Shapiro, and Angela Cheng Caplan (my agents, who made it possible for me to have a writing career); Nic Cheetham and his staff at Head of Zeus (UK edition); Lauren Jackson (publicity); Madison Penico (manuscript assistance); Valerie Shea, Steve Boldt, and Alexandre Su (copyediting); Michelle Marchese (design); Kaitlyn Snowden (production); John Vairo and John Yoo (art direction and cover); Jennifer Bergstrom and Jennifer Long (publishers); Caroline Pallotta and Allison Green (managing editorial); the various editors who published these stories initially; the friends who encouraged me to keep going and generously gave me advice; and the readers who found these stories to be worth their time and told me—without you, I would have given up.

Finally, I'm grateful for my family. They make all this worthwhile.